TJ GREEN

STORM
MOON
SHIFTERS
(BOOK 2)

DARK
HEART

Dark Heart

Mountolive Publishing

ISBN eBook: 978-1-99-004775-6

ISBN Paperback: 978-1-99-004776-3

ISBN Hardback: 978-1-99-004777-0

Cover design by Fiona Jayde Media

Editing by Missed Period Editing

www.tjgreenauthor.com

www.happenstancebookshop.com

Contents

One

Maverick Hale, alpha of the Storm Moon Pack, studied the river card, his own hand of cards, and then his three opponents.

He was playing poker in his spacious flat above Storm Moon, his club in Wimbledon, London. The lighting was dim, the corners of the room lost in shadows, and the fire in the wood burner blazed, keeping the chill February weather at bay.

His opponents were friends and employees, and one of them was a new member of his pack. Hunter, another wolf-shifter, had recently moved to London from Cumbria. He was tall and cocky with an undeniable flare for poker, and a brawler, if given half a chance. Grey was the Deputy Head of his security team; he had a shaved head, was packed with muscle, and was ex-Forces. As such, he was watchful and resourceful, and very good at poker. And he could drink—a lot—without it hardly ever seeming to affect him. The other poker player was Jet, a petite, dark-haired waitress who was also a spy in his club, paid to find out secrets. Nothing nefarious, of course, just things that would enable his pack to keep Storm Moon running smoothly, and life in general settled in their area. Both Jet and Grey were human. All looked at him now, expressionless.

Maverick weighed the options of possible hands, then slid his chips into the middle of the table as he stared at Jet. Her bet was ridiculously high, and he was sure it was because she had nothing of value in her hand and was hoping to bully out the opposition. He didn't have much either, just three of a kind, but that was hardly the point. "I'll match your bet."

Her dark red lips pouted as she leaned back in her chair, studying Maverick just as intently. "Are you sure you want to do that?"

Maverick smirked. "I just said so, didn't I?"

"Risky!"

"Hardly."

"Oh, I think it is. You are far too calm."

Maverick refused to break eye contact. "I'm always calm."

Grey snorted and almost spit his whiskey out. "That is not true! But," he slid a sideways glance at Jet, "let's not upset the boss too much."

Hunter laughed. "I thought Maverick was always in control."

"That's because you haven't been around long enough yet," Grey said. "Trust me, when he loses it, it's big. And I'm out. That bet is too rich for my taste."

Maverick glared at Grey. "I do not *lose it*. I express anger when necessary. It's healthy. Hunter, are you in or out?"

"In, obviously." He counted out his chips and pushed them forward. "Show us your cards, then, Jet."

She smiled as she placed her cards down. "Straight flush."

Maverick groaned. "You've got to be kidding me."

Her smile broadened. "I warned you. Hunter?"

"Bollocks. I have a flush." He eyed her appreciatively. "Well played."

She leaned forward and dragged the chips towards her. "Thanks. I know."

Grey threw his cards onto the table and eased his chair back. "It was an insanely risky bet, and could easily have backfired."

"But I'd still have won, just with less of Maverick and Hunter's money." She checked her watch. "Well, seeing as it is now almost three in the morning, I'd better get home. Money, please!"

"But we're not done yet!" Hunter complained.

"Yes, we are," Maverick said as he stood and reached for the cash. "It's been a long day, and a longer night, and I need to run before I sleep. Let's cash up the chips."

By run, he meant he wanted to shift into his wolf and race across Wimbledon Common, and maybe Richmond Park beyond it. He'd been cooped up all day in the club, ironing out issues with the pack, and then stayed all Thursday night, one of the busiest nights of the week—and they had a full weekend ahead, too. They had a big band booked for Saturday night.

"You want company?" Hunter asked, standing, stretching, and cracking his neck.

"Thanks, but no. I need some head space, too." Maverick pocketed his meagre winnings. "You need a hand getting home, Jet? I don't like you walking on your own at this hour."

"All sorted," Grey said. "I'm dropping her off. Hunter?"

He shook his head. "My flat is just down the road. I'll be fine."

In a few more minutes, Maverick was alone. As the alpha, he was quicker and stronger than the other shifters, and he needed to stay that way. Part of that role meant he needed to argue his way out of things—*or into things*—and be able to control a large group of shifters, all with big egos, and keep their respect. It was a hard job, but he did it well. Playing poker with friends was a good way to decompress, and to get to know the newer members, like Hunter, in a more relaxed setting.

He was impressed with Hunter that night. He was easy going and didn't lose it when he lost—especially to Jet. Not all shifters were comfortable being bested by a woman. Maverick was just as his name implied. He was not an old-fashioned shifter alpha who demanded subservience from everyone, especially women, and his pack knew it. If they didn't like it, they could leave. And yet no one did, which meant he must be getting something right.

Besides, he was already impressed with Hunter. He'd first met him a few months before, in November, when they were investigating the death of his friend, Kane. At that time, Hunter was living in Cumbria, part of the pack there. However, after a breakup with a witch, he needed a change. It seemed London and the Storm Moon Pack was it. He'd arrived just after the New Year, bringing his crazy shifter friend Tommy, too. Maverick wasn't sure what he thought of Tommy. He was a beast of a man, definitely a brawler, and some kind of demolitions addict. But he had no aspirations for leadership, only a good time. So far, both of them were working out well and had settled into the pack as part of the security team.

Did he really want to go out? It was mid-February and cold outside, his apartment was warm, and his bed beckoned after barely four hours of sleep in the past twenty-four. But he was also wound up and needed fresh air, and if he didn't shift now, he wouldn't be able to until Friday night.

Maverick shook off his introspection and headed downstairs to check on the last of the staff that were tidying up the club before they locked up. Then he would hunt.

Domino, Head of Security at Storm Moon and senior member of the pack, watched two of her security staff stroll through the darkened club, checking the toilets and small seating areas to make sure no one was still there before they locked up. In another few minutes they would be finished, and then they could secure the exits and go home.

There were three floors to the building, and Maverick owned all of it. His flat was on the first floor, the bar was on the ground floor, and the club was below it, in the basement. Domino was in the office that overlooked the club's dance floor. It was elevated above the main floor, with a large, one-way glass window that enabled the staff to watch the customers unobserved. The bar was at one end, the stage at the other, and a huge dance floor stretched between them. Out of sight was a series of seating areas in small rooms off a corridor that led to the office. They had security cameras everywhere, and the feed led to a few monitors in the corner of the room.

She turned away from the window to watch Arlo, Maverick's second in command, count the cash they'd taken for the night, ready to put it in the safe. "Good night's takings?"

"Very. I thought tonight would never end."

Domino laughed. "It's not even the end of the week yet! Saturday will be big."

Arlo rolled his shoulders. "I'm just tired. Saturday will be great. Mystic Banshees is the biggest band we've booked for a while. Are you putting on extra security?"

She nodded. "Another half a dozen. I thought it would be wise. An extra couple on the doors and through the club and pub." She was looking forward to the band, but the place would be packed, and that undoubtedly meant a higher risk of trouble from a crowd they wouldn't normally get. "Fortunately, Tommy and Hunter are happy to take on extra shifts at the moment."

"Good. I like them. They fit in well." Arlo made a note of the cash before placing it in the safe. "Done, and now I'll sleep like a baby."

"Snore and grunt, more like."

"Want to find out?"

"No! Besides, it's hardly like you make me feel special."

Arlo flirted with everyone. It was like breathing to him, which was why no one took it seriously. He stretched and winked, revealing a glimpse of flat, toned abs, and then ran his hand through his dreadlocks. He had a Jamaican dad and an English mum, and had skin the colour of milky coffee, with dark dreads that fell to his shoulders. "Dom, you know you're special!"

She leaned against the window, arms across her chest. "Be still my beating heart! You're cheesy, and your flirting is meaningless."

"But so much fun."

She laughed. "Idiot." She wanted to add that his heart still belonged to Odette, one of the Moonfell witches, but decided not to sour the moment.

Arlo, however, was not averse to teasing, and he smirked. "Besides, I wouldn't want to step on Hunter's toes. Working out all right with him, is it?"

"We have a perfectly good professional relationship. Are you insinuating something?"

"Just noticed that you seem to like *his* flirting, that's all."

"It's banter. Just like this is."

"Sure it is."

"Piss off!"

There was only so much she could say. Arlo was right. So far, Hunter wasn't making any obvious moves, but he definitely flirted with her more than anyone else. He'd made his interest clear while they were investigating Kane's death in November, but he wasn't part of the pack then, and now he was. That changed everything. She could do without messy relationships in her pack. Plus, she had her position of authority to consider. She was effectively Hunter's boss. So, he could flirt and she would enjoy it, but that was it.

The door opened and both turned, knowing it was Maverick before they even saw him. His alpha dominance radiated around him, and Domino had scented him from halfway down the hall.

Maverick brushed his hair away from his face as his long strides ate up the room. "All good here?"

Domino nodded. "We're almost ready to lock up, and the money is in the safe. How was poker?"

"I lost. Jet is annoyingly good."

"What about Hunter?" Arlo asked. "Can he play?"

"Very well." Maverick poured a shot of rum and knocked it back. "I'm going to have to up my game."

"Competition's good though," Domino pointed out. "It's better than getting complacent."

"I never get complacent."

Domino just laughed. That was true enough. Maverick never presumed anything, never dropped his guard, and was always fitter and faster than everyone else. His position depended on it.

He rolled his shoulders, "I'm going for a run, but I was thinking we should all head out tomorrow night. It's a full moon."

He didn't need to qualify that. There were no formal arrangements, but it was common for the pack to run together every full moon, depending on availability.

Domino collected the glasses and headed to the sink in the kitchenette. "Works for me. Richmond Park, I presume? We'll have more space there. I was thinking we should make it fun. Split the pack and have a hunt, of sorts. I could hide some steak or chicken in the daylight tomorrow. It will give the adolescents something to focus on."

The younger wolves who had only just started to shift needed to hone their hunting skills, and setting targets and making it a game was a good way to do it. If there was live prey available, like rabbits, badgers, foxes or birds, that was better, but it was sometimes a bit ambitious for the teenagers. At the moment, there were only seven of them, but they needed a firm hand.

"Great." Maverick headed back out the door. "Get the word out, Arlo, and let's make it happen."

The door slammed behind him, leaving Arlo and Domino alone again. Domino grinned. "Need help organising it?"

"I am very used to Maverick's requests. I have texts and email and messenger apps! I'm Pack Second, Dom. It's what I do. Do you need help burying bait?"

Only half-joking she said, "I'm Head of Security. Burying things is my job."

Hunter didn't want to go home yet. Maverick might not have wanted company, which was fair enough, but Hunter wanted to hunt, too.

He'd found it harder than he thought to move from Cumbria to London. He missed the familiarity of home, and the wide-open moors that stretched around Keswick. The wildness of the landscape was soaked into his bones after generations of his family had lived there. He had taken his first tentative steps as a shifter on those hills.

He missed the place more than he did his family, which was a terrible thing to admit. Of course, he missed the easy comfort of being around them and his lifelong friends. Although unexpectedly, Tommy, his big, brawny shifter friend, had moved with him. In his usual, brusque Tommy way, he just said he wanted a change too, so why the hell not. For all that he'd dreaded it at the time—Tommy was large, loud, and occasionally annoying—he was also funny and reliable. And so, for the first time in years, Hunter was flat sharing. With Tommy. It was all taking some getting used to.

Fortunately, Maverick and the Storm Moon Pack had lots of contacts, and finding a flat hadn't been hard. One of the shifters managed properties, and always prioritised renting to pack members. The flat wasn't cheap, but it was a decent size, and in Wimbledon. Hunter had money coming in from the family business, and both he and Tommy were paid as part of Storm Moon's security team. All in all, it had been a good move. The late hours and easy camaraderie suited him. Plus, there was Domino, the hot, sexy Head of Security who was doing a very good job of keeping him at arm's length. *That was fine.* He could wait.

After Hunter exited the club, he walked through Wimbledon Village to the green space around Rushmere Pond, stripped and hid his clothes under a bush, then shifted to his wolf. The night air was crisp and sharp, and he inhaled the scent of damp earth and grass, and the myriad scents that carried to him on the breeze. He immediately raced towards Wimbledon and Putney Commons, his long legs covering the ground easily. Hunter was a big wolf, his pelt dark grey. Beyond the commons, over a main road, was Richmond Park, extending to almost two and a half thousand acres, and filled with ancient woodland, wetlands, and grassland. There were lots of ponds, birds, wildlife, and even a herd of deer—although hunting the deer was strictly forbidden by the pack. It would attract far too much attention. In general, it was perfect. It was enclosed by a wall, but there were plenty of gates, and it was easy for a wolf to enter. Storm Moon Pack had chosen their base well.

Throwing off the close confines of Maverick's luxurious flat, he raced onwards, relishing the landscape unfolding around him. He ignored the time. It would be dark for hours. He zigzagged back and forth, investigating new scents, then hunting rabbits and foxes, mainly for the pleasure of it rather than to actually catch them.

Until he caught the scent of something quite different. Something foul, rotten even.

Hunter scanned the area and dropped low to the ground, hackles raised. Whatever it was smelled unnatural, and was certainly very different to the odd fey-shifting Pûcas they had come across only a couple of months before. Keeping low, he tracked it, following the scent across grass and into a stand of ancient trees. The scent of blood was strong there, and beneath all of it was a whiff of sulphur. He paused, ensuring that it wasn't a trap, and then edged forward again.

Ahead, there was a dark shape against the shadowed trunks, and he waited for it to reveal itself. For long minutes, nothing changed, and Hunter wondered if it had seen him. Then, with startling swiftness, the shape vanished. Hunter waited, scanning all sides, but whatever he had seen had gone.

When he reached the spot, the only thing to show for its presence was a dead fox.

Two

"Where were you when you saw it?" Maverick asked Hunter. "I was in that park last night and didn't detect anything odd."

"Close to Duchess' Wood. Not far from the Queen's Ride. I swear, I wasn't imagining it."

Maverick observed Hunter's earnest expression and direct stare. Hunter was a good friend of the Cumbrian alpha and used to being listened to. It wasn't a challenging stare, but he certainly wanted to be heard. "It's fine. I believe you. I was out southeast, in the Isabella Plantation."

It was just past midday on Friday, and Arlo and Domino were with them, all gathered in the Manager's Office, which was situated behind Storm Moon's ground floor bar. It was half the size of the Security Office in the club, but perfect for Arlo's needs. Maverick didn't have an office anywhere. He didn't need one. If he wanted a meeting with his senior staff, he either used their offices or his apartment.

Domino was perched on the corner of the desk. "We must cancel tonight's plans, that's obvious. Can't have a bloody hunting game when there's something out there that we don't understand."

"Agreed." Arlo leaned against the door, effectively blocking anyone else from entering. "We should head out there this afternoon. I know we can't shift because it's daylight, but it will be useful. We can chat to the staff, see if there is anything odd happening."

Maverick nodded. "Then we go back with a search party tonight. It could have been a visitor, of course. Something we won't see again." He narrowed his gaze at Hunter. "You said it smelled odd?"

"Yeah, sort of fetid. Rank. Like stale, brackish water. Bit of a whiff of sulphur, too. Probably some kind of decay." He huffed. "It was nothing like anything I've scented before."

"But some kind of paranormal creature?" Arlo asked.

"Had to be," Hunter reasoned. "It vanished instantly. I couldn't even find a trail of where it might have gone!"

"Did it fly?"

"Not that I saw. It was there, and then it wasn't. Like a ghost. But ghosts generally don't smell. Although..." he paused, thinking. "Avery's ancestor in White Haven appears every now and again. She carries a faint scent of violets and woodsmoke, but that's fleeting. Last night it was strong."

Maverick dropped into the chair behind the desk, annoyed that he hadn't scented anything. He had paperwork to complete that day, but nothing that couldn't wait. An unknown predator so close to their pack and on their claimed land was worrying. They might not own Richmond Park, but the North London Pack knew it was their hunting ground, and unless they were actively seeking trouble, wouldn't trespass. As for any other paranormal creatures in London, they could do what they liked there, but at least the pack normally recognized the scent.

"How did the fox die?" he asked.

"Its heart was ripped out, and something had drunk its blood. Chewed half its face off, too."

Domino groaned. "Are you sure it wasn't a vampire?"

Hunter snorted, crossing his arms over his chest. "Hell no! I know those. I hunted one in Cornwall. Ripped its throat out. No, it wasn't a vampire."

"Thank fuck for that," Arlo said, rolling his eyes. "I hate them. The rat-infested dive we hunted that last nest down in, was the worst."

Maverick couldn't forget that particular hunt. It had taken weeks to chase down their lair, and there were close to a dozen of them inside. They'd managed to hunt down a few individually, but had to find their base to kill them all. Then they'd burnt it. Vampires were cold-blooded killers, feral, and without reason. Of all the paranormal creatures, they were the worst, by far. He hoped Hunter was right.

"So it's something unknown—at least to us. No sign of human blood, Hunter?"

"None."

Maverick stood up, sending the chair wheeling backwards into the wall. "Then let's head out now. Arlo, stay here and let the pack know what's happening. Cancel the event tonight. Domino, organise a crew. About ten. After dark, we'll split up across the park, in two groups, maybe."

Domino frowned. "You don't want me to come with you now?"

"No. Let's keep it lowkey this afternoon. Just me and Hunter. After all, it might be nothing. Maybe whatever it is was just passing through."

Arlo crossed to the desk, sitting in his seat that was vacated by Maverick. "True. And it may be no risk to us, anyway. I'll contact everyone now and play it down. No point in panicking everyone."

"But stress that the park is off limits," Maverick instructed. It was always hard to find the line between maintaining safety and scaring the crap out of his pack. Parents of young shifters were always jumpy. Just because they were wolves, didn't mean they didn't care about their young, or that they thought they were invincible. "I'd rather play it safe than sorry."

He swept out the door, Hunter in his wake.

Maggie Milne, Detective Inspector and lead officer of the London Paranormal Policing Unit, was pissed off at being called out in the cold weather, especially to this stretch of the Thames.

It was frigid, clouds were gathering, and there would be rain soon. *Fuck it.* She hated winter. Not even hot toddies and fires could make it better.

"Who called this in, Conrad?"

Detective Sergeant Irving Conrad was one of the two sergeants on the team. He looked as pissed off to be out in this weather as she was. *Mainly,* she thought uncharitably, *because he was overweight and hated having to walk anywhere.* And this was a nightmare place to find a dead body.

"The Director of Ham Polo Club, Mr Huntingdon-Smythe. That man over there." He pointed out a well-dressed man in an immaculate suit who was sitting on a bench, being comforted by a PC. Maggie inwardly groaned. Posh men in smart suits were always trouble, in her opinion. *Bollocks.*

Why here? she asked herself again. This was an exclusive area, just beyond Richmond Park, and right next to Ham Polo Club, Park Lane Stables, and Ham House and Gardens that was owned by The National Trust. Not far from there was an activity club, and despite the cold weather, people had actually paid to go on the river today. *Madness.* Further up the road was Richmond Yacht Club situated on Eel

Pie Island. The whole place was all manicured lawns and well-tended borders; it reeked of cash and outdoorsy wankers. Maggie hated it.

And now one of these wealthy denizens was dead.

Unfortunately, this fresh mystery guaranteed that her annoying boss would be all over this case. If only it wasn't her team's responsibility. Unfortunately, while she had no idea who had killed the unfortunate sod at her feet, it was undoubtedly paranormal. The man's heart had been ripped out of his chest, his rib cage cracked and broken, and blood was splattered everywhere. A human could have done it, potentially, but there was a strange smell around the corpse that had nothing to do with damp earth and blood. Besides, there were claw marks—*or maybe teeth marks*—and Maggie was pretty sure they weren't human.

"Any idea what could have done this, Conrad?"

"A wolf?" He cocked an eyebrow. "The shifter kind."

"Are you trying to be funny?"

"They have sharp teeth and are supernaturally strong. And they hunt."

"They also rip throats out, not hearts. Plus, neither Maverick's pack nor Castor's would dream of doing *this*." Castor Pollux was the alpha of the North London Pack, and while he was undoubtedly a shady piece of work, he wasn't this stupid; nor would he tolerate this behaviour from his pack. As for Maverick Hale, Maggie thought it highly unlikely that he would be responsible. She had a high regard for him after their collaboration a few months earlier when they had to battle Pûcas and therians. For all that he riled her up with his rock star swagger, she dismissed him as a suspect immediately. "No. It's someone—*something*—else."

"Could be rogue," Conrad reasoned.

"No. It doesn't feel right. And it smells of the river."

"The body is dry."

"Which makes it even odder. You must be able to smell it?"

"Of course. It smells like something has been dredged from the depths. Maybe the creature from the Black Lagoon."

Maggie took a deep breath of resignation and immediately wished she hadn't as the stench of brackish water filled her nostrils. However, her sergeant's witticism prompted a question. "Could it be lake water, rather than river?"

"Bloody hell, Guv! I don't know." Conrad hefted his trousers' waist band up, but it was an unequal match for his beer gut, and it subsided beneath it again. "But the river is much closer than the ponds in the park, so my bet is the river. Maybe it's some kind of sea creature that's headed upstream."

"A killer water creature that likes human hearts? Interesting." Maggie looked towards the Thames that ran sluggishly a short distance away. "It's a busy stretch of water. Isn't the ferry terminal close to here, too?"

"A few hundred yards upstream." He pointed, but the place was hidden by trees that edged the river. "This place would be quiet at night, though. Secluded. None of these places," he gestured behind him to the polo club and stables, "would be open."

Maggie finally turned her attention to who the victim was rather than the area and the culprit. The man was well dressed in casual clothes that reeked of money, and was middle aged with thinning hair. "Who is he?"

"Mr Skelton. He's a member of the stables, and a co-owner. Mr Huntingdon-Smythe who found him says he knew him quite well. Apparently, he often swings by to check on the horses at night. A bit obsessive. Ex-British show jumper."

"I guess that answers why he was here, then." The grassy area where the body was found was a few minutes' walk from the stables. "How did he find the body?"

"He saw it from the clubhouse windows and came down to investigate. Didn't actually realise what it was until he was here."

"But why was he *here*?" Maggie asked. "Maybe he heard something, or something had spooked the horses. Are they okay?"

"From what I've gathered so far, yes they are—at the stables and the polo club."

"I'd rather not presume. We should check while we're here."

Conrad frowned. "Do you think they were the target?"

"I have no idea right now, but we should keep an open mind."

Across the field she saw her team's specialised Scene of Crime Officers arrive in a large white van. The SOCO team always took a little longer to get on scene than a regular team, as most of the members were engaged in other activities across the force. Unfortunately, the Paranormal Policing Team was not always busy enough for a dedicated SOCO team. She'd had enough trouble securing these.

Right behind them was Layla Gould's car, the doctor from the Paranormal Department, a government team situated in The Retreat, the sprawling underground headquarters beneath Hyde Park and Kensington Palace. Since the events at Christmas when Maggie had investigated the deaths caused by the Deputy Director of the PD, she had kept in touch with Layla, and had managed to secure her as their regular pathologist, something she was beyond pleased about.

Maggie rolled her shoulders in an effort to ease the crick out of her neck caused by the cold wind. "We'll hand things over and see what the doc says. Then we'll start nosing around."

The team had parked on a narrow lane that ran under the trees, and they crossed the grassy expanse quickly. While Conrad dealt with

SOCO, she pulled Layla aside. She was a small, birdlike woman in her sixties, and was immaculately dressed as always in a smart wool coat and leather gloves over her plaid woollen trousers. She'd even pulled on posh Hunter wellies with paper shoes over them. She fitted right into this environment.

Layla greeted Maggie briefly, her sharp eyes already appraising the body. "Well, what a mess. You always like to make life interesting, Maggie."

"I know you don't like to be bored."

"Fat chance, at the moment. New staff at The Retreat are driving me mad. Never mind, I'll get over it." She crouched to examine the body. "Where's all the blood?"

"On him!"

Layla huffed. "Oh come on, Maggie. His heart has been ripped out of his chest. This place should be swimming in his blood."

"It could be in the earth beneath him."

"But it's not. You'd see it. No." She shook her head. "Some of it is missing. *Interesting*."

"Any idea of what could have done it? Has the PD had any weird reports?"

"We're always getting weird reports, but nothing that match-es this." She looked up at Maggie, blue eyes flashing with intrigue. "Something new, perhaps. Or very old. Lucky you."

Maggie snorted. *Yes, so lucky.*

Grey groaned as he leaned back in the chair, hands behind his head. "Don't tell me we have shit to deal with when we have the biggest act we've booked in months turning up tomorrow."

"Well, I could lie, but that wouldn't do us any favours," Arlo admitted with a smirk. "Do you want to join us tonight?"

Grey shook his head. "I'd just slow you down. Besides, if you're taking a lot of our senior staff, I should stay here. Who's going?"

Domino studied the roster that was printed on the wall in the Security Office. "Maverick wanted ten, but that will be pushing it."

"Take Tommy and Monroe. They're both big enough to count as four," Grey said, laughing. "Are you both going?"

"I'd like to," Domino admitted. "It would be good to hunt, but it's Friday, and who knows what may happen here."

Domino always worried and hated to delegate. That's what made her such a good security chief. She took her responsibilities very seriously. Sometimes she missed out on the fun stuff because of it. Not that searching for a killer was fun...well, for normal people anyway.

Grey crossed to her side. "Go. I'll handle it here, but maybe leave Vlad, too. He's Deputy Manager now, and leaving him in charge tonight will be good for his ego."

"I doubt he'll see it like that," Arlo said, filling the kettle with water to make them a drink.

"You'd be surprised. He's enjoying stretching his legs in the role." Some people didn't handle leadership well. It went to their heads, and they became insufferable. Vlad was a pro, and Grey enjoyed working with him. "The staff—especially the shifters—respect him, so there won't be any issues while you're gone. We'll keep John on the door. He's a regular face there and the punters like him."

Domino ran her finger down the roster. "Jax is off tonight, so I'll call him. You sure you can spare Monroe? Hunter is already with Maverick, so he should come."

"Sure. Take Cecile, too. She'll be pissed if you don't," Grey said, smirking. "I'd rather not have Cecile grumbling all night. Especially if you take Xavier."

Cecile and Xavier were French cousins. He was dark-haired and olive-skinned, while she was a sharp-tongued honey blonde who fought as well as any of the men.

"You don't mind?" Arlo asked Grey.

"I'm resigned to it. I'd rather you weren't vulnerable on the hunt. Leave me Rory and Fran too, and I'll promote one of the younger shifters to man the club doors."

Rory was one of their older staff members who'd been travelling with his family for over a year and had only recently returned to London. He'd slipped back into his old security role easily, and Grey was glad of it. However, they couldn't forget the younger shifters. Balancing the need to give them more responsibility over leaving the club vulnerable was always tricky, but it was something they did daily. It was pack life, and although Grey wasn't a shifter or a pack member, he knew as much about it as if he was. Being in the army was a bit the same. Handling aggression and giving shifters an outlet for their natural urge to hunt and kill was essential. No matter how affable most of them were, Grey could never forget that they were aggressive killers at their core. It was a credit to them that they reined it in so well. He almost forgot until tempers smouldered, and the yellow light glowed within their eyes. At that point, the predator became all too obvious. Grey also knew the club could function with their less aggressive, mature shifters. In fact, they helped settle the junior staff more. They were less competitive.

"Who are you thinking for the door job downstairs, then?" Arlo asked, handing him and Domino a cup of coffee. The club entrance was inside the building, accessed by the stairs from the ground floor bar. It was where the cloakroom and club ticket area were situated, manned by a couple of female human staff—usually Jasmine and Jade—and of course whichever shifter was on the door, too.

"Hal." He cocked an eyebrow at Domino. "He's itching for more responsibility, rather than skulking around the bar all night. Fran can cover the loading area and back door. Sound good?"

Hal was the oldest son of one of their shifter families and had been eager to work at the club rather than his father's business. He thought it more exciting than working on cars, and Grey couldn't blame him.

"I'm happy if you are," Domino said, eyes on the roster again. "So that means our team is me, Arlo, Mav, Hunter, Tommy, Mads, Jax, Monroe, Xavier, and Cecile. Ten. Perfect."

"Sure that's not overkill for one dead fox?" Grey asked.

"It's a big park," Arlo pointed out. "Maverick suggested teams of five. I think teams of two. We'll cover more ground. I guess it depends what Maverick thinks after he's been to the park. Time will tell."

Grey sipped his coffee, thinking over what the dead fox could portend. He was playing it down—it was his way—but he was unsettled and worried. Plus, it was a full moon that night, and all the crazies loved a full moon.

Three

"There it is," Hunter said to Maverick, pointing at the base of the tree where the dead fox was still sprawled.

In the afternoon half-light of a cloudy winter day, the brutalised carcass looked even more horrific than it had the night before. Not that Hunter was squeamish. He killed his own fair share of foxes while he was hunting, but he usually ate most of them. The poor fox had been sacrificed. At least, that was the word that came to mind.

Maverick didn't speak; instead, he crouched and sniffed the body, face expressionless.

It had taken them almost an hour to reach the spot after parking the car in the closest carpark by Upper Pen Pond. Everything felt different in the daylight, but the scent of blood still hung heavy in the air, and the other unusual scent, too—or unusual to a wolf, at least. In warmer weather it would already be decomposing rapidly, and Hunter wondered if the park staff would remove it. They probably would. It wouldn't do for regular visitors to find it.

Hunter searched the area while Maverick investigated the body, hoping to pick up a scent he had missed the night before, and a way to track the killer. Unfortunately, it was as if the responsible party had vanished into thin air.

What kind of creature would take a heart? Not an animal, surely; therefore, it was something or someone supernatural. *Perhaps it would be used for black magic.* Witches might know, but even all these months after splitting up with Briar, the earth witch in White Haven, he wouldn't phone her. He could call Reuben or Alex, the male witches in the coven, but it would be weird, and he didn't want that. Although he missed them, especially being called Wolf Man by Reuben. *Silly bugger.* He was so preoccupied by his own thoughts that he barely heard the growl until the air was humming with it.

Alarmed, he looked around and found Maverick on his feet, staring wildly around, his eyes molten gold. One wrong move now and he'd rip Hunter's throat out. Or anyone's, for that matter. Hunter's eyes were the only thing that moved as he scanned the area like Maverick. Fortunately, no one was there, and it was dark and lonely beneath the trees.

Hunter kept his voice low. "Maverick, what have you seen?" Maverick's wild gaze swung to Hunter, and knowing how to deal with an enraged alpha, he adopted a deferential tone. "Have you scented something? Can I help?"

A full-throated roar ripped from Maverick, and he threw his head back, jaw open wide.

Herne's horns. He was going to shift. Here in broad daylight! *Was he possessed?* He looked out of control.

But no. He had enough wit about him to strip before he shifted to his wolf—a huge, brindled-brown animal that was the size of a small horse. Hunter had no idea what was happening, or why, but he did the same. He was either going to be fighting for his life or following Maverick, because there was no way he could leave him on his own now. Hunter wasn't sure which was the worse option.

Fortunately, Maverick had no interest in fighting Hunter, and he raced through the woods, a rippling shadow in the gloom. He travelled quickly, zigzagging back and forth, but there was no trail that Hunter could discern. All the while, Maverick kept growling, a throbbing pulse of sound that to Hunter's ears was horribly loud. Hunter could barely keep up, but he followed him through Duchess' Wood, into Deer Park, and then along the Queen's Ride to Jubilee Plantation. Every now and again he slowed down, but not for long. He finally halted at the perimeter of Saw Pit Plantation, and Hunter drew level with him, keeping a respectful distance. He settled on his haunches, wary of every sound and movement.

They had passed a few people, but had skirted around them, Hunter grateful that the cold February afternoon and impending rain kept visitor numbers low. He risked a quiet bark, a question. *"What's going on?"*

Maverick levelled a long stare at him, and Hunter looked away. Movement in his peripheral vision showed Maverick was shifting back to human, and Hunter shifted, too.

Surer of himself now, Hunter didn't stand on ceremony. "What the hell was that, Maverick?"

"You dare to question your alpha?"

"I do when you risk exposing us both." Hunter met his eyes, this time refusing to back down. "There are people here. And dogs!"

"You didn't have to follow me."

"Yes, I bloody well did, and you know it. Now we're stark bollock naked in Richmond Park and risk being seen. Or arrested. What is going on?"

"I recognise the scent." Maverick's eyes were still molten gold, and it looked as if he was hanging on to his self-control by a thread.

Understanding suddenly dawned. "This is personal."

"You could say that." Maverick studied Sidmouth Wood a short distance away.

Chastened slightly, Hunter said, "You know what—or who—this is."

"Not exactly. It's a scent I hoped never to smell again. It was all over my parents when they were found. Dead."

The enormity of his statement left Hunter temporarily lost for words. He rubbed his stubbled jaw, fumbling through what he knew about Maverick. "I'm sorry. But I thought a witch killed your parents, and that's why you hated them."

"A witch was partly responsible, as well as whatever this scent belongs to. We never found it then, but I swear that I will find it now." Maverick stared at Hunter. "By any means necessary."

Arlo didn't like surprises, and this was one big fat surprise. "Are you sure you're not mistaken? It was a very long time ago, Maverick."

"I'm not mistaken. I will take that scent to my grave."

He was in Maverick's flat early on Friday evening. Maverick had been back for an hour or two, but hadn't wanted to be disturbed, and no matter how much Arlo had wanted to ask him questions, he had respected his privacy. Hunter had informed them of what had happened, racing into the office as soon as they returned, flushed with worry, and angry after chasing his alpha around Richmond Park.

Impatient, Arlo had continued to work, finding it hard to focus, until he finally received the call from Maverick that he knew would come. He had expected to find him seething with fury, or chewed up with memories, but instead it was worse. He was ice cold with tightly reined anger.

"I need to find whatever it is," Maverick continued, fingers gripping his glass of rum, eyes on the fire. "It's time to stop these endless questions that have been circling my brain for more than twenty years."

"I agree, and we'll do everything we can to help."

"We will keep my personal connection a secret from everyone though, except for you, Domino, and Grey. And Hunter, of course. The rest of the team know nothing."

Arlo hated to question him in this mood, but... "What about Vlad? He's Deputy Manager now. We can trust him, or he wouldn't be in the role," he added when he saw Maverick's shoulders tighten.

He sighed. "Okay. Tell Vlad. But that's all!"

"That's fine, but there might come a time—"

"I'll decide when."

"Of course." It was already dark outside, and light rain was falling. They would be lucky to see any of the full moon that night, but perhaps that was in their favour. They would stay hidden while they hunted. "It may have gone already, whatever it is." He squared his shoulders, ready to share what he'd seen on the news reports. "A dead man was found nearby, did you hear?"

Maverick whirled around, rum sloshing in the glass. "No! Who? How?"

"I don't know the details, but he was found by Ham Polo Club. Close enough to the dead fox, wouldn't you say? Maggie is the leading officer."

Maverick huffed. "So it's paranormal, then."

"It seems so. Do you want me to call her? I can ask for more details," he clarified in answer to Maverick's narrowed eyes.

"All right, but keep my connection out of it. Just say that it's in the pack's interest to know."

"Of course. This whole scenario raises more questions, though. If it is the thing that—"

Maverick cut him off. "It *was* involved with my parents' death. I am not mistaken."

Arlo nodded. "Then the obvious question is, why is it here now? Has it come for you? Or is this just a weird coincidence? A new hunting ground, perhaps?"

"I'd like it to be a coincidence, but I doubt it is. Perhaps it has come for me. Or is a warning to me, for some reason. Or even maybe a taunt."

Arlo's worry magnified, out of fear for Maverick's safety and that of the pack. Not many things would take on a shifter and win, but it had killed two shifters in the past—and maybe more. "I'm sorry to keep asking questions, Mav, but I'm confused. You have always said that a witch killed your parents. That's why you hate them so much, but now you're saying that this creature is involved—this *something*. Is it a witch disguising itself? I just don't get it!"

"It's complicated, and right now you don't have to get it. You just have to trust me."

"Of course I trust you, but some context, some explanation of what the fuck happened would be good! It could help us now!"

Maverick virtually snarled. "When I'm ready."

Deep in the back of his eyes a yellow glow started to smoulder, and Arlo's wolf answered. He could feel it struggling within him, no matter that Maverick was his alpha. Secrets were fine, until they risked killing someone.

Arlo needed to leave before he did something stupid. "If that's all, I'll go and call Maggie."

"Are the staff organised for tonight?"

"Yes, ten as you requested. Vlad will stay here to support Grey."

"Good. Tell them we'll go at ten o'clock, leaving together from the carpark out back." Maverick turned away, his broad shoulders straining beneath his t-shirt, and Arlo knew he wanted to shift again. Could smell the charge in the air.

"Of course."

Arlo didn't trust himself to say any more, and he stalked down the stairs, fury building. When he reached the flat's entrance door, he burst through it to the rear carpark and took deep inhalations of cold air. His eyes would be molten gold, he knew, and he had to get it under control before he went inside. *Fuck it! Maverick was infuriating sometimes. He was hurting, of course, memories of his dead parents and his childhood would be painful, but for fuck's sake...*

"Bad meeting?" Fran was at the corner of the building, overseeing the band that just arrived to set up for the evening show.

"You could say that." He took another breath. He certainly wasn't going to badmouth the alpha to Fran. "You've heard about what's happening tonight?"

Her mouth twisted in displeasure. "Yes, and I'm stuck here." Fran was of medium height, attractive rather than pretty, with short auburn hair clipped in a pixie cut, and large almond eyes that missed nothing. Plus, she was pure muscle. Her human partner, Evelyn, ran a gym that they all used, but Fran frequented it daily. She was ripped, and on her best days wasn't overly communicative.

"Not stuck, Fran," he said curtly. He moved closer, finally getting his anger under control. "Whatever that something is, could have it in for this pack, so you being here tonight, on this door, is very important. You're one of the only senior security staff left, so you need to be vigilant—and calm-headed. Understand?"

She straightened, new resolve in her eyes. "You think it might come here?"

"It's unlikely, but certainly possible. I trust you to do the right thing."

"You can count on me, boss."

"I know." He shouldn't take his anger with Maverick out on Fran. She'd sustained some serious injuries fighting Pûcas a few months earlier, and she was highly trustworthy. He softened his stance. "I have phone calls to make. Any concerns, call me. I'm here for a few more hours."

He headed into the club, nodding at the band members who were carrying their equipment onto the stage, crossed the empty dance floor, and pounded up the stairs to the office.

Domino was seated at the desk, as impatient for answers as he was. "Well?"

"He's a stubborn, secretive, pain in the arse."

"Not our usual Maverick, then?"

Arlo slammed the door behind him so hard that it rattled in the frame. "No! And that worries me. I mean, I know this is awful! This is about his dead parents, but keeping secrets..."

"So, we cut him some slack," Domino said, leaning back in the chair. "He needs our support. If necessary, we pick up more things here. This is his priority now."

Arlo walked to the fridge and grabbed a beer. "Want one?"

"No, thanks. I want to stay fresh for tonight."

"It's one beer!"

Domino rolled her eyes. "Fine."

Arlo popped the caps off the bottles and walked over to the desk to hand it to her. On the computer monitor were more reports of the dead man that Maggie was investigating. "Any updates?"

"No."

Arlo took a few sips of his drink, and then pulled his phone from his pocket, ready to call Maggie. "How old was Maverick when his parents were killed?"

"Fourteen."

"Did he tell you why they thought it was a witch who killed them? Because this is a creature, from the sound of what Hunter says."

"No. He just told me that it was complicated, and that there was some sort of issue with the pack that his family belonged to."

"In Kent, right?"

"Yes. Just outside Canterbury, I gather. That's all I know, though. It's a subject he keeps very quiet about, and I don't blame him. It's in the past. I *do* know that he grew up with his aunt after that."

Arlo nodded and settled in the chair across from the desk. "Yeah, I heard that. His older brother ran wild, took off to France on a ferry when he turned eighteen. Pretty much abandoned Maverick. Not that he says it in quite those terms." Arlo suddenly felt very mean and guilty. "I shouldn't be so hard on him. That's a lot of shit to have dealt with."

"You're dealing with a lot too," Domino reassured him. "It's your job. How did everyone take the news today?"

Arlo huffed at the memory. "The usual acceptance of some and worry of others. Especially those with kids. I know Maverick wants to find the creature, but I'm hoping whatever it is just blows through."

Domino looked guilty. "I don't. I want to help him find it, or the witch that was involved—and still could be." She sipped her beer. "I can't complain. I had a nice, easy upbringing, and I know you did too, with your cosy bedtime stories that your mum used to read you."

Arlo laughed. He should never have shared that information. "We were lucky."

"Too true." She eyed his phone. "You going to call Maggie?"

"I'm summoning the courage."

Domino almost spat her beer out in a snort of laughter. "Want me to handle it? Woman to woman?"

He was tempted to hand her the phone. "No. I'll win her over with my smooth ways."

"Yeah. Good luck with that."

Arlo decided to just get it over with, and leaving Domino at the desk, strode to the window and watched the flurry of activity in the club below while he called Maggie. The band was setting up, and the usual staff were behind the bar, restocking supplies before opening. Hal the shifter was chatting to the door girl, no doubt getting familiar with the set up for the night.

Maggie answered quickly, her voice clipped. "DI Milne."

"Arlo Weir here, Maggie, from Storm Moon."

"Fuck. Don't tell me something is wrong there!"

"Lovely to chat to you, too." He smiled. Maggie had a foul mouth and a short temper, but she was brilliant at her job. "No, nothing going on here. I just wanted to check a few things about the body you found earlier."

"I didn't *find* him! He wasn't a lost handbag!"

Domino sniggered, no doubt able to hear Maggie's strident voice from across the room.

"Bad choice of words, sorry, Maggie." He rolled his eyes at Domino. "I'm sure you're busy, but you can understand that we're worried about the death. Clearly it was paranormal, or you wouldn't be involved. Anything you can tell us?"

"Other than the fundamentals, not much. The PM will be done tomorrow. His heart was ripped out, and a lot of his blood was missing. I assume it's just the juicy details you want, right?"

"Anything. It's on our patch. We want to help." He winced. Actually, it wasn't what he should be saying at all. They would look for it, obviously, but Maverick wouldn't thank him for actually offering assistance. "We want to stop it. Catch it and kill it if necessary. Any idea what it is?"

"No. I was hoping you might be able to tell me."

"If you can tell us more, we might find out. No one wants an unknown killer running around, especially us."

"Are you holding out on me?"

"No." *Technically true.*

"If only I could believe that. There was a strange smell on the body. Brackish. Watery. No water on the victim, though. But that's it until the PM."

"And where was it found—exactly?"

She ran through the details, and Arlo nodded as he pictured the place. "Thank you. Will you call me tomorrow with an update?"

"I guess so. It's a full moon tonight. You going to hunt for it?"

"Of course."

"Already?" she sounded impressed.

"No point waiting."

"No. I don't want to deal with another death tomorrow. I was thinking I might have to call you guys. You've pre-empted me." She huffed and he heard paperwork rustling.

"Are you still in the office?" He checked the time. "It's past seven."

"I'll be here for a lot fucking longer yet." She paused, and then said, "It was a nasty death, Arlo. Vicious. I know the victim was human, but he wasn't a little man. You lot should be careful."

"So should you. No midnight excursions, Maggie."

"You don't have to warn me. Stay safe, Arlo." She rang off abruptly.

Arlo turned and found Domino watching him. "It must be bad. Maggie sounds shaken."

"Then we hunt in bigger teams," Domino answered.

"Do you think Maverick can hold it together tonight? He was barely hanging on earlier. Hunter is pretty laid back, and not averse to a wild chase, but he was *not* impressed with Maverick's behaviour."

"It was a shock. He'll be fine. He just needs to...acclimatise."

"Will you go and check on him?"

"He will not appreciate me coddling him."

"It's what friends do."

"You're his friend, and now you have news from Maggie. Suck it up and go see him. You two should work on your issues." Domino smirked.

"They're not *issues*!"

"You're his second. Go and remind him why you are. And make sure he's not drinking too much rum."

Four

Maverick knew he was being abrasive, and that he'd lost his head in Richmond Park. He hated himself for it, but he couldn't seem to control his mood either, and that just wasn't okay. As the alpha, he needed to be in control of himself all the time. Or at least in front of his pack. He had a reputation to uphold.

But that scent...

He was still in his flat, sitting on the sofa in the dark, only the firelight from the wood burner illuminating the room. The darkness suited his mood as he rifled through his memories.

He had seen his parents' bodies, and the image was still seared into his mind. At fourteen he'd just started to join the nighttime hunts. He was in control of shifting to his wolf, and was already tall for his age. His brother, Canagan, was seventeen and eager for more of a role in the pack, but he was also headstrong and enjoyed drinking and partying with the other teenage shifters. There were usually four of them who used to take off together, three boys and one girl. He could remember their faces, but not their names.

They weren't a large pack; probably ten families and a couple of lone adult males. From what he could recall, though, it was a good group. Friendly and family-orientated. They all lived in the villages to the southwest of Canterbury, situated on the vast expanse of the Kent

Downs. Places such as Bossingham, Waltham, and Anvil Green. It was idyllic, until the unthinkable happened.

There had been no warning. No sign that anything had invaded their hunting grounds.

His parents, both shifters, would sometimes hunt at night on their own, and Maverick had been left at home for a few hours while his brother was out with his own friends. But when Maverick woke at three in the morning and realised his parents weren't home or his brother, he'd called the alpha, a shifter called Droug. That set off a huge search, but hadn't stopped Maverick from going out, too.

He'd set out on his own, even though Droug had told him not to, aiming to meet the pack at Denge and Pennypot Wood, a place where his parents liked to hunt at night. Maverick was always headstrong, even then. Plus, he'd been worried, too. His parents were usually back by two in the morning at the latest, unwilling to leave him too long, even though he was a teenager. He knew something was wrong. He could feel it.

He arrived just as the group found his parents in a tangled grove of trees, close to a stream. He'd caught sight of their bodies, and smelled the blood, but the pack had intervened before he saw anything else. His parents were in their human form at that point, and the alpha had called the police once they'd concocted the story, of course.

But their deaths had changed everything. His ordered life had been upended, the police asked endless questions, and Maverick's mood veered between rage, grief, and disbelief.

His aunt, Abigail, lived close by, his father's sister, and Maverick and his brother had gone to live with her. His brother and three friends had been vague about their whereabouts that night, just saying that they were hunting a few miles away, in a hollow in the downs. There was no reason to doubt them. Canagan was a little wild, but not bad.

There hadn't been any tension between him and their parents, beyond the usual teenage crap.

The police had been thorough, but no one had been identified as the killer. The pack conducted their own investigations, and that's where things became a little murky.

A knock at the door interrupted his thoughts, and Maverick returned to the present with a jolt. It was Arlo. He flicked the lamp on next to the sofa, trying to appear more rational, and called, "Come in."

Arlo looked wary when he entered, coming in only a few feet before pausing, eyes skimming the room before settling on Maverick. "I called Maggie. The PM is tomorrow, and she'll know more then. She was able to give me some information, though."

"Join me for a drink, Arlo?" Maverick asked, rising to his feet. "You can update me in comfort."

"If you want company, or I can make it quick."

Tension radiated from him, and Maverick realised he'd pissed him off. "Sorry I was abrupt earlier. I've got a lot on my mind."

"I know."

"But I was a dick, and I shouldn't have been rude." He laughed dryly. "So much for staying in control. I sort of annoyed myself for losing it with Hunter. Is he all right?"

"Pissed off, but he's fine." Arlo joined him at the kitchen counter. "It's always unnerving when your alpha strips off and goes hunting in broad daylight."

"Not my finest moment." Maverick handed him a measure of rum. "Need a mixer?"

"No. Sure you should be coming tonight?"

"Yeah. I'll be fine, although to be honest, I need this as much as a hole in the head." Maverick squared his shoulders and sat on a bar stool, glad to see Arlo finally relax and join him. "What did Maggie have to say?"

"That the attack was vicious, and the man's heart was missing. Ripped from his chest. She also said that there should have been more blood there."

Maverick's heart quickened at the news, his pulse pounding in his ears, and he took a deep breath and another slug of rum. "Just like my parents. And the fox, of course."

"Which supports your theory that they're related. I'm really sorry, Maverick. This is obviously raking up horrible memories."

"It was a long time ago. I thought I'd come to terms with it, but obviously not. Now it feels like it was only yesterday." Arlo didn't speak, and Maverick knew he would have to explain what he had refused to discuss earlier. "The reason that we thought a witch was behind their deaths was because there were two witches who lived in one of the small villages outside Canterbury. A brother and sister. They were odd, no doubt about it, but they kept to themselves. Until one day they approached Droug, the alpha—they knew all about us, of course—asking for shifter blood."

"Why?" Arlo asked immediately, forehead creasing with concern.

"Great question. That's exactly what Droug asked, too. They didn't tell him. Said it was for a spell, but refused to elaborate."

Arlo cursed under his breath. "You never willingly let a witch have your blood. That could be a disaster."

"Exactly. He said no. They had a big pack meeting. I wasn't invited to it, I was too young, but my parents came back and warned me and my brother. We were told to keep our distance from them." He shrugged. "That was fine. It wasn't like we hung around with them, anyway. They were older than us, in their late twenties, maybe thirties. Not married. No kids." He took another sip of rum, his mouth suddenly dry. "And they lived in this really weird cottage. Proper witchy, you know? Like you'd see in a fairytale."

"The sort you'd tell stories about as kids."

"Yeah! Well, they weren't too happy about the refusal. From what I recall, they tried approaching a few shifters while we were just minding our business. Like a dog with a bone. Things got tense very quickly. The thing is, no one really wanted to threaten them. They were witches, after all. We just wanted to keep the peace. We certainly didn't want to be cursed."

"Had they been threatening before?"

"No. Seemed fairly harmless—crazy witchy cottage aside. They did their business, we did ours."

"But you said they were odd."

"They were uncool...to me, at least. They wore unfashionable clothes, and were a little intense. Awkward."

"Did they approach your parents?"

"One night, after dark. The brother, I think his name was Owen, came to our house. My parents met him at the door. Refused to let him in or give him blood. I think they asked about why he needed it, he again refused to say, other than it was really important. There were raised voices. My dad told him that they could be just as dangerous and not to threaten him. Then the witch left. It was less than a week after that they were killed, and the two witches vanished immediately."

"I can see why you thought they were behind their deaths. But no one else died?"

"No. Although to be honest, lots of precautions were taken after that, and obviously with the police involved, I guess they were just scared off." Maverick's memories of that time were jumbled, because he'd been kept out of much of it. His aunt didn't want to talk about it, and his brother ran even wilder. Maverick had pieced things together from whispered conversations he'd overheard, or the scant information he had been given. "I was hoping it was something me and Canagan could work on together, but," Maverick gave a bitter laugh, "he wasn't interested in me. My aunt tried to handle his moods, but in the end, they drove each other mad. My brother took off after his eighteenth birthday. I haven't seen him since, but for a while we'd receive the occasional postcard from tiny places in France with the barest of information on them." It was a painful memory. A feeling of rejection. "We knew he was alive, and that was it."

"You haven't seen him since?"

"No. Or heard from him in years."

"What about your aunt?"

"She moved to Rye on the south coast after I left home. I kept in touch, but she died a few years ago. Cancer."

"I'm sorry. And the pack?"

"All gone their separate ways, I think." He was suddenly curious about them. "A few would have stuck around, I guess."

Arlo drained his glass and placed it on the counter. "Depending on what we find tonight, perhaps you should try to locate them. Fill in some of those blanks in your memory. Those gaps of information you were never privy to. Then again, maybe let sleeping wolves lie."

"I'm not sure that I can anymore, actually." He finished his drink, and realised he didn't want any more. He was filled with new resolve for action. "Hunt with me tonight, Arlo. I need a level head with me."

"Of course, but I have complete faith in you."

Maverick laughed. "Liar, but thank you for saying so. Now, let's talk about our plans."

Domino had volunteered to search the riverbank with Monroe, Xavier, and Cecile, and now all of them were having last minute discussions by the cars, which they'd parked close to the polo club, planning to fan out from there.

Maverick seemed more like his usual self, and she was pleased that Arlo would be with him. In addition, Hunter was joining their search group. They were focussing on the grounds around the polo club and stables. Ground zero.

Tommy, Mads, and Jax were searching beyond the club, around the borders of Richmond Park. They'd decided to keep the search to where the dead body had been found rather than the fox, although there had been some argument about that. If the creature needed more blood, the park would be a good place to hunt. There were deer there, and lots of open space.

"Where was the body found, exactly?" Domino asked Arlo.

He pointed across the grassy area. "Over there. I think I can see the police tape. We should all head there first to get the scent before we split up."

Maverick had been studying the polo club's building a distance away, but now he turned to Tommy, Mads, and Jax. "If you think it's important, head further into Richmond Park. I don't want us to miss anything because we're too focussed here. But be careful! I don't like that we don't know what this is."

"If we find it," Jax said, a lean blond man, "I presume you're happy that we'll kill it?"

Maverick paused for a split second before saying, "Only if you have to. Otherwise, catch it. I want to see what it is. Speak to it, if possible." He added after everyone looked puzzled, "I need to know if there are more of whatever it is."

They split into their various groups, and Domino said to her three companions, "Once we have the scent, let's separate into pairs. Me and Monroe can head west, you two," she said, nodding to Xavier and Cecile, "head east. But not far! If you need help, howl, and we'll come running."

Cecile stripped while they talked, revealing long legs and toned abs, as unconcerned about her nakedness as they all were. "Why are we so worried about this thing? It killed a human. We are shifters, and more than a match for whatever it is."

Domino wished she could share about the connection to Maverick's parents, but instead she said, "We shouldn't presume anything. Ever."

"I never do, but it's like you and Arlo are extra jumpy around this."

"Just worried about the pack and the club, like always. And the fact that we don't know the scent. That's all." She shrugged nonchalantly.

Cecile just snorted and shifted to her wolf. She and Xavier, her cousin who had shifted at the same time, raced after the others, leaving Monroe and her alone.

Monroe had stripped his t-shirt off too, revealing his huge muscles and rugged chest. He towered over her, and she was a tall woman. He was easily twice her weight, his black skin seeming to dissolve into the night. "You're hiding something, Dom."

"I'm really not."

"I'm sure you have your reasons to. As long as they don't compromise our safety."

"I would never risk that."

He didn't answer, instead shifting into his huge wolf and following Cecile and Xavier to the scene of the attack.

Hunter had hung back to talk to her, and they were the only ones now still by the cars. He was clad only in his underwear, and she was in her sports bra and jeans. His scent enveloped her, and it was all she could do not to step into his embrace. She could clearly smell his attraction to her.

But he hadn't stayed behind to flirt. "I don't like keeping secrets from the team who are hunting this thing. It's not right."

"I agree with you, but they're Maverick's instructions, so we follow them."

His eyes were on Maverick's wolf. "But when family is involved, things get murky. It's only been a few months too since one of his best mates was murdered. It's a lot to deal with."

"He's the alpha. He can cope."

"You didn't see him this afternoon."

"We all have a lapse in judgement, Hunter, even you. I'm sure he's fine now."

"Yeah. But for how long?"

Without another word, Hunter stepped out of his clothes, shifted, and ran to join the others.

Five

Vlad couldn't help smiling as he weaved through the customers who populated the basement club.

They paid no attention to him, despite his height and commanding demeanour. He earned a few admiring glances, but most customers were either talking to each other, flirting, or watching the band that had just started their set. He nodded at a few familiar faces as he scanned the crowd, wary of any disturbances, but so far, the evening was going smoothly.

Vlad enjoyed his new job. He liked the responsibility and the change of pace from doing security work. There was nothing challenging about that, other than risking life and limb, of course. The Deputy Manager role involved more paperwork, which was a downside, but it challenged him in other ways. He'd had to get used to liaising with the kitchen staff about food orders, and the breweries who provided their beer. He'd been in meetings about menus, new craft beers, and wine selections. He was also fielding requests for shift changes, holiday leave, and navigating staff complaints. That was the challenging part, negotiating staff needs. *That* was a pain in the arse. But being part of what he called Storm Moon's Inner Circle was the best part of his new role.

He certainly wouldn't have heard the details about Maverick's past otherwise. The alpha hadn't been present when Arlo had updated him and Grey. Vlad's problem was the fact that he couldn't share everything with his younger brother, Mads. Since the day they'd joined the pack together, they had shared everything—including the not so pleasant memories of their brutally controlling ex-alpha. They had both worked on the security team, and still shared a flat, although more and more recently Vlad felt the need for his own place and more privacy. Fortunately, Mads had been pleased about his promotion, but there was no getting away from the fact that it had changed the dynamics of their relationship.

However, the new role made Storm Moon more of a home than it already was. He felt a greater degree of responsibility for the staff, the pack, and the customers, so despite his pleasure with the new job, he was on full alert for any potential issues that night, especially with an unknown killer in the area. He spotted Jet at the bar chatting to a customer, and headed towards her, hoping their spy might have heard something of use. The staff had been warned to be on the lookout for anything, and she, more than anyone, would have heard any rumours.

Spotting his approach, she ended her conversation and crossed to his side, tilting her head back to look up at him. "Everything okay?"

She was petite in every way, and Vlad had more than once considered asking her out. He liked her raven dark hair, her tattoos and piercings, and the way her hips swayed when she walked. He especially appreciated her full lips that were always painted in dark red lipstick, just asking to be kissed...

Realising he was staring, he snapped his focus to the present. "Fine, so far. What about you? Any whispers about the death?"

"More than whispers." Her gaze drifted to the people surrounding them, a mix of men, women, and shifters. Her eyes narrowed as she assessed them. The scent of perfume, sweat, and intrigue was strong. She finally looked at Vlad again. "Plenty of gossip and speculation, but nothing I'd say was valid. A few people think it's another type of shifter. Some think it's a water creature that came from the Thames."

"Like what?"

"A kelpie was one suggestion." He nodded. A weird, shape-shifting horse that would drown its rider in the river. *Eat its victim's heart, though? Unlikely.* Jet continued, "Or a mermaid that has found itself far from the sea." She frowned. "Is that how mermaids kill?"

"I think they're more likely to drag you under the water to become their mate," Vlad said. "Sounds bloody awful. So, mostly bullshit, then?"

"So far. It's hard to discount anything, though, when we know so little ourselves, right?" She watched him with amusement, as if she knew that he knew more.

He just shrugged. "True. Well, if you hear anything that warrants more questions, let me know."

"You, rather than Grey?"

"Either of us."

She raised her fingers to her forehead in a mock salute. "Always, Captain."

He laughed at her sarcasm, rather than taking offence. "I like that. You can call me that more often." *Preferably while naked, her limbs wrapped around his.* He quickly banished that thought from his head and waded back into the crowd, but not before he saw her giving him the middle finger salute instead.

He found Hal at the club's entrance, back to the wall next to the door, a calm, watchful eye on the customers paying their entrance fee and depositing their coats. "Any problems?"

"A couple of drunks I refused entrance to, but that's all." Hal cocked an eyebrow and smirked. "Thought they were being charming to Jade and Jasmine, not realising that leering and slurring double entendres was deeply disrespectful. I wanted to punch them, but didn't." Hal ran his hands down his jacket, smoothing the lapel of his smart, dark grey suit that he'd paired with a black shirt. He had shoulder-length, light brown hair that he'd tied back in a top knot, and he looked very professional. "Almost mussed up my jacket."

Vlad laughed. "You managed both of them on your own?"

"Walk in the park, boss."

He looked over at Jasmine, who gave him an impish grin. Clearly, Hal was suited for this job. Knowing that Rory was in the office over-looking the dance floor and monitoring the camera feeds, he walked up the stairs to the ground floor bar, the rhythmic *thump* of the bass guitar disappearing with thick sound insulation, and entered a completely different atmosphere.

The lounge area stretched from the double-fronted entrance doors, currently shut to keep out the chill February night, to the long bar at the rear of the room, covered with copper and backed by mirrors with rows of spirits. The seating in between was a mix of plush velvet teal benches in private booths situated around the edge, and tables and chairs in the centre of the floor space. It was as full as the club was downstairs.

Soft music played in the background, and the hum of chatter filled the air. As he was about to head to the bar to find Grey, the front door opened, and John stood on the threshold, the Scottish, red-haired shifter who acted as their regular doorman. An unknown man stood next to him, with short, clipped hair and a certain wild-eyed expression on his face that spelled trouble.

John caught his eye with relief and called him over with a brusque nod of his head. When all three stood in the small entrance hall that acted as a buffer zone between the bar and the street, both doors firmly shut, John finally spoke.

"This gentleman caught my attention as he was trying to enter, because he looked, well, a little intense, and fear was rolling off him like a tidal wave. I thought—all things considered—we should have a chat first."

"I really don't know why!" the man shot back. "I've been perfectly polite."

John ignored him. "It seems he's looking for Maverick Hale. I advised him that he was out right now, but he insists that it's important. He refuses to elaborate on why he needs to see him. However, as I detected the unmistakable air of magic about him, I thought we should investigate."

The man was of average height, but he looked malnourished. His skin hugged his cheekbones, and he appeared exhausted. And yes, fear did roll off him in waves, despite his attempt to look composed. He narrowed his eyes and clenched his jaw. "Seeing as I'm not running away, or trying to defeat you with magic, there is no reason to be so rude."

"We're not being rude," Vlad said easily, although all his senses were on full alert. The unknown man was potentially a witch. "We're taking precautions after certain recent events. I'm Valdermar Rasmussen, the Deputy Manager," he said, extending his hand.

Unnerved by the introduction as Vlad knew he'd be, he blinked rapidly. Politeness was always unnerving if you were on the offensive. It took the wind out of your sails. "Owen Radnor," he said, accepting the handshake. "I know exactly the events you're referring to. A dead man, and probably countless dead animals, too."

"If you know anything about that, you better speak quickly."

"Which is exactly why I want to meet Maverick." He sneered as the yellow light in Vlad's eyes kindled, quickly on the offensive again. "You're shifters. Yes, I know all about you, as you know that I'm a witch. I thought this club was welcoming to all of us paranormal types."

"It is, normally, but to be fair, you don't appear that harmless right now. I can feel your magic swelling." Vlad was keeping an eye on the man's hands, and John was ready to act next to him. A swift punch would end any attempt at a spell.

"I have no intention of harming you. My magic is my protection. I need your help, actually. Or rather, Maverick's. Whatever you're detecting from me is more akin to desperation than aggression." He took a breath, his shoulders dropping, and gathered himself together. "I've spent weeks looking for Maverick, and I must see him. I know for a fact that he'll want to see me."

Vlad considered the man's age, the fact that he was a witch, and the accent that suggested he was from Kent, and suddenly had a horrible feeling as to who this man might be. "Do you have a sister?" he asked.

The man's eyes flared with surprise, pupils constricting as Vlad leaned in. "I did. She's dead now."

One thing was certain; they couldn't let this man leave. This could well be the witch Maverick thought had killed his parents.

"I'm sorry to hear that. You can come in, but try anything, and you'll be dead, too, quicker than you can blink. Wait here." He opened the door to the street and stepped outside with John, one eye on the witch. A queue was already lining up to enter because the doors had been shut, so Vlad made it quick as he scanned their surroundings. He now wished that so many shifters hadn't gone with the search party. "Anyone with him?"

"Not that I could see. He's scared."

"He should be." Vlad wouldn't elaborate. He couldn't. "Be careful."

"Always." John turned back to the queue, all smiles.

Vlad escorted the witch inside, heading straight to the bar. "Take a seat. Drink?"

Owen shook his head, sitting warily on the stool, picking one where he could see the whole room. Vlad was torn as to whether to take him into his office behind the bar, a smaller version of Arlo's, or let him stay in the main room, where the crowd would likely deter him from doing anything stupid. Being herded into an office like a prisoner wasn't likely to make him feel more relaxed, either. However, he did need to consider that this man might be a killer. Although, looking at him now, Vlad didn't buy it.

He pulled his phone from his pocket and called Grey. The question was, should they bring Maverick back from the hunt, or leave them to it?

Hunter inhaled the crisp night air, but was unable to banish the strange, brackish scent from his nose, or the strong smell of blood.

If it wasn't for that, this would be a perfect night. The earlier clouds were rolling away, and a star-pricked sky promised a frosty night. The full moon was cresting the horizon, honing his instinct to hunt. The moon didn't govern their shift to wolves, but it did enhance them. It was like a super boost to their preternatural abilities.

And that's when Hunter detected another strange scent.

Sulphur.

He froze, paw lifted mid-stride, nose raised. A low growl emitted from his throat, and Maverick and Arlo, only a short distance away, stilled too.

The faint scent vanished, and Hunter adjusted his position, angling back towards the stables behind him. Slinking to his side, Maverick arrived before Arlo. His lips curled, a question in his eyes. Hunter indicated he'd picked up a new scent, and sinking low to his belly, crossed the ground to the stables.

However, the scent was elusive, and although he picked up faint trails, he couldn't fix on where it was coming from. The horses were becoming aware of them, their snickering becoming more audible. It was clear the scent wasn't from there, and Hunter doubled back, fearing he'd gone in the wrong direction. This time, all three wolves tracked back and forth, and then Arlo snarled, snout fixed on the riverbank.

Hunter caught the sulphurous scent again. It was cloying, somehow dirty, and all three loped towards the river, Hunter wondering where Domino's team was.

Then a howl split the night, and caution vanished as they raced across the grassy expanse, vaulted the fence that bordered the river path, and landed on the other side just in time to see Xavier crash into the water. Cecile followed him in.

Something—an unidentified blackness, like a void of light—seemed to be in the water, too. It thrashed amongst the tangle of limbs and fur that were Cecile and Xavier, and without a second's thought, Hunter and his companions raced to their position and leapt into the water, too.

Wolves were excellent swimmers, but it had been a long time since Hunter had been in the water. The river that seemed so sluggish on the surface actually had strong currents, and they tried to tug him under. That was the least of his concerns, though. The strong, sulphuric scent was overwhelming here, and the unidentified attacker was wrestling with Xavier, pulling him deeper and deeper underwater and out into the centre of the river. Relentlessly, all the wolves followed him, strong limbs cutting through the pull of the current.

Maverick, not surprisingly, reached them just after Cecile, and his huge jaws sank into the attacker, trying to pull it away from Xavier. But whatever it was clung on stubbornly, and they were all caught in the thrashing circle that tumbled them around and around.

It was dark and hard to see anything, despite Hunter's excellent eyesight, but the void of darkness made it easier to see the creature, in a strange way. He looked for the absence of light, and snapped at whatever part of it he could decipher. However, he was running out of air, his limbs getting heavier, and blood was around them all now. Wolf blood. Only adrenalin kept him going. Through the haze of the attack, Hunter realised other wolves had arrived—Domino and Monroe.

And then suddenly, it was over.

The dark wraith vanished, streaking upstream, and Hunter was dragged roughly to the surface by Domino, where he greedily took long breaths. Xavier was next to him, supported by Maverick, and Arlo appeared next, quickly followed by Cecile. All swam to the bank, scrambling up the muddy slope to reach the path.

They had drifted downstream in the fight, and their splashing and heaving breaths seemed loud in the night, but the bank was empty and silent. Monroe was nowhere in sight, but upstream a sleek, dark shape was pursuing whatever it was that had attacked them. Domino paused long enough to see that everyone was okay, and then plunged into the water again.

Maverick shifted. "Everyone back to the cars, look after Xavier. Wait there." Then he shifted again and leapt into the water, too.

Hunter turned his attention to Xavier. He was streaked with blood, and huge gashes were down his forelimbs and flank. Cecile had claw marks down her left side, too, but Hunter and Arlo had only minor injuries. Although, now that his adrenalin was wearing off, they were stinging badly. Cecile nosed her cousin, licking his face, and he staggered to his paws, legs wobbling beneath him. But he was mobile, and that was enough.

Six

G rey settled on the seat in the small booth by the bar that was reserved for the staff, and assessed the witch, Owen Radnor, who sat next to him.

He didn't need to be a wolf to detect his fear. Owen's eyes darted about the room, hand gripping the brandy he'd finally accepted. However, as he sipped it, he steadied himself.

"You're safe here," Grey told him, "as long as you play by our rules." He nodded to Vlad, who sat opposite Owen. "My friend here tells me you want Maverick. What for?"

"I need his help."

Grey didn't see the point in mincing his words. "Are you the witch who killed his parents?"

"No!" Owen jerked back in shock, almost sloshing his brandy, and his emphatic reply made the bar staff look around. He calmed down and replied quietly. "No, I was not responsible. Not directly, anyway."

"But you and your sister were the witches who asked them for blood."

"He told you that?"

"Yes. Vlad and I need to decide if you're a risk to anyone here. You're a witch with undefined motives, and that means I don't trust you." Grey had no idea how powerful this witch was. He could turn him into a toad for all he knew, with one word of command.

"As I told your friend here, I haven't come to fight. I need Maverick's help."

"That's a big ask, considering what happened to his parents."

Owen licked his lips, eyes darting nervously again until they finally settled on Grey. "That's because he doesn't know all the details. When he does, he'll understand."

"Just out of curiosity," Vlad asked, "when did your sister die?"

"About six weeks ago."

"Is it related to what's happening now?"

"Yes, but that's all I'm saying until I speak to Maverick." Defiant in voice but not his mannerisms, he retreated to the corner of the booth.

It wasn't good enough as far as Grey was concerned. "My friends are hunting that thing right now. Anything that helps them is important. *What* is it?"

Owen hesitated, and then as Grey leaned closer, finally relented. "It's a type of demon."

Grey's blood ran cold. *They weren't prepared for that. Not even close.* He slid out of the booth, saying to Vlad, "I'll make the call while you keep Owen company."

Vlad, his emotions well under control, just nodded and settled back in his seat, a watchful eye on the witch.

Grey entered Arlo's office, wondering how this news would be received. He had visions of Maverick tearing through the door, feral and eyes glowing, which is why he had every intention of keeping Owen in full public view. It was close to eleven o'clock already, and they would be open for a while. And even if they were closed, they would still sit with Owen until Maverick returned.

He called Domino first, but her phone rang and rang. Not surprising. The phone would be in the car while they hunted. He left a message asking her to call him urgently, and then tried Arlo, who answered within seconds.

"Hunt over?" Grey asked, hoping the demon was a ruse.

"Not entirely. Something attacked Xavier. Pulled him into the river."

"Is he okay?"

"Yeah, but he's injured. So are a few of us, actually. Maverick, Domino, and Monroe are still hunting it." Arlo's voice was tight, betraying his worry. "And before you ask, I have no idea what it is."

"I do, and I have more information that Maverick won't like, so you've got your work cut out. I'm relying on you to keep Maverick calm, and to get everyone out of there safely."

Maverick stalked through the entrance of the bar, senses on full alert, trying very hard to keep his emotions under control.

Their attempt to track the fleeing creature had failed, which had infuriated him, but when Arlo took him aside to tell him the news about Owen and the demon, his fury had exploded. Arlo, sensibly, let him vent. After his initial response he calmed down, took stock, and locked his fury under an icy exterior.

His mood wasn't helped by his worry about Xavier, whose injuries seemed to be worsening over time rather than improving, according to Arlo, who had sent Xavier and Cecile to Moonfell with Hunter. He then waited with Tommy, Jax, and Mads, who had returned to the car after being summoned by Cecile's howl. By now, the three injured shifters were hopefully being tended by Morgana, the Moonfell witch who was employed as their healer. Moonfell, their huge, Gothic mansion, was on the edge of Richmond Park, so it was quicker for them to reach her there.

Maverick took a deep breath, smoothed his still damp hair into submission, and crossed the floor to the corner booth, flanked by Arlo and Domino. As soon as he laid eyes on Owen, everything came flooding back, the past jarring with the present. Owen was diminished, somehow. A shrunken man compared to the image he'd had in his mind. Someone he could break without hardly trying.

"You've got a fucking nerve," Maverick said, standing over him, his low voice almost a growl.

To his credit, Owen didn't shrink back, but instead stared at him apologetically. "I know, but I have my reasons, and I want you...would like you to hear me out. Please."

Grey and Vlad were seated in the booth, waiting patiently. He gave Grey a knowing stare. *Well played*. Being in the bar was a good move. An annoying one, but wise.

The seconds ticked by while Maverick considered his options, but ultimately, he didn't have any. Not if he wanted information—especially about this so-called demon, news he'd barely wrapped his head around. Unfortunately, it did make sense. The stench of sulphur had already raised that suspicion. *But did he want anyone else to hear their conversation? Did he trust himself on his own?*

"Vlad, Grey, thanks, but you can leave. Arlo and Domino, take a seat." Vlad and Grey nodded, pausing only to receive brief instructions from Domino, then left without a word. Maverick slid into the seat opposite the man whose memory had haunted him for years. Domino sat next to him, Arlo next to Owen.

"Thank you," Owen began.

"This better be good." Maverick leaned closer smelling the witch's fear. "Because right now, I want to kill you, and only my good friends here are stopping me."

"I know." Owen's hand clenched around his glass, knuckles white. "First of all, I want to say how sorry I am that your parents died, and that I couldn't tell you so at the time."

"Because you ran away, out of guilt."

"Not because of what you think. Neither I nor my sister killed your parents. However," he licked his lips, "we were partially responsible, as were a few others. What you need to understand is that everything we did was based on one stupid summoning that went horribly wrong. We needed shifter blood to put it right. That's why we were so persistent."

Maverick held a hand up to stop him. "Are you here just to apologise, or does this have some relevance to the fact that a man has died today, and one of my pack is badly injured?"

"Everything that is happening now is tied to that event in the past. What started then is not over. It's why my sister is dead."

"The creature who attacked tonight killed your sister? Or the demon, as you call it." Maverick, uncharitably, felt some victory in this.

"That creature *is* my sister. Her name was Ivy, if you remember."

"*What*?" Maverick felt the world tilt. "How is that possible? You said it's a demon. Hell, it stinks of sulphur, so that makes sense. How is it also your sister?"

"Ivy has been consumed by it." Owen choked up, tears threatening, and unable to meet Maverick's stare any longer, he dropped his head, staring at his drink instead.

Maverick was dumbfounded, floundering for words, and it was Arlo who recovered quickest. "You talked of a summoning, all those years ago. You summoned it. On purpose?" He looked incredulous.

"Yes. We had always been fascinated by the ancient Latin spells used by necromancers and priests in the Medieval Church. We thought they were jokes, to be honest, and then," he dragged his gaze from his glass to look at Arlo, "we found they weren't. You must understand that we weren't powerful witches. Still aren't. We have no lineage that goes back centuries, like some families. We came to our magic through discipline and years of work, taught by our mother. We don't have elemental magic. Most of our magic is based upon ritual. That was what drew us to the ancient documents and old books that talked of demon-summoning. If we were successful—and we didn't think we would be, I must stress that—we thought we could control our own demon. Get it to do our bidding and by doing so, enhance our magic. But as I said, we really thought it futile."

Arlo gave a dry laugh. "So, you summoned one and then found that you couldn't control it."

"We could for a while, but unfortunately, the demon trap that we kept it in was damaged accidentally. We managed to contain it, but by then it had attacked my sister, and she was injured. The demon itself was a lesser creature, from the lower order of demons."

"Lower order?" Domino murmured. "They have orders?"

"Hierarchies, yes. Fortunately, ours was not of the earth-shattering, bring the end of the world type."

"Just the murdering, rip the heart out of body type?" Maverick said, pinning Owen in place with a vicious stare. "I presume that was what killed my parents. It finally escaped you." And then he had another thought. "Your sister killed my parents?"

"No!" Owen was emphatic. "She was still herself at that point. It was the demon. But there's a reason it tracked your parents." A film of sweat covered Owen's forehead and upper lip, and the stench of his fear increased. "We needed shifter blood because we had read an old

rite that said shifter blood, rather than human blood, could control
it."

"But no one gave you shifter blood."

"Actually, that's not true. Your brother did. So did his friends."

Maverick leaped to his feet, leaned across the table, and gripped
Owen's throat. "You're a fucking liar!"

He was oblivious to the stares, and his pulse thundered in his ears.
All he wanted to do was see the life drain from the man who had
destroyed his family.

And then he felt Domino's hand on his arm, and her urgent en-
treaty. "Not here, Maverick."

He slowly came to his senses and found the bar staff turning away
as if they hadn't been staring at all, and the few customers at the closest
tables twisting back to their companions.

Maverick released his grip on Owen and sat down, ignoring the
brandy pooling on the table from the glass he'd tipped over. He took
a deep breath, in and out, settling his wolf. Owen looked terrified,
sitting as far back in his seat as he could. Arlo and Domino were sitting
again, but were on full alert.

"I'm not lying," Owen said, almost whispering.

*Was this why his brother had gone off the rails and vanished from his
life with only the occasional postcard? Guilt?*

"What is it that you want from me?"

"I need to send it back to the other dimension, but for that I need
your brother's blood, and his friends' blood, if possible. I tried without
it and failed. I don't know where they are. If that fails, then," Owen
took a breath, eyes furtive, "then your blood might work. It is tied to
your family, after all."

Maverick signalled for more drinks and sat back in his seat. "Tell me
everything."

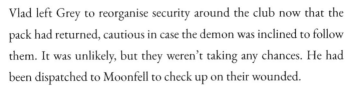

Vlad left Grey to reorganise security around the club now that the pack had returned, cautious in case the demon was inclined to follow them. It was unlikely, but they weren't taking any chances. He had been dispatched to Moonfell to check up on their wounded.

He had heard much about the Gothic mansion that belonged to the three witches, but had never been there before. He knew the witches well enough, of course, and was glad that Odette dispensed with her usual theatrics when she answered the front door and ushered him down the hall and into the large kitchen, which was now doubling as a sick room.

A sheet had been draped over the kitchen table, and Xavier lay on it, his modesty protected by a towel. Long, raking claw marks scarred his thighs, right rib cage, upper arms, and shoulder, and they were filled with a disgusting yellow pus that stank of death. Xavier was in his human form, his face contorted in pain, and barely conscious.

"No wonder his wounds are so bad," he said, watching Morgana tend to him, ably assisted by Birdie. "A demon probably has poisons we know nothing about."

"Fortunately," Odette said, "we have spells and plenty of salves that should counter its effects. He looks bad right now, but Morgana is confident he'll be much better in a couple of days."

Morgana glanced across at Vlad, not looking as confident as Odette made out. "No more fighting for a while, though!"

"Thanks, Morgana. We really appreciate this. Where are the other two?" Hunter and Cecile were nowhere in sight.

"In the shower." Odette filled the kettle. "It's the easiest way to clean their wounds before we dress them. Plus, they stink of the river. Tea?"

"Coffee, if possible."

She nodded and headed to the coffee machine, and Vlad took a moment to calm himself down. The night had been chaotic, a combination of their usual Friday night business, the hunt, and the arrival of Owen. He had driven recklessly, worried about his friends. He had known Xavier a long time, and his imagination had run wild thinking about demon injuries. *If Xavier died...*

Part of him had wanted to attack Owen, but he had restrained himself, aware of his role, the crowded bar, and the fact that Grey needed him. And they needed Owen. Anything that he could tell them would be useful, and hopefully Maverick was getting as much information as he could.

Vlad leaned against the counter, arms folded across his chest, watching Morgana, and wincing with every groan that Xavier made. Morgana was dressed in another of her long, black dresses, but an apron was over it, bloodstained, and her hair was tied back. A stack of cotton swabs was on the table, and Birdie, the new, glamourous, sixty-something version with her mane of grey hair, was busy handing over various pots and salves, and fixing dressings in place. Odette was barefoot, dressed in jeans and a long jumper, her hair tied carelessly back, long curls escaping. The kitchen itself eventually drew his eye. It was magnificent, all black tiles, dark wood, and gleaming stainless steel. The high, arched Gothic windows were only partly covered by blinds, and he could see the spotlit gardens beyond. His wolf longed to explore. The garden promised secrets.

The scent of coffee pulled him back to the kitchen, just as Hunter and Cecile entered the room through a door in the far corner. Hunter wore only a towel wrapped around his waist, revealing his muscled body, but Cecile was wearing a thick bathrobe, displaying the lower half of her shapely legs. Her long, honey blonde hair looked darker now that it was wet. Both had visible wounds and claw marks sustained in the fight.

"Hey, guys. How are you two?"

"I've been better," Hunter said, wincing with pain as he twisted to show claw marks on his back, then held his arms out to display his wounds there. "The shower helped for a few minutes, but now they're stinging like a bitch. Burning, actually. There's something on my shoulder, too."

"A bite," Odette informed him as she crossed the room to examine them. "Looks nasty. You too, Cecile, below your neck." She eased the top of the bathrobe back, the edge of the bite just visible above the collar.

"I know." She reached for it, and her hand came away sticky. She sniffed and recoiled. "Gross. It's getting worse, too. The ones on my legs are itching." She shook her head as if to clear foggy thoughts. "I feel woozy, but forget about me. It's Xavier who needs help."

"You all need help. You've been wounded by a demon." Vlad gently guided Cecile to a seat.

"Don't worry, you're next," Morgana told her, frowning. She took a moment to crouch and examine her leg wounds, keeping her hands high like a surgeon as they were still covered in Xavier's blood. "They're red around the area, which means the infection is spreading."

"Is that bad?" she asked.

"Well, it's not good, but I can handle it. We'll have to find you some clothes. You too," Morgana said as she visually inspected Hunter's shoulder. "I haven't had a half-naked man in my kitchen for years."

Hunter smirked. "What a pity."

"You can come and wander around mine anytime," Birdie shot back, eyes lingering on his chest.

"Good grief, Birdie!" Odette said, thrusting Vlad's coffee at him. "The Goddess is playing with your hormones."

"No, Hunter's impressive abs are playing with my hormones."

Despite everything, Vlad laughed, glad of the witches' humour. He needed levity after all the drama. "What's happened to your clothes?"

"Covered in pus and blood," Cecile explained with a grimace. "They are in the wash."

Hunter winked at Birdie. "I'll drop the towel if you want."

"You better not," Cecile warned him. "I have seen enough of you naked lately. And we're in the kitchen! Be civilized." Her French accent became more obvious as she scolded him. "Honestly!"

"Spoilsport." Hunter laughed as he said it. "Just lightening the mood."

"I'll be happier when I know Xav is okay."

Morgana finished his final dressing and washed her hands in the sink. "He needs to stay here tonight, where I can keep an eye on him. You two should stay, too."

"Mine will be fine," Hunter protested.

"I decide that, not you."

Vlad felt his responsibilities ease as Morgana took control and the caffeine kicked in. He caught sight of his reflection in the window, the darkness beyond turning it into a mirror. His blond hair was sticking up rakishly, and he took a moment to smooth it down. His phone buzzing in his pocket, however, reminded him of his duties.

"It's Arlo. I'll take it in the hall."

Odette's eyes flickered with interest, but she just nodded as he left the room.

After they'd exchanged pleasantries, Vlad listened in silence as Arlo related their conversation with Owen. It all sounded insane. "Let me get this right. The demon is now Owen's sister? Is that even possible?" *Why was he asking? It wasn't like he knew anything about demons. They could turn into bunnies, as far as he knew.*

"It happened, so it must be." Arlo sounded tired. "Maverick is furious."

"Owen could totally be lying. It could be a way to gain sympathy. Deflect Maverick's anger. Especially because of his brother. Do you think it's true? That his brother gave his blood? What a moron."

"Maverick doesn't know what to think right now, but I don't think Owen is lying. However, we need to find out, one way or another. We also need to find more about demons and controlling them, and ultimately getting rid of them."

Vlad knew with blinding clarity what was coming next. "You need Odette to see Owen." The witch was well known for her ability to see to the truth of things.

"Yes. Would she come here, do you think? I don't want him anywhere near our injured pack, or think it's fair that he should know where the witches live. I still don't trust him."

"Something tells me that Moonfell would eat Owen alive, but leave it with me." He silently added, *Odette will do anything to help you, Arlo, and if you can't see that, you're an idiot.* However, he promised to call him back with news and ended the call.

When he returned to the kitchen, Morgana was working on Cecile's injuries, and Birdie on Hunter's. Xavier was wrapped in a blanket, still prone on the table.

"Will Xavier really be okay?" he asked the witches.

Morgana barely glanced at him as she said, "I think so, but he'll need constant attention for the next twenty-four hours. So will these two. I don't like how Cecile is behaving."

"I'm just tired," she complained.

"Lying doesn't help me diagnose what's wrong," she said sharply. "Bloody shifters and your egos. Same goes for Hunter. You stay put."

"If you say so," he said evenly.

"Well, I have news," Vlad said, sitting astride a kitchen chair that he dragged from the table. "And a request. First, we know more about the demon. Apparently, it's a lesser demon, whatever that is," he said, trying to recall Arlo's terminology. "But it's taken over a witch. Killed her, I guess, essentially."

All three witches' attention snapped to him. "Go on," Odette said, fixing him with her strange, far-seeing eyes.

He outlined Owen and his sister's experiments, and what had ensued in the past, and Birdie hissed with annoyance. "Rank amateurs playing with forces beyond their control."

"He admitted they weren't skilful witches…"

"Even more reason not to summon a demon! Did he think it would be like a puppy on a lead!" Birdie was outraged, Hunter's wound forgotten. "We need details. It means we can tailor our magic and healing spells to better deal with their injuries."

"And catch it," Morgana added, levelling her stare at Vlad. "You won't be able to. We have to do that."

That hadn't even crossed Vlad's mind. He had been focussed on killing it.

As if she'd read his thoughts, Odette said, "No, you can't kill a demon with teeth and claws. You need to banish it, and for that you need magic, power, and a demon trap."

"Even though they used shifter's blood to do...whatever it was they used the blood for?"

"Yes. That just makes it worse," Morgana said, brow furrowed with worry. She repeated Birdie's words. "Absolute amateurs."

Vlad turned to Odette. "The trouble is, we have no idea whether this is truth or lies. Or if he's trying to trap us into something. Plus, Maverick needs to know if his brother was really involved. Arlo asks if you'll speak to him. Owen, I mean."

"Of course. I'll go now. We need as much detail on his rites as he can remember if we're to trap it and send it back where it came from, including the spell he used with the shifter blood. All of it. There is much he won't have told you. Even if he did, you wouldn't understand."

"Can you save Owen's sister?"

"No. She's gone forever now."

As much as Vlad wanted to stay at Moonfell and relax in their kitchen, he also knew he needed to return to Storm Moon. There was nothing he could do at Moonfell. *Unless...* "Do you need me to stay here? Added protection in case the demon returns?"

"You're very sweet," Birdie told him, "but I can assure you that we do not need your protection to keep a demon at bay."

He smiled. "No, I didn't think so. I'll get back to the club, then." This house was filled with magic. He could feel it, like a current of electricity, humming everywhere. Plus, the Moonfell witches were powerful, from a bloodline that ran back centuries. "Can I at least carry Xavier to a bed before I go?"

"Yes, please," Morgana said, still tending to Cecile. "Odette, do me a favour and show him the way. And if you need to bring Owen here after you've spoken to him, don't hesitate. It may be that we need him, as well as his rituals."

Seven

Arlo experienced the familiar tug of attraction when Odette walked into his office where they had relocated Owen, swiftly followed by the pain of remembered arguments, harsh words, and the failure of what had been something so promising.

He greeted her with as much equanimity as he could muster. They had seen each other several times now over previous months, and it was getting less awkward every time. Perversely, he now looked forward to it, as if one day, everything might change and they could be friends again. For now, though, she just nodded at him with a cool greeting, reserving her smiles for Domino, who sat behind the desk. Maverick had returned to his flat to mull over the information Owen had shared, declaring that if he spent one more second in Owen's company, he would kill him.

"Thanks for coming," Domino said, giving her a brief hug. Domino had already showered and freshened up after her swim in the river. She pointed to Owen, who sat beside Arlo on the small sofa. "That's Owen, the witch who summoned the demon. We need to know if he's telling the truth."

Immediately Odette focussed only on the witch, crossing the room to sit in a chair that she pulled closer to Owen. She hadn't bothered to change for the club. She still wore her old jeans and jumper, hair rakishly tied back, and still looked dazzling. She was like a perfect flower compared to the overdressed and over made-up customers in the bar.

"Give me your hands, Owen." He leaned forward, looking nervous as Odette clasped his hands within her own. "I'm Odette, a witch like you."

"I can already tell that you're nothing like me," he said, eyeing her warily. "I can feel your power."

"The Goddess has blessed our family."

"What are you going to do to me?"

"Nothing except listen. I already know a little about what has happened, but I want to hear it from you. Tell me about your sister and the demon rituals. There was more than one ritual, wasn't there?"

"Yes, we tried several summonings, and all failed, until one day...well, it happened." He licked his lips.

"You found the rite in an old book?"

"Yes, several of them, actually. Histories of Medieval demonology, filled with rites."

"I know the rituals you refer to. They were used by priests in the Church?" She meant the Catholic Church, the only one that existed in England at the time. It was long before King Henry VIII had created the Church of England.

"Yes, they were arcane and fascinating, and we decided to experiment."

To her credit she didn't even blink, even though Arlo knew she would be furious at such cavalier behaviour.

"One day you were successful. The demon's name?"

"Brokaz—or that's as near to how we could pronounce it, anyway." Owen relaxed as he talked, his attention solely on Odette. It was as if she was hypnotising him.

"You say he was a lesser demon? How do you know?"

"It was in the summoning itself. The title, actually. *To summon the demons of the third tier who can help to achieve your earthly desires, and to bind them to your power for the purpose of magic.*"

"And what was the purpose—for you and your sister? What magic did you want to achieve?"

"We wanted to make money. To have influence."

"You tell half-truths, Owen. I think your purpose was uglier than that." Odette gripped his hands tighter as he tried to pull away, and Arlo laid a restraining hand on his arm. Odette said softly, "There is no need to restrain him, Arlo. He cannot break our connection yet." She leaned forward, the slender woman controlling Owen, and he mimicked her actions until they were only inches apart. "Owen, don't lie to me. You wanted a demon. Why?"

"We wished it do our bidding." A sweat was on his brow and upper lip as if he were struggling to resist answering.

"How you prevaricate. What bidding?"

"For help with a money spell. We wanted to be rich."

"There was more than that. You wanted to control other demons...I see it now. He would be the gateway to others who had greater power." Odette frowned. "You wanted an army."

"No! We wanted respect."

"There was a coven who refused you. You wanted to hurt them."

Arlo exchanged a surprised glance with Domino. *This was new.*

"Lies!"

"*Truth*. You wished to join a coven, and they denied you. You decided to hurt them with a demon." Her eyes were hard now, like flint, and they bore into Owen, who squirmed but couldn't move. "You would have harmed others in your desire for power. They saw this in you. In both of you. That is why they refused you. And they were right. You *did* harm others. Why shifter blood?"

Owen was stuttering with shock, eyes narrowed. "You have it all wrong."

"Stop lying!" Odette shouted, her voice like thunder as power snapped around the room, the lights flickering wildly. "Revenge is burned upon your heart. But I do not see it all yet." She fell silent, her strange, unearthly stare still fixed on Owen, and also through him, as if she were seeing the past scroll before her.

Arlo had the perfect view of her expression: unblinking eyes, calm face, unlined by time or grief, but her lips uttered silent words. All the while she continued to grip Owen's hands, such slender hands that had such a powerful grasp. Hands that also caressed and teased.

But she was oblivious to Arlo's observations and memories, and she took a sharp intake of breath. "Now I see it. You sought to change its nature with shifter blood. To make it more powerful—at its request—using arcane blood spells. When you did it, the demon resisted your bonds, injured your sister, and escaped, killing Maverick's parents."

Arlo leaned forward, horrified and fascinated, and glad that Maverick wasn't there to witness this. They would have to tell him, of course, but best not to see the writhing, squirming Owen, or hear the strange tale that Odette was seeing unfold within her uncanny Sight.

"You were desperate," she continued, "unable to send it back, unable to control it, and your sister bound herself to it—her life blood to keep it contained. And you refused to help."

"I couldn't help! One of us had to remain rational and human to maintain the rituals."

"Always so weak, Owen. Always grasping. Now you are here, grasping again."

Odette finally released his hands and flopped back in her chair, eyes slowly becoming focussed on the present again. Owen scuttled back in his chair, blazing with fury and shame, the stench of fear strong beneath it all. Domino was closer now, bristling with energy and ready to pounce if needed, but Owen wasn't making any attempt to escape or retaliate; he just looked defeated.

"There is more, but I can't see it yet. Can I have a drink?" Odette asked. "Hot, sweet tea, if possible."

"I'll get it," Domino said, gesturing for Arlo to stay seated.

Arlo didn't give a crap how Owen was, instead asking, "Are you all right, Odette?"

"I'll be fine. It's always hard when someone tries to block the truth, but we have some of it now, in all of its ugliness. There is more to discover, though."

"What do we do with him?"

"He should be guarded at all times, but he has little power now. The demon has drained most of what he had. He was telling the truth about that. He has no natural magic. I still wouldn't trust him on his own, though. You should check his pockets for charms and amulets. Jewellery, perhaps."

"I'm still here!" Owen protested. "Do you think I'm deaf?"

"Your needs have no weight with me," Arlo informed him, "not now that I've heard the sordid truth. Don't worry, we won't torture you or kill you—yet."

"We'll discuss it with Maverick," Domino said, handing Odette her drink. "In the meantime, I'll get Monroe and Tommy to take him downstairs to the Security Office. They can search him and guard him down there."

Arlo waited silently, while Owen sulked and Odette sipped her tea. She had told him that truth-seeing sometimes drained her energy, and that sugar was a good way of returning her equilibrium and closing her third eye. Domino made a quick phone call, and within moments

Tommy and Monroe entered, their size intimidating Owen even more. They hustled him out the door, heading to the rear entrance, no doubt to save escorting him through the bar.

Arlo checked his watch. Almost closing time, although it felt like it was much later.

"I'll update Maverick," Domino said, and before Arlo could object, she left him and Odette alone, flicking the overhead lights off on her way out.

Only soft lamplight spilling from the desk illuminated the office, and silence settled around them, as the noise of the bar receded. Despite his awkwardness at being alone with Odette, he relaxed for the first time in hours. He stretched out, his feet on the coffee table, hands behind his head that rested on the sofa back, and stared up at the ceiling. This was his office, so it had been designed to his style. It was painted peacock blue, and dark wooden blinds covered the only window that overlooked the side of the building; it was made of safety glass, with bars outside as it was on the ground floor. There were a few art prints, the desk in one corner with the office chair in black leather behind it, one two-seater sofa, and two modern armchairs in leather and steel with a low coffee table at the centre of the arrangement.

For a while neither of them spoke, but then Arlo felt compelled to start a conversation. Odette might not speak otherwise, and he wanted to breach the gulf that had opened between them. Domino, sneakily, had gifted him some time with Odette, and although he'd avoided her for years, he now craved contact with her.

"Thank you," he said. "We appreciate you coming out so late on Friday night. You can see our dilemma."

"It's fine. You know I will always come when needed. Especially after seeing Xavier's injuries."

Arlo immediately felt terrible. He hadn't even thought about his three injured friends since she'd arrived. He shifted position to look at her. "He'll survive, though?"

"With Morgana's help. Demons have claws and teeth—of a sort—and they carry poisons from their world that are very different to ours."

Arlo shuffled to sit up. "Did you see anything that would help? The type of ritual or demon?"

"I saw the demon. A lesser one, certainly, but powerful enough. They were fools to think they could contain it. As for the rite, I saw glimpses...nothing specific, but I will speak to Owen again. Once I've recovered, and he has. I've drained him, too."

"It's his own fault. He shouldn't have lied."

She smiled, meeting his gaze properly for the first time since she entered the room. "True. To resist makes it harder for both of us. He didn't expect it though, and he isn't strong, so it wasn't so bad. The tea is helping."

"Why did you hold his hands?"

"To attune to his energies. He's scared."

"Does that make him more dangerous?"

"Perhaps, but he won't escape. He doesn't want to. He thinks the demon will come for him, and it might well, even though it's his sister. Well, was. I doubt she retains any of herself anymore." She curled her legs under her to get more comfortable. "It's the shifter blood that most intrigues me. That's the spell I need to understand. To try to change a demon's nature is either ballsy or insane."

"Or both. You didn't ask him about Maverick's brother. He'll want to know that."

"I saw it all. I didn't need to ask. That is how the demon broke free."

Arlo's tiredness vanished. "His brother really gave them his blood?"

"And his three friends. Their part in the ritual and their paths afterwards were not revealed to me though, although I know they fled out of fear and guilt."

"You don't know where to?"

"No. It may be that we need some of their blood to send the demon back, but I'm unsure at this stage."

"Owen and Ivy's blood?"

"Owen's *and* the shifters."

That possibility hadn't even entered Arlo's head. "We need to find them after all these years?"

"Perhaps. Maverick will want to find his brother anyway, surely."

"Yeah, he probably will. Maybe that means someone should go with him."

"He won't want that."

"I know him better than you do," he said, suddenly riled at her calm prediction.

"I know, but there are some things better done alone, like sorting out murky family business. You would be the same."

"I suppose I would be, but it might be dangerous. Who knows where his brother is or what's he's involved with."

"He might be married with kids, for all we know," Odette said, laughing.

Her smile disarmed him, and he wanted to call a truce to their years of...what, enmity? Resentment? Hate, perhaps? Not on his behalf, certainly.

"Can we be friends?" he asked softly. "It doesn't seem right to be treading warily around each other now that you're back at Storm Moon regularly. Well, Morgana at least."

"Is that what you want? Or is that what you think should happen for the pack?" She regarded him over her mug, unblinking like an owl, and with a sudden flash of insight of his own, he realised that was her other side, the animal half that she carried within her. *Why had he never seen that before?*

"It's what *I* want. It's nothing to do with the pack. I miss this."

"Us sitting in the dark, drinking tea?"

"You know what I mean. Us talking like civilised adults that were once lovers and have now moved on. I miss our conversations." He missed those more even than sex, although that was always great; it was their feeling of connection, more than he'd had with any woman before or since that he really missed. She *knew* him.

"I miss it, too. But it's easier said than done."

"Is it? Or can we both just move on? It's been a while now. Three years."

"And four months."

For some reason, he liked that she knew it was longer. Like it mattered to her more than he thought. "Yes, three years and four months. I could probably work out the days, too. Long enough, though, yes?"

She smiled. "Let's be adults, then."

Relief washed over him, and the tension that he'd seemed to carry for years ebbed away. "Thank you."

"Perhaps you shouldn't thank me yet. You might change your mind."

The lamp cast her in a golden glow, igniting her milky skin, and making a nimbus of light around her hair. "I doubt that."

He decided to be really, truly selfish for a few moments, knowing that Owen was guarded, and that the injured shifters were being cared for, and that Domino was with Maverick. The staff could clear the club. It would all run like clockwork, and security was high.

He sat back again, watching her with a lazy smile and feeling the need to connect properly. "Tell me what you've been up to. All the Moonfell madness."

She sniggered. "We'd need a week. But only if you tell me Storm Moon madness."

"Deal."

Eight

"So that's the whole sorry tale that we know so far," Domino told Maverick after she'd related Odette's success. "It's ugly. Horrible. I'm sorry."

"You have nothing to apologise for."

When Domino arrived in Maverick's flat, she had expected brooding silence and darkness, but instead she'd found the place filled with lamplight, music, and a spread of old photos across the coffee table. Maverick had listened intently while she relayed Odette's news, but as soon as she finished, he shuffled through the photos again.

He held one out to her. "This is my brother. The stupid fool who caused such destruction. Looked pretty harmless then, didn't he?"

The photo showed a gangly-limbed teenager with dark brown hair, wearing grubby jeans and a t-shirt, sitting on a waist-high wall, grinning at the camera. "He looks a bit like you, around the eyes. Was this your house?"

"Yes. Our childhood home. That was early summer. He'd have been about fifteen then, so I'd have been twelve or thirteen."

"A couple of years before everything happened."

"Yes. Before they died."

His mood was calm, his natural, even temper had returned, and Domino was relieved. Maverick had been so intense earlier. Burning with fury. "You've regained your balance quickly. Are you okay?"

His charming, rakish, alpha grin illuminated his face. "I am. Am I happy about the news? No. I still want to rip the witch's throat out, and my brother's, too. I won't though, don't worry. Not yet, anyway. But I know what I need to do. I need to track down my brother and speak to him."

"You want answers."

"Hell yes! Wouldn't you? I need to look in Canagan's eyes and find out what the fuck he was thinking! And his friends." The news seemed to hit him again, and he raked his hand through his hair, leapt to his feet, and headed to the kitchen. "Do you want a drink? I'm making coffee."

"Seeing as we're likely to be up for hours yet, sounds good. Do you mind?" She gestured at the photos.

"No, go ahead. There's some of me in there, looking ridiculously young."

Domino studied the images of family gatherings, and several photos of a young Maverick, skinny and long-limbed like his father and brother, too young to have developed the broad shoulders that he had now. They looked happy. "This looks a beautiful place."

"The Kent Downs. Have you ever been?"

"No, but if you want help tracking him down, I'll see them then. I'm not sure this is something that you should do alone."

"No, thank you. I *want* to do this alone." He handed her a cup of coffee, fixed with milk and sugar, just as she liked it, and sat on the sofa. "As to when it happens, I guess that depends on this demon. I'm not leaving the pack until that's dealt with. Did Odette suggest how we could do it?"

"No. I didn't hang around to hear more. I just sent Owen down to my office and left Odette with Arlo."

He smirked. "Alone?"

"Yes." She sipped her coffee and with every mouthful felt a little more revived. The plunge into the freezing river was now almost a distant memory. "I'm hoping they at least start acting normally around each other."

"Are you matchmaking?"

"I wouldn't dream of it. But I hate working around awkwardness, and those two... Ugh!" She rolled her eyes. "The worst thing is, I think they actually want to be friends again. I'm just nudging them in the right direction."

He laughed as he leaned back and put his feet on the coffee table. "Yeah, you're matchmaking. Good. I think it's driving us all a bit mad. I hope they work it out."

"Arlo back with Odette? But you hate witches."

"I hate *some* witches. I can't criticise the Moonfell bunch, can I? They've been nothing but helpful."

He looked disgruntled, and it was Domino's turn to laugh. "It's hard to put aside such long-held beliefs, isn't it? You can still hate Owen and Ivy, though. They deserve it."

"You know, as big a shock as this news is, it actually feels good to be looking into it again. At the time, my parents' death divided the pack. Broke our family up, obviously, and the police got involved—they didn't know that we were shifters, of course. My aunt was grieving and angry. It was...*huge*! And when the attacker was never identified, that made it worse. Then my brother took off, although technically he'd been absent for a while. For a long time the whole thing dominated everything, until I made myself move on."

Maverick had never been so open about this subject before, but now there was an air of confession, and Domino wondered if she was supposed to offer some kind of absolution. Or maybe just listening was the important thing. She settled more comfortably in the armchair, feet curled beneath her, trusting that Grey or Vlad would come for them if they were needed.

"Is that when you came to London?"

"Yes, looking for big city excitement. And women, of course. I found that sex offered far more comfort than drowning my sorrows in alcohol."

"You certainly seem to balance that particular minefield."

"I never promise anything. That's fair, right?"

"It's fair, although I bet they aren't half so happy about it as they make out." Although at some point she was sure he'd meet his match, and then he may sing a different tune. Wolves could be possessive, and alphas perhaps even worse. They were used to getting their own way. A woman treating Maverick as disposable may not go down well at all. However, Domino decided to keep those thoughts to herself. "You joined this pack then?"

"Not initially. I lone-wolfed it for a while, but I needed stability, to return to the feeling of family I once had. That's when I joined this pack, although it was different then."

Domino knew their history. She'd been a member for over ten years, although Maverick had been around for longer. She'd been in another pack in the east of England before then. But there were things that she still didn't know. "How did you get the money together to buy this place? It's prime real estate."

"The family home was sold and split between me and my brother, although we couldn't touch the money until we turned twenty-one. And then my aunt died, and left me everything."

"Nothing to your brother?"

"Nope. She was pretty bitter about his behaviour, and with good reason. The year or two that he did stick around, he was a shit. He stayed out late, picked arguments, drank too much, and was generally a nightmare. He pretty much abandoned me, which was devastating, to be honest, and I couldn't understand why. I thought that grief would have brought us closer together. Now, of course," his face twisted into a wry smile, "I understand why. It was guilt. So that's something."

Domino felt devasted for him. Of course a young boy would have looked to his older brother for comfort, and to be rejected must have been like experiencing the death of another relationship. Anger flared for Maverick, and all that he had lost. But of course, his brother wasn't much older, either. "It would have been hard for him to spend time with you," Domino said, thinking how horribly guilty he would feel. "I wonder if he wanted to tell you and couldn't face it."

"There were awkward conversations." He shrugged. "Such a long time ago. I'm probably mis-remembering things."

"Your aunt must have been young when she died. I sort of presumed that she was still alive."

"No. She died of cancer. I always kept in touch, obviously. Went to see her as often as I could, but I felt powerless. I tried to get in touch with my brother. I thought he should know, but he never left a forwarding address. I could feel everything I'd achieved start to slip away again." He stared at Domino, as if willing her to understand. "I had a good place here, and was earning respect, but I don't know, all of a sudden, I felt it could go at any moment. I'd been renting a flat, but then when this place came up for sale, it seemed like fate. I had the money, and I wanted stability. I wanted to build something."

"A safe place for you and others." Domino felt emotional, and she suddenly had newfound respect and understanding for her alpha that she'd never had before. He'd always had her loyalty, for believing in her and not being a sexist wanker, and now she knew she'd support him to the death if she had to. "And then you became the alpha. From my perspective, I think you have created a great pack, and a great club. The important thing to know is, has it worked for you?"

He smiled. "Yes."

"Good. You didn't have to share all that, but I appreciate that you did. Thank you."

"You caught me in the right mood, and," he shrugged again, a little awkward, "you're my friend. A good one. You deserve to know what all this crap we're about to face is about." He sat up, placing his empty coffee mug on the table with an air of purpose, and the intimate mood broke. "So, we need to speak to Owen again, and decide what to do with him long-term. I'm certainly not turning him loose. We could put a camp bed up in the office, put a couple of shifters on guard."

"That would work. And we need to ask Odette about blood rituals and demon-summoning. According to Vlad, Morgana says we cannot do this alone."

Maverick sighed. "No, I didn't think we could."

Domino had been mulling about Odette's revelations, and things that had been unsaid, but insinuated. "You know, we might even need your brother's blood. Maybe his friends, too. I just don't get how Owen and Ivy changed the demon's nature, although maybe that's the wrong word. For all that he says he has no natural magic, he must have got something right!"

"Let's question him again. Perhaps I will need to find my brother sooner rather than later."

"Have you any idea where he is?"

"The last postcard I received was five years ago, at least. From Italy." He rummaged in the box and withdrew a thick, slightly dogeared envelope. He opened it up and thumbed through a few postcards. "These are the ones he sent me over the years, and this is the latest. He was in Rome."

Domino took the postcard from his outstretched fingers. "I went there as a teenager. Beautiful city. What was he doing there?"

Maverick shrugged. "No idea. Working? Maybe he found a pack that suited him. Although, I think it's more likely that my brother is a lone wolf. He never liked rules, and after what he did? Even less so, I would imagine."

Domino handed him the card back. "I doubt he had any idea of the consequences of his actions, you know. He'd have been too young to really see it. The one good thing is that the postcard might help with a finding spell."

Maverick nodded. "True. I didn't consider that. Come on. Let's see what Owen has to say, and how Odette can help us."

Nine

"You've done a good job with those dressings," Hunter said as he looked into the garden from Morgana's living room window. He'd been led there after he'd dressed himself in Morgana's son, Lamorak's, clothes. Weird name, but at least his clothes fit him. Morgana was clearly a fan of King Arthur. "The sting has gone, for now."

Birdie handed him a tumbler of whiskey on ice. "That will be Morgana's salves. She's always been skilled at healing."

"Aye. I knew a witch like that. Could heal anything. Except for my broken heart."

"Like that, was it?" Birdie patted him sympathetically on the arm. "It's mending though, I see."

"Slowly."

"Anything going on with Cecile?"

Hunter shook his head. "Beautiful, but not my type. It's Domino I've got my eye on."

"Like a challenge, then? Good for you."

Rather than pursue that particular conversation, he asked, "Will Xavier be okay?"

"He'll survive—at least I think so, but I can't promise anything, I'm afraid. They were nasty injuries, and despite Morgana's skills, they may take a while to heal. However, she'll watch over him all night now."

Once Morgana had finished dressing Cecile's wounds, she had cleaned up the kitchen, and then headed to Xavier's bedside with Cecile. Despite being offered a bed, Cecile had insisted on watching him with her for a while. Hunter, however, was too wired for sleep. His encounter with the demon kept running around his head.

"I never thought I'd see a demon again," he confessed. "Not in the flesh, if that's even the right expression. It doesn't really have flesh, does it?"

"You've seen one before?" Birdie asked, surprised.

"Through a portal. Actually, a scrying mirror. It was a big, ugly bastard. It roared and sent me straight into my wolf. Never had that happen before." *Over a year ago, now. Another world.*

"You had no control over your shift?"

"None. I hated it. But it looked nothing like that thing we saw earlier. Although to be fair, it was thrashing about in the water, so it made it hard to see anything." He considered the odd scent of brackish water that smothered the scent of sulphur. "I didn't know demons could swim, either."

"They are creatures of another world, so I doubt swim is the right word," Birdie mused. "Although that is a good point. Why was it in the water? They are drawn to fire—that's their natural element, but I'm no expert in demonology. I presume they can, to a certain extent, occupy any element they want, if only for a short time. Perhaps that might help us work out a way to trap it."

"A demon trap, I presume?"

"Yes. They are complex things, of sigils and runes and magic. Usually blood, too. I hope Odette can find out more. The more I think about it, the more I think she should bring Owen here."

"I don't like that idea at all." The three witches may be powerful, but it didn't seem right to Hunter's protective instinct that they should invite such a devious man into their home.

"We'll contain him. We can ward a room, even a couple of them, so that he can't leave them. We'll see what Odette thinks." And then Birdie turned away abruptly, attention on the garden, her eyes narrowing. "Hades! Are you okay?"

Hunter looked outside, alarmed. *Who was she talking to?*

Birdie, however, didn't speak again, instead closing her eyes, and pressing her forehead to the window. Hunter focussed on the garden, trying to discern shapes amongst the foliage. The spotlights that had been on earlier were now off, and the garden was swathed in darkness. He needed to be out there, hunting. Injuries be damned. There was something alluring about this garden. It beckoned...

Birdie squeezed his arm with sudden force, and unexpected speed. "It's here."

"*What?*" He pressed his face to the glass. "The demon? I thought this place was protected!"

"It is. It's on the boundary. Hades has seen it."

"Who the fuck is Hades?"

"My familiar." Birdie headed to the patio doors, grabbing a wrap from the sofa. "Let's go see."

The distant hoot of an owl greeted Hunter as he stepped outside, and his hunting instincts came to the fore. Birdie led the way unerringly along the twisting paths, and Hunter asked, "Should I shift?"

"No need, and you'd ruin your dressings. We'll watch it—if we can."

Birdie headed north, skirting the edge of a long yew hedge before following gravel paths that wound between shrubs. The sharp scent of earth and greenery was all around them, and something else. Something timeless and omniscient, like a sentient presence. It seemed to be interested in him, almost stalking him. He turned, wary, eyes scanning the undergrowth.

"It's just the garden," Birdie said softly. "Nothing harmful."

"What do you mean? It feels like something is following me."

A gentle smile played on her lips. "You're new here, and the garden is interested, that's all. Now hush, and get a move on. And stay close!"

She continued at a surprisingly fast pace, sure of the paths, and Hunter had no choice but to follow. Now he had even more questions. The garden that watched him, the demon that lurked on the perimeter, and Hades. He grinned to himself. *This place was awesome.* A huge moon gate loomed before them, and they passed under it and through a collection of ferns on the other side.

Birdie paused, eyes vacant for a moment. "It's moved west, by the pond."

She veered left, almost backtracking, and after a few minutes he saw a large pond in the distance, and a summerhouse beyond it. The air felt damp here, and Birdie paused again, studying the wall that formed the boundary a short distance away. Trees softened its hard planes, as did a sprawling mass of ivy. Perched on top of the wall was a large cat. A *very* large cat. Hunter blinked, as if his eyes were deceiving him.

"What the fuck is that?"

"Hades. And stop swearing!"

"Hades is a cat?" Hunter whispered, transfixed on it. His immediate instinct was to hunt it, but that was quickly followed by fascination. That was no ordinary cat. He inhaled. It smelled of cat, and looked like a cat, but the spirit was something quite different—and he had no idea what it was. "*What the fuck?*" he muttered.

"Shush, we're talking."

Birdie sat on a bench that was almost submerged by foliage, her expression vacant, eyes fixed on Hades. "I see it. It's ugly, and it reeks of water."

"You see it through Hades?"

"Yes."

"I'm going to see it too, then."

"Don't step beyond the boundary!"

Hunter ran to the wall as stealthily as he could, unwilling to scare the demon off. *Had it tracked them here? Or was it drawn to the water in the pond?* In a few minutes, he had hauled himself up the thick ivy and jutting stones to sit on the wall, but he kept low, glad of the overhanging branch that cast him in shadow. He was a few feet away from Hades, and for the moment, ignored him to focus on the demon.

It took him a moment to see it, even with his good eyesight. It wasn't until a breath of wind stirred the leaves of the shrubs below, that he saw the unmoving darkness next to them. Slowly it took shape. It was smaller than he'd expected, an amorphous blob, very unlike the clear, distinct features of the demon that had confronted his friend, Alex, the White Haven witch. It absorbed all light, but it was slowly and steadily oozing forward, like slime. A very different kind of movement to earlier. Perhaps being in the water made it quicker.

The demon moved towards the wall, but a flare of something barely seen or felt made it withdraw again. However, as it oozed clear of the shrub, it seemed to have two arms and two legs before they merged into a blob again. A human shape. *Ivy, Owen's sister?* The bitter, brackish smell mixed with sulphur wafted around him, and Hunter's injuries suddenly started to itch. He jerked, almost falling off the wall, but steadied himself in time. However, the burning in his wounds intensified, and his vision swam.

In seconds, Hades was next to him, his clear, golden eyes looking into his, and through some strange animal magic that was utterly unlike how shifters communicated, Hunter could understand him—his voice in his head. *"It knows you're here, and it's making your injuries worse. You need to go."*

"I just wanted to see it."

"And now you have. Go, before you do something stupid."

Hunter hung on to his reason, despite his aching wounds and muddled head. *"Has it followed us here? The shifters, I mean."*

"It's followed the magic, but it can't get in."

"Can we stop it now, somehow? It's right there!"

"How?" Hades was calm, unhurried. *"We are not ready. We have no trap. Now go, before you fall on the wrong side."* He nudged him gently.

But Hunter had other questions. Hades felt old. Very old. *"Who are you? You are no ordinary cat."*

"Not now, my wolf friend. Time to go."

This time, he nudged Hunter to the garden with unexpected strength, and he grabbed the ivy to save himself, quickly scrambling down the wall.

Birdie was waiting for him. "Come on, back to the house."

"Who is Hades?" he persisted as she hustled him along the path that led around the pond.

"My familiar, I told you. Now get a move on. You're in pain, I can tell."

"It's fading again." Not entirely true, but close enough.

"Liar."

"Hades?"

"The honest truth is that I don't know much about him at all. But enough of that. You need to rest, and I need to speak to Odette."

The atmosphere in their office was tense when Grey entered it after completing his perimeter check with Vlad.

Jax and Mads had joined Fran and Rory outside, shifting into their wolf to watch the club from the trees that edged the carpark. Grey thought it highly possible that the demon might find the club, searching for either Owen or Maverick, and hadn't wanted to take any chances. Their customers and the rest of the staff had gone home, and the place was locked up. He had instructed the shifters not to engage with the demon at any cost. They were only to watch, and call them if it arrived.

Grey glared at the man responsible for it all. *Owen Radnor.* He was currently seated on the sofa in the corner of the office, surrounded by Domino, Maverick, Odette, and Arlo, all peppering him with questions. Monroe and Tommy were watching silently. Monroe had shifted to his wolf, an enormous, thick-furred beast that watched Owen's every move. If it was a deliberate move to unsettle Owen, it was working. Owen kept shooting him nervous glances. Tommy was still human.

Vlad leaned against the door to watch, while Grey pulled Tommy aside. He'd taken a liking to the Cumbrian man. He admired his no-nonsense attitude, his willingness to get involved in everything, and his ridiculous sense of humour. He looked more like a bear than a wolf, with his shaggy mane of hair and beard. "What's going on?"

"Trying to discern the nature of what they're dealing with." Tommy growled, an unpleasant sneer on his face. "I've met men like him before. All talk and no action."

"He conjured a demon, Tommy. That was action."

"He sets the ball in motion and then steps back and watches the shit fly."

"Is that a mixed metaphor?"

"I don't fuckin' care. You know what I mean."

Grey smirked. "Yeah, I do. I do not like the idea of him being here all night."

"I'll watch him. He won't get by me. I'll rip his head off if I have to."

"Let's hope it doesn't come to that." Grey shuddered. He'd heard all about Tommy's fight with the old alpha and his supporters in his previous pack. Tommy was not a man to be trifled with.

"What have we found out so far?"

"That he has a book of rituals in his hotel room. He doesn't seem particularly keen to share it, but he'll have to."

"Why won't he share it?" Grey asked, confused. "He came to us for help."

"Because there's other dodgy shit in there, I reckon. We'll probably find out he sacrificed his sister to save himself."

That might well be true, Grey reflected, watching Owen fidgeting. He was still hiding something. Grey didn't often feel out of his depth, but he felt it now. He was used to dealing with paranormal creatures and threats, but demons? They were something else entirely. He wondered what Maggie was making of all of it.

Maverick raised his voice, and Grey and Tommy fell silent to listen.

"Do I need my brother's blood? It's a simple question, Owen!"

"Yes. No! I don't know." His hands twisted in his lap. "Probably."

"But," Odette intervened, "you didn't use their blood to summon it, did you? Just yours and your sister's?"

"Yes, that's true."

"It was the shifters' blood that was used to change its nature after the summoning?"

"Yes. Weeks after."

"Does that make a difference?" Maverick asked.

Odette considered his question. "In theory, no. To catch a demon means setting up an effective trap. But this one has been changed—according to Owen—and I need to see the rituals used for that. I think to be on the safe side, yes, get your brother's blood. If you can't get it, then we try to catch it without." She paused, thoughtful. "I think we can contain it in a trap regardless of any blood. A trap is a trap, and it's still a demon! But, to banish it might be harder. I think we should err on the side of caution and get your brother's blood. Second best would be your blood, Maverick. You are family, after all."

"You can have it. Anything to get rid of this thing."

"Hold on, though," Grey said, catching their attention. "It was over twenty years ago when your parents died. Why is the demon killing people now? Where's it been for the last twenty years? I mean, it clearly escaped from you, Owen. How did you recapture it back then?"

"My sister bound it to her!" Owen glared at Grey. "I've already said this. We had to track it into the woods. We had to act quickly before it struck again. We knew it had escaped, obviously. We were already searching for it."

Odette was staring at Owen in her uncanny way again, the look that made Grey shiver. "You've been feeding it with blood all this time."

"Animal blood!" Owen insisted.

"But it became greedier. You fed it human blood at the start, and had to continue."

"No! That's a lie!" Owen was pale and sweating now.

Odette grabbed his hands again, and Arlo and Domino restrained him to stop him from struggling free. "The witches you wanted revenge on. You killed them." The room was deathly silent, all attention fixed on Owen and Odette. "I see it. If we search, we will find their bodies." Her breath caught in her chest, and her eyes widened with horror. "It has a taste for witches. Their blood is more magical. It sustains it for longer. You found that out, and you hunted witches."

"No! Not true!"

"Very true. Oh, Owen. You betrayed your own for a little power."

"But I am not a witch, am I? Not like you." Owen was almost spitting with fury. He would have lashed out if he could, but Arlo and Domino were gripping him tightly. Tendons strained along his neck, and his jaw clenched.

"This puts a whole different light on things," Odette said, surprisingly calmly. "I must warn Morgana and Birdie."

A mobile phone started ringing on the desk, and Domino called to Grey. "It's mine. Can you answer it, please?"

Grey retreated to the corner, seeing Hunter's name on the screen, and he kept his voice low so as not to disturb the conversation. "Hunter. Everything all right?"

"My wounds are flaring up again, but I'm okay. So are Cecile and Xavier. But I thought you should know that the demon was on Moonfell's boundary. It can't get in, though." His voice was strained. Tired.

Dread filled the pit of Grey's stomach. "You saw it?"

"Yes. From the wall. Moonfell magic is keeping it out."

"Hang on, Hunter." He interrupted the group and relayed the information. "Do you think it will feed off Moonfell's protection spells?"

Odette's eyes clouded with worry. "I don't know. It shouldn't be able to, but tell Hunter what I've found out. I'll return home soon. Tell them to prepare a room for Owen."

While Grey talked to Hunter, Owen was struggling even more, and half of Grey's attention was on him. "No! I will not go with you! I have a hotel room!"

Grey hurriedly ended his call and joined the others. By now, Monroe had leaped on to the table and was snarling in Owen's face while Arlo and Domino restrained him on the sofa.

"You cannot be trusted," Maverick said, calmly. "I'll send a shifter with you, Odette. I know you will contain him with spells, and that you have three shifters there already, but they're injured. I need to help. I'll focus better knowing that everything is okay here."

"Me," Tommy volunteered immediately. "I'll watch the bastard."

"Excellent, thank you," Maverick said, starting to pace the room and ignoring Owen. "I need another favour, Odette. A finding spell for my brother."

"We'll do what we can." She rose to her feet, ready to leave. "I have more questions for Owen, but they can wait until we have both rested. He has many secrets, but he is holding them back well."

Grey caught a glimpse of Owen's forearms as he still struggled to break free, his cuffs riding up his arm. Strange marks were either tattooed on them or drawn on. "Odette! Owen's arms. Are they runes?"

Tommy hurried around the table and pulled the long sleeves of Owen's jumper higher to reveal twisting shapes on his forearms in the form of a thick bracelet. There was one on each arm.

Owen roared. "Get off me, you animal!" He started a guttural chant under his breath, and without a second thought, Tommy punched him. Owen's head snapped back, and then fell forward on his chest.

"Little fucker, trying spells on me," Tommy said, satisfied. He lifted Owen's head up, but he was unconscious.

"Nice one, Tommy," Domino said, finally easing her grip on Owen. "Thanks for not killing him."

"It was tempting."

"What are they, Odette?" Maverick asked.

She ran her long, slender fingers over the marks. "Rune spells. I need to examine them properly later. I think he must have been trying to activate them. I'm not sure what they would have done."

"Why now and not earlier?

"He thought he would walk out of here, that's why," Vlad said. "He's more dangerous than he's making out. This pretence that he has no magic anymore...I don't believe it."

"I can't feel it, though," Odette said, puzzled. "Or maybe that's what the runes are for—to hide it. This just gets weirder and weirder. Let's get him to Moonfell before anything else happens."

"Tommy, Monroe," Maverick said, calling them to attention. "You two will rotate at Moonfell. You both need to sleep and rest, understand? Tommy is up first. Monroe, you take over midday tomorrow. Can you hold out that long, Tommy?"

"No problem."

Monroe just growled and showed his teeth.

"If things escalate, then we'll re-evaluate, but I'll leave that up to all of you," Maverick said, staring at them each in turn. "Once I know where to search for my brother, I'll leave. Refer everything here to Arlo or Domino." Everyone nodded and Maverick stretched, seemingly unconcerned by the prospect of what lay ahead. He had obviously decided to include Monroe and Tommy in his family secrets, which was a relief. The more that they knew the better as far as Grey was concerned. "Let's call it a day, then. I need sleep. I'll be around in the morning for the finding spell, Odette."

"We should keep the patrol on the club," Grey said to Maverick. "Just in case the demon comes calling."

"If he comes for me, I'll deal with it. But I doubt he will. We've told everyone not to engage, so they can go. No one else is dying tonight, especially for me."

Grey didn't like that idea at all, but if that's what's the alpha wanted, so be it.

"Then you better come home with me," Odette said to Tommy.

He winked. "Thought you'd never ask." He steadily ignored Arlo's narrow-eyed stare.

Odette just laughed as Grey asked, "Need another shifter for the journey?"

"No. If he stirs, I'll just hit him again."

It was with a sense of relief that Grey locked up the club and got in his car to go home. All he wanted to do now was sleep, and pretend a demon wasn't prowling London. He had a feeling though that sleep wouldn't come easily that night, or for the days to come.

Ten

"He's still in Italy?" Maverick asked Birdie, surprised. He watched the tendril of smoke coil above the spot on the world map that was spread over the table. For some reason, he'd decided that his brother would be in another country by now.

Birdie nodded. "South of Naples. I'm not sure where exactly, though. I'd need a bigger map of Italy to make sure. Sorry! This is the biggest I have." She gave a dry laugh. "Ridiculous, I know, considering the size of this library. The other maps are ancient, or little things in guidebooks."

"It's fine." Maverick brushed aside her concerns. "I'll find him."

They were in Moonfell's vast library on Saturday morning, a weak February sun filtering in through the long windows. Birdie had burned part of the postcard to cast the finding spell, and the remnants smouldered in the silver bowl. It was nine o'clock in the morning; Maverick had risen early after sleeping heavily, eventually, and had awoken refreshed and filled with new purpose. Seeing Owen again had been cathartic, and hearing the details of what had happened to his parents was actually a relief after all the years of knowing very little.

If Birdie had a late night as well, she showed no signs of it, either. She looked full of energy and purpose, and was dressed in a dark blue woollen dress with leather boots, her thick, white hair bound in a long plait. She had answered the door and let him in, and so far, he hadn't seen the other two witches who lived there.

Birdie put away her spell ingredients, a collection of herbs that she'd burned with the postcard. "Are you sure you should go alone?"

"Very sure. I spend my time surrounded by the pack, the club staff, and endless business responsibilities. A break will do me good."

"A chance to tidy up loose ends. What if he avoids you? Attacks you?"

"He won't. Canagan may have neglected me, run away, and behaved badly, but he never hurt me or threatened me." He placed the map on the bookshelf again. "I see his behaviour now for what it was. A young man overwhelmed with grief and confusion—and a big dollop of guilt, of course."

He had two reasons for finding his brother. The first was to get his blood for the ritual; the second was the need to see him and ask questions. To try to understand his motivations back then, and what he was doing now. After years of not wanting to have anything to do with him at all, suddenly it seemed very important that they reconnect, despite everything. He was his only remaining family member, after all

.

Maverick considered his next actions. He wanted to get on the road quickly. "I'll book a flight to Naples. I presume that's the closest international airport, and then hire a car. Hopefully I'll find a pack that can help."

"Do you know any shifters in Italy?"

"No. We haven't even got any Italian pack members."

Birdie slapped her forehead with the heel of her hand. "What am I thinking? My niece is in Sorrento. She can help. Hopefully." She rolled her eyes. "Jemima is a strange one, but she has plenty of magic. Or maybe Como, her son, can help if not, but he's just coming into his magic, really."

That sounded hopeful. "Your niece is a witch?"

"Yes, of course. Most of our family are. Magic runs strong in our blood. Jemima is my sister's daughter. She doesn't like Moonfell, is a bit put out that her mother isn't the coven head, but," she shrugged, "she can do magic. She can narrow down your brother's location once you're there. She'll probably even know a local pack."

Maverick didn't think he'd ever feel happy to have a witch helping him, but now... "Thanks, Birdie. I really appreciate it."

"Any time. The sooner you banish this notion of hating all witches, the better."

"I don't hate all witches. Not anymore. I still hate Owen, though. How's he doing?"

"I'm going to see him now, so you may as well come, and we'll check on your friends, too. By the way," she gave Maverick a sheepish smile, "Maggie will be here soon."

"Maggie Milne? Why?" The thought of having to argue with the DI was not pleasant.

"Because she needs to know what's going on, of course." She cocked her head to study him. "She's investigating this. The more she knows, the better. She's coming to see Owen. She might even be able to find some of your brother's missing friends."

"I hadn't considered that."

"See? You don't have to do it all alone. Can you remember their names?"

"Not really. Nicknames, perhaps? I'll give it some more thought."

He followed Birdie along the labyrinthine passages of Moonfell, the gentle waft of incense seeming to be everywhere in the gargantuan house. She reached the end of a passageway and started up a winding stone staircase. "We decided to put him in one of the tower rooms, well away from the rest of the house."

"It feels like I'm in the Tower of London."

Birdie giggled. "I assure you that he's in a very comfortable room, not a cell. Tempting though it was."

"You have cells?" He honestly wouldn't be surprised.

"We have *cellars*! Very dark and damp they are, too!"

As they reached the next floor, Maverick felt a tingle on his skin; the flare of magic. "What's that?"

"A protection spell, of sorts. It traps him here, and also dampens down his magic. He most definitely has more than he's admitting to having." She opened a heavy wooden door made of thick oak planks with a door knocker on it. "This was someone's private quarters once, hence the door knocker."

"This place is full of surprises."

"You haven't seen anything yet!"

The door opened on to a plush, decorated landing, surprisingly large, with a thick Oriental carpet on the floor, and heavy brocade curtains at the long window. Two doors opened off it, and both were open. One revealed a bedroom, the other a decadent bathroom with a claw-footed bath under an arched window, an extensive view of the gardens beyond. Seated opposite the open doors, on a winged back chair, was Tommy, looking like the Lord of the Manor. He stood as Maverick entered, shaggy hair falling into his eyes that he quickly swept back. "Morning, boss."

"Morning, Tommy. Everything all right here?"

"As good as can be expected." He gave a wry grin. "He's not very happy to be here. Especially because the doors are warded, too. At least he has his own bathroom."

"With an open door!" Owen shouted from within the room. "I have no privacy!"

"But you're alive, you scrawny-bollocked little man," Tommy roared back.

Moving to the open door, Maverick saw that Owen was seated at a table under the window, the remnants of breakfast in front of him. He was still wearing the clothes he'd worn the day before, and they were rumpled and creased. All sign of his diminished, beaten personality had vanished, and instead Owen was brimming with anger.

He glared at Maverick, bruises blooming around his eyes from the impact of Tommy's punch. "You can't keep me forever!"

"Stop being dramatic. You can leave when the demon has gone."

"That could take weeks!"

"Hardly," Birdie informed him. "We have no intention of letting it drag out that long. If your book of spells doesn't provide the answers, we have other options. We will collect it from your hotel room today."

"Well, I have to go with you!" He stood and crossed to the door so there were only a few feet between them. "They won't let anybody into my room."

"I am not just anybody, and you're going to give me the key," Birdie replied. "You will stay here. We'll bring your baggage, too. I presume you want us to catch this demon? It is what you sought Maverick out to do."

"Yes. Of course."

"Or did you just want his blood, and you hoped to trick him with your apologies? You've been feeding the creature witch blood as well as shifter blood, from what Odette told me last night." A dangerous edge entered Birdie's voice. "You're playing a dangerous game."

"I have been doing what I needed to do to control it. You have no idea what it's been like all these years."

"And yet you didn't send it back?"

"We couldn't!"

"I doubt that. Tell me which hotel."

He shuffled, eyes darting to the floor. "It's just a little one. I can't remember the name right now."

Birdie looked at Maverick and rolled her eyes. "He thinks I am a fool."

Tommy laughed. "Perhaps he prefers Odette dragging the information from him. You can't hide it, little man."

"All right! It's the Hotel Café Royal in Mayfair."

Tommy snorted. "Bloody hell! You're rich!"

Maverick sighed as things started to make sense. Owen and his sister never had much money all those years before. None of them had. When Owen said he wanted power, that meant money, too. "The demon made you money. Lots of money. You fed it blood like a pet to keep it happy, but now that you've lost control, it's consumed your sister, and now it wants you." The layers of Owen's deception just kept piling up. "Why keep holding things back? You want help! We're giving it."

"Leave him," Birdie said, walking away. "I'll deal with him later. I'm already sick of seeing him, and I barely know him." She paused at the door to the stairs, eyes fixed on Owen. "Your dark heart will kill you, Owen, and it will happen by your own hand."

Maverick watched Owen's face contort with anger and then confusion, then followed Birdie, leaving Tommy to watch over him. Birdie didn't speak again until they were on the second floor of another wing, and here the normal noises of the house returned. Conversations, doors opening and closing, distant music, and the general disorder of life, far different to the looming silence of the tower room.

"We've put Hunter, Cecile, and Xavier next to each other. It means they can keep each other company. This place can get rather overwhelming sometimes." Birdie's eyes twinkled with mischief.

Morgana stepped out of the far room, relief crossing her face as she saw Birdie and Maverick. Her long hair was unkempt, and her eyes were dark from lack of sleep. "Oh good, you're here. I'm not happy with Xavier's condition, at all!"

"Why?" Maverick asked, stalking to her side. The stink of infected wounds hit him before he'd even reached the door. "Holy shit. Is that Xavier?"

"Yes. The salve isn't as effective as I'd hoped. His wounds are getting worse. I've changed his dressings half a dozen times over night, but they seep with blood and pus every hour."

From the doorway, he could see Xavier lying motionless beneath fresh sheets, the window partially open to let in fresh air, despite the chill weather. Beneath the scent of rot, the stench of sulphur was faint but unmistakable. Xavier already looked half dead. Spell books were piled on a table, evidence that Morgana had been searching for something else to help.

"Is there anything you can do?"

"I have other options," Morgana said. "Spells, rituals... I'm wondering if the demon is still close. He murmurs in his sleep. Screams, occasionally." She looked at Birdie. "I'll need you and Odette later. There's a spell that will help stabilise him."

Birdie nodded. "Anything. We'll collect Owen's spell book today. That might help, too. I know where to go now."

"Perhaps a shifter should go?" Maverick suggested. "Leave you free to work here."

"I don't trust him not to have put protection spells on his book. I would," Birdie said.

"At least take someone with you." Maverick felt responsible for this, in a weird way. Owen had come looking for him, after all.

"I'll think on it, thank you."

"What about Hunter and Cecile?"

"Sleeping in their wolf," Morgana told him. "So far, they are okay, but their wounds weren't as severe. I'm hoping that if we banish the demon, its influence will go and therefore help them all recover."

"There's no doubt in my mind," Birdie agreed, "that Hunter seeing the demon made him worse last night."

"Why isn't Xavier a wolf? We heal quicker that way."

Morgana shook her head. "I let him try it for a few hours last night. There was no discernible difference, and it made it harder for me to treat him."

A new sense of urgency hit Maverick, and he pulled his phone from his pocket. "I'll book my flights now. I need to find my brother."

"Come downstairs and have coffee," Birdie urged him. "I sense that Maggie is already here. Tell her everything you can. We need all the help we can get with this."

Early on Saturday afternoon, Maggie finished the last of her notes on the whiteboard in the corner of her office, tapping her lip with the capped marker.

"That's as much as I have on the teens that Maverick can remember. As yet, we don't know if we need them, but my instinct is to find them—just in case."

"We need the old case files," said Stan Walker, her DS. "We can match up the names with the families, check ages, addresses. They'll all be shifters, and they will all have been interviewed."

"We can't presume that," Irving said, the other DS. "They didn't have paranormal teams then. They wouldn't have known they were shifters. Unless their families were present when they found Maverick's parents, there would have been no need to interview them."

"But they'd have been local families," Stan pointed out.

"But why interview them if they weren't involved? From what Maverick said, they lived in several villages in the area, with no obvious connection at all."

"Enough!" Maggie yelled, their bickering threatening a headache. "Let's get the files and go from there. Their blood might make a difference now!"

"What if they're dead?" Stan asked.

"Well, there's not fucking much we can do then, is there? Unless family is still around." Maggie took a deep breath. Stan had made a valid point. "I fucking hate cold cases! It was bloody years ago. God knows where they are now!"

"They might still be in the area. Some people never move far from home," Irving said, reaching for a chocolate digestive to dunk in his coffee. "You want me to chase up the file? I have a contact. Handy for a weekend."

That was a surprise. Irving had spent most of his career pissing people off, not cultivating relationships. "How did you manage that?"

He tapped his nose, smearing chocolate on his face. "Never you mind, Guv. I'll get on it now."

"Any news from the doc?" Stan asked Maggie while Irving reached for his phone.

"I'm heading to The Retreat now. I doubt that anything she has to tell us will change the direction of the investigation. We already know more than I anticipated at this stage, thanks to Birdie and Maverick." She gathered her bag and coat, ready to leave. "Poor Maverick. I actually feel sorry for him. All that business with his parents, and now he has Xavier to worry about. He'd lost a little bit of his swagger when I saw him this morning. Had a dangerous glint in his eye, though."

Stan leaned back in his chair, frowning. "I can't believe you didn't interview Owen. Very unlike you."

"I figure he won't tell me anything new. I might even antagonise him. I'd rather leave him to the witches. However, that reminds me. See what you can find out about Owen, and his sister, too. Where he's been, what money he's got...anything. Birdie thinks he's holding back, and although spooky Odette has seen things, it would be good to fact check."

Over an hour later, after battling the crowds on the tube, Maggie met Layla in the morgue at The Retreat. The last time she'd been there was just before Christmas, walking into a fight she didn't expect with Russell Blake, the PD's lab manager. After that, there had been a shake-up there with new staff and security measures. She'd been kept in the loop by her friend, Jackson Strange, who worked for them, in and around his occult hunting business.

"It's quiet in here," she remarked when she met Layla at the security checkpoint, having been scanned and had her bag searched.

"Always the same on Saturdays. Some things are new, though. Security is constant now. It never used to be." Layla moved at a fast clip as she led them to the morgue, a good distance from the main entrance. "It's annoying, but for the best. I'd rather not have to shoot anyone else."

It was Layla who had shot Russell, just before he tried to kill Maggie. It was a debt Maggie doubted she could ever repay.

"Anyway," Layla continued, sweeping into the corridor that housed the labs and her offices, "I have started the PM. It's very disturbing. Poor Mr Skelton might be dead, but his wounds are worsening. And I have to warn you that the stench of demon rot is quite overpowering. My air filters are working overtime."

Maggie grimaced. "I can smell it already. Anything you can share would be very helpful. Xavier, one of the wolf-shifters, has appalling wounds, apparently."

"Caused by the same demon?"

"It better be the same. Finding out we have two demons would be a bloody nightmare!"

"And no other deaths, I presume?"

"No. Fortunately, it has appeared at Moonfell's boundary...or perhaps, unnervingly. The witches are working on a way to trap it now."

Layla threw open the door to the small mortuary and Maggie nearly gagged. The stench of decay and sulphur was overpowering. "I thought the air filters were on?"

"They are." Layla passed her a face mask. "Let's make this brief. I just want you to see the injuries."

"I saw them yesterday!"

"Humour me."

Begrudgingly, Maggie put the mask on, leaving her coat and bag in Layla's office further along the corridor. When she entered the morgue, Layla had already removed the body from the freezer, and it was displayed in all its horrific glory. The torso was open from the neck to the pubic bone, peeled back to show the cavity where organs had been. Pus was pooling and festering. In fact, it looked like it was bubbling.

"What is going on with *that*?" Maggie was appalled, hand clasped over her mask to try to block the smell.

"It's acidic. Mildly so, or it would have eaten through the corpse by now. It's the sulphur. I should just be able to flush it out with an alkaline solution, but I can't. I've had the lab scientists helping me, but nothing doing so far. I'm probably going to have to send him for cremation sooner rather than later."

"But what about his family?"

"I'll explain it as best I can. You can see my dilemma. As fast as I flush it out, it comes back. Damn demons."

Layla put the body back in the freezer, after wrapping it carefully in a body bag, and led Maggie to her office where she could finally breathe without gagging. She hadn't seen Xavier that morning, but if this was what it was doing to him...

"I need a solution, or Xavier will die. Does alchemy help at all?"

One of The Retreat's labs was dedicated to alchemy, using old methods that had proven resourceful and unique.

"The staff are in there now brewing up something that might work. If it does, I'll let you know."

"Thank you. Morgana, one of the Moonfell witches, is looking after Xavier, and she's using magic on his wounds, but she's struggling to make headway, from what they told me this morning." Maggie made a few notes while Layla filled up a kettle from the sink in the corner and put it on to boil. "Have you dealt with demons before?"

"A very long time ago. It didn't hang around like this one, though. It entered and vanished through a portal, summoned by a necromancer." Layla fixed her sharp eyes on Maggie. "Why hasn't it killed again?"

"Maybe this one moves through a portal too, and Owen is holding out on us."

"Or the sister has some influence?"

"Over a demon?"

Layla shrugged. "Or maybe Owen does? I bet he didn't expect to be imprisoned in Moonfell and guarded by witches and shifters. For all we know, he wanted to sacrifice Maverick to it. He might be scrambling now to adjust his plans. Whatever is happening, we can't afford to have more deaths on our hands. Ready or not, they need to trap this demon."

Eleven

Arlo entered the Hotel Café Royal in Mayfair, Birdie at his side, after meeting her at the entrance.

Maverick had already updated him with everyone's plans, and after one long phone call, in which Arlo had been at his most persuasive, Birdie had finally agreed to go to the hotel with him. As far as Arlo was concerned, going alone was madness. He had no concerns about Birdie's magical abilities, but he didn't trust Owen an inch. Plus, he might see something Birdie would not.

He'd half wondered if Odette might go too, which was an added incentive, but Birdie wanted Odette to stay at Moonfell with Morgana. If the demon tried to breach their defences, she wanted someone there to respond. Although, she doubted the demon could get in. She had insisted that their protections spells were strong. However, she admitted that they had never been tested by a demon before—not in recent memory, at least.

"Bloody hell," Arlo exclaimed as they crossed the hotel's sophisticated reception area. A huge chandelier that looked like a glittering waterfall drew the eye. "This place is seriously posh!"

"Isn't it just? Owen has been putting his pet to good use."

"He could have earned that money legitimately. How do you get a demon to make you money?"

"Good question. I confess, I don't know." Birdie crossed to the lifts and pressed the button. "Third floor."

"You have his key?"

"Yes, but magic will work if this doesn't."

Even the silence of the hotel was luxurious, and it followed them all the way down the corridor to Owen's room. The place oozed glamour and refinement, utterly unlike Owen, unless he'd affected a very different persona to the one he was showing them. They saw only one couple exiting their room, and they smiled as they passed, finally pausing before Owen's door.

"Let me assess it first," she murmured to him. She placed her hands on the wall, feeling for any magic.

Owen had placed a *Do Not Disturb* sign on his door, which made Arlo wonder what he didn't want the hotel staff to see. Arlo cocked his head as he listened, but he heard nothing to suggest what might lie inside.

"Feels fine, at the moment. Do you hear anything?" Birdie asked.

"All good so far."

"Good." Birdie slid the electronic key into the lock, and it opened with a soft click.

Arlo pushed the door wide, scanning the large room before entering. It was decorated in neutral tones, restful and intensely boring to Arlo's eye. He liked colour, and knew Birdie did, too.

"Good grief," she groaned. "Endless biscuit tones. Kill me now."

"Depressing, right?" The bed dominated the room, and Owen's clothes were strewn over it. However, his suitcase was nowhere in sight. To the left was a large wardrobe. A leatherbound book sat on a bedside table. "Looks harmless so far. That must be his grimoire. Happy if we go inside?"

Birdie nodded. "Careful, though."

Shutting the door softly behind them, they explored the room together. Arlo had expected to see occult paraphernalia as well as the grimoire, but so far the room looked like any hotel room—well, apart from the expensive finishes.

Birdie was examining the grimoire. "There are a lot of demon-summoning rituals in this. It makes my skin crawl."

"Do you think your ancestors would have summoned some?"

"I know they did. It was all the rage, at one point. Fortunately, not many did. It's a hazardous pastime. We have a large collection of summoning spells that I'll be comparing this to later."

"I'll grab his bag and pack his clothes and toiletries. I presume you want to take them?"

She nodded. "May as well. He'll be with us for a few days."

But Arlo paused as he drew close to the wardrobe, his highly sensitive nose detecting the faint odour of blood. He eased the door open, but other than the few clothes hanging up, and the suitcase and overnight bag on the floor, the wardrobe was empty. He sniffed again, but the scent of blood was unmistakable, and it was stronger now.

He picked up the overnight bag, something bulky rattling within it, and placed it on the bedroom floor. Inside was a large wooden box, approximately twelve inches square, heavily carved in runes and sigils. A hinged lid that was a couple of inches deep had a keyhole in the centre.

Carefully, as if it might explode, he lifted it out and placed it next to the bag. "Birdie. Come and see this."

Birdie grimaced as she joined him. "The runes represent arcane knowledge, but I don't recognise the sigils."

"Is that bad?"

"Anyone can make their own sigils. You just combine pertinent runes. I wonder if Owen made this or bought it."

"He didn't mention it was here?"

"No. He must have hoped we wouldn't find it. Idiot." Birdie eyed Arlo. "What do you think? Open it here or at Moonfell?"

"Either could play into his hands. I presume we don't want him to open it?"

"Absolutely not."

"I'd put money on there being blood in it." Arlo inhaled again. "Not much, but some."

"It reminds me of a medicine case. I know," Birdie said decisively, "let's cast a little protection spell around it first, and then open it."

"I'll search the case for a key. Although, it's likely he's carrying it on him."

Arlo hauled the suitcase onto the bed, searching the pockets methodically, and then all of Owen's clothes, too, piling them back into the suitcase as he worked. These clothes were of better quality than the ones he had worn to the club. He had definitely been playing down his wealth. There was a lot that Owen was hiding about himself, and Arlo didn't like it one bit.

"No key," he said. He blinked with surprise to see the box in the middle of the room surrounded by glowing runes and a pentagram. Birdie was still finishing the design, painting the marks magically with her finger, casting a spell as she did so. "You work quickly."

She didn't answer for a moment, but when the last sign was in place, a shimmering blue shield appeared around the box.

"No point wasting time, Arlo. It might be unlocked, so a simple *flip* should do the trick." She gestured upwards with her hand, directing the gesture at the box, but it remained stubbornly sealed. "Okay, now for a few simple spells." However, several minutes later, the box was still shut tight, and Birdie sighed. "Arlo, sweetie, can you bring me the grimoire?"

"Sweetie?" He grinned as he headed to the bedside table. "What did I do to deserve that?"

"You've come to some sort of understanding with Odette. That makes me happy."

"She told you?"

"She didn't have to. She has a lightness about her that she hasn't had in years. So do you."

Trying not to feel ridiculously happy at that news and what it might mean, he picked the grimoire up, the feeling of magic crawling over his fingers as he did so. He hurriedly handed it to her.

Birdie paged through the book. "Nothing obvious suggests itself for this box. I wonder..." She paced around the box, studying the runes again. "Let's try a different kind of spell."

Arlo was getting restless. *What if they unleashed something huge and caused a massive incident in the hotel? Or spent another hour here, and then had to take it to Moonfell, anyway.*

"Ah ha!" The lock clicked and the lid opened an inch.

"What did you do?"

"Used a little elemental magic to circumvent the rune spell. Devious, but effective. Remember, according to Owen, he does not have elemental magic. He might actually be telling the truth, for once."

Birdie made a scooping motion with her hand and flicked the lid up. It flew open, settling back with a judder onto well-oiled hinges. Inside were lots of small vials of a thick, dark substance. They lined the lid and the compartment below. There appeared to be another compartment underneath the top one, hidden from view.

"Blood!" Arlo said as the scent intensified. "What is that? A mini blood bank for pixies?"

"A selection for his summoning spells. Maybe to control the demon?" She shrugged. "Nothing good, I'm sure. I expect these are samples from lots of different people."

"Can you drop the protection spell?" Arlo asked.

"I think it's safe to."

With a few gestures, the shimmering blue shield vanished, and Birdie reached inside to lift the top compartment off. A porcelain jar with a lid, covered in runes, lay in the bottom of the box. She carefully lifted it out and removed the lid, revealing a shrunken, desiccated organ within it. Arlo knew what it was in an instant.

A human heart.

"How are you feeling, Cecile?" Hunter asked as she joined him on Moonfell's east-facing terrace with a coffee.

She slumped into a wicker chair next to him, pulling her coat around her. "Pissed off and worried. I hate being injured, and my wounds are throbbing like a bitch, but I'm worried sick about Xav. He looks awful." Cecile's long, honey blonde hair looked a little unkempt, which was unusual for her, and there were dark circles under her eyes. She'd been staring at the garden, but now she directed her gaze at Hunter. "Do you think he'll die?"

"It's possible," he said, unable to lie, "but Morgana knows what she's doing. I think without her, he'd already be dead."

"That's what I was afraid you'd say." Her eyes filled with tears. "He's like a brother to me, Hunter. I'm not sure I'd cope without him."

"Of course you would. You're strong, and we would support you, but don't think like that. There's plenty we can do yet."

"Like what?"

"Catch the demon and send it back to whatever literal Hell hole it came from. Use Owen's book that Birdie has gone to find. We have options." He wanted to add that they could use Maverick's brother's blood—if he could find him—but he wasn't supposed to mention that to her.

"But how long could that take? He could be dead by then."

"He's still alive now, and he's strong!" Hunter didn't know Xavier that well yet, but he'd seen enough of him to know that he was stubborn and a fighter.

"But he looks so weak, and he can't even sleep in his wolf!"

"We'll chat to Morgana later. Persuade her to let him change, even if for only a few hours. You need to be patient. His injuries are way worse than ours."

She gave him a small smile. "I know. I'm tired, and that means I'm not rational. I slept so well, too. Whatever Morgana gave me knocked me right out."

Hunter nodded. "Me, too."

Morgana had offered them herbal tea the night before, and Hunter, used to his old girlfriend's healing teas, hadn't questioned it. He'd drank it and shifted to his wolf, and was out cold for hours, curled on the huge bed in the guest bedroom, only waking an hour earlier. He'd made his way downstairs, resisting the urge to peer into every room he passed, drawn on by the scent of coffee, and finally found his way to the kitchen. The garden had beckoned. It was a cold afternoon, the sky a mix of pale blue and high cloud cover. Hunter could scent spring just around the corner. Snowdrops were already appearing in Moonfell's garden. Remembering the sitting room where he'd been with Birdie the night before, he'd retraced his steps and headed to the terrace for fresh air. He hadn't seen any of the witches.

"I didn't tell you what I saw before I went to bed, did I?" he said to Cecile.

"No." She turned to face him, adjusting the cushion behind her. "You saw something here?"

"The demon, lurking on the boundary."

"It followed us?"

"Maybe. Or Owen. Hard to know, right?"

"Can it get in?"

"Nope—at least not yet." He stretched, needing to explore. "I met Birdie's familiar, too. A massive cat that's not really a cat at all."

"What is it then?"

Hunter grinned. "Great question, but it's old. *Very old*. Want to come and explore the garden with me? I think it will do you good. We might find one of the witches."

"Morgana is with Xavier. I checked on him before I came downstairs. She said Birdie is out with Arlo, getting Owen's grimoire." She looked uncertainly back towards the house. "What if Morgana needs me?"

"She's resourceful. She'll find a way to contact you."

Cecile huffed. "I suppose you're right. I must admit, this garden calls to me, and I need to stretch my legs."

Hunter chose a route he thought was roughly where Birdie had led him the night before, but headed more directly west, wanting to find the area of the garden where the demon had been. He had a good sense of direction, but paths that led west vanished into undergrowth, and he realised that they were actually being directed to the north. A large moon gate made of blocks of stone appeared to their left, but although he tried to reach it several times, he ended up being redirected to a grove of trees.

"Are you sure you know where you're going?" Cecile asked him, her natural disdain that she carried for most things that weren't French reappearing. *She was definitely feeling better.*

"This bloody garden has a mind of its own."

"Of course it does," Odette said from up ahead of them, looking like a half-seen, fey-like creature in the depths of the wood. "It led you to me."

Her voice acted as if to unveil her, and suddenly Hunter could scent her, where before there had been nothing.

"That's clever," he said, arriving at her side. "How did you do that?"

"Do what?" she asked, mischief sparkling in her eyes.

"You know what. It was like you weren't there. I couldn't even smell you. Some kind of shadow spell, I presume?"

"Something like that."

Cecile, however, was focussed on what lay ahead. The garden boundary was just visible through the trees, and she froze, sniffing. "*Mon Dieu.* It is here?"

"Yes. It hides on the far side of the wall. Risky in daylight, but the trees on the far side are particularly dense."

Hunter could only presume that his sense of smell had been affected by his injuries, because he couldn't detect a thing. "The demon is still here?"

"Yes, and that surprises me," Odette said softly. "It's either confident in our inability to catch it, or it's compelled to stay here. Either way, we should take advantage of its proximity and catch it. But that means setting up a trap and getting it on this side of the wall."

"You'd have to remove your protection spell."

Odette nodded. "It's the last thing I want to do. I'm not even sure I can. They are baked into this place."

"Then we catch it out there, and carry it here."

"Over your shoulder, like a caveman?"

He smirked. "That wasn't exactly what I was thinking!"

Cecile shook her head. "It's madness. We can't risk getting close to it. It's too dangerous."

"But we can't leave it running loose, either," Hunter said. "Can you make a portal and send it back to where it came from? I know a witch who can do that."

"I have never attempted such a thing," Odette confessed. "It takes a particular skill to do that, but we have extensive family who potentially could. I guess it is not beyond the realms of my magic, though. But the issue is that the shifter blood seems to have changed it. It's been here for many years, if we're to believe Owen, and I don't think it would be straightforward. That's why we need the blood that bound it here."

Cecile frowned. "Is there something I don't know about?"

Hunter shrugged, feeling awkward. "It's Maverick's business, Cecile."

Her jaw clenched. "Is that why our wounds are so bad? Is it responding to our shifter nature?"

That thought hadn't occurred to Hunter before. "Is that possible?"

"Anything is possible," Odette said.

Cecile swung around to face the boundary again. "You have also failed to mention another possibility as to why it's here. It could be waiting for your protection to fail. Owen could be hatching some kind of plan right now to destroy your protection spells."

"Owen had no idea that he would be brought here," Hunter reminded her. "Hell, we didn't know until last night."

"Really?" Cecile rolled her eyes. "He could have pre-empted all of this. He could have known of our links to Moonfell, and engineered this whole thing. You said that he fed the demon witch blood. There's plenty of it here. Who's watching him now?"

"Monroe," Odette said, glancing back towards the house. "Tommy is sleeping in another room."

"Is he?" Hunter asked, surprised. "I thought he'd gone home."

"With so many beds, and him needing to be here later, it seemed silly not to offer him a bed."

"Forget Tommy's sleeping arrangements!" Cecile said, annoyed. "Owen could just be extremely resourceful. He finds himself in an unexpected situation, and decides to take advantage of it. Like you said, Odette, this house is steeped in magic. Could he steal it?"

Odette snorted. "What a ridiculous notion. If he tried, this house would retaliate—strongly."

And then an enormous, blood-curdling howl ripped through the chill afternoon.

Monroe.

Twelve

"Perhaps we should cancel the band tonight," Domino said to Vlad and Grey. "It seems insane to open, knowing that a demon is on the loose with a taste for our blood."

They were seated at the corner booth in Storm Moon's bar, snacking on dumplings and sweet chilli sauce prepared by the kitchen staff. Domino had checked the club's emergency exits to ensure they hadn't been tampered with, and set up extra security patrols, but she still wasn't happy.

"Not a chance," Vlad said immediately. He was sprawled across the seat opposite her, seeming to take up twice the space of a normal person. That was shifters for you. "The biggest band we've booked in months will be here to set up in less than an hour. We have sold out all advance tickets, and there's more on the door! No way! This is going ahead. We have to make it work!"

Grey, annoyingly, agreed. "He's right. This is a huge gig. If we cancel, we look like dicks. Besides, nothing might happen. Like Cecile said, the demon is stalking Moonfell. As long as it's there, we're okay."

"That seems rather chillingly put," Domino said, "but I guess you have a point."

"Well, I'm not happy about it, obviously, but we know where it is, and it can't get in!" Grey snagged the last dumpling off the plate.

"Besides, Mystic Banshees are a great band! I've been looking forward to this for months."

Vlad, at ease in his new role, stretched back, offering a tantalising peek at his well-defined abs as his t-shirt rode up. "We're down five staff who are stuck at Moonfell, but we have the rest."

"Six," Domino reminded him. "No Maverick!"

"What if we get Birdie to add a little more protection to our doors? She's out with Arlo now. Get her to swing back this way!"

Domino fell silent, mulling over their options, but unfortunately, Grey and Vlad were right. They couldn't cancel at such short notice. The band might claim damages, and it would put the club in a bad light. Of course, a demon wreaking havoc and murdering customers, the band, and shifters would also be bad. But that might not happen.

"Fine. Call Arlo!"

"On it!" Vlad grabbed his phone and strode across the room to make the call.

"It was a good move, that," Grey said, nodding in Vlad's direction. "Like a duck to water."

"I know. It doesn't solve tonight's issues, though. You're remarkably calm about all this!"

"No other way to be, Dom. We have to open, and we'll take as many precautions as possible!"

"Can we at least plan for the worst? Like maybe have a demon trap on the grounds."

"Like we put one on a tarpaulin and roll it out when needed?"

"Sarcasm is not helping."

He grinned. "I think it is. It's actually not a bad idea, either."

"Oh, piss off! Like we say, 'just step over here, Mr Demon. There's a nice trap ready for you.'"

"It could be a Mrs Demon. It's a bit sexist of you to assume, actually."

Domino laughed. "There is no dealing with you when you're in one of these moods."

"I can't help it. When things look really bad, I use humour as a defence mechanism."

"Seriously, if the patrol spots it, what do we do? We can't fight it like we'd normally do! Look at what happened to Xavier. Our only option is to retreat, close the doors, and then what? Hope it gets bored?" The more she thought about it, the more ridiculous it seemed. "And then how do we explain to the customers that they can't leave? What about those trying to get in?"

Grey licked the chilli sauce off his fingers, regarding her like a commander looking at a rookie recruit. It both irked and amused her. "Calm the fuck down! It can't be on all sides of the building at once, and we have several exits. If necessary, we lock down. Then we distract it somehow, maybe dangle a little shifter blood in its direction. Then we let whoever needs to leave use the farthest exit."

"That sounds remarkably simplistic."

"Sometimes, the simplest things are the best."

Domino had so many more objections, but maybe Grey was right. There were only so many scenarios they could plan for. After that, they just had to think on their feet. She pinched the bridge of her nose and closed her eyes. This was her job, and she just had to deal with it.

"Good news," Vlad said, and she opened her eyes as he slid back into his seat. "Birdie is on her way. They found Owen's grimoire in his hotel room, and something else. Arlo didn't say what." He raised his eyebrows. "Sounded suitably ominous. And the band is here. I saw them pulling up around the back."

Domino rose to her feet. "Great. Let's pretend everything is perfectly normal, then! Just like any other Saturday night..."

Morgana was the first to arrive in the tower after Monroe's chilling howl, but Tommy was right behind her as she threw the door open, magic balled in her palms, ready to deal with what might lie inside.

However, she wasn't expecting to see Owen suspended in midair in the middle of his room, body twisted and contorted, face frozen in horror. He looked like a fly trapped in a spider's web, his body encased by filaments of golden light. Monroe was in his wolf, an enormous, growling presence, transfixed on Owen. He stood as high as Morgana's chest, broad and powerful, his lips peeled back to show his snapping teeth.

"Holy cow," Tommy murmured.

Odette had cast the spells on the tower rooms, but Morgana was pretty sure she hadn't cast any that would do this. "Monroe! What happened? Are you all right?" In seconds he shifted, and stood naked before her, muscles rippling, and Morgana kept her eyes fixed firmly on his face. *Good Goddess. Do not be distracted now.* "What happened?"

Monroe, however, was utterly oblivious to the effect his naked body was having on Morgana. His eyes were fixed on Owen. "He started some weird chant. I called over to him, told him to stop, but he just looked at me with this weird, devilish grin. He looked possessed. And then," Monroe shook his head, "something just seemed to rip through the room, catching him and lifting him, and well, he was left like *that*." He finally looked at Morgana. "That's as much as I know! Did you do this?"

"Odette spelled the room so he couldn't get out, a sort of binding spell, but I think the house intervened, because I'm pretty sure that the spell shouldn't have done that."

Tommy snorted, rubbing sleep out of his eyes. He was only half naked, displaying an impressively hairy chest, but at least he had his jeans on. "The house? You're talking like it's alive!"

"It's complicated." Morgana walked closer to the doorway, aware that the spells sealing Owen inside were still in place. "The house has a way of looking after its own."

"Are you saying it has a brain?" Monroe asked, horrified. "Because that's freaky as shit."

"No. Not really. Forget the house! What was he saying?"

"Sounded Latin, but I don't know. Some kind of chant." He shrugged, and his pecs popped.

Only look at his face. "Well, what was he doing before that?"

"Nothing, other than sitting and looking out of the window occasionally. Every now and again, he'd goad me. Asked me if I was a pet wolf to do a witch's bidding. When I ignored him, he offered to pay me money to switch sides. I told him to fuck off."

Tommy huffed. "Wanker. We should just kill him. Get it over with."

"No!" *Bloody shifters.* "He might be the only thing controlling that demon. We can't risk it. Neither, however, can we leave him like that."

"Spoilsport," Tommy said, looking askance at Morgana. "He can't do much damage like that, can he? I think this place knows what it's doing." He patted the wall. "Good job, mate!"

"You're a bloody idiot, Tommy," Monroe said.

The clatter of footsteps and voices on the stairs announced the arrival of Odette and Cecile.

"After me!" Odette insisted. She appeared in the doorway first, flushed from running.

Cecile was right behind her. "Thank the Goddess! You're all okay."

"Apart from Owen," Morgana pointed out. "Where's Hunter?"

"Keeping an eye on our boundary. The demon is still there."

Cecile pressed a hand to her heart. "I thought Owen had escaped." She hugged Monroe. "I was so worried about you."

Morgana ignored them, addressing Odette. "Did you cast a spell that could do that?"

"No, although it was a binding spell, as you know. It was aimed to stop him from casting spells and escaping."

"Then I was right. The house did that to him. I can only presume he was trying to communicate with the demon, from what Monroe said. He was speaking Latin."

"A common language to invoke demons." Odette stepped to the doorway. "I think it's safe to go in. Do you?"

Morgana nodded, and Odette broke the seal. They crossed the room to his side, the others fanning out around them, and Monroe shifted back to his wolf. Odette's magic hummed, tickling her skin. Up close, Owen was covered with a sheen of sweat, and his eyes were wide open, fixed and staring as he spun slowly in the air. His jaw, however, was clenched tight, lips sealed in a thin line as if to lock his words up ti ght.

"I can't even tell if he's conscious or not," Morgana said.

Cecile was looking out of the north window, one of the two windows in the room. The other faced east. "He has a good view of the garden up here. I wonder if he watched us cross to the boundary?"

"It's hard to know what he was doing," Morgana mused. "He hasn't got his grimoire or any obvious spell ingredients. I can only presume he knew the summoning spell by heart."

"Wait!" Odette lifted the sleeve of Owen's right arm as he spun around. "What if that is what these runes are for? Part of a summoning spell. I was going to look them up later. *Damn it*. I knew I shouldn't have put it off!"

"We have a lot on our minds. We can't do everything at once. They could have a few functions. Personal protection, memory spells... Runes are very versatile."

Tommy crossed to their side and leaned in, sniffing. "Sulphur again. Faint, but it's there."

Owen was more closely linked to the demon than they had realised, and that was a sobering thought. At least they knew they could trust their protection spells.

"Elemental air is keeping him spinning," Morgana said to Odette. "I'll release it now. Tommy, can you carry him to the bed?"

He grunted in what Morgana took to be agreement, and she deftly banished the elemental spell, but left the gold threads that bound Owen's limbs, and the binding that sealed his jaw. Tommy caught him as he fell, and roughly placed him on the bed.

"I think that for now," Odette said, watching Owen through eyes that had taken on a faraway gaze again, "we leave him like this. It won't do him any harm. He can breathe. Anyone got their phone handy?"

Tommy dug his out of his jeans pocket. "I have."

"I'd like to take a few photos of his rune bracelets."

Tommy held Owen's arms in position, and while Odette took photos, Morgana scanned the room. Nothing looked untoward. They had checked every drawer and shelf, careful to make sure nothing magical or dangerous was left in it. There was nothing more they could have done to make the room safer.

Within a few minutes, Odette was satisfied. "All good. Everyone out."

Once they were back in the small antechamber, Monroe shifted back to human, and Odette sealed the room again.

"Happy to keep watch?" Morgana asked Monroe.

"Sure," he said reaching for his jeans, "but I'd love a cup of tea."

"I'm sure I can rustle up some cake, too. Don't hesitate to call if he stirs again."

"I'm heading straight to the library," Odette said, full of purpose. "I'll get those photos printed. It will be easier to research them that way."

"In which case," Cecile said, "I'll visit Xavier."

"If you point me in the right direction," Tommy said, cracking his knuckles, "I'll find Hunter. I'd like a good look at this demon. Maybe, Odette, you should work on a few personal wards that might protect us. Is that possible?"

"Leave that one with me," Morgana said, heading downstairs and contemplating a session in the glasshouse. "This might be where a strong potion could come in handy."

"What have you found out about Owen?" Maggie asked Stan as she entered the office.

She felt guilty at seeing him there, already after six in the evening, the remnants of a sandwich on a plate next to him. She knew he had a family that he'd much rather be with, but it couldn't be helped. They had to find out more about Owen. He was the key to everything.

They had only two offices in their department, hers and the one that Stan and Irving shared. Her own was in darkness, as was most of the main office. Only lamps on the desks lit the gloomy space, although lights from the city provided some illumination, too.

Stan leaned back in his chair, brushing crumbs off his chest. "Not a fat lot, unfortunately." He looked gaunt in the light, shadows pooling beneath his eyes. "I know he still lives in Kent, though. A little village called Bodsham. He's fifty-four, has no criminal convictions or driving offences. He's as clean as a whistle. No known employment, though—not for ten years—and he doesn't claim unemployment."

"So he's independently wealthy. Have we got his bank records yet?"

"Nope. The sister however, Ivy, is far more interesting."

Maggie pulled a chair to Stan's desk. "Why?"

"Because she's been dead far longer than Owen suggested."

"Really? Why would he lie about that?"

"Sympathy, perhaps?" He looked pleased with himself, despite the late hour, a smile playing about his lips. "Or perhaps he didn't want to say how she'd died."

"Go on!"

"In a major house fire, ten years ago. The house they originally lived in. She was trapped in it, Owen escaped."

"Was it suspicious?"

"Not according to the investigation. Looked to be an electrical issue. It was an old house, apparently."

Maggie snorted. "An electrical issue, my arse. If he has been handling that demon for over twenty years, I bet that it had something to do with that fire."

"It was a thorough investigation, though," Stan pointed out.

"Yeah, well, demons don't need accelerants. The question is, was it an accident, or did Owen deliberately kill her?"

Stan tapped his pen idly on his desk. "Perhaps it was to disguise the fact that the demon had taken her soul. They found her charred remains."

"I need to speak to him. I know what he told Maverick, but I'm not satisfied. He seemed to suggest that she'd willingly sacrificed herself. Now, I'm doubting that."

"You think he sacrificed her."

"Yes. And if he sacrificed his own sister, what will he do to virtual strangers? What *has* he done?"

"I've started looking into deaths in the area, bearing in mind that Odette thinks he killed witches for their blood, but it will take me a while to narrow down what sounds likely."

"Thanks Stan, you've done well. Go home, get some rest, and we'll come back fresh tomorrow. In the meantime, I'm heading to Storm Moon to pass on the news."

Stan stood up, ignoring the spread of papers and empty plate, obviously eager to go. "You could just phone them."

"No. I want to get down there. That's the only way to pick up intel. They'll hold stuff back on the phone. Besides, there's a big gig on tonight. I might get in for free!"

"Didn't think you were the gig type."

"If it comes with free drinks, I'm the anything type!"

Thirteen

By six o'clock on Saturday evening, Maverick had landed in Naples, courtesy of a cheap flight from Stansted. By nine o'clock, after navigating through customs and hiring a car, he was in Jemima De Luca's elegant lounge that popped with colour and elegance, much like Jemima herself.

Jemima was slender but shapely, her low-cut dress skimming over too pert breasts and rounded hips. He guessed she was in her early fifties, but she wore it well. Perhaps she was using glamour, or maybe the Italian lifestyle just suited her. She ran a hand through her chic, brunette hair cut in a bob, eyes sweeping over him. Maverick instinctively knew that this was a woman who was used to getting her own way, and hated it when she didn't.

"So," she said, after handing him a gin and tonic, complete with ice and a slice, "you're Maverick Hale. You're not what I expected of a werewolf."

"I'm a wolf-shifter, not a werewolf. We're very different. Werewolves are governed by the moon. I am not."

"I would imagine not much governs you at all." Maverick was used to being ogled by men and women alike, but Jemima was almost predatory. Despite her self-assured behaviour, there was something almost brittle about her. Dangerous. Maverick found he liked it.

"Well, I am the alpha of Storm Moon. I give orders, not take them. I'm not sure how much Birdie said…"

"Oh, Birdie." She rolled her eyes. "Yes, our Illustrious High Priestess said you need to find your brother. I gather he's here somewhere."

"South of Naples. That's as much as we could narrow it down to. I understand that you're a witch."

"I certainly am. I can cast finding spells, but I need something personal."

"I have postcards that he sent. That's all I've got from him that's remotely personal."

"If it worked for Birdie, it will work for me. The thing is," she stepped closer, her gaze sweeping over him again, "what do I get out of this?"

"My eternal gratitude?"

Maverick had a feeling she wanted much more than that, but he was pretty sure Birdie had said that she was married and had a son. At present, though, they were nowhere in sight. Not that he cared that she was married. Maverick had no qualms about sleeping with a married woman; as long as he wanted to and she did, well, that was fine by him. Although, he suspected that sleeping with Jemima might bring more trouble than he cared for.

She laughed. "Oh, you're funny. I always like that in a man."

"If you can find my brother, I'm very willing to negotiate." He fixed her with a smouldering smile, eyes full of promise. "And I never back down on a deal."

"Good to know." She opened her palm. "The postcard?"

He reached into his leather jacket and passed it to her, a finger grazing her palm deliberately as he did so. Her pupils dilated with desire, but she turned and led him to a table beneath a long window that overlooked Sorrento's steep streets lined with houses. It was dark, and the hillside glittered with the lights. No doubt there would be bars and restaurants, chatter and laughter, but in this house, all was silent expectation. A map was spread across the table, a detailed one of the area, and a selection of herbs and a silver bowl waited to the side.

"I'm sorry," he said, feeling like the house was far too silent. "I've intruded on your Saturday evening. Should you be out somewhere?"

"My husband's away on business, and my son is out with friends and won't be back tonight. He's barely home anymore. He wants to embrace his magic and go to Moonfell. If that's what he must do, I will let him, of course."

"Can't he learn magic from you?" He watched her prepare the postcard and kindle the dried herbs.

"I don't use it that much. Well, not in the way that Como wants me to." She shot him an amused look before continuing her preparations. "That probably surprises you."

"It's your magic to use as you choose."

"And I choose to use it for my business. Only an elite few are chosen to live at Moonfell."

Maverick was pretty sure that wasn't the case, but he now understood why Birdie said Jemima was odd. Jealous and full of resentment was how he would put it. "They are happy to have Como there, though?"

"So it seems. But enough of that place. It's large and gloomy, and I'd rather live in sunshine."

Moonfell was far from gloomy, but Maverick just nodded. "From what I can gather, my brother has been here for years. He must share your sentiments. Do you know any shifter packs, or do you keep away from paranormal affairs?"

"I know of some. We keep a respectful distance. There is one in Amalfi, a short distance from here, and of course a couple of very large packs in Naples. Right, I'm ready. Watch the smoke."

Jemima lit the square inch of postcard she'd torn off and placed it on the herbs, casting a spell as she did so. Maverick knew what to expect now, and he watched the lazy swirl of smoke idle up and across the map. As expected, it settled below Naples, and then streamed further south until it pooled above a place called Salerno.

"That doesn't surprise me," Jemima said. "It's a big town, and I'd expect a pack to be there. I know the place well."

"But you don't know *them*," Maverick surmised. "I could shift and hunt the streets. I'd pick up their scent sooner or later."

She leaned back against the table, picking up her glass of gin and tonic again. "Do you speak Italian?"

"No. I was hoping they would speak a little English."

"I happen to be fluent, and that will get you much better information."

"You want to come with me?" Objections were already forming in his head. He hunted alone.

"I told you that I have contacts in Amalfi. They will know who to contact in Salerno. They might have even heard of your brother. That will save you pacing the streets. It's a big place!"

The last thing Maverick wanted to do was to take Jemima. For a start, he guessed she'd want more payment. She didn't strike him as the sort to help as a favour. But, there was no doubt that her help would enable him to find his brother much quicker.

"Okay, thank you. But I can't wait. I have to go now, so if that doesn't work..."

She cut him off, eyes sparkling with humour and excitement. "It works perfectly. I'll phone him so he expects us, and then get my keys."

Vlad was at the end of the bar drinking a well-earned beer when he saw Maggie Milne enter Storm Moon.

The room was packed, spirits were high, and drinks were flowing. The band was due to start downstairs any minute, and there was still a steady flow of people heading to the club.

Birdie had already been and gone, after casting spells and painting strange, shimmering sigils on all the entrances and emergency exits. Vlad didn't know exactly what she'd done, only understanding that they would offer some protection against the deathless minions of the Otherworld, and that it was temporary. Birdie had said she'd need a coven to make really strong protection, but that it would suffice for one night. Apparently, it didn't help that they were a public building that catered to the paranormal. *Whatever*. It made Vlad feel better. Although, part of him relished having a chance to fight the demon himself.

Maggie made a beeline for the bar and sat on the stool next to him. She looked annoyed—her usual expression—and he said, "Hey, Maggie. One on the house. What do you fancy?"

"A very large red wine. Thank you." She slipped off her coat and sniffed her shirt. "Ugh. I stink of rot. I should have showered first."

"Where have you been?"

Checking that they couldn't be overheard, she said, "The morgue. I saw the victim's body. It's still swimming in demon infection. Disgusting."

"Well, you'll be pleased to know that Birdie has warded our doors for a little extra protection. Have you heard about the heart in the box?"

Her face drained of colour. "What fucking heart?"

"Ah! They found it in Owen's hotel room." He explained the details of what Arlo and Birdie had discovered.

She took several large gulps of wine before answering, and then glared at him. "And where is it now?"

"At Moonfell."

"Just fucking great! It should be in the morgue!"

Vlad shrugged apologetically. "I think they need it. Witch stuff. Demon investigation stuff. You know..."

"The Gods give me strength." She took a deep breath. "So, where is your illustrious leader?"

"On a plane right now, heading to Naples. Actually," he checked the time, "he should be there."

"Already?"

"Can't afford to waste time, can we?" The key to keeping Maggie happy, as far as Vlad could tell, was to continue making progress. "Birdie suggested he meet her niece, Jemima, who should be able to put him in touch with local shifters."

"Well, that's something. I gather you have a big band on tonight?"

"Yep. Mystic Banshees. Downstairs is full, hence the extra security and protection."

She didn't look happy about that. "Let's hope the demon doesn't have a passion for rock bands."

"We discussed closing, but it's impossible." Vlad decided it was time that he asked a few questions before he disclosed more news from Moonfell. "Have you found out any more about Owen?"

"Not much, yet, but what we do know is interesting." She related the news about Owen's sister's death. "Suspicious, isn't it?"

"The more I hear about him, the worse he gets."

"I need to interview him. Try and crack the shell of lies he's constructed."

"You don't trust what Odette has seen?"

"It's my job to interview people, regardless of Odette's abilities. I'll head to Moonfell tomorrow. I presume he's still there?"

He had a feeling he was about to witness an infamous Maggie outburst. "Well, yes. But he's currently trussed up in a binding spell, unable to speak."

"He's fucking *what*? Why?" She kept her voice down, but she was obviously furious.

"Self-inflicted, by the sound of it, after he tried to do some kind of ritual in his room."

She spluttered, fumbling to find words. "Well, they'll just have to unbind him! I need to question him! Fucking necromancing bloody witches. Why wasn't I told?"

The bar staff were watching the heated exchange, clearly amused, but Vlad took it in his stride. He'd endured his grisly old alpha screaming at him in the past, before he moved on to violence. Maggie was a pussycat in comparison. "I'm sure it's first on the agenda for tomorrow. They're working on a demon trap, so they're sort of sidetracked."

Mollified, Maggie calmed down. "Well, that's good, too. At least he can't manipulate the demon, I suppose. I thought they needed Maverick's brother's blood?"

"If we can contain it, that will be a start. What you need, Maggie, is to let your hair down. You know, your mate, Harlan, is here, with some woman named Olivia, and a guy called Jackson."

"Is he?" She looked shocked, and a little miffed. "He didn't mention they were coming!"

"You might want to check your messages." Only an hour earlier, Harlan Beckett, the American Occult Collector who worked for The Orphic Guild, had been complaining how useless Maggie was at checking her phone. He'd introduced his friends, and Vlad had been more than interested in Olivia. She, however, was giving off distinctly not-interested vibes, which was disappointing.

Maggie reached for her phone, and then paled. "Fuck it. I've had it on silent, and then I was in the morgue, and the Tube…" She looked dejected, and then pleading. "Damn it. I bet all the tickets are gone, right?"

"Maggie Milne, it's not every night you pop in here for a drink. I think you were after a free pass anyway, right?"

She smirked. "You're right. I *need* it. And I need more wine! Anything to distract me from bloody demons."

Vlad grinned and gestured to the bar staff. "Another wine for Maggie, please. Why don't I escort you down there?"

"Vlad, you might just be becoming my favourite shifter." She pulled a makeup pouch from her handbag and applied some lipstick, and then ran her hands through her hair. "Am I respectable enough for your club?"

"Of course. And I'll bear that in mind if I ever get into any trouble."

Circumventing the queue to get in, he led Maggie into the club, and then left her to find Harlan and her friends while he headed backstage. The band was due to start soon, and although he'd met them when they first arrived, he hadn't spoken to them at all since. Part of his job as Deputy Manager was to make sure that all their needs were catered to, especially ensuring that the correct rider had been supplied and the band was happy.

He glanced up to Bacchus, their resident DJ, who also looked after the light and sound on band night. They were operated from the controls in the DJ's Pulpit, as they called it. Bacchus, of course, wasn't his real name, but he suited his pseudonym. He was a wild-haired Greek man in his thirties who sported a variety of beards, and was covered with tattoos. He loved to drink and to dance, and his parties were legendary. Vlad waved to catch his attention, and he signalled a thumbs-up in response. The band's soundcheck had been extensive, and they had been demanding, but at least it was all done now.

His skin tingling with anticipation of the set, Vlad headed backstage and found the band on their feet, finishing their drinks. The singer was a striking woman called Nova who had dark red hair the colour of ripe cherries.

"Everything okay?" he asked her.

"Perfect so far."

"Are you sure, because you look like you might be sick."

"Typical last-minute nerves. I'll be fine when I'm onstage. Is everyone ready out there?"

"It's electric. The place feels like it might ignite." Unlike backstage, where it felt like it might implode. They were all nervous, and Vlad had seen enough acts come and go to know that was typical. He needed to give them their space. "Break a leg, guys, and I'll see you later."

He was halfway across the dance floor when Nova walked onstage, followed by the rest of the band, and the screams and shouts from the crowd almost deafened him. He waited for a few minutes to watch the start of the opening song, and then headed to the office. It was a relief to enter the relative calm of the space. Grey was standing in front of the monitors, arms crossed, while Domino scanned the dance floor from the observation window.

"All good so far?" Vlad asked, joining Grey. The feed was in colour, and of a good quality. They had recently upgraded all of their security hardware, and added cameras to the outside of the building.

"Yeah. Jax and Mads are keeping to the trees at the back. Fran is on the rear door, but that's shut tight now. No sign of a demon." He grinned at Vlad. "I highly doubt it will saunter up the main street. I reckon John has the easy job right now."

The camera at the front of the building showed John chatting to a group of young women, no doubt explaining that the club was now full, and no further tickets would be sold.

"You know," Vlad said, "we should move the club entrance outside. It makes the bar really busy, having people streaming in for the big bands. It unsettles the customers to have people constantly passing them."

"Only happens early though, doesn't it?" Grey said. "After that, it settles down. Besides, if you're having a few drinks first, you'd have to go outside and around to get in."

Vlad knew there'd be objections, but it was something that had always bugged him, and now that he was in the new role, he'd decided to raise it. "We could keep both. It would cut the foot traffic down."

"And double the staff."

"It's not like we're not making money," Vlad pointed out.

"I like the idea," Domino said, joining them. Domino was dressed in black jeans and a Storm Moon t-shirt that hugged every curve. She looked like she should be in the rock band, not Head of Security. "You should suggest it to Maverick when he gets back." Her eyes narrowed as she studied the screen. "Is that Jax, or a demon?"

Grey laughed. "Jax, you noodle. "I think they'd have let us know if a demon was watching. You're jumpy."

"Of course I am. I'm waiting for a demon to arrive."

Vlad remembered Maggie's news. "Shit. I should have told you what Maggie's found out about Owen. She's here now, with Harlan and two other friends, downstairs. Owen's sister died years ago, in a fire."

"So what's all that bullshit about her dying recently?" Grey asked, the cameras forgotten.

"I don't know, but I'd better tell Arlo. He's still at Moonfell, right?"

Domino nodded. "I'll phone Maverick, too."

Fourteen

Arlo liked being back in Moonfell's kitchen, hearing the back and forth of magic-based discussions, and watching Morgana brew up a potion. The mixture simmered on the hob top in a large copper pan, and an unusual scent that Arlo couldn't quite place filled the room.

Everyone was there except for Cecile who was watching Xavier, and Monroe who was still guarding Owen. Birdie had summoned Tommy and Hunter from the garden, saying that Hades would keep watch on the demon and inform them if it moved. He had a feeling she didn't want them in the garden alone at night.

Not that they were complaining. Morgana had cooked a huge pot of beef chilli, and Tommy was on his third helping, washing it down with beer. Most of them were still seated at the table, but Birdie was on the sofa in front of the fire, the large wooden box on the table in front of her. The heart, still in the jar, was in a fridge in the herb preparation room off the kitchen, where Morgana kept most of her supplies.

"I should return to the club," Arlo said reluctantly. "They might need me. Especially with what we now know about Owen."

"He's unconscious," Hunter said. "What damage could he do?"

"But we don't know how he's linked to that demon! What if he can still direct him in that weird state he's in upstairs?"

"That's true," Odette said. "I've been in a couple of times since he triggered the binding spell. I think there's a lot going on behind those motionless eyes. I just wish I knew whether it would be safer to bring him out of the binding spell or leave him in it."

"Well, Maggie wants to see him in the morning, so you'll have to release him then," Hunter reminded her. "You should be there for that, Odette. You might be able to tell if he's lying."

"He's doing a very good job of subverting my skills so far."

"Rubbish," Birdie piped up. "You found out a lot last night. And it's not always a skill you can govern exactly."

Arlo smiled at Odette's annoyed expression. She hated to be thwarted. "What about those rune armbands? Any news on them?"

"I've identified a few of the runes, but they have so many interpretations that I'm not sure how they work together. I'll compare them to the summoning circles in Owen's grimoire."

"Do you know which one is the one he uses?" Hunter asked.

"There's one that has the most annotations on it, so perhaps that one. I can see myself staying up all night, working it out."

"Not on your own," Morgana called over. She was stirring the potion again, a glass vial on the counter ready to decant it into. "Our most pressing need is to set up the demon trap and decide how to get the demon in it."

"You should stick it in a demon cage," Tommy suggested, finally pushing his empty plate away. "Then we can carry it in."

Arlo shook his head. "That's seriously the nuttiest idea I've heard yet, and you come out with so many!"

"What's wrong with it? I meant a *magical* cage. Something we can pick up and bring in." He shrugged at their puzzled faces. "Well, if it can't get in here, and we need to catch it, you need to do that out there to bring it over, right? After all, Owen is in a magical cage right now!"

Birdie twisted around in her chair, lips pursed thoughtfully. "That is an interesting suggestion!"

"You mean it actually makes sense?" Hunter asked. He grinned at Tommy. "Wonders will never cease!"

Tommy extended his middle finger. "Piss off!"

"Actually," Birdie said, rising to her feet. "I think we're getting far too caught up in what Owen does." Arlo still couldn't get over how she looked now compared to just a few months earlier. She'd been a wizened old lady then, bent with age, although still powerful; now she was a magnificent elder. "I don't trust that man one little bit. We now know his sister died years ago in a fire that he might have set himself. He might have needed to destroy all sorts of things he was up to. The upshot is that I don't want to use his summoning circles and traps. We have a perfectly good one in our spell room, and the original is written in one of the family grimoires. We can recreate that."

"But what if he has changed the demon somehow with shifter blood, or even witches' blood?" Odette asked, perturbed. "We could fail."

"I'd rather fail from my mistakes than sacrifice myself using his magic. As for your suggestion, Tommy, I like it. I have an idea that will involve your binding spell, Odette. How's that potion coming on, Morgana?"

"It's done. It's for painting on sigils, rather than for drinking," she explained to the shifters. "Wards that should prove effective at deterring the demon. Arlo, I can do you first, if you're leaving?"

"I feel I should stay now, if you're going to be catching demons. I can't leave you on your own. And Hunter and Cecile are still injured."

"I'm feeling okay, mate," Hunter said. "Well enough to shift and fight."

"And if you need bait," Tommy said, a wide grin spreading across his bearded face, "I'll be it. You can cover my naked body all over with sigils. Works for me!"

"I don't think you'll need to be naked," Morgana said, amused, "but thanks so much for offering!"

"And," Birdie added, "I have no intention of fighting it. We will funnel it into the trap. Hades will help. Thank you, Tommy. You acting as bait might work perfectly!"

Arlo felt that if he were to protest, he'd be making a big deal of it, so he just shrugged. "Okay. If you're sure."

"Over here, then, Arlo," Morgana said. "Strip your shirt off. Just painting your upper body will be fine. The effects will last a few days, as who knows what will happen with this demon."

Arlo did as she requested, standing with his arms outstretched as Morgana used a paintbrush to paint the sigils on his skin. He wasn't sure if it was the sensation of the brush or magic that left a tingle on his skin. The images shimmered before vanishing. "What about the rest of the pack? Can they get this done, too?"

"I don't see why not. Although, I'm not one hundred percent sure of its efficacy, just to warn you. I suggest you don't court danger with a demon."

"Not likely." When she'd finished, he pulled his t-shirt and jacket back on. "I'll see Xavier before I leave. Do you think he's getting better?"

"I don't need to change his dressings as often, but he's not out of the woods yet."

"Does that mean he can change to his wolf now?"

She sighed, resigned. "I guess so. See what you think when you see him."

It took Arlo several minutes of walking up ornate staircases and down long corridors to reach Xavier's room, and he found Cecile on a chair by the fire, reading a book in lamplight.

"How's he doing?" he asked, crossing to the bed. The room was warm, and Xavier only had a sheet draped over his naked lower half. The sheet was stained with smears of blood, as were the many dressings on his arms and torso. Fortunately, his face was uninjured, but he still looked horribly pale, and his hair was sticking to his head with sweat. Arlo tried to breathe through his mouth, but there was no getting away from the smell of his injuries.

"He's sleeping easier now. That has to be good, right?" Cecile crossed to Arlo's side, the book still in her hand.

"I think so. Have you spoken to him?"

"I chat to him occasionally, but he hasn't responded."

"I still don't understand how the demon first attacked you," Arlo said. "Was it in the water?"

She nodded. "We were walking along the bank when it emerged so swiftly from the water that we couldn't react quick enough. It pulled Xavier in, and I went in after them. It was like a damn Octopus. It seemed to have so many limbs." She looked haunted by the memory. "It was like trying to bite a flame. It was so elusive. So weird!"

"It's a *demon*. I think they're meant to be weird. But it's a good thing you couldn't bite it. It could have been disastrous."

"I know, but at the time, I didn't even think! I just reacted. I was luckier than Xav. My wounds are better. They still sting, but at least they're healing. I had a few hours' sleep in my wolf this afternoon."

"Well, if you can get through to Xav, Morgana is happy for him to shift, too."

Cecile finally smiled. "That's good news. What's happening downstairs?"

"They're making plans to catch it in a trap. Tommy is the bait. He volunteered."

"Why doesn't that surprise me?" she said, smirking.

He laughed too, glad to relieve the heavy mood. "We'll get through this. Maverick is working on a plan, too."

"He's being secretive. So are you!"

Arlo hated lying to his pack. Especially when they'd been injured because of Maverick's past. "Sorry. I'll tell you everything when I can. In the meantime, stay here, and stay safe. I'm heading back to the club. Apparently, they don't need me to catch the demon." He couldn't help the resentment creeping into his tone.

"The club needs you, though, and the pack. These are uncertain times, so look after them."

Although Cecile was right, he couldn't banish his mood, and it was with a heavy heart, that he returned to Storm Moon.

Maverick had presumed that he'd be driving to Amalfi, but Jemima had insisted that she would because she knew the area better. She also had a much nicer car than the one he'd hired. She owned a sporty little Alfa Romeo, and cocooned within its warm interior, they had chatted about the area and what had led Jemima to live there.

A desire to escape Moonfell and England appeared to be the motivating factor. It seemed Moonfell spread a long shadow, at least for Jemima, although Maverick couldn't quite work out why the place annoyed her so much. It certainly didn't seem as if love had drawn her to Sorrento. Not for her husband, anyway. She might have been fond of him, but it seemed to be more of a business partnership than a love match. Or maybe it had been once, and now it wasn't. Or perhaps that's just what she wanted Maverick to believe. Mostly, however, they talked about Italy, rather than anything personal.

It took an hour to reach the small town of Amalfi, another spectacularly beautiful place on the southern coast of the spit of land jutting out beneath Pompeii. The town tumbled down to the sea, backed by rugged cliffs. Maverick hadn't travelled much for years, and now he wondered why not. He felt he'd been missing out. He suspected he also knew why his brother had stayed in the area. *Why leave all this?*

Jemima hadn't said much about the alpha they were visiting, except that his name was Giovanni, and he was the head of a shifter family who had made their money from wine.

"He's not the head of a pack, then?" Maverick asked, wondering whether he was marching into some kind of mafia family.

"He has a big family. That's his pack." They crested the road that wound down the steep cliffs, the town spread below them, but Jemima turned left up an even narrower road that switched precariously above the bay.

"He lives up here?" Maverick asked.

She pointed up. "Oh, yes. He lives in that wedding cake."

Maverick peered through the window, craning his head to look up. "Good grief. That's massive! I can see why you call it a cake."

"A wedding cake, darling. No ordinary cake for Giovanni. I helped furnish some of it."

A few minutes later, they swept through imposing iron gates, along a drive, around a fountain, and halted in front of the vast villa. The drive was littered with other cars, and the house glittered with lights that bounced off pristine white walls.

"He's having a party?"

Jemima exited the car, smoothing her cocktail dress around her hips and adjusting her cleavage. "Always. He loves to entertain."

"But he's expecting us, right?"

She nodded. "I phoned."

He looked down at his dark jeans, boots, t-shirt, and leather jacket. "I hope there isn't a dress code."

"As if anyone would ever refuse you entry anywhere." Her eyes ran across him again before heading to the front door. "Nope, never."

Maverick couldn't see any obvious sign of security, other than cameras mounted on corners and above doors, but he sensed shifters out of sight, somewhere in the garden. They were in their wolf, patrolling, and he knew they had scented him.

The door was opened by a middle-aged man dressed in a dark suit, and he bowed his head. "*Signora da Luca*. A pleasure to see you again. The master is in the rear garden terrace room. You know the way." He spoke in English, but his Italian accent was strong. "*Signor* Hale. A pleasure."

"Leonardo," Jemima murmured, "thank you. I doubt we'll be long. No need to move the car."

"*Si, Signora.*"

"He has a butler?" Maverick asked as they walked down the hall, distant chatter drawing them onwards. He could sense the shifters ahead. He felt their power, magnetism, and effortless dominance.

"And cleaners and chefs and gardeners." Jemima smiled, tucking her hand into Maverick's left arm. "They're all human."

The walls were painted white, the floor made of marble, but artwork—paintings, as well as sculptures—worth millions, Maverick estimated, lined the walls and filled rooms on either side. The furniture was modern, the materials of bright colours, and it was obvious the white walls were designed to be a backdrop for everything else.

They eventually reached double doors that opened onto a grand conservatory, sparkling with light from several chandeliers. Approximately a hundred guests circulated the area, champagne flutes in hand, and within seconds of them entering the room, a waiter passed by, and Jemima snagged two glasses. Soft music played, something classical, and beyond the long windows was a huge swimming pool that glowed an azure blue.

All eyes turned to them, and an older man exuding lethal but controlled power, strode through the middle of them all, hands outstretched in greeting. "Jemima, what a pleasure to see you again."

"Thank you for agreeing to see us, darling." They exchanged kisses on both cheeks, and then Jemima said, "Giovanni, this is Maverick Hale."

Giovanni appeared to be in his seventies, shorter than Maverick, but with a boxer's build. He had well-groomed white hair, tanned skin, and wore a black tuxedo, impeccably tailored with cufflinks glittering, which served as a partial disguise for the shifter beneath, because his suit was the only civilised thing about him. Giovanni's eyes shone as he took in Maverick, and Maverick was on high alert. Giovanni was a fighter, and although no doubt he would have minions to do his dirty work now, Maverick was pretty sure he'd have been neck-deep in it in the past.

Maverick shook his hand. "*Signor Moretti*. A pleasure to meet you."

"Likewise. Is this your first time in Italy?"

"I'm afraid it is. I feel I've missed out. It's beautiful."

"The best," he said, nodding and guiding them through the crowd.

There were numerous human guests, but it was obvious who the shifters were. They were generally taller and broader, with an air of controlled violence. He met their eyes, an acknowledgement of who

DARK HEART   151

they were. If they thought they could intimidate him, they were idiots. He half wondered if they'd rustled up the party just for that purpose, but surely Jemima would have said so.

Giovanni paused in front of a whip-thin woman with dark hair and intense eyes, and a tall man, with the typical broad shoulders and narrow waist of a shifter. "My daughter, Carla, and my son, Rocco. I have four other sons, but they are all around somewhere." He waved his hands vaguely. "My grandchildren, too. I am blessed to have seventeen of them."

No wonder he didn't need a pack. That was a big family. "A pleasure to meet you both," Maverick, said, already sick of this meet and greet. He hadn't got all night to spend chatting, and he was pretty sure Giovanni knew it, too.

"You are here on business or pleasure?" Carla asked.

"A little of both, actually," Maverick said. "I'm catching up with family."

"Pleasure, surely then," she said, teeth bright against her tanned skin. She was a similar age to Jemima, but Maverick was pretty sure they weren't friends. *Acquaintances with mutual interests, perhaps.*

"I hope so." Maverick glanced around, aware that normal conversations had resumed, but everyone still glanced at them furtively. The rumour mill was already in overdrive. *Or did they know who he was here to find?* He now wished he had asked Jemima exactly what she had told Giovanni.

But what did it matter? His brother might be a nobody who no one had heard of.

For a while they made small talk, talking of Amalfi, and wine, and what Maverick did for a living. Jemima added to the conversation, witticisms dripping from her lips, until finally she said, "Giovanni, perhaps we could talk privately? Then you can continue your party without us."

"Of course." He kissed her hand. "Let us go to the pool house."

Great, Maverick mused. They were going outside the main building. *For privacy, or something else?*

The pool house was an innocuous name for a building that was the size of a small family home. It sat across from the conservatory, table and chairs arranged on the patio outside it, a light gleaming in the window. When they stepped inside, Maverick realised that two of Giovanni's sons, and two grandsons, had been waiting for them in here. All four were fit and athletic. The younger two were not much younger than Maverick, it appeared.

"Is this some kind of trap?" Maverick asked immediately. "I only need to ask you a few questions, and yet you seem to think you need bodyguards."

Jemima's eyes flashed him a warning, but he ignored it. Giovanni, however, merely smiled.

"You read too much into things," he said, hands gesturing expansively. "I am merely ascertaining that there is not a threat to my family."

"I'm here on my own, just looking for my brother. I haven't brought anyone from my pack with me. It's purely family business. I'm sure you can appreciate that. If you can point me in the right direction, I'll leave, and you'll never hear from me again."

"The thing is," Giovanni said, eyes never leaving Maverick's face, "your brother works for a very dangerous alpha in Salerno, and has an illustrious job in the pack's business."

"How do you know that? I haven't even given you my brother's name. I didn't even mention it to Jemima...and I only decided to come today!"

"But I had your name, Mr Hale, and with even one hour's notice I have ways of finding out what I need to know. Information is currency in my world."

Vineyard owner? Not bloody likely. Or not just that. He resisted glaring at Jemima, refusing to look away from Giovanni, despite his intense stare.

"So, what's my brother's name? I'm curious to see how good your network is."

"Network! Nothing so official. Your brother is Canagan Hale—known here as Matteo Noakes."

Interesting. It was the Italian version of his father's middle name and his mother's maiden name. Not that Giovanni needed to know that. "He changed his name?"

"He clearly wished to stay hidden. His boss can ensure that. Fortunately, I do extensive research on all the shifters in this area. I don't like surprises. I will say, however, that you look like him—although, he is darker, with a tan after being here for so long. A little rougher around the edges."

Maverick looked at the other four men, hoping for confirmation. One man, his dark hair flecked with grey, nodded. "He speaks correctly. What you should be asking is why, and who he works for?"

"I suspect I know why. It's the reason I'm here."

"Maybe," Giovanni said, drawing Maverick's attention back to him. "Or maybe it was the trouble he found himself in when he worked in Naples."

This man loved his secrets, and Maverick was over it. "Fine. He's hiding from a dodgy past. *Again*. Where does he work?"

"He's the Pit Boss for the casino in Salerno. *Casino Signora Fortuna*. Or the Pit Manager, as we call it in these more civilised times. It makes him sound less like a bulldog."

Maverick wasn't sure what he'd expected to hear about his brother. *That he was on the run from trouble in Naples? Perhaps. That he had a very good job? Not so much.*

"Sounds like he has his life in order now. I'll go find him. Thank you. I have all I need to know."

"No, *Signor* Hale. It's not that simple."

His stomach tightened. "Why not?"

"The alpha is also the owner of the casino, and demands absolute fealty. She's ruthless, and she won't like you walking in to talk to your brother."

Maverick had many questions. "The alpha is a *female*? In Italy? I hate to point this out, but you guys are known for your patriarchal attitudes."

"I hope that wasn't an insult," one of the grandsons said, a low rumble in his throat.

Giovanni shushed him. "Not now, Bernardo." He smiled wolfishly at Maverick. "You are right. It's unusual, even more so here. But she is ruthless. That's how she got to where she is now. In exchange for the name change, your brother was obliged to work there for ten years for terrible pay. It's the standard deal. But then, things developed between them. They are now together."

At least now he knew why Giovanni and his family were interested in him, if his brother had those types of connections. The casino could be a front for of all sorts of things. "My brother is the alpha's mate?"

"*Si*. That makes her more possessive. But it's not just her. He's bad news. The whole pack is. They're not mafia, but they are close enough. You should walk away."

"Absolutely not!" *What the hell was going on? So much for trying to reconnect with his brother and forging some kind of relationship.* "I won't be there long. One conversation, and then I'm gone. Hell, an hour will do it. How big is the pack?"

Giovanni shrugged. "Most recent estimates, about sixty. They'll all be in the casino. It's a big one."

Fuck. "Well, I haven't come all this way to just turn around now. And I'm sure they're used to other paranormal creatures frequenting the place."

"Of course, but your brother will be in his office, and I doubt you'll get to see him."

"I'm his *brother*. I'm sure they'll make an exception."

"I wouldn't bet on it. In fact, I wouldn't bet on anything in there."

"I'll wait outside on the pavement if I have to. Thank you for your help." He turned to Jemima, who was waiting silently. "Let's go. I have what I need."

"I had a feeling you would say that," Giovanni said, shaking his head. "I'd offer to help, but we keep our distance from them. I advise you don't go, but if you insist... Jemima, I suggest you stay away, too. Witches are not allowed inside."

"Is that right? How intriguing." She smiled, eyes alight with excitement, and she reached up and kissed his cheek. "It's been a pleasure, Gio, and I value your advice and your time. Thank you. We'll let you get back to your party. Have a good night."

"Does that mean you're coming with me?" Maverick asked her when they were alone in the car, the house fading into the distance as she roared down the road. "Despite his warning."

"Of course it does. I've heard of the casino, but didn't know it belonged to shifters. It sounds thrilling." Jemima squeezed his knee, and her hand slid up in his inner thigh. "I wouldn't miss it for the world."

Fifteen

"Bloody hell, Tommy!" Hunter said, watching Tommy's sigils glowing faintly in the dark as they stood on Moonfell's terrace. "Are you sure you want to offer yourself as bait for a *demon*?"

"We need to catch it. I trust the witches to do it."

"But if it gets to you first?"

"I'll make sure it doesn't." Tommy had always been reckless, but this was another level. His eyes smouldered gold, a feral gleam that once kindled would be hard to put out. "Plus, I've got sigils for protection."

"Untested protection!"

Tommy winked. "Worried about me? Bro, I'm touched."

"Yes. I can't afford the rent on my own."

"So funny! You know you'd miss me!"

Odette interrupted them as she stepped onto the terrace carrying a large backpack. "We're ready."

Hunter looked over her shoulder. "Where are the other two?"

"They'll meet us at the wall. Morgana is taking the ladder." She laughed at his confused expression. "It's quicker than walking around the perimeter."

"Are you sure you don't want Monroe, too?"

"No. I want him watching Owen. He's still bound and unconscious. I feel a bit mean leaving him like that, but well..."

"Bollocks to him. It's his own fault." Tommy said, extending his hand towards the garden. "Lead on, Odette."

For a few minutes no one spoke as they navigated the paths to the perimeter wall. Hades was sitting on top, focussed on a spot a short distance away. In another few minutes, Morgana and Birdie arrived. Morgana had the ladder, and Birdie carried another full backpack.

"How many ingredients do you need for this spell?" Hunter asked. He reached to take the pack off her. "It looks heavy."

"Enough," Birdie said, relinquishing it with a smile of gratitude, "but I have the ritual, too. Demon traps are tricky, and we need to mark it out on the ground. Hades!" she looked up to the cat. "How far away is it?" She nodded at his unspoken response. "Several minutes away, and it seems unconcerned by our presence right now. I wonder if it's sleeping...like Owen."

"Then how can we make it chase Tommy?" Hunter asked.

"I'm hoping that we can provoke it by our proximity, but otherwise we unbind Owen. Like I said, a work in progress," Odette said.

They all clambered over the wall, which was straddled by the gnarled branches of well-established climbing plants. Tommy and Hunter climbed up easily and steadied the ladder for Birdie. Once they were all perched on the wall, they dragged the ladder up and positioned it down the outer wall. Outside the confines of Moonfell's garden and its protection, Hunter was aware of the lurking presence of the demon. Feeling safer as a wolf, he stripped and shifted, and his senses immediately improved. The demon was several hundred yards away, a void beneath the trees. A prickle of fear and anticipation crept across Hunter's skin, but his normal wish to hunt was tempered with caution. His wounds started to ache again, and he wondered if he'd been too eager to help. *Too late now.*

Tommy had shifted, too and he sniffed the air, settling on his haunches to watch the demon.

The witches had found a patch of flat, bare earth under a tree, and they worked quickly, marking out a trap in salt as directed by Birdie. It was a pentagram within a circle, and as soon as that was complete, they started to mark out convoluted sigils around the edge. But Odette was already shaking her head.

Hunter shifted back to human and kept his voice low. "What's wrong?"

"I'm not convinced that these will be accurate enough. The sigils aren't as crisply drawn as I would like. This has to be right, or it will be a disaster."

Birdie nodded. "Perhaps we keep it simpler. After all, we'll be adding a binding spell to the demon once it's inside. The trap is temporary. Simple runes will suffice."

"But how do you bind the demon safely enough to transport it?" Hunter was beyond confused, and now that the time was close, doubts were setting in.

"Like we said earlier," Morgana said. "We bind it in a magical cage. Three of us can work quickly."

"But what if the salt circle is disturbed? The ground is uneven! Anything could happen."

"We're burning it into the ground once it's done," Birdie explained as the other two continued to work. "Scorching the earth with it. We'll leave an opening for the demon, and seal it once it's in. You know about salt circles, then?"

"My ex-girlfriend was a witch. I picked up a thing or two."

After a hurried discussion, all three witches adjusted the runes they used, simple lines that intersected and that were easy to mark on the ground, but Hunter's skin prickled with unease. This might be a so-called lesser demon, but it was still dangerous, and who knew what the shifter blood had done to it.

And then Tommy growled.

Hunter focussed on the demon again, and for a horrifying moment, couldn't see it. Then he saw it was edging away. He was about to warn Birdie when Hades leapt down from the wall and headed to her side.

She looked at him, alarmed. "Have we spooked it?"

"What does he say?" Hunter asked. He was unable to understand Hades in his human form.

"He doesn't know, but as Owen is still bound, it has to be us!"

"And yet it's not attacking us," Hunter said. "Perhaps it knows what we're doing. Are you ready for it?"

"No!"

"We'll track it," Hunter said immediately. "Circle around it and draw it back if it goes too far."

He shifted without waiting for her response, and nudging Tommy, they set off together in a wide, looping circle that left enough distance between them and the demon, but kept it within sight. It moved quickly, slinking along the ground without any obvious limbs. It was like a drifting cloud made of poisonous vapour.

Hunter let Tommy run ahead, keeping pace with it, while Hunter hung behind, making sure it couldn't double back to attack the witches. Hades was pacing along the wall again. But the demon was showing no signs of returning. It seemed it had a new destination in mind, and its pace quickened so much that both wolves had to race to keep up with it. At times it blinked from view, as if passing from one world to another, but every time it reappeared, it was further away.

Hunter had a deep sense of foreboding. It was heading toward where Richmond Park lay alongside Wimbledon Common. With another minute it was away from Moonfell's perimeter and was in open park land. He and Tommy raced to intercept it, but it slunk past them, leaving traces of sulphur in its wake.

In seconds, Hades's voice was in Hunter's head. *"It's leaving the park! We have to get it back."*

"We can't keep up. But I know exactly where it's going. To Storm Moon. Tell the witches. We'll meet them there."

Grey was drinking a cup of strong tea and feeling relaxed about the evening as he studied the security cameras' feeds.

The band was a huge hit, the club was heaving, and they were making a lot of money. And even better, there were very few issues for security to deal with, and no sign of the demon.

"Looking good so far," he said, turning to Domino.

She was at the window observing the dance floor, but she looked at him and smiled. "This band is great. I wish I was down there."

"Why don't you go? I'll be fine for ten minutes."

She shook her head. "No. I'd rather not get distracted. Besides, there's a small group by the bar I'm keeping my eye on."

He crossed to her side. It wasn't hard to spot them. They'd carved out an area for themselves to the left of the bar. A tight knot of half a dozen men. "I see them. They're just drunk and having fun."

"And pestering the bar staff."

"Rory is close by. He'll sort them out," he said, spotting his dark hair and familiar build. He had absolute faith in Rory. He was old and wise enough not to overreact to a bunch of drunk idiots, but neither would he tolerate them if they got out of hand.

"I think I'm just tired and overwrought. It's been a busy twenty-four hours." Domino shifted her stance and ran a hand through her mane of hair. "I need coffee."

"Any news from Maverick?" he asked as she headed to the coffee machine.

"No. I'm sure he's just busy tracking down his brother. Let's hope Birdie's niece is helpful."

"And his brother isn't a dick."

"He has to find him first." The door swung open, and Arlo came in, a disgruntled look on his face. He had been back for a few hours, mooching around the place, and generally looking miserable after being told the witches didn't need him. "You're a ray of sunshine," Grey told him. "No fun upstairs?"

"No. It's all quiet."

"Which is good news, you fruit loop!"

"Is it? The witches are demon hunting, and I'm stuck here."

Grey didn't dare tease him about Odette. *Too soon.* "Well, we need you, so suck it up! Plus, you get to watch a killer band."

"Whatever." He huffed and headed to the monitors. "They should have let me help. Everything is okay here."

Grey was just about to offer some contrived rubbish in an effort to appease him when his phone rang, as did Domino's and Arlo's. With an uneasy glance at the others, Grey listened to Morgana's hurried, short message. He knew it must be the other witches calling his colleagues.

The demon was on the way, and so were they.

Neither shifter was tired nor bored now. Both were on high alert as they ended their calls, killer instincts on full display. Grey had worked with shifters long enough to recognise the signs. Their shoulders were thrown back, they seemed to have increased in stature, and already a golden light kindled deep within their eyes. Grey's own adrenalin levels spiked, and his thought processes sharpened, too. Years of training in the army kicked in naturally.

Grey thought quickly. "Okay. We send as many shifters as we can outside, and we clear a space at the back of the carpark. The witches need to set up their demon trap."

"And if customers leave the club? The carpark is too obvious," Domino said.

"It's a small carpark that generally only the staff and the visiting band use. You know that! Most people get here by the bus or the tube. Plus, the band is still playing," Grey pointed out. "No one is leaving yet except maybe from the bar upstairs, and everyone will leave by the main door anyway, which is right on the street."

Arlo directed his attention at the feed of the carpark. So far it was all quiet there. "I doubt there's enough room. They'll need a big space for a trap."

"And we risk our pack in confined spaces," Domino complained. "Don't forget, a lot of the pack are here tonight just for a night out! It's not just our security staff at risk."

"We keep them inside with everyone else. No one else knows about this except our team."

"How? Lock them in? Are you insane?"

Grey tried not to lose his cool with them. "Both of you, shut up. I get it. There were injuries last night, but we haven't got time to fine-tune this. We act now. We need to warn the team already out there, and we need to move cars to create space. Circle the wagons, like in an old western." He grabbed his keys from his jacket and handed them to Domino. "You focus out there. Leave in here to me. I presume that's what you'd prefer? We still have to make sure everything stays safe in here."

Domino nodded. "We leave Hal and John on the doors and pull everyone else."

"Take Hal from the club entrance," Grey suggested. "No one else is coming in now. All the tickets are sold. The girls are still in the cloak room. Who cares if a few late stragglers get in now."

"Great idea," Arlo said. "I'll gather security up and meet you outside, Domino."

Domino and Arlo were already striding out the door as Domino said, "Thanks, Grey. Round up a few more car keys and we're in business."

The staff room was behind the bar upstairs, and that's where everyone's personal items would be. Grey knew just who to recruit for that. *Jet.*

And then he groaned. Maggie was here. He had to tell her. *Bollocks.*

Maggie was a little tipsy, if she was honest, but the news about the advancing demon was like having a bucket of cold water thrown over her head.

"Oh, for fuck's sake, Grey! I was having a really good time!"

Grey smirked, but it made him look sexier rather than annoying. *Yes, she was definitely tipsy.* "You can pretend you don't know. Enjoy the band, kick back. Get really drunk. I'm telling you only because I thought you would want to know! All of you, actually. You bunch of whacky occult collectors."

She was with her friends—her *pack* as Jackson now called them all—Harlan, Olivia, and Jackson. They had been watching the band, but were now in one of the small lounge rooms off the corridor that led to the Security Office. Normally, they were full of people seeking out a quieter spot to chat, but the band tonight held everyone's attention and it was empty, apart from a couple snogging in the corner who were oblivious to everything.

"In fact," Grey continued, "I don't want you to do anything. The shifters are outside and dealing with it. I'm keeping the door staff informed. I'm telling you out of courtesy."

Maggie wasn't sure if it was the wine, or maybe her raging peri-menopause hormones, but Grey was looking particularly good that night. His jeans hugged his muscular thighs and his biceps bulged very nicely. She took a deep, calming breath. She needed coffee. "I can't just sit here. I have to do something."

"Actually," Harlan said, "I think Grey is right. We're not exactly equipped to hunt demons. And Olivia is pregnant."

Olivia, glowing with health and positively thriving in her early pregnancy, glowered at him. "Stop bringing that up like it's a disease! It's been barely ten weeks. I'm very capable of helping! And I'm sober, unlike you."

Jackson, her tall, scruffy friend, shrugged. "I work for the PD. I can hardly sit this one out."

Grey held his hands up, backing towards the doors. "Hey, I've told you, and now I suggest you keep out of it. You're welcome to stay in our office, or just keep watching the band. I'll be upstairs coordinating if you need me."

"Wait!" Maggie commanded. He wasn't getting out of this mess that easily. "What about the other businesses on this street? You might be locking down, but they won't be."

"Unless you can exert your influence to get them to lockdown too in record time, there's bugger all that I can do."

"Fuck!" Maggie said, exasperated. There was no way she could organise anything official now. This was just going to have to play out. But they could help here, at least. "Cars! We can help by moving them."

"Whatever, but you get in the way, and Domino will kick your arse!"

Maggie, fuming, turned to the others once he'd left. "I cannot sit this out. Let's see what we can do."

"Maggie! Think this through," Harlan said, blocking the way to the door. "This is the big 'D' we're talking about, and in case you've forgotten, I saw one earlier this year. They're terrifying. We should stay out of it. My pathetic human flesh can't cope—and neither can yours."

"We have to do *something*!"

Olivia nodded. "I agree. We can definitely move the cars, and then we'll keep humans away, if nothing else."

"Good, now let's find Jet with the keys." Maggie ignored Harlan's eye roll and strode out of the room and to the emergency exit at the side of the stage, the quickest way to the rear of the building. She slammed the bar down, pushed the door wide, and strode outside.

Fran was at the stage entrance, having an argument with one of the band's entourage. From the expression on Fran's face, Maggie wouldn't have argued with her, but the young man was clearly not in his right mind.

"I don't care that you want a smoke," she virtually growled at him. "This area is off limits for the next hour. Security issue."

Maggie knew Fran from their raid beneath Brixton Market when they had fought Pûcas together. She headed to her side, flashing her ID at the young man with black eyeliner and piercings. "Back inside, no arguments. We'll let you know when it's safe."

"But I wanna smoke!"

"Tough shit. Do as you're fucking told!"

"You can't talk to me like that!"

"Listen, you little scrote, we're trying to keep you safe. There's a mad gunman on the loose. Get inside!" He backed up, mouth open in shock, and Maggie slammed the door after him. "Wanker."

Fran snorted. "Mad gunman?"

"Better than a demon. And you're welcome!"

"Give it two minutes and he'll be back. I know the type."

"You have my permission to punch him."

"Tempting, but no thanks. Sure you should be out here, Maggie?"

"I'll do what I can to help."

"Perhaps you should mind this door while I head up there. That's where I would be if that idiot hadn't come outside."

Maggie took pity on her. Fran was desperate to get in on the action, plus guarding the stage door would be a legitimate reason for Maggie to stay close to the action. "Give me five minutes, and I'll be back."

Maggie raced to the top of the stairs. Jet was handing out the staffs' keys to the others, and a couple of cars were already being moved. She stuck her hand out. "Tell me where to."

"We're clearing that corner." She pointed to the left where the carpark ended under an overhang of branches. "It can't be seen from the street. The witches need a large circular area for the trap, so that's it. We'll ring the cars around it."

"What will that do?"

"Create a barrier, and more privacy. It's better than nothing, Maggie!" Jet frowned, impatient. "Any better suggestions?"

"No."

Maggie did as she was told, and within a few minutes, half a dozen cars formed a semicircle at the corner, the trees and a wall behind it. Beyond that was the rear of other buildings and some small gardens.

Shifters were everywhere. Most were in their wolf, pacing the perimeter. Domino and Arlo were talking under the trees.

A wolf raced around the corner from the front of Storm Moon, paws skittering on the concrete, and shifted in front of Domino and Arlo. It was Vlad. "It's on the way. But it's coming from the other direction. It left Wimbledon Common and is cutting through gardens. And it's fast."

"It's coming from the wrong way!" Domino said, anguished. "I thought it would come from behind us!"

"It's the most direct way for it to travel. At least it's not coming down the bloody High Street," Vlad pointed out. "Tommy and Hunter are right behind it."

"We need to divert it," Arlo said, starting to strip. "I'm covered in protective sigils. I'll try to draw it around the back. If not, well then, we manage."

"I'll come with you," Vlad said.

In seconds, leaving no room for argument or discussion, both shifted and raced away.

"Where are the witches?" Harlan asked Domino. "If they're not here soon, we're all screwed! We need to get inside," he said, addressing his human companions. "Being at the front of the building is not an option right now."

Domino nodded, pulling her phone from her pocket. "I agree. Get inside. I'll call."

But the roar of a car engine and the squeal of tires cut through the dull thud of music and announced the witches' arrival. They all turned expectantly, rewarded seconds later by a battered Range Rover screeching to a halt on the carpark. The witches virtually fell out of the doors, not even bothering to shut them as they raced over, hefting large bags.

"Where do you want us? There, I presume?" Birdie said, spotting the ringed off area. She was desperately trying to hang on to her composure, but her hair was loose and flying over her shoulders, and Morgana and Odette appeared much the same.

It was their attitude that struck terror into Maggie more than anything else. They were worried—*frantic*—and the shifters were aggressive. Domino looked incandescent, her eyes full of fire. There was a palpable air of panic, and it all became horribly real to Maggie as the last of the alcohol left her system, and the snarl of wolves rose in volume.

A demon was coming for them.

But while she was temporarily struck by shock, the witches were already in action. Bags were upended as they started to mark out the demon trap on the ground, and most of the shifters circled to the front of the building.

Jackson grabbed her arm, pulling her down the steps to the stage entrance, Harlan and Olivia right behind them. The emergency exit had slammed shut, but Fran was already a wolf, guarding the stage door.

Maggie finally came to her senses. "We've got this! Go!"

Sixteen

Domino stripped and shifted, and in seconds raced to the front of the building, desperate to head off the demon and bring it round the safer back route.

She ran across the road, leapt over the fence behind the opposite building, and kept going until she reached gardens behind the neighbouring houses. She could smell the demon approaching, the sulphurous scent drifting towards her on the wind. Vlad was ahead but not far, and she leapt the final fence, almost crashing into him as he halted, the demon only a short distance away. But their presence wasn't stopping the demon. It lurched towards them, all smoke and flame, a snarling, twisting mass of shadows.

Unable to stop her primal response, she howled, and Vlad took up the call, too. A chorus struck up around them, her team advancing from all directions. The demon ran headlong towards them, and Domino braced herself for pain.

But then Arlo appeared from their left, leaping in front of her and Vlad. Whatever the witches had done to him seemed to work, because instead of advancing, the demon changed direction, heading right. Tommy jumped a fence behind it, barrelling into it with snarling, snapping teeth. For a moment, it seemed as if they had become one, and then the demon wrestled free and smashed through a fence.

Tommy, seemingly uninjured by his fight, followed it, and the pack changed direction, too. The demon seemed unfazed by the new course. For a second, Domino couldn't work out what she was seeing, because the demon suddenly vanished. She hesitated, perplexed, and then ran on regardless, and as soon as she was over the hedge, she saw it again at the far end of the next garden.

How the hell could it do that?

The chase continued, several wolves now homing in on it. Blood-lust was running high, but it was tempered by fear. Everyone knew how badly injured Xavier was, but equally they cast the knowledge aside. Domino howled a warning. They were herding it, not attacking it. However, although they had succeeded in changing its direction slightly, it was still heading for the front of the club, not the rear.

And then, just as they were approaching the street, Hunter vaulted over a wall in front of it, and the demon changed direction again.

Morgana raised her hands with her coven, arcane words rising on the air as they chanted the spell.

The trap, crude but hopefully effective, blazed in flame, and the marks scorched into the concrete. They had left a small section of the circle incomplete so that the demon could enter it. They would have to be quick to complete it once it was inside.

If they could get it inside.

Morgana banished all doubts from her mind. They had to succeed.

"I'll complete the circle," Odette said, scanning the carpark for any sign of the demon. A distant howl was the only clue that the shifters were hunting it. Only Jax remained close by, nose lifted, pacing the area behind them. "You two close it. Then I'll cast the binding spell at the same time."

"Can you hear Hades?" Morgana asked Birdie. "Is he following?"

Birdie nodded, eyes vacant for a moment as she located her familiar. "He is, but he's not as close as the wolves. It's changing direction again."

"But what's its purpose here?" Morgana asked, questions racing through her mind. "Why wake out of whatever state it was in to come here? To cause destruction? To kill shifters? And is it being *directed* here?" She kept seeing Owen's unconscious form, bound in magic in his room, and wondered what was going on in his head.

"No time for that now," Birdie said as a howl ripped through the air, sending goose bumps along Morgana's skin. "It's here."

Arlo didn't follow the demon and his team; instead, he headed directly to the front of Storm Moon.

Fortunately, it was late now, and the road the club was situated on was quiet. John still stood in front of the doors, Maggie next to him, and as soon as he saw Arlo, he nodded in understanding and hustled Maggie inside. They had agreed to say the police had ordered everyone to stay indoors due to a security incident. Now, no one would leave that way.

That was as much as he could do before the huge, hulking mass of the demon suddenly manifested in front of him, absorbing all of his attention. Its shape had changed, and with horror, Arlo realised that it looked like a wolf. A huge, towering wolf that continued to swell in size. Tommy jumped over the wall a few buildings down, and Hunter flanked from further along. All three advanced together, snapping and snarling as they raced at the creature. Arlo swallowed his fear. There was only one way to direct it now, and that was around the front and down the side of Storm Moon.

Everything was wrong for the trap, but there was nothing they could do.

Unfortunately, the demon had no intention of staying outside. It headed straight for Storm Moon's door, tongues of flames whipping around it. Tommy raced in front of it, blocking its way, and Arlo and Hunter attempted to herd it to the carpark. The rest of the pack arrived, and although the demon tried to attack them, Arlo, Hunter, and Tommy closed in.

Arlo's bloodlust and protective instincts kicked in immediately. His protective sigils were working, and the demon was keeping away, but Arlo could sense its cunning as it looked for a way to attack the unprotected wolves or get inside the club. He, Hunter, and Tommy ran closer and closer, making sure to keep between the demon and the team. Inch by inch they forced it into the carpark, but the cars were now between it and the trap.

They were screwed.

Harlan had been keeping track of what was happening on the carpark from the stage door, despite his deep misgivings about the whole situation.

He knew the stakes and understood that they couldn't fail. Maggie had gone to the front door in the bar upstairs to monitor the situation from the street. She was worried about the other businesses, and had decided that was the best place for her to be. If she could split herself in two, she would have. Olivia and Jackson were keeping an eye on the other emergency exits. Their main job, though, was to keep the band's crew distracted and also keep the band on stage. While they played, no one would leave.

Harlan edged the stage door open, Jet at his side. "What's going on?" she asked, trying to squeeze under his arm.

Dread filled him. "I can hear wolves, and the witches are shouting. Damn it. There's a lot of noise coming from the front. The keys are still in the cars, right?"

"Yes, why?"

"Because we need to move a couple of them." Harlan hadn't imagined that one day he might face one demon, never mind two. He must be cursed. "You stay here. I'll do it."

"You can't move two cars at the same time! We'll do it together."

With no time to argue with her, and knowing that logically she was right, they ran up the stairs, sprinted to the middle cars in the semicircle, and fired up the engines. The witches were in position by the trap, and Harlan reversed, twisting the wheel hard to get it out of the tight spot they purposefully made. He hit both cars on either side before he got free, he and Jet driving as if they were at the dodgems. Together, they squealed out of the way to make room for the demon to get through.

And then it was there. The creature of nightmares. All swirling darkness, shadows, and flames. And it looked like a *wolf.*

Harlan was suddenly thankful he had seen a demon before. It made it easier to handle the situation now. He jammed his foot on the accelerator and shot forward, blocking its retreat to the front of the club. The demon-wolf aimed straight for the witches. Harlan spun the wheel again, the smell of burnt rubber mixing with the sulphurous stench of the demon. *Could you actually hurt a demon with a car?* Fuck knows, but he was determined to try.

With wolves leaping over the car and around him, and the witches chanting, he floored the accelerator again and drove at the demon. With a satisfying smack he thudded into it, and it rolled across the ground, through the gap, and directly into the trap. He followed it in the car, trying to seal the space as Jet roared in next to him.

Odette leapt forward, steady hands closing the circle with salt, and with a flash of flames, the trap was complete.

But now the real work began to bind the demon.

Vlad shifted back to human, running forward to help Jet out of the car, as Harlan stumbled out of his.

Jet virtually collapsed in his arms, face etched with terror, and he lifted her up and carried her to the top of the steps that led to the stage door.

"Wait," she murmured struggling to free herself. "Let me see it."

"Are you sure?"

"I need to see this through." Her face was pale, making her makeup stand out even more, but her jaw was set, eyes hard.

He understood her need and lowered her to the ground, but he kept his arm around her to support her. She didn't object, and it comforted him just as much. He was gripped by a similar grim compulsion to watch the creature from another dimension. Hunter had shifted, too, and had pulled Harlan away from the action and joined Vlad and Jet.

However, the rest of the wolves circled the demon trap, and the low rumble of their snarls mixed with the steady beat of the band.

The three witches circled the snarling demon and the trap blazed again, the simple runes etched on the floor now seeming to dance in the air. The demon tried to attack them, whips of flames flicking like tongues, but as soon as they struck the circle boundary, gold light flashed, and it retreated. Now Vlad understood why the witches had made the trap so large. The demon had swelled in size, and even now it pulsed with power.

They took a few moments to prepare themselves, holding black candles in front of them and positioning themselves equally around the circle before Odette began the binding spell. She sketched images into the air, runes again, all sharp strokes that hung on the air and then vanished. The other witches repeated the incantation, and the air was suddenly alive with twisting, curling runes. Odette shouted something unintelligible, and a gust of wind swept across the carpark. It carried the runes into the trap, smothering the demon.

It writhed, twisted, and roared in some hideous, guttural language that Vlad was convinced would make his ears bleed. The wolves howled and retreated, but the witches didn't budge.

Odette next threw water into the air from a small bottle, following it up with another chant, and the runes formed knots around the demon. The chanting intensified, and the knots tightened and multiplied, until the demon was completely encased in a shimmering ball that looked like a giant web. The guttural noise of the demon vanished, the chanting stopped, and for a moment, the world fell silent as if they had all stepped into a void.

Vlad wondered if he'd gone deaf, but in seconds, normal night sounds returned: the rumble of cars on the main road, the thump of music, a police siren in the distance. The witches stepped back and lowered their arms, stumbling slightly.

"It's done?" Vlad asked, leaving Jet with Harlan. "Is everyone okay?"

"It's done," Odette said, the ghost of a smile crossing her face. "Well, almost. We have to get it back to Moonfell...somehow. Can we borrow that van?"

Cecile's van formed part of the semicircle of vehicles, left there from the night before when she'd gone to the river in Arlo's car. Vlad nodded. "Sure, the keys are in it. It's Cecile's, so just keep it at Moonfell for when she's ready to leave."

"I'll go back with you," Hunter said immediately.

"Me too," Tommy said, shifting back to human at the same time as most of the other wolves. "I'll sit in the back of the van with it."

"I presume we can touch it?" Domino asked, circling it warily.

"Yes, but not for long," Morgana warned. "We pick it up and deposit it in the back of the van, and then don't touch it again until we have to. The binding is secure, but even so, the damn thing is toxic."

"Those of us who are warded, then," Arlo ordered. "Me, Tommy, and Hunter. The rest of you," he addressed the pack, "will head back inside and continue as normal—but stay on full alert. I don't trust Owen, and I wouldn't put it past him to be behind all of this. He could well be planning something else next."

Seventeen

"I confess that is not what I was expecting," Maverick said, eyeing the building down the street. "I thought it would be more garish."

Jemima laughed. "This is Salerno, not Monte Carlo."

Salerno was a large port town, gritty in some areas, more touristy in others. Not that he had seen much of it. Jemima had navigated with ease, and they parked in an accessible area before walking into the older part of town where the casino was situated on a narrow, winding street that led off one of the large squares. Despite the chill February evening, restaurants and wine bars were full, and the streets were busy.

The casino was a discreet-looking affair in an old building with half a dozen windows on each of the three floors. The ones on the lowest levels were comprised of smoked glass. It had a grand entrance door, but very little in the way of signage, other than gilt letters over the entrance, and two shifters in well-cut suits standing either side of the door. They had talked about it on the journey, and Maverick had checked the website on the internet. Details were kept to a minimum, creating mystery and allure, but it seemed the ground floor was full of slot machines, and gaming tables were on the first floor.

"You've never been here at all?" he asked Jemima.

"No. I'm not a gambler. Lucky, I guess, since witches aren't allowed in."

"Of course." Maverick had forgotten that detail with everything else he was thinking about. "So you can't come in, then."

"Of course I'm going in. I have very effective ways of masking my abilities. Are you a gambler?"

"I enjoy poker for fun, but I've always thought gambling in a casino would be like diving into shark-infested waters. I work hard for my money. I want to keep it."

"Keep your wits about you then, Maverick. Now, let me just muffle my magic." Jemima muttered to herself, and a ripple of *something* passed over her. All of a sudden, her magic—that faint trace of power she emitted—vanished. "Success?"

"Completely."

She smirked. "Always a handy trick."

They crossed the road at the same time as a cluster of people who were also aiming for the casino. One of the shifters opened the door wide, smiling in welcome, and they filed inside. Maverick thought they'd also get in unchallenged, until the other man, a tall, black-haired shifter with typical Italian looks, stepped in front of him and Jemima.

"You're a shifter." It wasn't a question. He didn't look at Jemima.

"Yes. I gather you welcome everyone here," Maverick replied, keeping his temper in check.

His eyes flashed a warning. A challenge. "As long as you're here to gamble and not make trouble."

"Of course not. This evening is all about fun with this beautiful lady." He gazed at Jemima, exaggerating his attraction to her.

Jemima smiled broadly. "And we have *lots* of fun."

"See that you do," he said, blocking their way for a moment more before stepping aside. "*Buona fortuna, Signora.*"

Jemima continued to smile broadly, her hand gripping Maverick's elbow possessively. "*Grazie, Signor.*"

Once inside, the soft lighting, rich decor, and warmth wrapped around them like a cloak. A reception desk stretched across the entrance hall, but beyond it was a flight of steps to the first floor, and doors opened to rooms on either side. The hum of conversation mixed with the jingle of slot machines. The place was popular. The people they had followed inside were now going through security and having bags checked before they entered.

Jemima reached up to whisper in his ear, her breath warm. "I forgot to mention, do not mention your brother here. We'll wait until we're upstairs."

He nodded. "That was my plan." Aware that curious eyes were on them, he leaned in and kissed her, and she responded enthusiastically. *Oh yes, Jemima would want more once this evening was over.*

They checked their jackets in, and Maverick made sure his wallet remained in his jeans pocket. He'd left nothing to identify him in his leather jacket. He exchanged money for chips, enough to look like a genuine player.

"Where first?" Jemima asked, her lips still flushed from their kiss. "He's likely to be on the floor upstairs where all the serious gambling is done, but I suggest we stroll around first."

"In case this all turns to shit, I want to find all exits and cameras."

"Planning a fast escape?"

"If I have to. How handy are you with magic?"

"I'm a Moonfell witch. I can hex, bless, and raze buildings as well as any good witch."

"No need to raze any buildings just yet, but good to know."

The lower ground floor was made up of lots of interconnected rooms, all filled with different slot machines. There was a bar that provided food, and a small dining area that overlooked the floor so that you could watch the gambling, but Maverick sensed much of the drama would be upstairs. Most of the gamblers here were casually dressed, and a mix of all ages, the clientele mostly human. Maverick stopped to buy them both drinks, and when he was satisfied that he'd seen enough, they walked up the flight of stairs to the first floor, the noise growing steadily louder until they reached the broad landing covered with plush carpeting. Ahead were wide open double doors leading into a generous, open plan room that stretched the length of the building. Again, the lighting was low and intimate, and tables offering all sorts of gambling games stretched in all directions. Black-jack, roulette, poker, craps, and baccarat. The room was full of people, it was loud, and the energy was high.

They started to circulate, and again he checked for exits. Several doors led to private gaming areas, the windows were locked tight and covered with thick green velvet curtains, and the bar at the end was as busy as the tables. Cameras were above every table, and in every corner. So far it was no different to any other casino, except for the overwhelming presence of shifters, of course. There was only one other obvious exit, and that was an emergency one in the corner of the room. He tried to shake off the unease that Giovanni had instilled in him. He just wanted to see his brother. *Easy.*

"I don't see any point in wasting time," he said when he'd seen enough. There was no sign of his brother, but no doubt he'd be in an office somewhere. Unless he had the night off. He wondered if the upper floor of the building was where he lived with the alpha, or if it contained offices. "Let's have a word with one of the staff."

"That one," Jemima said, pointing to a middle-aged, well-dressed shifter who was liaising with several members of staff. "Let me. I speak fluent Italian, and it's an easy way to earn a little goodwill. I won't mention you're his brother, and I'll use his new name, okay?"

Maverick nodded. He was nervous about meeting his brother after so many years, which was ridiculous.

When the man finished his conversation, Jemima stopped him with a smile, and launched into a rapid discussion Maverick couldn't follow until she introduced him. "This is Maverick Hale. We'd like to speak to Matteo Noakes. We understand he's the Pit Manager here."

The man had appeared relaxed, indulgent even, until he was introduced to Maverick and Jemima mentioned the Pit Boss. His eyes narrowed and he answered in perfect English. "No one works here by that name. I'm so sorry. You are mistaken."

Maverick stiffened, aware that they were now being watched by several shifters. "Are you sure?" he said softly. "Because I have it on good authority he works here. I'm an old friend, and I'm sure he'll see..."

The man cut him off, eyes not leaving his. "He does *not* work here. I suggest you walk away and spend some money. Another drink, perhaps."

Maverick's anger swelled. He hadn't come so far just to be turned away, and he was pretty sure Giovanni wasn't lying, unlike the man in front of him. He had good instincts. Tension mounted as Maverick straightened up, ready to argue, or even fight if he had to, but no doubt that would see him thrown out on the street. However, before he could respond, Jemima laid a restraining hand on his arm, and he felt her magic like a punch in the gut. But it wasn't directed at him. It was aimed at the shifter.

She almost purred as she said, "Take us to see Matteo now. You couldn't be happier about it. We are old, trusted friends, and it's quite safe. We have no intention of causing trouble."

It was a dangerous game. Shifters were harder to glamour than humans. Their paranormal abilities made them stronger, more resistant.

But Jemima had acted quickly, and that's why he felt her magic so strongly. Her voice was soothing even Maverick's anger, but she was a witch and she'd just outed herself. Their situation balanced on a knife's edge.

The shifter's eyes glazed as he struggled to maintain control, but Jemima continued to glamour him with honeyed words and persuasions, and her magic rolled around them, affecting the ones watching them, too. For a heart-stopping moment, Maverick could envisage an ugly scene in which they tried to make him leave and he resisted, until the man eventually nodded.

"Of course. Follow me."

Jemima's magic shut down like a steel trap, and the other shifters stepped away, their interest moving to the gaming tables. In seconds they were walking to a door by the bar.

"Another day, another demon. The fun never stops at Storm Moon and Moonfell!" Hunter grinned at the three witches, Arlo, and Tommy. "You guys should stop putting 'moon' in your home names. It's bound to attract the crazies!"

"I don't think demons are attracted to moons," Birdie informed him. "They are summoned by morons who can't control them."

"Looks to me like he knows exactly what he's doing," Hunter shot back. "It knew where to go! Do demons carry maps of Wimbledon in their back pockets?"

"No, demons use search engines, like everyone else," Tommy said, smirking. "Everyone knows that."

Arlo shook his head. "You're both wrong. I think the Wombles on the common directed him."

"You three are batshit crazy," Odette said, laughing. "Is this what dancing with demons causes? Insanity?"

Hunter grinned at her. He liked Odette, and the other two coven members. It was nice to have witches back in his life. They were fun. "I'm on a come down after my adrenalin high. What do you expect?"

They were in the old stable block at Moonfell. Part of it had been converted to a garage, and part of it was used for storage, although currently a large section had been cleared out for Morgana's son's art studio, apparently. And now it housed a demon. Another large trap had been burnt onto the ground, and the demon was inside it, still bound in runes. Every now and again it moved, like a nest of baby spiders waiting to hatch.

The drive to Moonfell had been precarious. The demon had been loaded in the back of the van, and Hunter and Tommy had travelled with it after strapping it in place with tie downs. They seemed ridiculously mundane things to restrain it with, but it was better than have it roll over them on the short distance to Moonfell. Arlo had followed in his car with their clothes, and all three were now fully dressed. Hunter was glad of it. It was cold outside.

"So what now?" Arlo asked. "And should we talk about the fact that it looked like a wolf?"

"Hades will watch it for us," Birdie said, pointing to the large cat who had crept up behind them silently. Hunter should have heard him approach, but Hades was uncanny. "As for its wolf appearance, I feel that's all too obvious. But let's think on it. We'll head inside for coffee, check on Owen, and then go to bed. I'm knackered after all of that."

"I still don't understand how you can get the demon in these grounds. What about your protection spells?" Tommy asked.

"It's bound in our magic," Morgana explained. "That makes all the difference."

"So if it gets out, it has free rein? I don't like that idea."

"Trust us," Morgana said, leading the way back to the house. "There are extra layers of protection here, so don't you worry."

While Arlo and Odette stayed in the kitchen to make drinks with Morgana, Tommy and Hunter accompanied Birdie. They found Monroe lounging in the chair that he'd positioned to see Owen, checking his phone while keeping an eye on the bound witch.

"Has he stirred?" Birdie asked.

Monroe stood and walked to the doorway to watch his prisoner. "He's been restless, but he's fallen still again now. I debated punching him if it got really bad, but he settled down."

"How long ago was that?" Birdie asked.

"An hour or two. About the time the demon was on the move, I reckon."

Birdie's mouth tightened into a grimace. "It has to be him." She withdrew and beckoned them all to the main door. "From now on, we say nothing about what's happening in front of him. Okay?" They all nodded. "Good. Monroe, head downstairs and have some food and drink, and then sleep. I'll take over here. I need some thinking time, anyway." She cast a long, thoughtful look at Owen again, and Hunter knew she was trying to work out what was going on.

"You need to rest too, Birdie," Hunter said. She looked tired, and he had no doubt that the spell had been hard on her. "All I've done is run around. I'm used to that. Let me take over."

"And your wounds?"

"Aching a little. I'll survive."

"No, you won't," Tommy said forcefully. "Give me ten minutes, Birdie, and I'll be back. It'll be my pleasure to watch the little scrote.

You all go to bed. I'll howl if there's trouble." He gave his big, feral grin. "I might have to punch him first, but I'll make sure he survives."

Grey waved the last of the human staff off, locked the front door of Storm Moon, and sighed with relief.

It was exhausting pretending there was no such thing as demons and the paranormal with their human staff. Grey had decided to change protocol, and he sent all the staff who knew nothing about the unsavoury events of the night home before any of the usual jobs had been done. They could handle it the next day. Right now, he wanted a debrief with everyone who had been involved with the demon.

He had watched most of the events unfold through the camera feeds, and had been desperate to help his friends, but it was impossible. The club had to keep running, and there had been a few incidents that had to be handled. In the end, though, the night had gone smoothly, the band had been a huge success, and the punters had left very happy, including the pack members they had kept in the dark.

The security team, and Maggie and her friends, were now seated in the bar in various places, unwinding, exchanging stories, and debating on what would happen now. There was a heightened air of alarm, despite their seemingly relaxed stances. Fran, Mads, Jax, Rory, John, and Hal all sat together, crammed into one booth in seeming solidarity. Vlad sat with Domino on a central table and chairs. Jet, Harlan, Maggie, Jackson, and Olivia all sat together on the table next to them. They had divided themselves by senior staff, humans, and the security team. Grey didn't like it. They were separated, and it suggested unrest.

Grey walked to the bar, poured himself a large whiskey, and sat next to Domino, who had turned her chair to face the next table, and was deep in conversation with Jet and Harlan.

"You two are awesome! Thanks so much for moving those cars. That was ballsy."

"It seemed insanity not to," Harlan said, gripping a glass of bourbon. "I wanted that thing in the trap as much as anyone. Moving cars was the quickest way for it to happen."

"And you hit it with the car, too!" Grey said, raising his glass. "Excellent. Not sure that Rory will be that pleased with the damage, though."

Rory was talking to Mads, but he now looked around in shock. "You did *what*? I didn't know about that!"

"Sorry!" Harlan quickly apologised. "I'll pay for the damage, don't worry. I didn't have time to think."

"I think you were amazing," Olivia said, squeezing his hand. "Both of you."

"And it made all the difference. You shunted it right where it needed to be," Domino said. "Are you both okay?"

Jet wasn't her usually bubbly self. She was quiet, hands clasped firmly around her drink, gaze furtive. "I've been better, if I'm honest. I just went for it earlier in a blaze of adrenalin, but now I can't get it out of my head."

"I was the same when I first saw one," Harlan reassured her. "They are so utterly unearthly that it's hard to actually accept what you're seeing. You keep doubting yourself. Like you'll blink and it's gone. But it isn't. And that one was different to the one I saw before, and not just because it looked like a giant wolf."

Grey had only seen the demon on the monitor for a brief time before the feed was affected by the demon's energy, but he knew exactly what Harlan meant. It was hard to wrap his head around its form. "Why is it different?"

"It seemed to jump. Like flashing in and out of existence."

Domino leaned forward, and other conversations fell silent to listen. "Yes, it did. It moved through space. One minute it was there, the next it had gone. How did it do that?"

"I'm not an expert. Like I said, I only saw one before, and it was in a confined space, but it seemed more fluid, if anything." Harlan shrugged. "Demons are not from this earthly plane. They are brought here. Perhaps jumping through space is something they do?"

"Or maybe," Vlad suggested, "it's to do with shifter and witch blood. The shifter blood must be the reason it looked like a wolf. But it was in the river last night, stinking of the Thames, and seemed happy enough there. Right, Domino?"

She nodded. "Yes. It was swimming! Do demons swim?"

"I thought they were creatures of fire and smoke," Grey said. "If it can adapt to water too, that does suggest a type of shifting. But we're just speculating. What's important is that we've captured it. Perhaps the witches can banish it after all, without the need for blood."

Jax asked, "Why do we need blood, again? And why isn't Maverick here, dealing with this? We need the alpha around when a demon is here! Xavier is severely injured. Any one of us could have been hurt tonight, too."

Grey tried not to show his surprise at Jax's words. Jax was usually one of the most loyal of Maverick's supporters, but they'd all had a bad shock that night.

Domino answered him, her voice firm. "Maverick is working on a solution to this. That's as much as I can say right now. Arlo as his second is now in charge, and he's doing a great job. The demon has been captured, and no one was hurt tonight. He's at Moonfell right now making sure it's secure."

Grey studied the security team while she talked. They were restless, eyeing each other nervously. Wolves were used to being predators, not the prey. Their eyes were veiled, expressions grim. They needed handling before things exacerbated.

Like Domino, he kept his tone firm, and made eye contact with each one. "You lot were brilliant tonight. You stuck together, and you handled it well. You worked as a team, which is what we always do. Tommy, Hunter, and Arlo all had protective runes painted on them. That is what kept them safe and deterred the demon. That's why they stepped between it and you. You will all get the same runes applied tomorrow, as an additional precaution. Even more importantly, tonight you protected the humans."

"But it was chaotic," Mads complained. "That thing was everywhere and nowhere! It could have been on top of us at any point."

"It's a demon! And you are wolves! Pack hunters. Predators. You herded it exactly where it needed to be. There are no hard rules in this life, especially in the paranormal world. I'm surprised at you. I thought you liked a challenge."

The room had gone very silent, and the humans looked distinctly uneasy. Adrenalin was peaking again, and more than one shifter had a golden glow to their eyes.

Domino broke the silence, staring at her team. "Of course we love a challenge. We thrive on it. It hones our skills, and makes us better hunters. We learn from this tonight. Have we ever faced a demon before? No. But we know more about it now. We know what can protect us against it. And importantly, we captured it. The next step is that we banish it. That's more complicated than you understand right now, but it's in hand."

"So, when will Maverick be back?" Jax asked, an air of belligerence about him. "Or Arlo? Or is he playing nice with Odette now? Does the witch's safety take precedence over ours?"

"Arlo's priority, as always," Domino said, fixing Jax with a hard stare, muscles tense, "is this pack. Ensuring the demon's capture and safe storage is an essential part of that. He will talk to all of you tomorrow. As for Maverick, he will be back when the job is done."

Eighteen

Maverick and Jemima were escorted to the second floor and along a corridor to a partially open doorway that led into a plush office.

The room connected to the huge security room, banks of screens providing feeds from all the cameras in the casino. There were dozens of them, and a huge number of staff to monitor them. It was a slick, professional operation, and Maverick had the feeling he had entered the heart of the lair.

He had a shock when he saw his brother. Canagan was no longer the slim, rangy boy with a mop of dark hair and a cheeky smile. Instead he was grizzled, with a scar down his cheek that disappeared into his thick, greying beard. His muscles were knotted, and he was ruggedly good looking, his dark hair cut short. But there was no levity in him. Everything about him was grim, from his expression to the way he carried himself.

And he didn't look pleased to see Maverick.

He'd been conversing with a colleague in fluent Italian. An argument, perhaps. But as soon as their escort edged through the half-open door, Maverick behind him, he froze. He dismissed the man he'd been talking to with a barked order, and addressed their escort with similar abruptness. Whatever he'd said wasn't good, because the man scurried away, shooting Maverick a confused look as he hurried down the hall.

Canagan didn't speak, his face devoid of emotion as he stared at Maverick.

Maverick broke the silence. "It's good to see you, brother."

"You shouldn't have come." His voice was rough, hard-edged.

"Is that all the welcome I get? Can we talk?"

Canagan walked to the door that led to the security room and shut it, then stared at Jemima, who had now moved into view. "Who's that?"

"A friend. She helped me find you."

"Wait in the hall," he instructed her.

Maverick hadn't been sure of how he would be received, but he hadn't expected this coldness. He nodded at Jemima. "Shout if you need me."

"Likewise." She left them to it, shutting the door behind her.

Maverick made a couple of hesitant steps into the room. He was used to being a commanding presence. Used to dominating everyone if he had to, but this was his older brother, who he had looked up to, emulated even, until he abandoned him.

"Why are you here?" Canagan asked.

"Because I wanted to see you. Needed to see you, actually. I have a lot of questions."

"This is not a good time or a good place."

"I don't care. I suspect from your attitude that this is my one shot. I need to make it count." As Maverick said it, he felt it to be true. His brother didn't want to see him. Didn't care about him, his life, or what he'd achieved, and he certainly didn't care that he'd been travelling all day to find him. *Who was he kidding?* He'd wanted to find him his whole life. Anger flared and he glanced at the windows into the security room. The staff were all preoccupied. No one was paying them any attention. "I'm not leaving until we've talked."

His brother picked up a remote control and aimed it at the blinds. They closed over the windows, giving them privacy. "Make it quick."

"I know the role you played in our parents' deaths. The blood you gave to Owen and Ivy, the witches. You betrayed us. Our whole pack."

Canagan crossed the room so quickly that he was a blur. He grabbed Maverick around the throat and thrust him against the wall, lifting him clear off the ground. "It's a fucking lie!"

"It's not," Maverick gasped out. "I can see it in your eyes. That's why you ran. You fucking coward!"

The next thing Maverick knew, he was flying through the air. He smashed against the next wall, rolled over a cabinet and bookcase, and slid to the floor. He regained his feet quickly, rose to a crouch, and crunched into his brother as he ran at him. They hit the desk, rolled over it and crashed to the floor. This time Maverick landed with more agility, and he twisted, pinning his brother to the ground.

"We *will* talk about this! I came to see you to try to understand why you did it! Even to sympathise with you for being tricked by that bastard, Owen, and his sister. But the big problem is that the demon is still killing people, and Owen no longer has control of it. And it almost killed one of *my pack*!" Canagan was struggling to rise, but Maverick had wedged himself between the desk and the wall, and he used that and his considerable strength to keep his brother pinned down. "Do you understand, brother? Owen unleashed a monster, and *you* made it worse! It's still here, walking the Earth and creating havoc!"

"And you are going to be the hero, are you? Save the day where your brother fucked up!"

Canagan reared up, eyes blazing with fury. He lifted Maverick and tried to throw him off, but Maverick refused to let go, and they rolled over, upending the desk so that everything cascaded across the floor. For a few minutes they fought recklessly, trading punches, smashing everything they touched, until Maverick was suddenly sick of all of it. He backed away, wiping blood from his cut lip. Both of them were bleeding and bruised, their clothing torn, both on the verge of shifting, and that wouldn't do at all. That way would surely lead to death or serious injury.

Maverick sat on the upended desk. "I didn't come here to fight you. I just wanted to see you, more than anything. You sent cards. It made me think you cared, but I see now that I was wrong. I'll leave you to your life here. But I still need what I came for. Your blood."

Canagan was still on the floor, but he dragged himself into a sitting position and leaned against the wall, eyeing Maverick warily. "How will my blood help? It was my blood that made it stronger. It tracked our parents because of it. It would have tracked you down too if Ivy and Owen hadn't managed to control it."

The possibility had crossed Maverick's mind, and he'd wondered if it had somehow tracked him to London all these years later. "Owen said it cannot be banished without the blood that changed it in the first place, so he said he needs your blood to send it back. The demon is different to how it used to be."

"I don't believe that for one second. He was lying then, and he's lying now."

"Why do you say that?"

"Because he's slippery. I presume he still has that weak expression. That air of desperation?"

Maverick nodded. "Yes, but we know not to trust him. A witch who helps our pack said he also used witches' blood to make the demon stronger. He used the demon to kill a coven that refused them a place all those years ago. He's a dark soul, we know that. It's why he summoned the demon in the first place. For revenge and to make money, apparently. But he says it has consumed his sister, and that he has lost control. He's scared of dying."

"Have you considered the fact he might want my blood to make it stronger again? That he has no intention of banishing it at all?"

"We have, but if we start the banishing spell and it fails, we could be in worse trouble. We need to prepare as best as we can." Maverick swallowed, needing to ask a question that he knew his brother would hate. "Why didn't you tell our alpha what was happening? We might have been able to do something then! Find witches other than Owen and his sister to help us banish it."

"Because our parents were dead, and I was responsible. I couldn't face it. And neither could my friends. We made a pact to keep quiet, and obviously, Owen and Ivy ran." His head fell back against the wall with a thump, and he closed his eyes for a moment. Maverick could see nothing familiar in his older brother's expression. He had changed in so many ways. He was hard, implacable. His eyes flew open, staring right at Maverick. "In the end, I couldn't stand to stay, either. The police investigation was a nightmare. We had to see that through, but that place had so many memories, and the guilt was suffocating me."

"But you could have helped afterward..."

"No! I'm not you, Maverick. I couldn't help. I left, and I put it behind me."

"Abandoning the only family you had. Nice."

"You were safe enough."

Anger flooded Maverick, but he fought to control it. "How could you know that? That demon could have come for me."

"Owen promised it wouldn't."

Maverick cocked his head. "You saw him after our parents died."

"Once. Straight after it happened. I went to find him, seeking answers. He grovelled and swore it was all under control and promised he would leave. And he did."

Maverick tried to organise the timeline of events in his head. They knew that Owen was behind their parents' deaths because of the fact they had been begging for shifter blood, and the fact that the sibling's scents were all over the area. But Canagan had supposedly found that out later, when Maverick did. As kids they'd been kept out of it.

Puzzled, Maverick said, "Some of the pack went to Owen's house as soon as the bodies were found. He'd already gone." Events dropped into place, and he stared at his brother in disbelief. "But you already knew." An ice-cold certainty rippled through him. "You were there at the ceremony when it went wrong. You didn't just give him your blood and walk away. You were *there*!"

"No!" Canagan leaped to his feet again, hands balled into fists, but his stare lacked conviction.

Maverick remained seated, arms folded across his chest, refusing to break eye contact with his brother, and beginning to exert his alpha control. "You watched it unfold. You watched the ceremony, you gave blood, and you saw it escape. Or did Owen control it, even then?"

"No! Fuck! Why don't you leave this alone?"

"Because your mistakes have come back to haunt *me*. At least have the balls to tell me the truth. I deserve that much."

"Fine!" he roared, voice wracked with pain. "I was there, with my friends. We took part in the ritual, and it terrified me! The demon was huge! It swelled in power, broke the circle, and ran! We followed it, but couldn't stop it, and that's when it happened." His brother covered his eyes with his hands. "I saw it all, and I couldn't stop it. Only Owen and Ivy could, but it took too long." He took a deep, shuddering breath, and finally looked at Maverick again. "I fucked up. I was young and stupid, and we thought it would be cool, and that we'd be doing Owen a favour. We thought he'd owe us. That we'd have a witch to use if we needed one. We were wrong. Horribly wrong."

Blood was dripping from Canagan's broken nose and he wiped it away with his hand, not caring that it still flowed over his chest and onto the floor.

Maverick didn't speak. He couldn't. He was full of conflicting emotions. Anguish, sorrow, frustration, but mostly anger. Hard, cold anger. His brother had lied for years while he stuck around, and then vanished suddenly, leaving confusion and grief in his wake. Maverick had come here to try to understand. To get blood for a solution, and to forgive, perhaps. Offer solace. Now, he just wanted to leave and never see his brother again.

He looked around at the devastated office. Everything was smashed, and silence had fallen heavy as lead. It took a great effort to speak. "So, this is where you live now, with the alpha. A female, I gather. You have quite the reputation. You changed your name, but I guess you kept something of our parents, though. *Matteo Noakes.*"

"I got into lots of trouble when I was younger. That's behind me now."

Almost. "Does she know what you did?"

"No one knows, except those of us who were there."

"And where are they now?"

"They're dead."

"What? How?"

"Fights. We all stepped on a dark path that day, Maverick. It's a miracle I'm still alive."

"Then we're screwed. I can't get their blood."

Canagan shook his head. "Actually, I was the only one whose blood was used. There was no time to use the others. The demon fled."

Maverick frowned. "Did they donate their blood? Would the witches have kept it all?"

"No. The blood offering was from my hand. Fresh. We didn't give any, or leave any with them."

"But why did Owen say that he did?" A thick, oily dread spread from the pit of Maverick's stomach. *Had Owen wanted him out of the way? Did he think his brother wouldn't tell him the truth and that he'd go on a wild goose chase looking for his brother's friends? Or was his brother still lying?* He leapt across the space between them and pinned his brother to the wall. "One of you is lying. It better not be you." Maverick exerted his alpha control again, eyes boring into his brother's, but there appeared to be no fight left in him.

"I'm not lying. Not anymore. You have the whole, shitty truth. But whether Owen sought them afterwards, I have no idea. We all kept secrets."

"I'll deal with it. Don't send any more cards. I don't want them. All I want is your blood." He strode into the adjoining bathroom, grabbed a towel, and thrust it at his brother. "Clean yourself up and I'll take it with me."

"Don't trust Owen, Maverick. Whatever he wants to do, do the opposite. Now I wonder if the demon escaping was even an accident, but that's just me. The events of that night were jumbled. It was confusing."

Maverick folded the towel, put it under his jacket, and took a few moments to tidy himself up. "I trust we'll get out okay?"

"I'll take you to the back stairs."

"Where's your alpha?"

"Out, which is lucky for you."

"Lucky for *her*. If she'd have got in my way, things wouldn't have ended well."

Canagan dusted himself off, somehow diminished. "You're an alpha now?"

"I am."

"You did well for yourself. I'm pleased."

It was too late for pleasantries, and Maverick exited the room, relieved to find Jemima waiting. No one was with her. She stood, calm and composed, and then she saw the room behind him. "Everything okay?"

"I've got what I need." He glanced up the corridor, but the door to the security room was still closed.

Canagan emerged a moment later, the blood wiped from his face, although his t-shirt was covered in it, and walked to the top of the back access stairs. He punched in a code. "The stairs lead to the ground floor, you'll come out behind the building. No one should stop you." Maverick nodded and held the door open for Jemima. He made to follow her, and Canagan said, "I really am sorry. It was more than I could admit to anyone. Especially you."

Maverick took one final long look at his brother's face, feeling it would be the last time that he ever saw him. He should say something to console him. Try to forgive him. He had been just a kid, after all, and had witnessed their parents' death, but he couldn't. The words stuck in his throat. He turned and left without another word.

Maverick brooded on the way back to Jemima's house, and she left him to his thoughts. Eventually, he fell asleep as exhaustion hit him. The hour-long journey seemed to pass in only moments, and it was a shock when she pulled up on the drive, the bay sparkling beneath her home.

He roused, blinking back sleep. "Sorry. I need to find a hotel." She didn't speak, instead exiting the car, and he followed her. "Did you hear me?"

"Of course I did. You need a shower and a change of clothes, and I can offer you a bed." Desire smouldered behind her eyes. "One on your own, if that's what you prefer. You've had a shock tonight. I'm sorry."

"You heard what happened?"

"Not a thing. I cast a spell to stop anyone from hearing anything after I heard the first crunch of smashing furniture. Why do you think no shifters burst in?" She opened the front door and stepped inside the empty house without turning a light on.

"Thank you. I couldn't have done it without you."

"Families are tricky. I know that more than most." She slipped her shoes off, and his gaze travelled to her shapely legs and ran up her body. He might be tired, but he wasn't dead yet. She smiled. "I'll fix you a drink while you shower. Top of the stairs, third door on the right."

"And your room?"

Her smile broadened. "Right next door."

Nineteen

"Holy cow. That's unexpected," Maggie said on Sunday morning, watching the demon writhing in its golden bonds. Not that she could really tell it was a demon. She could barely see any of it. "How long will it hold?"

"As long as we need it to," Odette told her, arms crossed and finger tapping her lip thoughtfully. "We'll have to keep renewing the spell, of course, and we'll make the trap more elaborate today. More secure. Hades told Birdie that it barely moved during the night, but it's more animated now."

Hades was at the side of the room, large amber eyes fixed on the demon as he sat sphinx-like on the dusty floor. He looked up at Maggie, blinked once, then looked away. She felt as if he'd seen through to her soul, and she shivered. *Another uncanny thing to add to this weird house.*

"You're sure you can't banish it without Canagan's blood?"

"We are skilled at many things, but demon banishing is not one of them. We're researching and preparing, and theoretically we know what to do, but we'd rather have his blood before we start. We heard from Maverick this morning. He's already got it."

"Has he?" Maggie looked at her, shocked. "That was quick...which is brilliant, obviously."

Odette shrugged. "A combination of magic and good local contacts. He'll be back here this evening. He was organising flights, the last thing we heard."

"Great!" A huge weight lifted from Maggie's shoulders. *Progress.* Her gaze shifted back to the demon. "So last night when you captured it, was actually very risky."

"Dealing with demons is always risky, even when you supposedly know what you're doing." She sighed. "Having to race to Storm Moon when we were setting up here was nightmarish. We rushed the ritual—we had to. It could have been a disaster."

Maggie suddenly felt guilty for every mean thing she'd thought about the Moonfell witches. Their brooding, Gothic mansion bred rumours and distrust. Perhaps they even courted it. But there was no doubt they were a force for good. She wished she'd met them years ago.

"Thank you, Odette. I really appreciate everything you did...and are doing. It's very generous of you to keep Owen here, and his pet demon."

"It's the safest place. We wouldn't have it any other way."

Maggie examined the huge stable block with its high-beamed ceiling and sturdy stone walls. It was a long building, divided into smaller areas by more modern walls. The garage was to the left, but this area was still large, and some of it was given over to storage. The remnants of the old stalls were still partly visible on the walls. "Will you banish it from here?"

"We're certainly not taking it into the house! We'll probably have to open a portal, and that will be big and dangerous."

"A portal?"

"A doorway to the Otherworld. To send it back, we need to open one up." Odette looked matter of fact about it. It should have been reassuring. It wasn't.

"So, you don't do this often?"

Odette sniggered. "Great Goddess! No! One of our ancestors was obsessed with demons, but we're not."

"What if something comes out of it? Another demon? Something *else*?"

"We must make sure nothing does. It's very complex."

Maggie had only drank one cup of coffee that morning. She wished she'd had a gallon now. "At least we caught it. Well, you did."

"Group effort, and you played your part. Let's have a drink, and then you can see Owen—and the box we found in his room, of course." Odette turned and led the way back to the house along a gravel path edged with emerging green stems peeking from the soil.

Maggie took a deep, energising breath, feeling that spring was just around the corner. It might be the middle of February and cold now, but promise was in the air, the unmistakable scent of change. It helped shake off her grim mood, and she found she had a bounce to her step as she followed Odette to the house. Purple and yellow crocuses were nodding from the garden beds, and a drift of snowdrops were just visible beneath a tree in the distance. Birds called, and there was a general sense of life across the garden.

She huffed. *What was the matter with her? Waxing lyrical over plants! Especially with a mild hangover and only a few hours' sleep.* Maybe it was the fun of the band, the involvement in the chase...although, she bitterly regretted being at the front of the club and not the back. *And maybe it was also the memory of Grey and his very impressive muscles and cheeky grin...*

Odette had been sidetracked, checking plants as they walked, but now she turned and grinned at Maggie. "You're cheerful this morning."

"Just pleased that we're making progress."

"He likes you too, you know."

"What?"

"Grey. I can tell." She grinned again. "You two would be firecrackers."

Maggie was lost for words, and she spluttered, feeling her face flush. "Why are you saying that? What do you mean?"

"I see the truth of things, Maggie, you know that. Don't worry." Odette tapped her pretty little nose. "I won't say a word. I thought you'd be pleased."

It was pointless to deny it. "It was just drunken thoughts!"

Odette tutted. "Maggie! This has nothing to do with alcohol. What's wrong with a little passion? And I'm not lying. He does like you. I can tell!"

"That's worse! Now I'm going to feel super self-conscious when I see him next time!"

"I haven't said anything to him. Us ladies must stick together. Although, if you want me to mention it..."

"*No*! Odette, don't you dare say anything to anyone!"

"If you say so."

The path had delivered them to the kitchen door, and before Maggie could threaten her with anything else, they entered the great Gothic kitchen. Monroe, Hunter, and Cecile were seated at the kitchen table, the remnants of breakfast in front of them. She knew Morgana was tending Xavier, and Birdie was researching demonologies. While Odette made coffee, they exchanged pleasantries. They all looked well. Cecile and Hunter had obviously recovered from their injuries, although scars still remained.

Monroe looked belligerent as he faced Maggie. "You interviewing that bastard this morning?"

"If I can. I have a lot of questions. Although," she checked her watch, "I'll phone my team first. I'm hoping they have some information for me. Background stuff on Owen."

He nodded. "Leverage."

"Sort of." Odette handed her a mug of coffee, and murmuring her thanks, she sat down. "I already know his sister died ten years ago. He lied about that."

"Really?" Cecile sat back, shocked. "How did you find out?"

"My DS was looking into her and found her death records. It was an easy find, as was the manner of her death. I'm not sure why Owen was lying, though—yet."

"He assumed we wouldn't be able to find out," Hunter said. "Idiot."

"How did she die?" Monroe asked.

"House fire. The whole place was destroyed. He's in a new house now. Same area, though. It was ruled as an accident. No accelerants were found in the house." Maggie gave a dry laugh. "I'm far more suspicious, though. I wonder if he sacrificed her."

Monroe frowned. "Which means she wasn't controlling the demon in the first place. That's what he suggested, right?"

Odette answered first. "That first night when I interviewed him, yes. He seems to be an accomplished liar, though. I'm finding it hard to read him. I really have to concentrate. Normally I get flashes of truth, or sometimes it's so obvious I see it even without trying, but with him... It's hard." She joined them at the table, placing a plate of biscuits in front of Maggie. Despite the fact that the shifters had just finished their late breakfast, all three leaned in and took a couple. *Shifters! As bad as bloody Nephilim.*

"I'm hoping," Maggie said, turning to her, "that you'll be there when I interview him. You might see something I won't."

"I'll try. I'll have to release the binding spell, anyway."

"I presume Tommy is watching him?"

Hunter nodded. "Couldn't wait. He's like a machine sometimes. Monroe will take over soon, though."

Monroe grunted in agreement.

"And Arlo?" Maggie asked. She was pretty sure he'd headed to Moonfell the night before.

"He went home when he knew we were okay and the demon was secured," Odette informed her. "He has a big day, talking to the pack later."

"Aye, this business has ruffled a few feathers," Hunter said, his Cumbrian accent getting more noticeable. "It's a good job Maverick is back so soon. Packs can get jittery without an alpha."

"More fool them," Monroe said with a huff, "if they start in on Arlo. And they shouldn't question Maverick's decisions, anyway. He's never let us down before. Some packs don't know how good they have it."

"A bad experience, Monroe?" Maggie asked him.

"Not me, but I've heard plenty."

He didn't explain, and although Maggie had questions, she let it be and considered her next actions. She hoped Stan and Irving had started work early. She needed more information on Owen. She pulled her phone from her bag, ready to make the call in the Poison Palace, as she liked to call the glasshouse situated next door, and then she saw the rune-covered wooden box that Vlad said had contained a heart. She pointed at it. "That's what you found in Owen's hotel room?"

"Ah." Odette grimaced and rose to her feet. "Yes, and that reminds me that I need to show you its contents. Prepare yourself. It's not pleasant."

Domino grunted in annoyance as she flicked through all the saved camera footage from outside the club. "Bollocks! There's almost nothing decent of that damn demon!"

"Hoping for a memento?" Grey asked sarcastically.

"No, moron! I'm looking for clues as to how it moves! How it does its weird jumps in space. All we've got is lots of flickering footage—and that's if we're lucky!"

Grey patted her shoulder in sympathy, his large, meaty hand almost jolting her off the chair. "Weird, Otherworldly energies were messing with our equipment." A sharp, staticky whine cut across his conversation, and Domino paused the feed.

"And why is it doing that? We don't even record sound!"

"Like I said, Otherworldly energies." Grey seemed blithely unconcerned about the grainy, static-ridden footage. Half a dozen cameras showed wolves and a flash of demon before everything vanished into a grey haze. "Besides, we have witnesses, including you."

Domino leaned back in her chair, rubbing her temple. "Yes, but I could barely believe what I was seeing, and there was so much going on! I just wanted to see it again." She pushed back in the chair and wheeled across the floor, accidentally hitting Vlad as he entered th e office. She bounced right off him, like hitting a wall. "Oops. Sorry."

Vlad shrugged nonchalantly and smoothed down his short, blond hair. "The pack has assembled. You ready?"

"Not really." Domino looked at Grey. "You coming? I think you should."

"This is pack business."

"And you're an honorary pack member."

"If you had human staff there, I'd come, but just wolves? No. I might antagonise them."

"But it was the security team who were pissed off last night, and you are part of that team."

"Domino..." Grey started, about to argue.

"No. You need to come. If anyone questions it, they'll answer to me."

"I agree," Vlad said, holding the office door open. "I think all senior staff should be there, and that's you, Grey. Besides, Jet will be there, too. "

Grey rolled his eyes and got to his feet, and Domino sighed with relief. She could hold her own with any of the shifters, and Arlo certainly could, too. He was in the bar now, getting ready to update the pack, but the security team needed to see that she valued Grey as her second, and that they needed to respect his opinion. Mostly they did, but she reinforced it at every opportunity.

When they entered the bar, the atmosphere was tense, and heads swivelled in their direction before staring at Arlo again. He was at the back of the room, leaning against the copper topped bar as he checked his phone. He looked casual enough, but he met Domino's eyes with a resigned look that acknowledged this was going to be hard.

Domino joined him, and Grey and Vlad flanked them. Jet was seated off to their side, apart from the pack, and she exchanged a brief, worried glance with Domino before watching Arlo.

Arlo put his phone away and faced the pack. "Thanks for coming here, everyone. I realise that Sunday mornings are precious, but I think it's important that I keep you updated. Fortunately, I have good news. We caught the demon last night. It's contained at Moonfell now, and we're working on a way to send it back where it came from."

An audible sigh of relief ran around the room. There were no children there, which meant that not all adult family members were present. Arlo must have asked them not to bring them. Demons were a hard enough subject for adults to deal with.

A few asked obvious questions, like how did they catch it? And how could they banish it? Arlo handled all of it well, but then Barrett, the older, grey-haired shifter who used to be the alpha said, "It ran through Wimbledon? Through gardens and streets?" He looked around the group, shoulders tight. "Why the hell weren't we told?"

"Because you're not on the security team, and you didn't need to know."

"I still live here, and I'm still a shifter. We should have been warned. I would have made it a priority in my day, or don't you care?"

"Of course I care." Arlo kept his voice even, his tone firm. Barrett had been a popular alpha, but he hadn't wanted the role anymore, and generally kept out of pack business now. However, he could still make waves. Tsunami-sized ones. "It was heading for the club. We had to make sure that it was locked down and secure."

"Not all of us were here, watching the bloody Mystic Banshees. Your priority should be *all* of your pack."

"It is."

"Then why weren't we told? You're the Pack Second, not the security team. Domino handles that. You," he jabbed a finger, at Arlo "should have thought of us."

"I did, and made the call that you weren't here and therefore safe. It was late," Arlo said, standing his ground. "Very late. Most kids and families would have been in bed, and it was cold out. It's not like they'd have been in the garden."

"But you don't know that, Arlo. You didn't think. We could have been leaving restaurants or cinemas. If that demon was searching for shifters, we could have been attacked, and we'd have been unprepared."

Domino felt tension rise, and she couldn't blame them. The team should have considered the wider pack in their planning. They knew pack members were watching the band, but everyone else had faded to the back of her mind. Many were at home with kids. They'd screwed up. One glance at Arlo showed he knew it, too.

To his credit, Arlo agreed. "You're right. I'm sorry. I should have informed you. But despite what you think, you *are* our priority."

"Well, we weren't last night. I thought Maverick had left us in safe hands." Barrett glared at Arlo.

Domino gritted her teeth. *The last thing they needed was someone challenging Arlo's role as Maverick's second.*

Arlo stepped forward, not breaking eye contact with him. "He did. Everyone is safe, and the demon has been caught. No shifters were hurt, nor any humans, and no one has commented on the fact that wolves were in Wimbledon last night."

"Apart from the howling," a woman called Frieda said. "I heard it. I wondered what the hell was going on. Will we have questions about that?"

"There were also the usual sounds of police and ambulance sirens last night," Arlo shot back. "Most people will have missed it. And the Paranormal Policing Unit was already here. There'll be no come back from the police."

"It's the pack that concerns me, and should concern *you*," Barrett said, weighing in again.

Jax, Mads, and Fran, who had complained the night before, looked pleased; vindicated, perhaps. Arlo needed to shut Barrett up and regain control.

Fortunately, Arlo went on the attack. "Have you ever had to deal with a demon, Barrett?"

"No, but—"

"Then you can have *no idea* what we faced last night. None of you have. And you have us to thank for that." He gestured to Grey, Domino, and Vlad, and then at the security team spread though the group. "The security team was brilliant last night. They put their lives on the line for all of you. From the second that demon left Moonfell, our team was tracking it. Hunter and Tommy followed it across Richmond Park and Wimbledon Common. Vlad met them at the town boundary and told us what was happening. They tracked it the *entire* time, and then the team surrounded it." He stopped staring at Barratt and focussed on the rest of the pack. "It didn't go where we wanted it to, but we knew where it was every step of the way. *Every step.* You weren't in any danger because we made sure of it. Grey coordinated everything in here, and John, on the front door," he nodded at the shifter in recognition, "made sure to lock the club up tight when he knew the demon was close. We even had five humans helping us! Jet and Harlan moved two cars last night, just so the demon could get in the trap. Five foot-nothing Jet!" He extended his arm towards her, and she shrugged, embarrassed at the public attention.

Arlo took a breath as they absorbed that information, and then he rounded on them again. "Xavier is gravely wounded at Moonfell. Morgana's skills are the only thing keeping him alive, and the witches also risked a lot last night to catch it." His voice rose with annoyance and indignation. "Tommy and Hunter travelled in the back of the bloody van to make sure it stayed in the binding spell. Monroe guarded the witch who is behind this mess all of last night while this was happening! And I have barely slept a wink, thinking on this. So don't, *Barrett,* tell me that I don't take my responsibilities seriously, or that we were unprepared last night, because you haven't got a fucking clue what was happening!"

Doubt flickered in Barrett's eyes, and Domino noted a wave of relief sweep over the pack as Arlo outlined the measures they had taken. She realised she'd been holding her breath, and she took one now, tension easing from her shoulders. But she didn't move, and neither did the rest of the senior team.

Arlo ploughed on, knowing he had their full attention. "Today, the witches will come here and apply you with the same protective runes they applied to Tommy, Hunter, and me. The security team will be first, then you—if you want it. I doubt you'll need it, but the offer is there. Then, taking your objections in, Barrett, we'll institute a new communication system. We can set it up today before anyone leaves. I have everyone's phone numbers. We'll create an alert system for pack safety. Agreed?"

Barrett nodded. "That's a good step. And Maverick? Where's he?"

"On his way back here with a way to end this for good. Any more questions?"

Another shifter spoke up. "So, the demon is secure for now?"

"Yes. It's contained, and within Moonfell's walls. Anyone else?"

There was a show of shaking heads and low mutters between people, and Arlo nodded. "Good. Be back here at three this afternoon if you want the protective runes. There is no choice for security staff." He levelled this particularly at Mads, Jax, and Fran.

Turning away, Domino caught Grey's eye, and saw the same look of concern she must have in her own. Crisis averted. *For now.* Arlo had more than earned his position then, and when they had some privacy, she'd tell him so.

As for Vlad, it must be hard for him, with Mads stirring up trouble. *Shifter crap. It never changed.*

Twenty

Hunter settled into his position just inside the door of Owen's room, waiting for Odette to release him from the binding spell.

Tommy and Monroe were also there, positioned on either side of the bed like prison guards. They were both huge and packed with muscle, of similar height and build, but where Tommy was pale-skinned, shaggy-haired, and bearded, Monroe was black, his hair shorn close to his scalp, and he was clean shaven. Owen would have a hell of a shock when he woke up with those two looming over him. Morgana had placed a plate of sandwiches and a jug of water on the table, and had retreated to the window to watch. Birdie and Maggie were seated at the table, Maggie with a pen and notepad next to her.

There was an air of expectancy and uncertainty, and Hunter was ready for Owen to bolt for the door when the spell was released. *He'd be an idiot if he tried that.* He rolled his shoulders, contemplated whether to shift to his wolf, and then decided against it.

"Ready, everyone?" Odette asked.

At their collective nods she cast the spell, her fingers weaving over Owen's body. The golden chains that bound him disappeared one by one, as if dissolving into thin air, and as the last binding vanished, Odette uttered a word of command and Owen's eyes flew open.

He took a sharp intake of breath and sat up abruptly, eyes wild. He tried to get out of bed, but Monroe and Tommy restrained him.

"Slow down!" Monroe commanded.

Owen looked around, confused and seemingly disorientated, and then as his panic settled, a sly, calculating look took root in his eyes.

"Welcome back," Odette said, standing at the foot of his bed. "How are you feeling?"

"What did you do to me?"

"I didn't do anything."

"Liar!" he spat. "Something attacked me in this room, and I did nothing!"

Monroe laughed. "Look who's lying now. I saw you start to chant something."

Owen twisted to look at him, mouth settling into a sneer. "You don't know what you saw, you oaf."

Monroe lowered his face to Owen's. "Call me that one more time, shifter killer, and I'll tear your head off your scrawny shoulders."

Owen inched back, but was stopped by Tommy's bulk. Hunter smelled his sharp bloom of fear before he gathered control.

Owen turned to Odette. "What happened to me?"

"The house doesn't like you. You not only triggered one of my spells, but something that is innate within the house itself." She tutted, amused, looking as if keeping prisoners in Moonfell was second nature. *Maybe it was.* "Owen. You really are very arrogant, and very dangerous. I presume you're hungry and thirsty. You've been trapped in the binding spell for twenty-four hours now."

"Twenty-four!" He tried to shake Tommy and Monroe off. "That's far too long. Has anything happened?"

"Oh, plenty. Why don't you refresh yourself first. Bathroom is that way. I'm sure you remember. Tommy and Monroe will go with you. Don't try anything foolish."

Owen looked as if he might argue, but instead, hobbled to the bathroom on stiff legs. Odette stood next to Morgana, and they waited silently for him to return. A few minutes later, looking slightly more alert, Owen entered the room, taking everyone in before he seated himself at the table. He didn't speak again until he drank two glasses of water and started on his sandwich.

"I don't know you," he said to Maggie. "I don't think you're a witch."

"No. I'm DI Milne of the Paranormal Policing Unit, and I have a few questions for you."

He paused, food halfway to his mouth. "I don't know why. I haven't done anything."

"Oh, I think you've done quite a lot, but by all means, finish eating first. I can wait." Maggie's voice was smooth, calm even, but the weight of knowledge hung behind her words. Hunter knew she'd had a long conversation with her sergeants, and she'd finished the call with a spark of malice and triumph in her eyes.

He waved his sandwich airily. "Go ahead. I can eat and talk."

"Fine. Let's start with this." Maggie banged the rune covered box filled with vials of blood onto the table, and then placed the heart in the porcelain jar next to it. "Unusual belongings for a man who hasn't done anything, no?"

A range of emotions ran across Owen's face. "It's not what it looks like."

"What does it look like?"

"It's an animal heart."

"Really? Because it looks remarkably human-sized to me."

"It's not. The blood is also animal."

"Well, I will be delivering all of it to the forensic pathologist later, so we'll soon find out. Even if it belongs to an animal, it's still very disturbing that you should possess it. What do you need all this for? Your demon?"

"It's not *my* demon!"

"That's not what you told Maverick and his team. You said you had conjured it and lost control, and that it had killed your sister. That's why you're here, isn't it? To get help to control it again. Use shifter blood to send it back to wherever you summoned it from."

"That doesn't make it mine."

Maggie, relatively calm up until now, exploded. "Well, it's not fucking anybody else's, is it?" She thumped the table, rattling his plate so violently that Owen jumped. "Do you think I'm fucking stupid, you odious little man? Your demon killed a man two nights ago, and went on a rampage again last night. You've endangered a whole community with your recklessness. Don't tell me it's not your demon! You're here, and you brought it with you!"

Hunter supressed a grin. He'd never seen Maggie let rip before. It was impressive.

"All right!" Owen held up his hands. "Yes, it's mine in that I summoned it many years ago. But I don't own it. No one owns a demon."

"It's still your fucking responsibility, and now it's also mine!"

"I came here for help!" Owen yelled back. "Instead, I am being treated as a prisoner. I could press charges. I've been kidnapped!"

"Press charges my arse," Maggie snapped. "You tell lies so easily, Owen. It's hard to know what to believe."

Owen took a deep breath and changed tack, sensing perhaps that he was doing himself no favours. "I'm grieving. My sister is dead because of that demon." He looked at the three witches and then back to

Maggie. "I was a greedy, foolish young witch, and we made mistakes. I've apologised to Maverick. I'm trying to make amends."

"For killing his parents and tricking his brother. How noble of you. And your sister. My condolences. When did she die?"

Owen licked his lips. "A few weeks ago. The demon was getting stronger, trying to break its bonds again. I use spells to control it. A trap I have constructed in my house. Obviously, it's not on this Earthly plane all the time. I summon it when I need it."

"Really?" Maggie leaned forward. "So, it goes back to its own plane of existence when you've finished using it."

"Exactly."

"And how do you call the same one each time? Brokaz, I believe it's called."

"All demons are individuals. I call that one particularly. I reward it." He squirmed again. "It's what makes it obedient, mostly."

"Until it's not," Maggie said coldly. "And you feed it with blood, I presume." She tapped the box. "And maybe a heart? Or will I find that this is the victim's heart from Friday, and that the demon gave it to you?"

"No! It's an animal's heart."

Hunter knew it was human. He could tell from the smell of it. So could Tommy and Monroe. The only thing that Owen could gain by lying was time. *But what did that achieve?* It wasn't like Maggie was about to take him to the police station. *What would they do with him?*

Maggie leaned on her elbows, hands clasped beneath her chin. "So, Maverick's parents' deaths were a terrible, unforeseen consequence of a spell gone wrong. An attempt to gain control with shifter blood. Is that right?"

"Yes! It was a *horrible* accident."

"How did your sister die?"

"She sacrificed herself, like I said. Again, the demon was struggling to escape, like it did all those years ago. I hadn't checked the trap carefully enough. There was a break in the circle, and one of the sigils had been damaged. It was my fault," he claimed magnanimously. "My sister, always selfless, sacrificed herself to it. It..." his breath caught, and he blinked back theatrical tears. "It consumed her. I was able to contain it again. But she changed its nature. It's different now. It's become stronger, and it escaped again."

"And that was a few weeks ago."

"Yes!" He nodded vigorously.

Maggie nodded. "Interesting. And yet, Owen, I have been doing a little digging on you." She referred to her notebook, flicking back through some pages. Owen leaned forward, eyes sharp, lips pressed tight. Tommy and Monroe stepped closer to him. "My sergeants found out that your sister died ten years ago in a house fire. You only have one sister, so she couldn't possibly have died recently."

"*No!*" he said sharply. "You're wrong."

Maggie sighed. "Don't be ridiculous. I have evidence. I think that you killed your sister many years ago. Maybe I'm being harsh. Maybe it *was* the demon! Either way, your house burned down, your sister died, you moved, and you continued to use the demon to achieve whatever warped aims you had. Money, revenge, power... All of that bollocks that people think is important, but isn't. My big question is, why lie about your sister? I think it was just a very convenient way to garner sympathy—risky, admittedly, but you like taking risks. You've been doing it your whole life."

Owen's face contorted into a demonesque mask, and he opened his mouth to speak. Odette raised her finger to her lips and uttered one word. Owen's mouth opened and closed, and he clutched his throat, face turning purple.

"You attempted a spell," Odette said calmly. "I don't appreciate that. And it's pointless, shaking your head. I know it to be true. It's also pointless to try to speak," she added. "You should concentrate on breathing. Your speech will not return until I will it. Do you wish me to bind you again?"

Owen tried to stand, but Tommy and Monroe pinned him to the chair, one hand clamped down on his shoulders, the other grabbing a flailing arm. Forced back into his chair, Owen took deep breaths, but his eyes were filled with fury.

Hunter sniffed the air and looked around the room. The air was charged with static, and the energy in the room was rising. He was unsure whether it was the house—*how weird was that*—or Owen. "Something is happening," he said, interrupting the interview. "I can feel it."

Birdie nodded. "So can I."

She leaned forward, pulling one of Owen's long sleeves back. Even from across the room Hunter could see they were glowing with a fiery light.

"Back, everyone," Birdie commanded, leaping to her feet. Her chair overturned, as did Maggie's, who almost fell over it in her attempt to get away.

But Tommy and Monroe struggled to break away from Owen, as if their hands were welded to him. Hunter watched in horror as their faces contorted in pain and confusion. "Let go!" he shouted.

"I can't!" Tommy ground out through gritted teeth.

Both shifters' bodies were contorting, their skin rippling across their features.

Hunter raced across the room. "Stop Owen! He's drawing on their shifter power somehow." He didn't know what he could do to help, other than rip Owen's throat out.

But Birdie reacted first. She chanted something incomprehensible, and Owen crumpled, unconscious, supported by Monroe and Tommy who still couldn't break free. She threw her hands wide, gesturing at Tommy and Monroe, and they flew across the room, the connection broken violently. Golden threads manifested out of the air to bind Owen again.

Hunter ran to his friends. "Are you all right?"

Monroe groaned. "That bastard was draining my shifter magic. How is that even possible?"

"I'm fine," Tommy protested, rubbing the back of his head. "Just give me a minute. Is that little bastard unconscious? That's all I care about right now."

"He's out for now," Hunter informed him. Relieved that they were okay, Hunter joined Maggie and watched the three witches, who had formed a circle around Owen. A shimmering light had encompassed him, and it was growing brighter. Hunter shielded his eyes and whispered to Maggie, "What's going on?"

"I have no frigging idea, but I want to wring his neck."

Within another minute, Owen was not only bound within shimmering gold threads, but also cocooned within a ball of golden light.

"That will do," Birdie said, stepping away from Owen. "It will keep us safe from him, and I think we have broken his..." she stopped, eyes becoming vacant. "Hades?"

It seemed that the room held its breath as everyone waited for Birdie to speak. Hunter headed to the window, trying to see the stables, but they were hidden from view.

"He's okay," Birdie finally announced. "The demon gained strength for a few minutes, but his bindings have held, and it stopped moving again."

"Which means," Morgana said grimly, "that we were right. He is connected to it somehow, and those rune bands on his arms are the key. We cannot risk waking Owen up again."

"Damn it!" Maggie returned to the table, frustrated. "I wanted to speak to him about the strange deaths in Canterbury a few years ago. I'm convinced he's responsible. I should have left his sister until the end. Rookie error on my behalf, but I wanted to rattle him."

"Well, you certainly achieved *that*," Hunter said.

"What deaths?" Odette asked.

"A handful of men and women died in a twenty-four-hour period within weeks of Maverick's parents' death. I wondered if it was the coven you said he wanted revenge on."

"What was mysterious about them?" Birdie asked, still keeping an eye on Owen.

"No known cause, other than massive heart attacks. Yet all had no history of heart disease, and they were all young and reasonably healthy. They literally died in their sleep." She huffed and collected her notes. "We're still investigating, obviously. Early days yet, but I feel we're running out of time."

Hunter dropped into a chair. He felt as if he had been sucked into Owen's spell too, even though he wasn't touching him. "Maverick is back later today. He has his brother's blood. Does that mean you can do the ritual to banish the demon?"

"In theory," Odette said. She watched Owen bound in his luminescent cocoon. "I'm not seeing all of it, though. He has some kind of barrier up that is blocking me. It's infuriating."

"You couldn't read anything at all, then?" Maggie asked her.

"No. He's strengthened himself somehow after I was able to read him the other night. It has to be the demon that allows him to do that."

Hunter idly looked around the room while they chatted, wondering if anything had changed after Owen's attempted spell. Everything seemed normal, though, other than the heightened tension and the hum of magic from the protective binding spell around his inert body. And then his gaze fell on the jar containing the heart. The porcelain was so fine that in the light from the window behind it, he could see the heart within.

"Holy shit," he exclaimed, and he leaned forward to see it better. "I think that heart is beating."

Twenty-One

Maverick arrived at Storm Moon at almost seven o'clock on Sunday evening.

It had been a long day. He couldn't get a flight until mid-afternoon, which had at least allowed him time to catch up on sleep and drive to Naples with plenty of time to spare. And also spend several more hours in bed with Jemima. He should perhaps feel guilty for sleeping with Birdie's married niece, but seeing as she had virtually declared it a marriage of convenience, why should he care? Plus, they had lots of fun. The night before, he had emerged from the shower and entered the bedroom to find Jemima clad only in a skimpy silk and lace wrap, and she had pushed him onto the chair and straddled him before he could even speak. The rest of the night had been similarly energetic. It was the perfect way to forget his brother.

Except, he couldn't. Their encounter still infuriated him.

He dropped his overnight bag in his flat and walked into Storm Moon. He'd spoken to Arlo briefly that morning, chatting long enough to learn that something had happened during the gig, but that everyone was okay. He wanted to hear the details in person. John was already talking to a customer, so he didn't interrupt him. The bar was busy, but he seated himself at the end of the long copper counter, and the bar staff placed a rum and coke in front of him.

"Good to see you back, boss," a young woman said, whose name he struggled to remember. Sometimes the human bar staff changed so regularly he had trouble keeping track.

"Thanks. It's nice to be home again." He smiled, taking a moment to drink in the mood. Nothing seemed amiss, and the place had its usual lively atmosphere. "I presume the band went well last night?"

"The best! The place was packed, and they played a really long set. There was a bit of trouble with the cars on the carpark, but nothing major."

"Like what?"

"A couple were dented somehow on the front and back, but Arlo said the club would cover it. They belonged to the staff, so that makes it easier."

The demon. Better cars than people. "But no injuries, I hope?"

"No. Everyone was fine. There was a bit of an issue with a gunman on the loose in the area, apparently, but it didn't really affect us." She shrugged, unconcerned. "Arlo even sent us home early last night. Right after closing. We'd been run off our feet! Don't worry," she said, laughing, "we made our time up and came in earlier today."

"However Arlo wants to organise things is fine by me. I presume he's in his office?"

"Yes, with Vlad and Domino, I think."

"Thanks. I'll go and catch up." Relieved that the human staff had not noticed anything amiss, he stood up and spotted Jet.

She gave him a beaming smile. "You're back! Good to see you."

"You, too." He drew her into a free booth to chat. *Time for some intel.* "I'm going to see Arlo now, but how is the pack? *Really.*"

"Tense, although that's probably an understatement."

"The demon, I presume?"

"Of course. The topic of all conversation. Although, the human staff don't know, of course, except me and Grey. Arlo held a pack meeting today, and Barrett challenged him about not thinking of the families, and putting the club first. It was along the lines of, '*Back in my day...*'"

"Of course he bloody did. Damn Barrett. Just when you need his support, he puts the boot in."

"Arlo was brilliant. Shut him down completely, and kept Jax, Fran, and Mads in line."

Maverick looked at her in shock. "They stirred trouble? I'm surprised. They're normally very reliable."

"Personally, I think Mads isn't half as happy with his brother's promotion as he makes out, and Jax and Fran are put out because Hunter and Tommy are in the thick of the action, even though they're newcomers." She shrugged. "Not their fault, is it? It's just the way things worked out. Hunter was injured! It was a miracle he could chase the damn demon across Richmond Park. And Tommy, well, he's just Tommy."

"I'll speak to them later—nothing about what you've said, obviously. I'll think of something."

"I think Vlad's promotion might be ticking Jax and Fran off too, but that's pure supposition."

"I trust your intuition, Jet. Unfortunately, there's only so many senior jobs available. I'll find a way to give them more responsibility."

"You should know that Jax accused Arlo of favouring Odette's safety over the pack's, too. He didn't," she stressed, "but again, Jax was just angry and wanted to mix things up."

"What *is* happening with Arlo and Odette?"

"They appear to have put their differences behind them." She laughed. "Maverick, seriously, the look on your face."

He leaned on his elbow, chin in his hand. "And in your opinion, is that good or bad?

"Good!" Her mood sobered. "The witches were brilliant last night. Things got really rough. Everyone was brilliant, really. It could have gone horribly wrong. Did you do what you needed to do?"

Maverick felt guilty that he hadn't told Jet about his brother and his parents. He trusted her, and always sought her out like he had now for her opinion on his pack. "I did. And I need to apologise. I've kept things from you that the senior staff know. Tommy, Monroe, and Hunter, too actually. That's really unfair of me. I was in a bad mood on Friday."

"With me?" Her eyebrows shot up in surprise.

"No. Never with you. With me, and Owen, and this whole damn thing." If there's one thing his encounter with his brother had taught him, it was to look after your friends, and Jet was a very good friend. "Come with me while I update them."

"Maverick, it's okay not to include me in things. I'm not a shifter."

"Even more reason to. While our egos run rampant, you keep a cool head. Thank you. You and Grey are both brilliant."

She looked puzzled, and she reached for his hand. "What happened last night?"

Unexpectedly, he found himself choking up as the emotions he'd been trying to suppress all day rose to the surface, and he took a deep breath, exhaling slowly. "I had a bad encounter with my brother. Very bad. On the plus side, I had a great shag with a gorgeous woman afterwards—but that's between you and me." He winked.

Jet squeezed his hand. "Sorry. Sometimes families are shit. I'm very pleased about the shag, though."

"Me too!" He stood, pulling her to her feet at the same time. "Come into Arlo's office with me. You can get up to speed."

"Are you sure?"

"Absolutely."

Morgana didn't want the human heart in the house. She certainly didn't want it near Owen, but she didn't want it near the demon, either.

They had, after a long debate, decided to keep it in the glasshouse. It sat in the middle of an empty raised bed that she had prepared for planting herb cuttings that had rooted over winter. It was surrounded with yet more wards, sigils, and protection spells.

The heart was suffused as if with fresh blood, and still slowly beating. It had been hours since it had reanimated—*if that was even the right word*—and although they had monitored it closely, nothing else had happened. Maggie was frustrated that she couldn't take it to Layla for analysis, so in the end, Layla had visited Moonfell and taken a sample herself. Morgana hadn't wanted that to happen either, fearing that it might provoke some kind of supernatural response. Fortunately, it hadn't. However, knowing who it belonged to was important, and there was no other way to find out.

In the end, it was Odette and Birdie who went to Storm Moon to paint the shifters with protective sigils, while she prepared the circle for the banishing ritual they would cast that night, now that Maverick had returned.

"You should rest," Monroe said, entering the glasshouse so silently that she almost jumped.

"You're quiet for such a large unit."

"Wolf stealth. I mean it. We have a big night ahead. Or rather, you do."

She smiled. "Do I look frail?"

"No. But I know spells take it out of you, and that you've been working all afternoon on that new demon trap."

"And you've been watching Owen." She tapped the mug she was drinking from, reluctant to admit how tired she was. "Restorative tea always does the trick." She sat on the edge of the raised bed behind her, her shadow stretching over the heart in front of her. It was dark outside, and the glasshouse had subtle lighting. It suited her contemplative mood.

Monroe sat opposite her, arms folded across his chest. "I think strong coffee would be better."

"It would give me a headache, and I need a clear head for what lies ahead." *And nerves of steel.* "Are you okay?"

He shrugged. "The connection to Owen was brief, thanks to Birdie. Was it our power, mine and Tommy's, that made the heart beat again?"

"Perhaps. If I'm honest, I don't really understand any of it, and that's a nightmare considering what we're trying to do. I'm wondering if we should delay until we really know what we're dealing with."

"But if we delay and it breaks free..."

"I know. We still don't know what connection Owen has to it...not really. If we try to banish it, will it wake Owen up? Will it give him power so that he breaks his bonds? I mean, that sounds impossible considering what spells we've wrapped him up in, and everything that this house offers, but this is totally new to us. It seems that Owen, the heart, and the demon are all connected somehow, and the root of it appears to be shifter blood." She huffed, frustrated. The wolves seemed to think the tiny vials contained shifter blood, but again, Layla would confirm through the lab. "We don't deal with demons.

I understand the basics only. The fundamentals. Over the course of my many years of witchcraft I have of course studied demonology, but that was a long time ago, and I have never put it into practice. None of our family has. Theoretical knowledge is all well and good, but witchcraft is not exact. It's intention and power, trial and error, and well, magic. Unexpected things sometimes happen."

Monroe laughed. "All the best laid plans and all that."

"Exactly, just like last night. The demon appeared to be dormant, and then it just took off!"

"Hunter said it moved oddly. Seemed to jump through space."

"Apparently, although we saw less of it because we had to drive here. Odette nearly killed us, she drove so recklessly. But how do we know it's odd? That could just be how demons move! There are too many unknowns!"

"But it did look like a wolf last night...which, by the way, sounds terrifying! I'm not sure if I'm relieved or disappointed that I didn't see it."

"Be very pleased. As much as I've tried to shake it, the image of a wolf-demon is stuck right here." She tapped her head.

Monroe nodded. "Our shifter blood must have changed it, and that makes it very unpredictable."

"Exactly." The more Morgana thought about the coming ritual, the greater her feeling of foreboding. She had learned to trust her intuition, and everything about their next course of action screamed that it was wrong. "I need to look at Owen's grimoire again. Compare his rituals to ours."

"You're not going to use his, though?"

"No. He was altogether too willing for us to find his book, so we don't trust them."

"Or him, obviously. You won't let him help you?" Monroe asked.

"No! I wish we could trust him, but seeing as he keeps trying to cast spells on us, that's impossible. We have made one decision, though. We're going to destroy the heart. If it acts as a connection, then we must sever it." She stood, ready to head back to the kitchen where they had spread the books out on the table, preferring the informality of that space to the grandeur of the library.

"Good plan. And what about us?" Monroe asked, standing at the same time.

"You patrol close by, as agreed, with Hades. Maggie and Harlan will watch Owen."

Monroe threw his head back and laughed, white teeth gleaming in the low light. "I knew you wouldn't talk her out of it. She's as stubborn as a mule! Handy to have around, though. So is Harlan."

"Well, let's hope they don't regret their decision. They have no supernatural powers, so if anything goes wrong..."

"Have a little faith, Morgana."

She checked her watch. They would begin at midnight. *Three hours to go.*

Twenty-Two

Harlan was positioned at one of the tower windows in Owen's bedroom prison, trying to get a glimpse of the activity by the stables, but the angle was too acute.

He and Maggie had decided that they wanted to be close to Owen if anything went amiss, preferring to be in the room rather than out. They didn't have the shifters' speed if they needed to react quickly. *But nothing would go wrong*, he told himself for the hundredth time. *Everything would be fine. Just summoning a demon portal. A doorway into the unknown. Hell, perhaps. Eternal fires and damnation. A horde of demons awaiting it.*

No big deal.

He started pacing again, glancing every now and then at Owen's spell book, his compendium of demon-summoning rituals that the Moonfell witches had returned to the room.

"You're making me nervous. Stop it," Maggie demanded from her position next to Owen's bed.

The witch was still glowing in his giant egg o'sphere, looking like a weird, extra-terrestrial creature who had landed in his pod. Harlan had maintained a wary distance from it.

"I can't believe," he exclaimed, "that I let you talk me into this!"

"Oh, come on," Maggie scoffed. "Like I had to try hard. I mentioned it, and you couldn't wait to jump in."

"I said I would help if it made you feel happier. That's hardly me leaping into action." Harlan had been looking forward to a lazy evening at home after the late night spent drinking and dealing with demon shenanigans. But no. Maggie came around, positively seething with annoyance about hearts, and vials of blood, and posturing wankers—her words. There was something about the look in her eye that made him think Owen would be in more danger from Maggie than the other way around, so here he was.

"Well, now that I'm here, I'm having second thoughts." He looked out of the window again and glimpsed the flickering flames of torches and a pall of smoke. *Fuckity fuck. This was insane.*

Maggie tutted. "It could all be over within the next hour. Then we'll be kicking back and celebrating."

"And what about him? The demon-summoner and murderer."

"I'll get the witches to bind his power forever. I gather such things are possible. Then I can arrest him and charge him. We're building a case right now." She leaned in and yelled at Owen. "I hope you can hear me, you little fucker! You're going to prison!"

"Yeah, well, I'll believe that when I see it. And maybe we shouldn't be talking about these things in front of him. He's twitching." Harlan moved closer, squinting into the golden light. *Yes. Definitely twitching.* He checked his watch. *If all was going to plan, they would have started the ritual by now.*

Owen twitched again.

There was something primal, Arlo thought, *about being in Moonfell's garden at night.*

Everything seemed alert with innate knowledge, as if the garden was an interested onlooker, a participant even, in the ebb and flow of life here. Beneath the normal night sounds and the breath of wind moving through the shrubs, he detected a steady beat as if the garden was visceral muscle, organ, and bone. He felt it as a human, but it was even more apparent as a wolf.

Perhaps the preparations for the upcoming ritual had sharpened his senses, or more likely, caused his imagination to run wild. The large demon trap had been marked out on the smooth tarmac in front of the stable block, impressive in its details. Elaborate sigils and runes ran in a double circle, the centre of which contained a pentagram. Tall pillar candles blazed at its five points and around the outer circle, and strong incense mixed with the smoke from the blazing torches that were thrust in the earth on the edge of the drive.

Outside the circle was a raised altar on a block of stone, where the witches had laid out their tools—a chalice of water, athame, salt, incense, a flaming candle, a small metal bowl, and the grimoire containing the ritual. And of course, the heart in the jar, and a piece of bloodied cloth that Maverick had brought back with him.

Maverick was there too, along with Domino, Vlad, Hunter, Cecile, Tommy, and Monroe. They ringed the area, ready to chase the demon should the worst thing happen, and it escaped. Surely that was unlikely, though. They had moved it earlier from the cruder trap in the stable, still wrapped in its golden bonds. The fact that the witches had been able to bind it was a miracle to Arlo; it had seemed so powerful, so brutal. It was testament to the witches' power.

Now, though, was the real test. The raising of a portal through which to banish it.

Arlo lowered himself to the ground, the scent of damp earth mixing with the acrid bite of smoke and stench of sulphur. He faced the circle. Odette, his ex-girlfriend and friend now, after all this time, was positioned at the altar to lead the ceremony. The witches had argued briefly as to who should have that responsibility, but Odette won the argument, stressing that she was closest to an elemental Spirit Witch who would traditionally lead such a rite. Morgana and Birdie flanked her

.

Odette began the spell that released the demon's bindings, and as each golden rope disappeared, the demon was revealed—a heaving, churning mass of shadow and flames. It swelled, straining against its remaining binding, and as the last one vanished, it multiplied in size so that it was twice the height of a man, the faint image of limbs visible within the darkness. It charged at Odette, two strides taking it to the edge of the inner circle. Immediately, the double layers of the trap ignited into a cold, blue flame, and the demon shrieked and retreated.

The sound was so unearthly, so shatteringly Otherworldly, that Arlo buried his head beneath his paws. However, the longer the enraged bellow continued, the more it pulled at Arlo. Suddenly, he couldn't control himself, and he bounded to all four paws, lifted his head, and howled into the starry void.

He struggled to regain control, fighting against every urge he had to keep howling. He wanted to hunt.

Needed to hunt.

He was drawn to the creature in the middle of the circle, and he lowered his head to look at it and crept slowly forward. The rest of the wolves were doing the same, edging forward as if summoned by the demon. Arlo fought against it, trying to see what Maverick was doing. He needed his alpha to draw them all into line. He felt as if he was being torn apart.

The demon paced within its trap. Where there had been only shadow and flames, a shape emerged. Eyes first. Burning balls of fire. An elongated head. Four long limbs beneath a bulky body. *Bollocks.* It was a wolf again, and as it released its unearthly, ear-splitting, brain-numbing howl, Arlo lost all reason.

The pack had been called, and its alpha was the demon.

The wolves had lost all control.

Morgana knew it in seconds.

She struck her staff hard into the ground and uttered the word that would activate the second circle of protection around themselves. The golden light sprang up around them just as Vlad, the closest wolf, leapt at her throat. He struck the wall and bounced away, but in a split second he was back on all four paws, teeth bared, eyes filled with molten gold.

"Stop the ritual!" Morgana yelled at Odette.

"I haven't even begun it! I've just released its bonds."

"Well, something is very wrong!"

"No shit!"

From Odette's other side, Birdie shouted, "Well, start the ritual then, and send it back."

"It will take too long!"

"It doesn't matter how long it takes. All that matters is that we banish it, and that we are protected."

Morgana didn't join the argument, instead watching the giant demon prowl the trap. It had fully taken on the form of a huge wolf again, like some kind of hellhound. It was enormous, twice the size of the tallest shifter, its bulk the size of a car. It filled the centre of the circle, its tail catching the inner circle and causing it to flare up time and time again. They had debated that this might happen. They had not considered it would command the pack.

And it kept on howling; a gut-wrenching, guttural sound that felt like it was trying to pull her inside out, and that made her feel sick and dizzy. A quick glance at Birdie and Odette told her that they looked as sick as she felt.

Even worse, the wolves had surrounded them, as if commanded by the demon to rip them apart. They were utterly feral and without reason.

Morgana shouted to be heard above the snarl of wolves and the demon. "Odette, I can barely think straight! We can't complete the ritual like this."

Odette threw her shoulders back. "Yes, we will!" She turned her attention to her other spell book. "I'm starting the spell to open the portal now!"

"At least destroy the heart!"

Maverick, easily recognisable because of his size, leapt at their protection circle, clashing with such ferocity that he bounced off it and landed in the midst of his pack in a tangle of limbs. He shook himself off and launched again. His jaws dripped saliva, and his eyes were fiery pools, brimming with the urge to destroy. The other wolves followed suit, until they were all throwing themselves at the witches' circle of protection, which suddenly felt all too fragile under their combined assault.

Morgana had the barest seconds to wonder how the demon was commanding the wolves and what Owen was doing, when the wolves suddenly changed tack and attacked each other. Blood and fur went flying.

If they didn't act soon, the shifters would kill each other.

"What the hell is he doing?" Harlan yelled, as Owen levitated off the bed, his golden protection spell fading to a dull grey.

Maggie leaped backwards. "Fuck! I don't know. The spell is failing. It must be!"

The sound of howling filled Moonfell, seeming to pierce the walls until it was like thousands of needles in Harlan's brain. He struggled to see, his vision blacking in and out, and he clamped his hands over his ears. The brief reprieve of dulled noise gave him well-needed thinking time. He struggled back to his feet, not even realising that he'd fallen over. Maggie was doing the same, hands clamped to her head, face contorted with annoyance.

The protection spell that had wrapped around Owen suddenly vanished completely, and in seconds he was conscious and on his feet, a malevolent grin etched on his face. He seemed impervious to the noise, and he ran across the room to his spell book. Harlan ran after him and tackled him to the ground, flailing wildly and trying to land punches while he sought to focus and keep the contents of his stomach down.

Owen, however, either had superhuman strength, or Harlan was weakened by the noise. The seemingly scrawny, weak man struck Harlan hard and wrestled him away. Harlan scrambled after him, wrapping his body around Owen's legs, and bringing him down again. They rolled across the floor in a tangle of limbs.

Harlan hated to be defeated, especially by a demon-conjuring madman, but Owen once again struggled free and kicked Harlan in the stomach as he regained his feet. He reached the table, flipped his spell book open, and began an incantation.

Morgana smashed the jar on the altar, grabbed the ritual knife they'd prepared, and plunged it into the heart as Birdie and Odette recited the spell to open the portal. She then placed the heart into the silver bowl where charcoal smouldered, ready to consume it.

She spelled it into flames, and the stench of burning flesh cleared her mind. The demon howled with renewed ferocity, and then seemed to falter for the briefest moment. Something was working. She focussed on putting all doubt out of her mind and joined the incantation with her coven. Once the portal was open, they could send it back, and it would be over. The wolves would calm down, and the whole nightmarish event would be behind them.

But it was hard to concentrate with the wolves tearing each other apart. They were her friends. They were each other's friends. They would hate themselves for this. Looking at her bloodied hands, she hated herself for this, too.

But although they were following the ritual, the portal was slow to open. *Everything was taking too long.* She broke off the spell, and the other two faltered. Breaking an incantation once begun was not advised. The build-up of power and intent would fracture, but she had to help their friends.

"You two carry on. I'll stop the wolves."

The demon-wolf charged the boundaries of the trap with renewed energy again and again, and with every *thud*, the trap visibly weakened.

"It's going to get out!" Birdie yelled, exasperated. "Why aren't the spells on the house helping?"

"Because it's in a circle of our making!" Morgana tried to reason through what was happening. They needed a solution, quickly. "The garden recognises our magic, and the demon is within its influence."

"And the protective circle around us is dampening our spell's effectiveness," Birdie reasoned.

Odette finally stopped her spell. Her face was pale, her expression anguished. "The trap won't hold for much longer, not with the way things are going, and clearly destroying the heart has not worked."

"I think we need to drop our protective circle if we're to have an effect on *that*," Birdie added, nodding at the demon. "And we *must* raise the portal."

"You two start the portal spell again. I'll join you when I've stopped the wolves," Morgana said, her brain finally clicking into gear. She needed to be outside their protective circle to use her magic on them, but she could leave the other two protected.

She grabbed the athame and cut a doorway into the circle, stepped through it, and closed it again. Immediately the roaring of the demon and the howling of the wolves intensified, hitting her like fists. The wolves' heads snapped up, blood dripping from their teeth, eyes molten as their attention switched to her. She thrust her hands out and cast the spell for sleep. It was potent, enough to fell a herd of elephants, but it had no effect.

Every single wolf dropped to their belly, slinking towards her. If one leapt at her now, they all would. They would tear her to shreds in seconds. Morgana had to focus and block out the horrific, guttural roar of the demon.

And then another strange feeling passed over her, and the sound of something slithering joined in the general cacophony. She risked a glance over her shoulder, and saw a dark void opening within the trap. Despite everything, Odette and Birdie were managing to open a portal.

Time to complete her part of the deal. Morgana focussed on the advancing wolves again. She must have missed a word or a phrase the first time. Mastering her fear, she repeated the spell with confidence, the middle-English words dripping off her tongue with honeyed ease. As Maverick leapt at her, she thrust her hand forward, summoning elemental air. He flew backwards, crashing into his pack. The force of the wind pushed the others back too, and as she finished the words of the spell, it finally had an effect. They collapsed in a heap.

With a word of command, Morgana dissolved the protective circle around Birdie and Odette, and then Morgana spun towards the demon trap. Her coven continued the spell, but the demon still prowled and fixed its eyes on her. For one heart stopping moment, it felt as if time was suspended. Then the demon-wolf charged. It hit the edge of the trap, and the blue protective shield flared and splintered. It charged again.

Subduing her rising panic, Morgana joined her coven, standing shoulder to shoulder, and repeated the words to open the portal. They had familiarised themselves with it earlier, but saying it now, and feeling the shape of the words and their power on her tongue, was odd. She had never thought she would be using her magic—magic that created and supported new life—to do *this*.

The void grew in size, releasing the feeling of endless time. Eons seemed to stretch before her. Flashes of fire and shadow swirled, and it seemed that shapes moved within. Her terror rose in her throat, threatening to overwhelm her. She grasped Odette's hand and felt her terror, too. But also her determination.

However, despite the vastness of the portal that swirled before them, the demon-wolf was refusing to budge. It charged the trap again. Worse, within the void behind it, something else was taking shape. Something large, with a glint of fiery eyes and heavy limbs that moved with slow but sure intent as it crossed time and space to reach them.

Something was coming out of the trap.

Every cell in Morgana's body screamed to shut it down, and fortunately, Odette agreed.

She broke off the spell. "Enough! We have to close it! *Now*!"

With hurried words, she began the incantation to close it instead. It shrank, but far too slowly for Morgana's liking. Just as something large came into view, something with horns and a snout and cloven hooves, the portal snapped closed, and they were left with a raging demon-wolf to deal with.

"We bind it again," Odette said, once again taking charge, and with relief Morgana joined her in something she was far happier to do.

Maggie saw Harlan lying winded on the ground, clutching his stomach, and struggled to her feet.

Owen, through either arrogance or stupidity, had his back to her, and was intently focussed on his spell book. He raised his hands and started to chant, and power swelled within the room.

Do something, she willed the house. But nothing happened.

She cast about for a weapon and seized the closest object at hand—the chair she'd been sitting on. She picked it up and charged at Owen, then swung it with all her strength. She smashed Owen across the back of his head, sending him sprawling. He fell against the wall, trying to right himself, but she charged again, full of fury and vengeance. She struck him again and again, hitting his head, his body, and his arms as he struggled to block her and defend himself.

She didn't stop. She couldn't. Their lives depended on it.

Owen fell to his knees, the power he had manifested only moments before vanishing. Maggie kept striking him, even as blood pooled from his head. She raised the chair, ready to bring it down on the crumpled man at her feet, only to have it wrested from her.

Harlan's calm voice was in her ear, "Maggie! It's done! Slow down, girl."

She rounded on him, heart pounding, blood beating in her ears like a marching band.

He grabbed her wrists in his strong hands, stopping her from punching him. "It's just me, Maggie. You're okay. *We're okay.*"

"But the noise! The demon! Owen was doing something..." But even as she was saying it, the horrific roaring noise diminished.

"See? It's going to be okay."

She fixed her gaze on Harlan's brown eyes that refused to look away, and she took a deep breath as sanity returned. "We're okay," she repeated. "Did I hurt you?"

"No, I'm fine. You've kind of beaten Owen to a pulp, though." He released her and crouched to look at Owen, and then reached forward to feel for the pulse at his neck. "He's alive, but out cold."

"Good! Bastard. Now what do we do with him?"

Harlan's hair was mussed, his face scratched and bruised, but he still had a twinkle in his eye. "We do things the old-fashioned way. Tie him up and gag him."

Twenty-Three

Domino winced as Morgana cleaned the bite on the back of her shoulder. "Ow! That stings."

"It's neat alcohol, so I'm not surprised. You wolves have almost ripped each other apart."

Domino didn't answer, studying her team instead. They were spread around the kitchen, most of them half naked as they tended each other's wounds. The only one not there was Hunter, and he was watching Owen. All were subdued, and all were a bloodied mess after they had inflicted deep, ragged wounds on each other. It was a miracle none of them had died. Deep down, Domino was sure some element of reason had remained, but it had been buried very thoroughly. Her memories of the fight were vague after the demon had become a giant wolf. She had never lost control like that before. Ever. It terrified her.

Arlo grimaced, then yelled, "Tommy!"

"Stop being a girl," Tommy remonstrated. "You've got a huge tear on the back of your bicep that I'm trying to stick back together."

"I know. It stings like a bitch!"

"Enough with the female insults, please," Birdie said, smacking Tommy across the back of the head. "Four women just saved your furry arses."

Tommy winced. "Birdie!"

She glared at him. "Do I have to hit you again?"

"No!"

Harlan held his hand up from where he sat on the chair next to an uncharacteristically silent Maggie. "I helped, too!"

"No insult intended to men in the room," Birdie said airily. "Thank you, Harlan. Maverick! Your turn."

Maverick was standing with his back to everyone, staring into the fire. His back was a mess of ragged bites and claw marks, and he held himself stiffly. Every muscle in his back was defined, his sculpted shoulders tense from anger. Domino knew he would be blaming himself. His injuries were bad, but he had inflicted a lot worse on others.

When he didn't respond, Birdie spoke again, more softly this time, as the wolves turned to their alpha. "Maverick, your turn."

He turned around, revealing the raking claw marks down his chest and his blood-spattered face. He addressed the room. "I failed you all. We could have died."

"You didn't fail anyone," Arlo said. "We underestimated the demon."

Monroe grunted in agreement. "We underestimated *Owen*."

"And I almost bludgeoned him to death," Maggie said, voice hollow. "So now we can't even question him at the moment to work out what to do next."

"Maggie," Maverick said, wearily, "he won't tell us a thing, anyway. I think he's been playing us all along, and I've been so caught up in my parents' death and my brother's involvement that I failed to see the bigger picture. I think he must have targeted me because I'm the alpha of a big pack. He needed shifter energy, and we delivered it." Maverick had dispensed with his secrets, and now everyone knew about his family.

"You don't know that," Odette said. She was cleaning up Cecile's injuries by the kitchen sink. "We could have screwed up the spell and made it worse. I should never have released the demon from the binding spell, but I thought it would stop us from being able to banish it. What a stupid idea that was."

"But I'm the alpha. I should have been able to resist a demon."

"You resisted killing me," Vlad said calmly, lifting his chin to reveal the extent of the deep teeth marks there. Domino recoiled at the sight. "Your jaws were around my throat at one point. They did this. One strong bite and you would have ripped my throat out. You didn't. You stopped yourself just in time. Like Domino said, deep down, we hung on to some kind of sanity."

Domino willed Maverick to see sense. He was on the verge of saying he wasn't fit to lead them, and that would be a disaster. She leapt in. "We need to stop this, right now! Yes, we fucked up, but we're okay. No one is dead! Even that arsehole, Owen, is still breathing, although right now I'd happily rip *his* throat out. The demon is contained again, and Maggie and Harlan stopped Owen from performing another spell, by the sound of it. He must have been trying to release the demon somehow. Or use it for another purpose. What spell was he reciting?" Harlan had brought Owen's grimoire downstairs with him, and it lay open on the coffee table. "Did you save the page, Harlan?"

"Sure, I'm not a complete dumbass. I've tried to make sense of it. It's in Latin, and I know some, but I'm a bit rusty."

"We'll look at it later," Birdie said, summoning Maverick again with a hooked finger and pointing at a chair. "Sit. We'll clean you up, then you can all go sleep it off in your wolf."

Domino cast about for anything that might help them as Morgana applied a cool paste to her wound, and then suddenly remembered Hades. She hadn't seen him since the fight. "Birdie, does your familiar know anything?"

"Nothing that will illuminate where we go from here, but he did confirm that the demon is enhanced with shifter blood. He doesn't know how it happened other than through the use of dark, ritual magic. Whatever Owen started years ago, he's perfected his process now. The presence of all of you tonight was enough to strengthen the demon even more, and that means that you will be nowhere near us when we try to banish it again. Disappointingly, destroying the heart wasn't as effective as we'd hoped."

"And my brother's blood?" Maverick asked.

"As yet," Odette said, "I am undecided as to whether that helped or hindered. Hindered, I think."

"So, me visiting my brother was a complete waste of time?"

"I wouldn't be so sure about that." Odette offered him a fleeting smile. "There are many layers to this, and we need to keep peeling them away. Potentially, I was using his blood in the wrong way."

Morgana finished treating Domino and moved to the sink to wash her hands. "I agree. Maybe we need to neutralise your brother's blood, or weaken it."

"Or use it as a weapon," Harlan suggested.

Morgana shrugged, thoughtful. "I think Owen was right in that Canagan's blood was the foundation of everything that came afterwards."

"A counter-spell," Odette said immediately. "We use Canagan's blood again, but this time it will weaken the demon. When we open the portal again, it won't be able to resist."

"But the demon trap was a good one, right?" Maggie asked. "You contained it, despite its efforts to escape."

"Yes, and it tried *really* hard."

Domino shuddered at her brief memory of the portal opening, and the vast, timeless pit that had opened beyond it. The memories of what lay beyond slipped over her mind like black ink. She was glad that Morgana had knocked them unconscious with a spell before she'd seen any more. "Shouldn't the portal have pulled it in?" she asked the witches.

"Not necessarily. You still have to banish it. It's a way out as much as in," Birdie said. She hesitated, lips tight, her gaze distant. "But we couldn't complete that part."

"You started the banishing ritual?" Maggie asked, surprised. "I thought you didn't get that far."

It wasn't surprising that she was confused. The witches weren't talking about it, and the shifters had seen very little. From what Domino could tell of the witches' behaviour, they were shocked by the events. They didn't have their usual confidence. Everyone was suffering that night.

Birdie nodded as she treated Maverick's wounds. "Oh, we opened the portal all right, and began the banishing spell, but the demon resisted, and the longer the portal remained open, the greater the chance that something would exit. In fact, something was trying to exit. We shut it down. We couldn't risk it."

Arlo's head jerked up in shock. "I don't remember that."

"No," Odette said, giving an involuntary shiver, "you were out cold by then. You were all lucky. The memories of that thing will haunt me for the rest of my life." She flashed her coven a brief look of relief. "I wouldn't wish what we saw on anyone."

Neither of them answered; their grim expressions said everything.

"Okay, now we're getting somewhere," Harlan said, starting to pace. "The trap is good, but the demon is strong. You opened a portal—another success—but it wouldn't go through. We're missing a final piece of the puzzle... I'm wondering if there's something in his house—some ritual object that he would have used that will work for us ?"

"Like what?" Morgana asked as she sat down next to Domino and poured herself another glass of brandy. The restorative tea from earlier had been abandoned. Cecile and Odette joined them, Cecile's wounds now also treated with salve. Morgana pushed two glasses and the bottle towards them. "We destroyed the heart, and the demon seemed to falter for a moment, but then its power returned."

"Maybe there's something else. Say it was Ivy's heart, and he preserved it for years. How?"

Maggie snorted. "Ivy, who died ten years ago in a house fire? Yeah, right!"

"Why not? He could have preserved it with magic. It was a dried husk when it was found. Maybe he kept a tiny portion of it separately, and it's still in his house!"

"To be honest," Domino mused, "that is a good idea."

Harlan was a handsome man, Domino noted, as he commanded the room. Tall, good looking in a mature, grey at the temples way. He looked after himself, too. She could see his muscles move beneath his t-shirt. If she wasn't so attracted to Hunter, she might be interested. *Or was she just tired?* She eyed her drink, realising she was already onto her third brandy. *Probably just tipsy.* Or perhaps it was her heightened feelings after fighting. Being in her wolf always gave her hormones a surge. She focussed on what he was saying.

Harlan was excited, his earlier fight forgotten. "Okay, I have a working theory, so just hear me out! Ivy really did get sacrificed to the demon, voluntarily or courtesy of her brother. The house fire was a cover. The demon and Ivy bonded somehow. But the demon also had shifter blood. Maybe it absorbed human characteristics too in some whacky ritual. Owen needed to retain control of the demon, so he took his sister's heart and preserved it, but when the witches destroyed it, he was alerted somehow, enabling him to throw off the witches' spells."

"Wow!" Tommy said, rubbing his beard. "You, my American friend, are nuts!"

He didn't seem the slightest bit offended. "Demons like blood, flesh, mayhem, and destruction, but are controlled by rituals and incantations that bind them to whoever summons them. The connection to Owen could totally be strengthened by a heart, especially one that has a blood connection to Owen."

"As working theories go, I think it's a good one," Maverick said, eyes narrowing at Birdie as she cleaned his biggest wounds. "I thought you'd lost the plot over the Wolf King, but you totally called that one."

"See? I have my uses. Hunting occult relics and figuring out what they do makes my brain work in different ways."

"And then there's the box, of course," Arlo said. "The one that contained the vials of blood and the heart. The runes must have preserved it, too. And the jar, as well. That had runes on it."

"Perhaps," Birdie said softly. "Let's not presume too much. Maggie's friend, Layla, will have more answers tomorrow."

"And destroying the heart," Domino reminded them, "did not stop the demon."

"But it might finally have broken Owen's connection to it. That means the demon isn't controlled by anyone. I'm totally happy to go to Owen's house tomorrow," Harlan said. "I might see something that's useful."

Maverick held his hand up. "Not so fast. Let's go through his book again and see what strikes us as unusual and get a better understanding of that box. We need to unpick this, rather than racing ahead."

Odette nodded in agreement. "I agree. I really want to make sure that if we open that portal again, it's the last time."

"And Owen?" Monroe asked. "What about him?"

"And Xavier?" Cecile added. She'd been very quiet throughout the discussion, and as strong as she was, it looked like she'd had enough. Domino decided that Cecile would not be involved in whatever happened next. The demon injury had taken enough out of her, and now the fight with her own pack and worry over Xavier... It was too much.

"He's getting better," Morgana told her. "He will pull through this, but he'll have some nasty scars. Fortunately, he was heavily sedated with my potion tonight, so he wasn't affected by the demon-wolf. Thank the Goddess."

Cecile nodded. "I'll head up there now to keep an eye on him." She took her drink and slipped out of the room.

"And get some sleep!" Morgana shouted after her.

Maverick stared at Morgana. "You're not lying about Xavier, I hope?"

"No. I would never do that. He is much better, and the scars will fade a little with time. His fever has passed, so that's something. As for Owen," she turned to Monroe, "we'll keep him tied up and play it by ear."

"I have another question," Maverick said. "Why didn't those sigils you painted on us work tonight? We all fell totally under that demon's influence."

"The sigils were to stop it being able to get close to you. A deterrent. They had no protective ability on your mind." Morgana shrugged. "Sorry. I didn't anticipate that." She drained her drink and stood up. "I am beyond tired, and I can't think straight, so I'm going to bed. We all should. That spell has taken it out of me."

The other two witches nodded in agreement, and Odette said, "I'm planning on an early morning to study those runes again, so I'm off to bed, too."

Birdie finished cleaning Maverick's wounds, and scanned the room, taking them all in. "Don't stay up long. You need to sleep and heal. Sleep in your wolf. But no hunts or fighting for the next few days. You've all got beds here, and you know where they are. Get some rest."

"I'm coming, too," Maggie said, and within minutes, they left the shifters alone with Harlan.

They rearranged themselves on the sofa in front of the fire or stretched out on the rug. Domino curled up in the corner of the sofa and pulled a blanket over her legs. The room wasn't cold, and the fire burned brightly in the hearth, but it comforted her more than anything. Sleep pulled at her, but she forced herself to stay awake.

"I meant it," Harlan said, kneeling next to the coffee table and paging through Owen's grimoire. "Owen has secrets. There'll be more in his house. I'll find them."

"You might be wrong," Maverick said.

"But I don't think I am. Neither do you."

Maverick huffed and leaned back in the armchair, head resting on the back of it. "He came for me."

"He came for your blood. Family ties are strong."

Vlad stretched his long legs out and rested them on the edge of the coffee table. "I think he must have connected himself to the demon. It's like a two-way thing. He doesn't just control the demon. He draws power from it, too."

"Agreed!" Harlan nodded. "He broke out of the witches' spell! The house didn't respond. Why? How? He's not a big man, but he had a lot of strength tonight."

"Say you do go tomorrow, Harlan," Maverick said thoughtfully. "You can't go alone. Wait for the test results first, so we really know what we're dealing with, and then take a few of the team with you. Not us!" he said before anyone could raise an argument. "We're a mess, and I'm going to contact the pack tomorrow and be very present. I also want to see Owen again. I think Jax, Mads, and Fran all need a job. Any objections?" He particularly looked at Vlad.

"None from me. It's a good idea. Although, do we really want to risk any more of us?"

"Can we afford not to?" Maverick said softly.

Twenty-Four

Maverick sat next to Maggie, Odette seated on her other side, while Owen sat opposite them.

They were gathered in the tower room that served as a prison cell. It was late morning, as most of them had slept in after an exhausting night. All of them were battered and bruised. Maverick's own wounds ached, despite his long sleep in his wolf, but he was pleased to see that Owen looked worse. Maverick's urge to seek retribution was high. His primal instinct to hunt and defend his pack was screaming at him to kill Owen right now. It would be so easy. He could pounce across the table and break his neck. His potent alpha power swelled outwards, and he knew Owen would feel it. He let it linger, seeing a sudden stiffness in Owen's posture before he quelled it again. *Not now.*

Owen eyed them all warily, paper stitches over the cuts on his face that had been inflicted by Maggie and Harlan. "I could press charges for assault," he said belligerently.

"Don't be fucking absurd!" Maggie shot forward on her chair, looking as if she'd like to strangle him. "You attacked *us*!"

"I was trying to help."

"Bullshit!"

Owen looked smug at Maggie's response. "Did something happen I'm unaware of?"

They had all agreed not to reveal what had happened the night before. They wanted to see if he knew about it already somehow. Perhaps through his connection to the demon.

Maggie took a deep breath, wrestling her emotions under control. "Well, obviously, you broke free of the binding spell, and Harlan and I dealt with you in another way, but other than that, not much happened."

"Really? I heard howling."

"Wolves howl," Maverick said with a shrug.

Odette didn't speak. She just watched Owen intently.

"The good thing is that I have news!" Maggie said brightly as she consulted her notebook. Maverick suspected it was more of an affectation. She knew everything that she wanted to say. "The heart that you kept in your little rune box was examined yesterday by the doctor I work with. She ran all sorts of tests on it, and guess what? The DNA shows a family match to you. It's your sister's heart, Owen! How very interesting, don't you think?"

His eyes narrowed. "She's made a mistake!"

"No. We don't make mistakes like that. She compared it to blood that we took from you. There's no doubt about that. We," she gestured to her companions, "thought about how that heart was a shrivelled little lump when we found it on Saturday, and then how it looked as if it had just been ripped from someone's chest it was so plump and full of blood. What grubby little ritual did you do to achieve that?"

"I've been locked in here. I have performed no '*grubby little rituals*.'"

"But before this weekend? Something you probably did years ago."

"You have a very active imagination, DI Milne. I came here for help, remember?"

"And yet you attacked Harlan and I, and then ran to your book and started a spell. That's not how I expect people who want help to behave!"

"I heard the demon and the wolves and knew I had to help. If I had stopped to explain, it would have been too late. I was trying to cast a spell to help you banish the demon." His eyes travelled from Maggie, to Maverick, and then Odette. "You didn't let me help, and you couldn't banish the demon. Correct?"

So he knew. How?

"However," he continued, "you managed to contain it, after all. I admit that I'm impressed." *And very disappointed.* Maverick could see it in his expression, even though he was desperately trying to hide it. He thought the demon would escape, the wolves would kill themselves, and that the witches would die, too. "I strongly suggest that you let me help next time. Tonight."

Odette regarded him silently for a moment, and then said, "You're connected to it. You feel what it's doing. It's symbiotic, actually. You nurture each other, yet act independently. But when the demon acts, you feel it. I dare say it works the other way around, too. It's clever magic, I'll give you that."

He didn't deny it, instead saying, "You still don't trust me."

"You hunted witches. So no."

Owen banged his tied hands on to the table. "You're wrong!"

"I know what I saw."

"And I know what my sergeants found," Maggie added, drawing his attention back. "A string of deaths after Maverick's parents were killed. We're still digging. But," she wagged a finger, "in quiet, sleepy Kent villages, I know that was you. I'll find out more."

"Like I said, you have an overactive imagination."

"Rune boxes, hearts, demons, and... Oh, yes." Maggie smiled. "The vials were confirmed as containing shifter blood. But interestingly, the blood was degraded. I think you were in desperate need of more, and that's why you came to Maverick. Perhaps time is running out, and the connection to your pet demon is weakening."

Owen glared at her. "Does it look like it is? I know everything that happened last night."

Another confirmation, and he didn't care that they knew.

"And yet, you're here. Why else come to the man whose parents you killed?"

"Their deaths were an accident! How many times do I have to repeat myself? I came to Maverick for help. I needed his brother's blood to banish the demon. You tried to do it without me and failed." He turned to Maverick. "You found him, obviously. I knew I was right to come to you." Owen looked smug once more.

Maverick smiled. "Who said I found him?"

Owen tutted. "Well, you left, and now you're back, and they performed the ritual last night. The demon became your alpha, didn't h e?"

Maverick's anger spiked at Owen's cocky amusement, but he reined it in. "You knew that would happen, and yet you didn't warn us."

"I would have if you had given me half a chance. But no, you wrapped me up in spells. Witches." He shot a malevolent look at Odette. "You're all the same."

"You're a witch," Maverick said.

"Not like them. There is a way to perform the ritual that wouldn't do that."

"Liar!" Odette said immediately. "You wanted it to happen. You wanted the demon to have control, and through it, you would control the Storm Moon Pack."

"You only see shades of truth, Odette," he said smoothly before addressing Maverick again. "Trust not the witch. Let *me* help you next time!"

"Not a fucking chance in Hell," Maggie said. "I'll see you swallowed in that portal before I let you do anything!"

Maverick leaned forward. "You're playing us, Owen. You say you want the demon banished, but that would take away all your power. No, you came here for one reason only. Shifter blood. Specifically, my brother's blood. It's at the root of your connection to the demon. Well, that and your sister's heart. It stops now." He didn't mention the fact they had destroyed the heart and Owen didn't either. He certainly wasn't going to enlighten him if he didn't know. He stood up, scraping his chair back. "I have things to organise. I'll leave you to Maggie and Odette."

"You think that's what you're looking for?" Hunter studied the image in the book of demon rituals. "It's a jar. Why is that exciting? We destroyed one last night."

"Because it's linked to this, here." Harlan turned a few pages and tapped a ritual. "It's towards the end of the book, after the rituals, and it references a heart."

"Several rituals do," Morgana pointed out.

Birdie scowled. "And they're all gruesome. This book is an abomination."

All four were gathered in the library, a sea of books around them, all referencing demonology. The witches had been busy for the first few hours that morning, and had pulled all of the most helpful looking reference books from their shelves.

"Why that ritual?" Hunter asked.

"Because it's the one that's cleanest."

"Wouldn't it be the one most annotated?"

"It's a rewrite of this one." Harlan skimmed back to a very grubby page. "I didn't notice at first, but I kept going over everything this morning, and I realised that he has incorporated the notes *here* into the new page. He experimented. Tested it, and then decided he liked this."

"Logical," Birdie admitted. "I've done much the same myself."

Harlan continued. "And look. It mentions a specific jar to contain the organ. There's even a little illustration of it. It looks like a canopic jar—just like the one on the other page."

"A what?" Hunter asked, confused.

"Canopic jars were what the Egyptians used to store the organs removed from a body prior to mummification. If I remember correctly, they kept the lungs, liver, stomach, and intestines in them. They were interred with the sarcophagus in the tombs."

"But not the heart?"

"No, it was considered the seat of the soul and remained in the body." Harlan tapped the pages again. "There are a few illustrations here of different jars. Traditionally, canopic jars were not illustrated in Egypt, but Owen seems to have evolved his own rituals. There are lots of other illustrations, too. Different runes on different circles, with different alignments. Ways to store blood and body fluids. This man is revolting. I think he's a serial killer, actually."

Birdie, Morgana, and Hunter looked at him, shocked. "Really?" Hunter asked, thinking Harlan had gone mad.

"He murders people and likes it, Hunter. He might use a demon to do his bidding, but it's the same thing."

"Bloody hell! I never thought of it like that." He ran through what they knew of Owen's past. It was sketchy, and yet death followed him.

Harlan continued, "We didn't think that way before because of the paranormal angle, but he killed shifters—perhaps other types of shifters, not just wolves, and maybe hunted down Canagan's mates. Canagan told Maverick they were dead because of the dark path they had chosen in helping Owen. Stupid teenage rebellion and curiosity. What if Owen actually killed them? Maybe he hoped Maverick would lead him to his brother. And, of course, he's killed others. Witches. Odette saw that. Maggie's team has found suspicious deaths in the area, and are looking for evidence to support that theory."

No one spoke as Harlan's words seemed to thicken in the air around them. It would be easy to accuse Harlan of having an overactive imagination, but he had seen many strange, occult occurrences. While they were in the thick of things, confused over Owen's connection to Maverick's parents, Harlan had come on to the scene later. He was disconnected from their emotional involvement, and perhaps seeing things more clearly and logically than any of them.

Morgana finally broke the silence. "By the Goddess, Harlan, I think you're right. We've invited a demon-conjuring serial killer into the house." She slumped back in her chair. "He could wield immense power, and we in our arrogance, knowing he has no elemental magic—knowing he is not a true witch—have presumed we are stronger than him."

"And our spells," Birdie added, a hand pressing against her heart, "failed to contain him last night. What have we done?"

Morgana and Birdie stared at each other, jaws tight, seeking reassurance in the other.

Morgana shook her head. "The demon gave him strength. It was a flaw. He's safe enough now. He's still tied up, and the demon is bound."

"Hold on," Hunter said, dread welling up. "He came to Maverick. We assumed for his brother's blood. It was the tale he sold the whole thing on. What if he actually wants *you*? Or even this place?" He gestured around him. "Moonfell. Full of ancient and powerful magic. We know he's greedy for power, money, status... All of it!"

"He cannot steal Moonfell's magic, or ours! It's impossible," Birdie said.

"But he could destroy the house, or damage it. You've invited him in. He's upstairs right now. Like Harlan said, your magic didn't kick in last night like it did the first time he tried to exert his power. They had to knock him out. Tie him up. What if he's biding his time again?"

All eyes drifted upwards. Morgana darted to her feet. "We should check what's going on."

Birdie grabbed her arm. "Wait. Think!" She ran her hand across her forehead. "I'm the High Priestess of our coven and I've let a monster in our house. The Goddess should strike me down! I'm a fool!"

"Woah!" Harlan remonstrated. "Slow down, all of you. He's playing the long game. He always has. Let's think this through a minute. He turns up to Maverick and lays his cards on the table. He knows where Maverick lives, that he's the alpha. He knows of the connection to you three witches. *Maybe*. But he can't have predicted everything! He might not have expected to be taken prisoner. Being here could be an unforeseen piece of luck. Perhaps he's added you three and this place to his goals. But, he needs certain things to happen first. Plus, there are downsides to his plan. You went to his hotel room, found his book, but also found the box hidden in his wardrobe. I bet he did not want you to find that. He certainly didn't tell you about it, right?"

Birdie nodded. "Right. He was actually really annoyed about it."

"Which means it's important to him, and now he's scrambling. Pivoting. Trying to make this work for him. He's not going to do anything right now. He's biding his time again...probably until you have your second shot at opening the portal."

Hunter thought they were missing something very important. "How did he escape your binding spell, and why didn't the house trigger to stop him? We have to know that and deal with it before anything else!"

"Damn it!" Morgana slammed the table with her fist. "It's the same reason that our general house protection spells didn't deal with the demon in the garden when he raged within the trap and dominated the wolves. Because it's surrounded by our magic, and our magic is part of the house. We brought the demon in. Same with Owen. The connection with the demon last night meant he passed under the radar—so to speak."

"And now?" Hunter asked.

"The same could still apply."

"So you've inadvertently protected him."

Morgana floundered, looking to Birdie for guidance. "I guess so. What do you think?"

She nodded wearily. "It's possible. Which means we need to adapt, too. Think of new ways to contain him and restrict his connection to his demon until we can sever the link for good."

"And that," Harlan said, paging through the grimoire, "is where I've had my next stroke of genius. Maybe there's more than just a heart in a jar. Maybe there are other organs in other jars—just like the Egyptians. This ritual references other organs, too. They will all need to be destroyed, either with a ritual or just burned."

"Which is why destroying the heart only had a slight effect," Morgana said, colour draining from her face. "By the Goddess! There are more."

Harlan checked his watch. "Maggie has his address. He's still living in Kent. I can be there in a couple of hours. Three by the time I've got my car, and picked up the shifters Maverick wants me to take."

Hunter desperately wanted to go with Harlan and see this through, but Maverick was right. He was aching and sore after fighting. But with Owen upstairs, the day might not be that quiet at Moonfell.

"You need a witch," Morgana said, breaking Hunter's train of thought.

Harlan shook his head. "No. You need to stay here. If you're right about him, it's not magic spells I need to worry about. It's demons. Maybe taking wolves is a bad idea, actually."

"More demons?" Hunter asked, horrified.

"Maybe. Or I'll just have to deal with a house of horrors. Just a regular Monday, I guess. I just hope my boss is understanding." He grinned. "I gave him a little bullshit excuse this morning, and besides, he owes me."

"No, you have to take someone other than three shifters," Hunter said, ignoring Harlan's optimism. "You have to have someone you can rely on. Someone who'll keep a calm head and is used to fighting and handling weapons."

"Who, then?" Harlan asked, puzzled.

"Grey."

Twenty-Five

W hen Harlan arrived at Owen's house that afternoon, he was very relieved that Grey had agreed to be part of the team.

He had a good sense of humour, was physically strong, understood the paranormal world well, and wasn't easily intimidated. It was also good not to be the sole human working with shifters he didn't know very well. In the small confines of a car, being so close to natural predators made Harlan uncomfortable. They weren't threatening to him, but they were threatening in general, and they didn't even realise it
.

They had travelled down in Mads's large SUV, the shifter anxious to be helpful and very grateful for being included in the team. Harlan knew that Arlo had faced a challenging pack the day before, but Fran, Mads, and Jax seemed relaxed enough now. They had chatted easily on the way down, talked vaguely about strategy, and had all wondered how the hell Harlan had managed to keep Maggie out of it. With grea t difficulty was the answer, until he had pointed out that she was way outside her jurisdiction, and that she needed to see Layla, and catch up with Stan and Irving. As much as Harlan liked Maggie, he worried about her tendency to go off like a rocket. Like almost killing Owen the day before. He did not want that now.

All five stared out of the window at the unassuming Victorian house situated at the end of a leafy drive. They had opted to park on the drive, thinking it would be less obvious than parking on the road, and Mads pulled in behind a sprawling shrub. The house was large, with dark windows, and was a little dilapidated. Owen's love of money obviously didn't extend to keeping his house looking nice.

"That doesn't look so bad," Grey said. "A little creepy maybe, but that's to be expected from Owen."

"On a pretty normal street, too," Mads observed. "Expensive neighbourhood."

Fran nodded. "Big house and garden. Potential for traps."

"Nah," Jax said easily. "It's his home. There won't be traps."

"Nevertheless, we'll proceed carefully." Grey grinned at Harlan. "Think of us as your security team. You lead the investigation."

"Sounds good."

Fran pointed at a security box. "How do we get around the alarm?"

"Leave that to me," Grey said.

They exited the car and Harlan and Grey hurried to the front door while the shifters scanned the front garden. Owen either wasn't a gardener or had deliberately let the garden become overgrown. Hardly any of the road could be seen from the house. The greenery, even in mid-February, provided privacy.

Grey used his skeleton keys, and after a little trial and error eased the front door open, and then tackled the electronic alarm. Harlan wasn't sure exactly what he did, but in moments it was deactivated, and they stepped fully into the hall, Jax closing the door once they were all inside. Harlan and Grey had brought shotguns with them. Harlan's was loaded with salt-filled shells, Grey's with regular ones. Harlan had no idea how demons might respond to salt, but at least he was prepared for ghosts.

The hall was dark because of the lack of natural light. The walls were painted pale green, and it had a high ceiling, picture rails, and deep skirting boards. So far, all very ordinary. They passed a door on the right that led to a large, blandly decorated living room, and one on the left that opened on a dining room that looked like it was never u sed.

Grey gave a dry laugh. "The presentable face of this house. I bet the rest of the place doesn't look so innocuous."

He was right. When they passed through a door at the end of the short hall and entered the back of the house, everything changed. Occult symbols were painted on wooden panelling that lined the bottom half of the walls, and runes marked doorways and arched entrances to another couple of passages that led left and right. The walls were painted dark red, and old-fashioned wall lights lined the hall. Harlan flicked them on, and they illuminated large prints that hung beneath them. Images of demons and classical renditions of Hell, all full of fire and brimstone.

"Holy crap!" Fran said as she examined them. "He's a cheerful bugger, isn't he? Talk about obsessive."

"Yeah, the true face of Owen." Harlan shouted, "Hello? Anyone here?"

They waited for voices, or the telltale creak of floorboards or doors opening, but the whole house was deathly silent.

"I'm shifting," Fran announced, starting to peel her clothes off. "If something happens and I threaten you, go gentle with the Taser."

"Yes ma'am," Harlan said, patting his pocket. Both he and Grey carried them, just in case something triggered the wolves to attack them. He took a moment to study the runes and pointed to a large one etched into panelling. "*Ingwaz*. Means seed. Interesting. It indicates stored energies and male mysteries."

"Excellent. Male fucking mysteries," Grey murmured, pressing on.

"And *Uruz*." Harlan pointed to another. "In fact, that sigil combines both of them." The sigil was carved above an archway halfway down the hall.

"And that means what?" Jax asked.

"*Uruz* is strength of will. Vigour. Endurance."

"So, male mysteries and strength of will. Is that how Owen sees himself?"

"Perhaps. Or he's imbuing the house with these qualities."

They passed another living room, this one looking well used, with a TV on a unit, and a stack of videos in shelves either side of the fire. Grey eased a door open to the left. "Looks like a cellar. Shall we?"

"Me first," Mads said. He was the tallest shifter, similar in build to his brother, but his hair was a darker shade of blond. He still had a large, square jaw though, and pale blue eyes.

"Careful," Grey cautioned.

They stepped warily, a single lightbulb overhead illuminating the way. Harlan steeled himself for the worst. Signs of blood, perhaps. Or a wall of jarred body organs. But the only things down there were damp, empty boxes and broken furniture. For the next few minutes, they explored the place carefully, and then progressed back upstairs. They found a kitchen and boot room at the back of the house, but nothing sinister. The back garden appeared to be as overgrown as the front garden, with little to be seen beyond the shrubs outside the kitchen w indow.

"Should we check outside?" Jax asked.

Grey shook his head. "Later. Let's search in here first. I want us all to stick together."

Halfway up the stairs to the first floor, Fran emitted a low growl and proceeded slowly ahead of them all, Mads right behind her. Jax brought up the rear. Harlan steadied his shotgun as they stepped onto the first-floor hallway and couldn't help but gasp at the sight ahead.

The walls were again painted a dark, blood-red, but the runes and sigils had multiplied, as had the demonesque wall art. Huge images of several varieties of demons lined the walls, and around all of them were gold-painted occult symbols. It was an assault on the senses. Even the floorboards were painted, and the faint odour of sulphur hit them like a tidal wave.

Mads sniffed and shook his head. "Not fresh."

"But up here must be where he conjures them," Jax said. "This is seriously creepy."

The hall split in two, one part running to the front of the house, and one to the back. Fran gave a sharp *yip* and sat facing the rear.

Harlan examined the sigils on the floor, noting they were different on the passageway leading to the back of the house. "It's a ritual path, I think."

"For what?" Mads asked.

"Preparation, perhaps, before you enter *that*!" He pointed at the door at the far end of the hall painted with another complex sigil. "I think that is his Inner Sanctum."

"Looks likely," Mads agreed. "But preparation how?"

"Mental, probably. You would have to prepare yourself, gather your energies." Harlan recalled his research on different belief systems. "Many ritual preparations require that you enter a different state of mind. I could spend hours in here."

"Let's not," Jax said, grimacing. "We find what we need and then get the fuck out of here."

"Let's check the front rooms first," Grey suggested.

The hallway to the front was short with only two rooms opening off it, and a large window was positioned over the front door. Harlan

checked outside, but the garden and the street beyond—what he could
see of it, at least—remained quiet. He headed into the room on the
right and found an unused bedroom, but there were photos of a
woman in there, and it had a feminine quality. Harlan picked up a
photo on a chest of drawers. Jax entered the room behind him and
whistled. "Are those photos of his sister?

"There does seem to be a family resemblance."

"But she'd died in a fire, right? Before he moved here?"

Harlan nodded. "According to the timeline of events, yes."

"So, what is this? A way of honouring her memory?"

"Perhaps. Or assuaging his conscience."

Jax picked up items idly. "Or she really did sacrifice herself, and he
misses her."

"But if the fire happened as part of that, and she died in it as
Maggie's investigation suggests, then how come her stuff wasn't destroyed?"

Jax shrugged. "Maybe he'd already bought this place and they started moving in together."

Dissatisfied, Harlan returned to the hall and found Grey and Mads
exiting the other room. "Owen's room," Grey explained. "Lots of
occult bedside reading. Dark décor, grubby sheets. It's like it belongs
to a teenage goth in the '90s."

"Maybe he's stuck in time," Harlan suggested.

Anxious to get on with it, he headed to the back of the house where
Fran sat, ears pricked outside the door. The feeling of unease he'd
experienced upon reaching the first floor grew as they headed towards
the shut door at the end of the corridor. There were no other rooms
to investigate.

"This corridor feels short considering the proportions downstairs," Mads mused. "I reckon he's either knocked rooms through, or there's a maze of horrors behind the door."

"I guess it's time to find out." Grey nodded to the symbols on the door. "What do they mean?"

Harlan consulted his book of runes. "The rune above the door is *Mannaz. Man.* Interesting. It means divine influence in life, and the psychic order of the Gods. The one on the door is...worrying."

"Go on," Grey asked darkly.

"*Thurisaz*, otherwise known as Giant. A sign denoting self-empowerment, breaker of resistance, and a reactive and directive force, amongst other things. And also danger."

"Great." Grey lifted his shotgun. "Jax, open the door, slowly."

The door opened on well-oiled hinges, and the room beyond was pitch black. The scents of sulphur and incense were strong in here, and the feeling of power brought goose bumps to Harlan's skin.

Fran, eyesight much better than theirs in her wolf, stepped into the room, hackles up. Rather than feel for a light switch, Harlan pulled the flashlight from his bag and flicked it on. The beam of light illuminated a devilish face in the far corner of the room, so bizarre that he almost dropped his torch, and also a wedge of a large summoning circle on the floor. He checked the wall to the side of the door and spotting the light switch, turned it on. Half a dozen wall sconces lit the room, their meagre light revealing a chamber devoted to the occult.

The windows were swathed in thick, black curtains and the dark red walls were covered in sigils just like the hallway, but it was the huge, horned, devilish statue in the far corner that dominated the room. It glared at the newcomers and presided over the enormous summoning circle on the floor. An altar of sorts was arranged before the statue, and jars were positioned in the curves of its body. Even more unnerving was the giant circle ringed with sigils drawn on the wall, positioned between the windows opposite the door.

"Well, this is something else," Jax said, cautiously stepping inside the room. "Why is there a circle on the wall?"

"It's to make a portal into the other dimension," Harlan told him.

"I thought that was the one on the floor?"

"That's the trap—I think." If he was honest with himself, he wasn't entirely sure. "But those are what we've come for. The jars on the statue. There's what, half a dozen of them?"

"You really think there are body organs in them?" Grey asked.

"I'm hoping so," Harlan answered. "Gruesome though that sounds. My entire theory depends on it."

"But look at the shelves," Jax said, skirting around the circle until he reached long shelves on the wall to the left. "What are these?"

"Ritual objects, by the look of it," Harlan said, briefly glancing at them, his attention on the canopic-style jars. By now they were all inside, and he headed to the statue to inspect the jars. But he'd barely crossed the space when the door swung shut behind them, and the clicking of an elaborate locking mechanism resounded across the ro om.

Everyone spun around. A complex system of moveable bars had dropped into place on the door, locking them in. But Fran's attention was on the summoning circle, and she growled as a dark shape began to manifest in the centre of it.

Mads raced to the door and tried to open it. "It's shut tight!"

"It's just a lock," Grey reasoned, shotgun pointed at the manifesting creature. "We can work it out!"

"Before that damn thing manifests?" Mads tried to move the bars, but they remained firmly locked in position. "No one is out there—I'd have sensed them—so how has this shut?"

"I think," Harlan said, "that we are dealing with higher powers here."

Fran was snapping and snarling now, her fur standing on end as she prowled the perimeter of the circle, watching the dark shape in the centre get bigger and bigger.

"Who is summoning that?" Jax demanded, hands on hips.

"We've triggered something, we must have." Harlan thought quickly, trying to discern their risks. "If a demon is being summoned, then in theory it can't leave the circle. Jax, help me get the jars! Grey, shoot out the locks on the door!"

"All of them? That's nuts!" Mads said, hurling himself against the door to try to open it.

"Move aside," Grey said, running to help him.

The boom of the shotgun echoed around them as Harlan reached the statue. Jax clambered onto it and grabbed the jar resting on its shoulders, next to the demonesque head. He lifted the lid and yelled, "It's a brain!"

Harlan nodded, assessing the jars placed across the statue. "The jars are placed where the organs would be in a human. Brains, liver, intestines, stomach, lungs. Four are the same as the Egyptians kept, but Owen has kept more. And there's a place where the heart would be. I was right!"

"Well, that's just fantastic," Jax said, lifting another jar and leaning down to pass it to Harlan.

They were covered in futhark runes, but Harlan didn't bother trying to decipher them. *Later.*

Another boom resounded as Grey yelled, "Enough chat! We need to go."

"Except," Mads said, sarcastically, "the door is still shut! Blast through the wall, Grey!"

"It's a gun, not a jackhammer!"

Harlan tried to block out their shouts as he focussed on collecting the jars and wedging them safely into his pack, wrapping them quickly within the newspapers Morgana had given him. They were larger than he expected, and his bag was uncomfortably full. Just as he loaded the last one, another book on the shelves caught his eye.

"Jax, grab me that book. The one with the old, cracked leather cover."

"Sure," he said sarcastically. "Narrow it down, why don't you."

"The oldest one! Oh, screw it, just grab them all!"

Fran howled, the urgency of it making Harlan spin around. An enormous demon was taking shape in the centre of the trap. It opened its mouth, revealing row after row of sharp teeth, and beyond them a bottomless pit. It emitted a guttural roar and jets of flames.

Jax dropped the books he was holding and shifted straight into his wolf, clothes tearing. Mads seemed to resist for a second longer, and then he shifted, too. At the same time, darkness swirled in the middle of the circle on the wall.

The portal had been activated.

Twenty-Six

Vlad was relieved that the second pack meeting had gone so well that afternoon.

Maverick's return put them all at ease, although he had kept the bulk of the news from them. He hadn't shared about his family's involvement, or the failed ritual the night before. Vlad wasn't sure that was the right approach, but Maverick was entitled to his privacy. He had reinforced Arlo's decisions, and stressed that the demon issue would soon be resolved. No one challenged him.

As the final members left, Vlad shut and locked the club door. There was still another couple of hours before they were due to open for the evening, and he joined Arlo, Domino, and Maverick at the corner booth.

Domino winced as she leaned against the plush velvet of the seat behind her. "Thank the Gods no one asked about our bruises."

"I presume," Arlo said, "they're attributing them to the fight a few nights ago."

"I think a few had more questions," Maverick said, "but decided against voicing them. Barrett certainly looked unconvinced, but he should know as the old alpha that some things are better left unsaid."

"He's changed his tune from the other day, then," Vlad pointed out. He checked his phone for messages.

"Worried about your brother?" Arlo asked.

Vlad nodded. "It's been an awkward few days, but yes, I am. I'm worried about all of them, actually. We changed all too easily last night." His fingers prodded the bite marks on his neck. They were mostly healed now, but still tender.

Maverick noticed and grimaced. "Sorry. I would have thought that I could have resisted the demon, but—"

"It's a *demon*," Arlo said, cutting him off. "Way more powerful than us. After what Hunter told us about his experience, we should have expected it. I've been thinking about tonight, actually. If Harlan is successful and the witches try again, we can't afford to be there."

Maverick rubbed his stubbled chin, dark shadows beneath his eyes. "No, I guess not, but it feels wrong to leave the witches to do it alone. This is my issue. I brought it to their door."

"They don't see it like that," Domino said. "This isn't your issue alone. It's ours. And they are right. We can't banish it. We have no idea how to do it, nor do we have the power to, either."

Arlo nodded. "I agree that it's a group effort. Owen is as much a danger to witches as us."

"And he's in their house." Maverick's fingers drummed on the table. "There has to be a way to help."

Vlad shrugged. "We're guarding Owen. That's something."

"But if their own magic is now protecting him, that's got to be an issue."

"Not protecting, as such," Arlo mused. "Insulating him. Regular cuffs and rope seem to be doing the trick, though."

Maverick didn't answer; instead, he brooded. Vlad wished he could suggest something that would be of use, but he was out of ideas. They were susceptible to the demon, and short of killing Owen, they were at an impasse until Harlan and the others returned. If Harlan was wrong, they would need to rethink their strategy.

And then a loud banging resounded from the front door of the club.

"I'll get it," Vlad said.

He presumed that one of the pack had returned, Barrett perhaps, but when he opened the door, a tall, brooding stranger stood outside. His dark hair, edged at the temples with grey, a scarred cheek, and his beard did nothing to disguise the fact that he was Maverick's brother.

Vlad stepped outside. "Canagan. I'm not sure that he'll want to see you."

Canagan's eyes were hard. "I don't think you're in a position to make that call and turn me away. I'm going to see him."

Vlad shook his head. "You misunderstand me. I'm not going to turn you away. Of course you must see him." Vlad understood all too well tension between brothers right now, but there was always time to make it right. "I just need you to understand that he's under a lot of pressure. Things are bad."

Canagan's expressions softened. "A loyal pack member. That's good. But I'm here to help."

"And if he doesn't want you here?"

"I'm not going anywhere until this thing is done. He'll accept my help, whether he wants it or not."

Vlad didn't move. He knew brothers. And he knew egos. "You go in with that attitude, and it's all over."

He sneered. "You're counselling me?"

"I speak from experience. Start with an apology."

"I already have apologised."

Vlad gave a dry laugh. Canagan had made bad choices and they had shaped him into a brawler and a bully, used to having his own way and blustering through the rest of it. He'd rather die than admit fault. He'd seen it before and recognised it straight away. "Apologise like you mean it this time, or I'll throw you out myself." He stared Canagan down, making sure the man saw he meant it, and then stepped back, swinging the door wide. "Welcome to Storm Moon."

"We need Owen at the ritual tonight," Morgana announced after careful thought. "It's the only way. And we must move him out of the house."

"To where?" Birdie asked. "We can't take him off the grounds."

"The stables."

"It's cold!" Birdie protested. "I know he's a nightmare, but that doesn't feel right."

Tommy snorted. "I couldn't give a flying fuck. I hope his balls shrivel up and drop off with the cold."

Morgana tried not to laugh and failed. "Tommy!"

"I mean it. Odious little man."

"You call everyone a little man."

"Well, he is, especially to me."

They were in Moonfell's library again, gathered around the table that was covered in demon reference books. This time, however, they had narrowed down their selection, and Morgana felt far more confident than she had the night before. There were only the three of them there now. Odette was watching Owen with Monroe, none of them now willing to leave him solely in the care of a shifter. Hunter and Cecile were patrolling the grounds, ensuring nothing was amiss. Nothing was, Morgana was sure, or Hades would have told Birdie, but they wanted to be useful, and extra eyes on the garden wouldn't go amiss. Xavier was finally in his wolf and sleeping, and his wounds looked much better.

Birdie tapped her lip with an elegant forefinger painted with dark red nail polish. She wasn't about to let a demon hamper her style. "We need a fire tonight, too. We burn the herbs we discussed. Cleansing herbs. And we smudge the room when Owen leaves it."

"Oh, yes," Morgana couldn't agree more. "With a smudge stick the size of a broom."

Tommy smirked. "You two are sexy when you get all witchy!"

Birdie, unexpectedly flirty, blew him a kiss. "All the time then, because I always have my witch on!"

Morgana rolled her eyes. Her grandmother was becoming outrageous with her newfound youth. "Tommy, do you think you can build us a fire near the demon trap?"

"Sure. How big?"

"Think bonfire night big. There's a pile of old furniture at the end of the stables, and there's a wood pile on the west side of the house."

"No problem. I'll get Hunter to help me. When are we moving Owen?"

"I think now. Let's make him uncomfortable."

Birdie nodded. "You're right, Morgana. We're being too nice to him. He did try to kill us, after all."

"Exactly. "

Twenty-Seven

"Harlan," Grey said, as he backed against the wall, "what's happening to the shifters, and what is going on with the portal?"

Harlan grabbed the oldest leatherbound book of demonology, ancient and written in Latin, and thrust it in his bag. "The demon has triggered the shift, just like last night, and I think the demon is opening the portal. I don't even know how..."

"Forget how! We need to leave!"

As Harlan looked up, Jax snarled in his face, only feet away, teeth bared. Harlan froze, edging his hand to his pocket where his Taser was. Jax took a step closer, belly lowering, ready to pounce.

Grey attempted to distract him. "Jax! Stop it! We're your friends!"

It didn't work, and Jax leapt at Harlan. He fired his Taser, and the wolf yelped and lay twitching on the floor. Grey turned around once he saw Harlan was in control, trying to work out a way to open the locks. He heard Fran howl as the Taser struck her too, but tried to block it out, until a menacing growl sounded right behind him.

Harlan yelled, "Grey! Behind you!"

Grey whipped around, and too late to grab his Taser, used his shotgun like a baton and smacked Mads with it as he pounced. Both fell, the shotgun skittering away. Mads, blood pooling from his mouth, leaped again, undeterred. Grey rolled out of the way, grabbed his gun, and gripping it with both hands, thrust it between him and a wild-eyed Mads as he pounced again. The bulk of Mads's weight pinned Grey to the floor, and his teeth snapped inches from his face. Grey used the gun to push the wolf away. But Mads was enormous, a huge, heavy beast that was probably twice Grey's size. Grey stared into Mads's eyes, willing him to recognise him and see sense, but all he recognised was the need to kill.

Harlan yelled, "Get ready to roll, Grey!"

"Just shoot it!"

"*Now!*"

With one enormous push, Grey rolled the wolf to the side just as the dart struck it. Grey let out an anguished shout at the same time as the wolf yelped.

"Are you okay?"

"I'm partially electrocuted, what do you think?" Grey said, scrambling to his feet. "Damn it, that hurt!"

"Well, at least you still have your throat. The door?"

"Sure, let me focus on that while my balls are still zinging from the Taser!"

Grey took a deep breath. *This was very bad.* The portal was swirling with shadows and flames, the demon was roaring, and they were trapped with three semi-conscious, twitching wolves. Even if he and Harlan could escape, they couldn't carry three enormous wolves. He just hoped that once they were back on their feet, they wouldn't attack again.

"I knew we shouldn't have brought them!" Harlan said, as breathless as Grey.

"A little late for that." Grey checked his gun, reloaded, and aimed it at the demon. "I may as well try." He fired at the demon, which only seemed to enrage it further.

"Let me try. Salt shells may work better."

Grey took one look at the door peppered with shots and the sturdy brick walls and knew they wouldn't get out that way. Not in time. While Harlan shot the demon, he ran to the windows, pulled back the curtains, and groaned. They had been bricked up.

"No way out the windows, Harlan."

"What about the floor? Can you shoot through the floorboards?"

"It's a shotgun, not a cannon! What is the matter with everyone? Have you got an axe?"

"Yes, packed in my bottomless pit of a bag! I need to think!"

"Well, do it quickly! Give me your gun!" Grey fired at the demon again, and it hissed as the salt shells struck it. "Excellent. It doesn't like that."

Harlan passed him the box of shells and focussed on the portal, but Grey had only fired a few more rounds at the demon when he realised that the effect it was having wasn't enough. However, for all of its roaring, the demon was still in the trap, but nothing would contain whatever emerged from the portal. They would be eviscerated or dragged back to another dimension, instant food for the demon hordes.

Grey joined Harlan, who was still studying the portal. "Any luck closing this?"

"I've got an idea. The portal, like a trap, needs to have exact sigils for it to work. If we can destroy the sigils and break the circle, surely the portal will close. Where's the other gun?" He spun around, spotted the discarded gun with the proper shells, and advanced on the portal.

Grey, keeping his eyes firmly averted from whatever was manifesting in the centre, studied the sigils. They had been scored into the wall and painted, each sigil carefully drawn, and they were now lit up with flickering flames. He wasn't even sure they could destroy them, but he liked Harlan's reasoning. Harlan aimed at the closest sigil and fired. The pellets peppered the wall, and took a chunk out of it, but the sigil remained stubbornly intact. He fired, reloaded, and tried again, concentrating on one sigil only. Grey checked on the wolves. They were coming around, but weren't attacking them—yet. The room was now doubly loud, with shotguns blasting and a roaring demon in the confined space. Surely it was only a matter of time before the police were here, too.

Despite trying not to look, his attention kept being dragged to the portal's swirling centre. That way lay madness. Grey resolutely turned away, willing Harlan success. Just as Grey was giving into despair, the sigil fractured under the fourth shot, and the wall cracked beneath it. Harlan lifted the gun and battered the wall with the butt pad, just as a clawed hand with twisting, razor-sharp nails appeared out of the wall, reaching for him.

Grey roared at him. "Move!"

Harlan had barely time to jump to the side when he fired, and salt struck the clawed hand. It shrivelled and darted back. Harlan smacked the plaster again, and it crumbled and slipped to the floor. He righted the shotgun and aimed at the next sigil, but the portal was already changing. The flames were diminishing and cooling as the circle closed itself.

Grey staggered away from it on legs that felt like jelly. *That was horribly, ball-shrinkingly close*. "Well done, Harlan!" He turned to the demon again. "Should we shoot out the trap, too?"

"No!" Harlan leaped forward, arms raised. "It could escape. Do not break the circle!"

"But it worked for the portal."

"It's different! The circle contains the demon. The portal is an entirely separate operation."

"Okay!" Grey's head was spinning, and his heart was thumping, but he was alive. Time to focus on the positive.

"Ignore the demon. Concentrate on the door."

Grey snorted. "And the wolves, of course."

All three were now staggering back to their feet, but they looked weaker—bewildered, even. However, the demon was still prowling the trap, and still roaring. It was surely only a matter of time before the wolves attacked again. Both he and Grey reloaded their Tasers.

"Watch my back," Harlan said, studying the locks on the door. "One of them has already slid open!"

"How?"

"I don't know!"

The lock consisted of bars that moved in and out from a mechanism on the wall. Upon closer examination, Grey could see that different sigils had been engraved onto the metal of each bar.

"I get it! Sigil magic again," Harlan said, looking relieved. "The sigils are tied to the portal. I have to shoot them all out."

He grabbed the shotgun and returned to the portal, and Grey faced the wolves, willing them to stay calm.

"I told you not to get in touch, and now you turn up on my doorstep?" Maverick glared at his brother, hands clenched into fists.

"I need to put things right."

"I don't need you to do anything."

"But *I* do!"

The brothers were in the Manager's Office, alone. Arlo, Domino, and Vlad were in the bar, a shout away if Maverick needed them. He wouldn't, though. He could deal with this.

"Maverick, please." Canagan stepped forward, arms outstretched. It looked as if he'd barely slept since the night they had fought. "I fucked up, and I'm sorry. I'm your big brother. I should have been around to protect you. I should have been able to protect Mum and Dad. Instead, I killed them. I should have confessed to the alpha what I'd done so we could put it right back then. I was a coward. You're right. It's the biggest regret of my life." He stepped forward, eyes never leaving Maverick's, appealing for forgiveness. "The others all agreed it was a stupid thing to do, but that to confess to our involvement was worse. Owen made it seem like one big joke—both him and Ivy! It was like this grand experiment. He even promised a share of the glory. He said we could have anything we wanted! I thought I could get more money for the family."

"Don't lie! It wasn't for us! It was for *you*."

"Yes, for me, too. And it seemed exciting." Canagan dropped his arms, urgency gone as he dropped into a chair. "It was so sleepy in Kent. We might have been shifters, but it wasn't exactly big city fun. I had raging testosterone and an urge for excitement! Mum and Dad didn't get it!"

"They kept us safe." Maverick sat down too, suddenly too tired to stand and argue. "Looking back, I realise now that our childhood was idyllic. We had the whole of Kent Downs to roam. A safe way to learn our wolf nature. I have never felt that safe again in my life. Even with Aunt Abigail."

"She hated me."

"Only because you were such a dick. At least I know why now."

Canagan shook his head. "She would never have forgiven me. I couldn't bear the thought of her knowing what I'd done—even more than telling our alpha. I sometimes thought she knew that I knew more than I let on. It was the way she looked at me."

"She certainly never suggested that to me."

"She wouldn't have. She was protecting you, and I was glad of that. I knew I could leave and that you would be all right. I did you a favour."

"No, you didn't." A wave of sorrow swept over Maverick so profound that it left him feeling empty and lost. "You left a giant hole in my life."

"I left one in mine, too." Canagan's face twisted with regret. "My life since then has been full of danger. Fighting, territory, pack positioning. I thrived on it for a while. I had to, or I would have died. I told myself that it was what I wanted." He gave a dry laugh. "Mostly, though, I wanted things to be the way they used to be. But I made the best of it, and then I met my mate. She offered me a lifeline."

"Not exactly a fine, upstanding pack that you're in though, is it?"

"No. That's not my lot in life. Not like you and what you've built here. I checked up on you, made sure you were okay. You've done well for yourself. I'm glad our aunt left you all the money. You deserved it."

Maverick's throat felt thick with emotion. He wanted to sleep for a week, and for all of this to be over with. He was emotionally and physically shattered, and dealing with his brother was the last thing he wanted to do. But maybe Canagan meant it. He looked genuinely sorry. "How do you propose to help? I'll be honest, last night's attempt to banish the demon went badly." He described what had happened.

"Sorry to hear that. It didn't affect us that way. I can certainly share what happened with your witches. I remember bits of the ritual. It could help." Maverick didn't answer, and so he continued. "I mean it. I want to help end this. End Owen."

Maverick took in his contrite expression, his desperate need, and realised that he couldn't afford to say no. He wanted his brother to make amends. They both needed to move on.

"All right. Let's go to Moonfell."

Twenty-Eight

Maggie entered Moonfell's vast library brimming with news and found herself in the midst of several different discussions happening all at once.

She had let herself in the house after Birdie had given her a key earlier that day. Now, seeing the scene in front of her, Maggie wasn't surprised that no one had heard her knocking on the door or ringing the doorbell before she used it. The conversations were loud and animated, especially from Harlan and Grey, who were talking to the group of shifters. Domino and Vlad were there, too, and even Xavier, although he looked pale and weak. He was sitting in a chair rather than standing like the rest. In addition, an unknown man with an earnest expression on his scarred face was chatting to Morgana, Odette, Maverick, and Arlo, who stood around a table in front of the fireplace. In the centre of the table was a collection of jars covered in runes. Everyone looked tired, but they carried an air of expectancy and anticipation. The only people not present were Tommy and Birdie, and she presumed they were watching Owen.

Maggie first joined Harlan and Grey. "You found the jars, then?" she asked Harlan, nudging him to get his attention.

He gave her a cocky grin. "Not without a few issues, but yes!"

Grey snorted. "Issues! Like a demon, a portal, and vicious wolves." He rolled his eyes at Mads, Fran, and Jax. "Thanks, guys."

Fran glared at him. "Do I need to show you my Taser marks again?"

"Nope. I've seen quite enough of your arse already today!"

"Tasers?" Maggie asked, looking over them all. Whatever had happened, they seemed to have shaken it off.

"We shifted without control." Jax shrugged, not appearing too bothered by the whole ordeal. "The portal was worse! In fact, the whole house was a nightmare."

"A regular demon-summoning lair, really," Harlan said with an air of teasing amusement. "I've seen worse. Not much worse, admittedly, but it comes with the job. All in a day's work for an occult collector."

Maggie smiled, feeling like he might have been exaggerating just a little. "Well, I'm just grateful that you got out of there alive. Who's the new guy?"

"Canagan," Vlad answered. "Maverick's brother. He's come to help."

Maggie looked him over, seeing the resemblance she'd missed earlier. "Are you sure?"

"He wants revenge as much as anyone," Vlad said. As if Canagan was aware they were watching, he looked over and then quickly away again.

"Do I need to get the local police to search Owen's house?"

"No!" Harlan recoiled. "Not until it's made safe. There are all sorts of weird symbols and occult traps in the main room, and maybe more on the grounds. Best not to mess with it. We were lucky to get out intact. We're joking about it now, but it was very bad, Maggie."

"Okay. The jars contain what I think they do?"

"Body parts. I don't know if they're all from the same body, but I suspect they will be. The heart was missing. Come and see what I think he's done."

Harlan led her to the other table, and she saw an old volume next to the jars, open to a page filled with a chilling drawing of a human body, with illustrations of various organs.

He kept his voice low so as not to disturb the others. "I found this book at Owen's, too. I suspect that the body parts continue to connect Ivy—if they're hers, big leap, I know—to the demon. We need to destroy all of them."

"And Owen is connected to them, too?"

"Yes. He's bound himself to them in some way. A blood ritual, we think." He flipped the pages in the book. "A few rituals are described here. I suspect he's used one of these."

"What if they're shifter organs?" Maverick asked, interrupting them.

Harlan looked at him, startled. "I hadn't considered that, but it's possible."

So, this was what Owen had driven them to, Maggie reflected. *Discussing who Owen had dissected. The man was a monster.* However it had happened, she would ensure his victims received justice.

Maggie took a breath and introduced herself to Canagan. "DI Maggie Milne."

He accepted her handshake warily. "Canagan Hale. Have you come to arrest me?"

"For being a moron? No. Prisons would be full in that case. I suspect you've done your penance already."

"Not yet, but I'm getting there."

"So, what's the plan tonight?"

Morgana answered first. "We've been trying to put together the original ritual that Owen did, and then work out how he might have built on it from there. We think, thanks to Canagan, that we know."

Odette nodded. "And we missed something fundamental. Owen's blood."

"He used his own in the ritual?"

"It seems so."

"Well, I learned something today, too," Maggie said. "My sergeants uncovered several deaths in the Kent area over the years. We investigated the names you gave us, Maverick. It was enough for us to find them. Your old friends," she said to Canagan. "They all died in unpleasant accidents. Nothing suspicious at the time, but now, in the light of our new knowledge, it all seems *very* suspicious. I suspect Owen was behind them. I also suspect," she said, watching Canagan's reaction, "that if you had stuck around like them, he would have killed you, too. You taking off and changing your name meant he couldn't find you. Even with his pet demon to help."

"Which is why, eventually, he came to me," Maverick said, nodding. "But why now?"

"For Canagan's blood. It has to be," Odette said. "We know that the blood stored in the rune box is unusable, and that he's desperate to maintain his connection to the demon. And everyone who was involved in that first rite is dead now—except you. He must have found over the years that the original blood is the most potent for what he wants."

"Can we banish it tonight? Have we got everything we need?" Maggie said "we" deliberately. A demon in London was her problem. An innocent bystander dead, injured shifters, and a trail of death in a madman's wake. This ended today.

Morgana and Odette looked at each other, a long, searching glance, and then nodded. "Yes," Odette said, "but the shifters—especially you, Canagan—stay out of it."

"No! I need to be there."

"You'll shift without wanting to and turn on us."

Arlo nodded. "You will. It's inevitable. Especially if the demon takes the shape of a wolf."

"But if he sees me, he'll think he's won. He'll let his guard down."

"Who cares?" Maverick asked.

"Let him think we need him. He'll see me and assume victory, and maybe he'll give something away. He's an accomplished liar."

Odette frowned. "He is holding back. Canagan might be right."

"You know," Harlan said, his joy at their earlier success vanishing, "something has just struck me. The demon trap in Owen's house was sealed, which means it didn't escape like he said. Unless, of course, he stuck around to repair it and make his booby-trapped room."

"Which seems highly unlikely," Hunter pointed out. "In theory, he'd have been running for his life. That makes me reconsider the whole encounter I first had in the park. If the demon needed shifter blood, why not attack me?" His gaze travelled around the group. "I was on my own. Surely it could tell I was a shifter."

"Fuck it! That's an excellent point," Maverick admitted. "Why didn't we consider that earlier?"

"Because you've had a lot going on." Canagan clapped his hand on his brother's shoulder to reassure him. "This is what Owen does. He confuses you by spinning tales, and you get so caught up, you fail to see the details."

"Even me," Odette admitted, "who sees the truth of things. It means he's controlled the demon all along—and clearly not just one. He might be right about it being weaker, though. Some things are true. Weaving lies in amongst the truth makes it harder to discern facts from fiction. I think," she paused and nodded to herself, "that the demon is weaker, that it does need shifter blood, and that it fed on the fox and the man to sustain itself. Maybe Owen allowed it to. He's kept it close, though, all this time. It was drawn by our magic to this house, or by needing to be close to Owen. What I don't understand is how a demon could become weak. It's a *demon*!"

Morgana shrugged. "Maybe he never sent it back to its own world and has always kept it in this one. Another lie. Maybe that has made it weaker."

"And he's made it crave shifter blood," Arlo added. "The whole thing is completely screwed up."

"So why didn't it attack me?" Hunter persisted.

"Because," Grey suggested, "Owen willed it not to. That was the night before Owen arrived, right?" Hunter nodded. "Maybe Owen didn't want to alert the pack before he'd had a chance to speak to Maverick. He had an agenda, a time frame, and attacking you didn't fit it. When it attacked you, Xavier, maybe it was provoked, or Owen just let it loose. A way to manipulate Maverick so that he arrived at Storm Moon needing answers."

"I want to wring his scrawny neck," Maverick growled, hands clenching. "If Canagan's staying tonight, then so will I." He held his hand up as the witches started to protest. "No arguments."

"Don't trust me, brother?"

"I don't trust any of it. Just us two, no other shifters. Arlo, don't even think about complaining."

"Okay, then," Maggie said, taking in the resigned faces of the shifters, and thinking the whole thing was becoming more convoluted by the second. "Now that's sorted, tell me how I can help."

"I don't want you there either," Morgana told her. "You can go home, or to Storm Moon, but you do not get involved. Even Hades will keep his distance tonight. The only other people I want are Grey and Harlan. Are you okay with that?"

Both men nodded in agreement.

"But I can help!" Maggie protested. She hated being left out of anything.

"No." Morgana gave her a regretful smile. "Sorry, Maggie. Not this time. I don't doubt your abilities, but this is about numbers. I have who I need."

"In that case," she said, staring at the shifters, "I'm hanging around with you tonight!"

Twenty-Nine

G rey hauled Owen onto his feet and out of the stable to the drive.
It was a cold night; clouds scudded overhead, and a chill
wind sliced through the grounds of Moonfell.

A fire burned to the side of the demon trap that was surrounded by
candles, looking horribly similar to the trap that they found in Owen's
house earlier that day. Grey shuddered at the memory. It had taken
them another hour to get out of that room. The sigils had proven hard
to remove from the wall, and they had used the Taser on the wolves
once more before they regained control of themselves and shifted to
help them. It had been a subdued drive home, despite their levity once
they arrived at Moonfell.

Grey wished he had been banished from the grounds like most of
the shifters, but in all good conscience he couldn't leave. Besides, he
wanted to see this through. He was invested now. But even Xavier had
left. The witches weren't taking any chances.

Owen was struggling to break free of his grip, and he shook him
roughly. "Pack it in, Owen."

Owen smirked. "I'm glad you've seen sense and included me. It's
the only way this ritual will succeed." He started to say more, and
then he saw the jars lined up on the witches' stone altar and his smile
vanished. "What are they?"

"I thought you'd recognise them," Harlan said, joining them. "We found them in your house."

"You *what*?" Owen's manner changed in an instant. His face flushed with anger, and he struggled to get free. "You went to my house?"

"Yep. You see, I figured," Harlan explained, "that you had provided extra safeguards to connect you to the demon, and that the heart alone wouldn't be enough. I mean, we destroyed it, and still your demon wouldn't budge. You're a sneaky bastard, Owen." He shook his head from side to side. "But clever. I'll give you that."

Owen struggled to speak, mouth opening and closing before he said, "But I set traps!"

Grey snorted. "Yes, you did! It was touch and go there for a while, but we made it out. Made a bit of a mess of your wall. You'll have to replaster."

Owen stared at him, trying to discern whether he was telling the truth or not, before studying the jars with narrowed eyes as if trying to work out if they were really his. Grey experienced a moment of grim satisfaction at the fact that they had succeeded in upending all of Owen's plans, and then Canagan stepped off the path and into view and Owen relaxed. Grey met Harlan's eyes. *What now?*

"Canagan! Maverick found you! I'm so grateful that you've come to help—"

Canagan cut Owen off. "Of course I'm here to help. You want to banish the demon—finally, after all these years." He stepped closer, looming over him. "After all this death and destruction. This thirst for power and money at the expense of all else."

Owen stepped back, stuttering over his words, and Grey couldn't blame him. Canagan exuded animalistic dominance, and he struggled not to step back, too. "I would have done it sooner, but... Well, it was h ard."

"Is it? Or could you do it right now? Because I have the feeling that you know exactly what you're doing. You are a master of manipulation, Owen."

"I'm not lying! I can't send it back."

Canagan's expression was neutral. Unreadable even, as he stared down at Owen. "I don't believe you. But no matter, the witches will send it back anyway. Although, having killed everyone who took part in that first, unholy rite, I'll concede that it must have made it harder for you."

"Is that what they're telling you? That I killed everyone? Lies!" He tried to shake Grey's hand off his arm, but Grey tightened his grip. "All lies."

"I don't really care what you have to say on the matter at this point. As long as justice is done, and the demon is banished." Canagan glanced behind him to where the three witches were finishing their preparations. "Just the demon to fetch now."

Canagan walked away to help Maverick haul the bound demon into the trap.

"Hey, Birdie," Grey shouted over, "where do you want Owen?"

"Here please, for his blood." Birdie looked magnificent in her ceremonial gown, her hair piled atop her head, and she wielded a sharp dagger etched in symbols. "I hope you don't mind," she said to Owen, who was struggling to escape, "I'll use your own knife for this. Harlan and Grey very thoughtfully stripped your altar. Of course, we will add our own additions to the ceremony."

Grey and Harlan forced Owen's arm to extend.

"You don't need my blood!" he protested.

"Not according to your own book." Birdie smiled as Morgana held a silver bowl beneath his hand. "Unclench your fingers, Owen."

"No! Screw you!"

"I'll cut your forearm, then. There are always options."

Birdie made the incision quickly, and blood poured from the wound into the bowl. When they had collected enough, she covered the wound in a dressing. She then daubed blood on Owen's face and cheeks, and then his arms, covering his rune bracelets with his own blood.

"Thank you," she said, nodding with satisfaction. "Strap him to the chair in the centre of the circle."

Owen yelled, eyes wild. "No! I need to be here with you!"

Everyone ignored him, and within a few minutes Harlan and Grey had secured him in the chair, also carved with runes, and a few minutes after that the demon was wriggling in its binding next to him. Odette inspected the trap carefully, making sure none of the symbols were damaged, and touching up those that were.

Finally she nodded. "We are ready. Time to begin."

Grey retreated behind the altar with Harlan and the two shifters, shotgun cocked—just in case.

Morgana stood next to Odette, who was once again leading the spell, but she and Birdie had their own parts to play.

Odette activated the trap, her words carrying clearly in the chill night air, and the sigils burst into flames, eliciting a cry of anguish from Owen. Morgana hardened her heart against his desperate pleas.

They had decided that he was too dangerous to leave outside the trap, although she knew they were condemning him to certain death.

Once the trap was activated, Odette uttered the words of the ritual, and Morgana painted over the runes on the jars with Canagan's blood. The porcelain warmed beneath her fingers, and as she completed each one, she passed them to Birdie, who repeated the ritual with Owen's blood. Once complete, all the jars were lined up on the altar, now glowing with an inner light. Morgana's skin tingled with the ancient blood magic, and with every word, power magnified. The blood runes that they had painted on Owen now also took on a fiery light, and he screeched and fought his bonds as if the runes burned his flesh.

It already felt different to the other night, and they had changed the order of the ritual to accommodate their new plans. They weren't sticking exactly to Owen's ritual. They had found another to combine with it that would meet their needs. They hoped.

While Odette began the incantation to open the portal, Birdie broke the golden binding spell. She slashed her athame in the designated patterns, and the demon flailed and swelled in size just as it had the other night, emitting a blood-curdling howl as the last of its bonds vanished.

Owen immediately began his own spell, breaking out of his restraints and leaping to his feet, the chair crashing to the floor. He seemed to gain power along with the demon. Luckily, they had anticipated that.

Morgana nodded to the four behind her. *Now, for the next stage.*

Maverick's hair rose on the back of his neck as the demon paced the circle, side by side with Owen.

He knew they had a bond, but to see it up close chilled his blood.

Owen urged the demon-wolf on, even as the portal began to form in the air above the trap. Each howl made Maverick shudder, but he was prepared to resist the change. The witches had strengthened their rune spells, and looking at his brother, he saw his eyes fire with determination, too. If the witches trusted them to be here, then he had to have faith that it would work.

Maverick stepped forward and accepted the jar that Morgana offered him, and one by one his companions accepted one too until all six jars were allocated. Along with Morgana and Birdie, they carried the jars and circled the fire. The jar tingled within his palms, and he was certain something moved within it.

Odette was still leading the ritual at the altar, so he watched Morgana for instructions, but she faltered for a moment, and he realised why. The portal that had been growing slowly in size, suddenly magnified rapidly as Owen conducted his own ritual. He pranced in maniacal glee as his power swelled and he challenged Odette, calling something forth.

Another demon.

Maverick was convinced they'd prepared for everything, but they hadn't considered *that*. He was using the portal against them.

A wild, Otherworldly wind ripped out of the portal carrying the reek of sulphur and rot, and distant howls and panting.

Something was coming.

Odette's arms were outstretched, imploring the universe as she uttered her commands, hair whipping around her face, her long dress almost floating around her.

"*Now*!" Morgana and Birdie commanded simultaneously.

They all hurled the jars into the flames. The jars cracked, and the contents spilled out. Blood exploded from the organs contained within, and the stench of burnt flesh rose on the smoke. The demon screeched and shrank, and Owen collapsed on the ground, his face contorted with anger and pain.

Odette redoubled her efforts, her voice a shriek on the wind. Columns of flames soared from every candle, and the fire roared as if it were alive, sending them all flying backwards. Flat on his back, Maverick stared into the portal rippling over them, a swirling vastness of darkness and ancient power. For a second, he couldn't breathe, and he struggled to look away, until movement in the trap summoned his attention.

Owen regained his feet, practically incandescent with rage now, and although the demon was diminishing in size, lifting off the ground as Odette cast it towards the portal, Owen seemed to be getting stronger. With increasing horror, Maverick watched Owen stride towards the edge of the trap, destroy part of it, and leave its confines. He glowed with an Otherworldly light, and advanced on Odette, who stood alone at the stone altar.

Maverick ripped his clothes off and shifted.

Harlan raised the shotgun slung at his side, and fired at Owen.

Owen stumbled and turned, enraged, and Harlan fired again, at the same time as Grey.

The blast knocked Owen backwards, a mixture of salt and live ammunition peppering him. But they seemed to hardly damage him at all. Harlan reloaded, ready to shoot again.

However, they weren't as quick as the shifters. Canagan ploughed into Owen, knocking him to the ground, already naked and shifting into his wolf as he straddled him. Unfortunately, Owen was encased in flames and shadow, appearing to be half-demon himself, and he grappled with Canagan as he rolled across the ground, both of them a tangle of limbs.

Another howl, unearthly and as old as time itself, came from the portal above them. Harlan looked up and froze. A face took shape, the same that he had glimpsed earlier that day, but it was closer now. He could see the narrow slits of flaming eyes, and the huge horns that spiralled from its long, narrow, skeletal head.

He wanted the sound to stop. He couldn't think straight, but he had to help.

The witches were together now, Morgana and Birdie chanting with Odette as they sought to banish the demon-wolf and stop the other one from getting through the portal, but Maverick was fighting Owen with his brother. Blood and fur were flying as the empowered witch resisted them. It was chaotic and terrifying.

Harlan ignored his fear, and he and Grey raced to help. They had to get Owen back inside the circle—or kill him. Unfortunately, the press of wolves around Owen made it hard to shoot with any degree of accuracy.

Harlan yelled at them, hoping they would hear him. "Pull back! We're trying to shoot him!"

Maverick twisted slightly, and Grey pressed the gun to Owen's side, the only part of him he could see clearly, and fired. Harlan felt the shot rocket through him too, and Canagan yelped.

But Owen, despite his injuries, had superhuman strength now, and although he was gushing blood from his many wounds, he fought strongly. He seemed more demon than human, his eyes glowing with fire and death. He flung Maverick and Canagan off him, and they struck the stable wall and crumpled to the floor in a heap. He then cast his hands out, trying to counteract the witches' spell. Harlan and Grey fired their shotguns simultaneously.

The combined blasts made Owen stagger backwards, but not for long. His focus was now on rescuing his demon and calling the other one through the portal. They were quickly running out of options.

The two men and two wolves circled closer, trying to edge him towards the trap. If they could get him inside it again, then the witches might just be able to banish him. The demon-wolf was suspended between the earth and the portal, and the new demon that had manifested from its interior was still struggling to get out.

But then something swept past all of them, and the next thing he knew, Harlan was knocked off his feet. Winded, he looked up and blinked in shock. A strange, ghostly figure had manifested over Owen. It was enormous, but definitely human in shape, and Owen's demeanour changed immediately.

He shrieked, his voice almost a rasp. "*No*! It cannot be. You're a vision, nothing else. Leave now!" He made some complicated gesture with his hand, but the spirit was unaffected and leaned forward, picking Owen up as if he weighed nothing.

"Holy shit," Grey said, crawling to Harlan's side. "That's a woman!"

"Not just any woman," Harlan said, suddenly able to place the half-seen features. "It's his sister."

The spirit was deformed, her barely visible, ethereal body a mass of wounds and incisions that showed the horrors that Owen had inflicted on her. She had come for her revenge. She picked Owen up and dragged him, kicking and screaming, into the demon trap.

It was what the witches had been waiting for.

All three clashed their staffs on the ground, and lightning forked from them and hit the portal. Light sizzled through it, the demon retreated, and with a final howl, Owen and his pet demon were cast into it.

The portal sealed shut with a boom that shook every bone in Harlan's body. An unearthly silence fell, and darkness engulfed them.

Morgana fell forward onto the stone altar as her legs buckled beneath her. She drew a deep breath, glancing at Odette and Birdie.

Both looked as shattered as she felt, but Odette's eyes rolled in her head, and she and Birdie caught her before she fell and lowered her to the floor.

"Is she all right?" Maverick asked, looming over them, magnificent in his nakedness. *Great Goddess.* These shifters played havoc with her hormones.

"She just fainted. That was quite a battle," Morgana answered as Birdie made sure Odette was okay. Morgana struggled to stand, and Maverick pulled her upright. "You're covered in injuries."

He shrugged off his own injuries, studying the witches instead. "Par for the course. I'm okay. Are you?"

"Nothing a good cup of tea won't remedy. We'll be fine."

"Of course we will be!" Birdie said. "Odette is already coming around."

Maverick smiled, transforming his bloody face into something younger, more boyish. "You were amazing. All of you. Even *her*. Is there anything you can do for her? Ivy, I mean."

Startled, Morgana looked across to where Harlan and Grey were sitting on the drive, watching Canagan pace around the trap. The sigils and runes still smouldered with a fiery light, but the trap was empty, except for the ghostly figure of a slender woman in the centre.

"She's still here?" Morgana had seen the spirit manifest above the fire as they battled to keep the demons under control, but had been completely focussed on the spell. "She helped?"

"During our fight. She hauled him into the trap. Didn't you see?"

"I saw him in it, but I didn't see how he got there."

"I think she's waiting for something."

Morgana crossed to the circle, Maverick next to her, and stood by Canagan. "She's waiting for you, I think, Canagan."

"Me?"

He looked down at her, a crease furrowing his brow. "I don't understand."

The spirit drifted closer, her horrible wounds all too clear, despite her spectral appearance. Ivy looked haggard, her long gown in shreds, her hair lank. "I think she needs your forgiveness." Morgana could feel sadness radiating from her, and her anguish. "If you can give it."

"I'm not sure I can. They took everything from me."

"They did." Morgana nodded, phrasing her words carefully. This was no time to pull punches, though. "But you have to admit your own fault, too, Canagan. You were young, and you and your friends made stupid decisions, but they were yours to make. Your pack had told you the risks. Ivy has paid a worse price than you in the end, I think. Her spirit has been tied to the demon and Owen for years. We can see what she suffered at her death. It's time to move on. Forgive her, and yourself, too."

His voice was thick with emotion. "I still don't know if I can."

"If you don't, you will never find true happiness."

"For what it's worth," Maverick said softly, "I forgive you, and her."

Canagan stared at Ivy, brimming with anger and confusion, and then he took a deep breath. "You're right. I've carried this for far too long." He squared his shoulders. "I forgive you, Ivy. Perhaps you were as young, stupid, and misguided as us. As misled by your brother. But you helped us tonight, so for that you have my thanks. Rest in peace now."

Upon hearing his words, Ivy's spirit instantly transformed, and a beatific smile spread across her face. She glowed with an inner light as her injuries vanished and she appeared whole again before she disappeared.

Maverick gripped his brother's shoulder. "Good. It's done." He turned around and grinned at the rest of them. "Time to celebrate at Storm Moon."

"I'm not sure," Morgana started to give her excuses. "We have all of this to clean up now."

"We'll help you tomorrow. It can wait. Odette, Birdie? What do you think?"

Birdie laughed—more of a cackle, really. "I always love a party, and Odette is all right now."

Odette nodded in agreement. "I really need a drink!"

"And I'm desperate for a bourbon," Harlan said, still sitting on the ground next to Grey.

"Bourbon!" Grey scoffed. "Whiskey for me."

"That's settled, then. Back to Storm Moon!"

"Clothes first, perhaps," Morgana reminded him.

Maverick looked down at himself and then grinned at her. "If you insist."

Thirty

"Thank the Gods! You're back!" Domino's gaze swept over the victorious group, particularly her alpha as he strode across Storm Moon's bar, his usually cocky swagger on display. "You're all okay?"

"Never been better! Drinks are on the house!"

Their arrival was greeted with cheers and applause. The last few hours had been tense, the excluded team loitering restlessly, unable to settle, especially once they had closed to the public. Grey had phoned with the news of their success, and since then a party atmosphere had descended.

Domino, however, needed to see all of them to really believe it. But Maverick's declaration seemed genuine. His brooding mood of the last few days had vanished, and he appeared to be his normal self. Even Canagan had an air of levity about him. The weight of guilt seemed to finally have lifted from his shoulders. She hoped it meant that their relationship would start to improve after all these years apart.

The team weren't without injuries, though. All the men looked battered and bruised, and the witches appeared tired. Odette, in particular, was pale, and with amusement, she noted Arlo as he crossed to her side in concern. *Oh, yes. There were still feelings there.*

Grey winked at her as he picked up his whiskey on the rocks, already prepared and waiting on the bar. "Mine, I presume?"

"Of course. How was it really?"

"As scary as you could imagine. Actually, probably scarier. Not one demon," he held two fingers up, "but two! And a ghost! Fun times." He picked Harlan's bourbon up next. "And this, my good man, must be for you."

"You guys are the best!" Harlan took a big gulp of his drink.

Maggie had been sitting at the bar talking to Vlad, but as he poured drinks for the others, she joined them. "I am still very cross at being left out," she complained.

"Don't be," Harlan remonstrated. "It was a shitshow! Two demons and a ghost—just like Grey said. And the half-demonic Owen, of course."

"Really?" Domino asked. "He changed, then?"

"Yep." Grey sat on a bar stool. "Drew power from the ritual somehow."

"And started his own," Harlan added. "Sneaky bastard. Tried to call another demon out of the portal. I don't think any of us expected that. I'm sure it was the one I saw in Owen's house, just before we closed the portal there."

Maggie snorted. "So, like he had a herd of them or something?"

Harlan nodded. "A regular demon wrangler."

Domino reached forward and lifted Grey's chin. "You're covered in blood."

"Owen's, not mine. We shot him, several times. He was bloody superhuman! I'm okay, though. Just bruised, and scared witless."

"What about the spirit?" Maggie prompted. "Who was that?"

"Ivy." Harlan took another swig of bourbon, but his hand looked steady enough. "I think we were right. He sacrificed her to control the demon, and I don't think she went willingly. She hauled his ass into that demon trap! Lucky for us. I've got to admit, we were struggling."

Domino tried to picture it; the fire and demon trap, the candles, and the portal swirling above it all. She was suddenly very glad that she didn't need to be there. "And Canagan and Maverick didn't shift unwillingly?"

"No. They kept control all the way through." Grey looked over at the three witches. Arlo was with them, along with Jet, Hunter, Monroe, and Tommy. Vlad was serving them from behind the bar, and they were all chatting and laughing. "Those three were amazing. We couldn't have done it without them."

She smiled. "Let's hope Maverick has finally dropped his aversion to witches, then."

"I think so, after this."

"Well, I'm just relieved we won't have to prosecute Owen," Maggie declared. "We were stacking up evidence, but with everything happening such a long time ago, it's proving hard to build a strong case. Of course, it's still early days. I'd like to complete the investigation, regardless. I still think it's important that he's held accountable for everyone's deaths, even though he's dead, too. I'm convinced there are more recent issues—the current death aside, of course—that he's been involved with."

Domino was surprised. "So you'll keep investigating?"

"In and around other work, of course." Maggie grinned. "I'm a rottweiler."

"Oh, no! You're a wolf, remember?" Harlan laughed as he explained to Domino. "We have our own little pack. Maggie is our alpha."

Grey sniggered. "Now why doesn't that surprise me?"

Maggie actually blushed. "Well, I didn't elect myself!"

Domino wondered where her own alpha was. For a moment, she couldn't spot Maverick, and then saw him talking to his brother in a booth on their own. She watched them for a moment, hoping they were putting their differences aside, and then looked away, thinking she was prying. She caught Hunter's eye and he winked at her, and then gave her his lazy, seductive grin.

Her stomach flipped, and she held his eyes for a moment before turning away.

As far as Hunter was concerned, that gaze said everything. It was full of promise. He watched Domino for a few more seconds, admiring her figure and her spirit, before turning back to the conversation around him.

Tommy nudged him. "I saw that. You should make your move."

"Not now, you oaf. It's not the right time."

"Yer cissy!" Tommy snorted. "I wouldn't wait."

"That's because you have a caveman mentality. I am savouring the chase."

"I do not have a caveman mentality, you cheeky shite. I just can't see the point in waiting. Shame Odette fancies Arlo. I might have tried my chances there."

Hunter rolled his eyes. "Maybe stick to the girls in the club rather than risk pissing off the witches."

"What about us witches?" Birdie asked, a twinkle in her eye.

"I was just observing how attractive you all are," Tommy said, a weird half leer on his face.

Birdie sniggered. "Oh, Tommy. As if I believed that."

In an effort to shut Tommy up, Hunter asked, "Are you sure you're feeling okay? It sounded like it was a big ritual." The witches had described what had happened in great detail.

"Oh, I'll be all right after a good sleep. Odette took on the brunt of it."

"Why didn't you? You're the High Priestess, right?" Hunter was aware of how the Moonfell Coven worked.

"We each have our areas of speciality, and Odette wanted to take the lead. It's more in keeping with her abilities. She was right to. She did an excellent job. When I was more elderly and incapacitated, she and Morgana took on more. I have to accept that now." She looked regretful, briefly. "It's good to feel myself again."

"So what now for Moonfell?" Hunter asked, as Tommy headed to the bar for a refill.

"Life will roll on. Clients will want spells. Morgana will help women conceive. Odette will paint. Me, well I shall enjoy it all. But enough about us, what about you? You're enjoying your new pack, I trust?"

"It's a good change. New opportunities and all that. I didn't expect demons here, I must admit, but I like the work. It's not Cumbria, but it's good enough."

Birdie considered him for a long moment. "You'll do well here. The pack likes you."

"They do?" Hunter suddenly felt like he was being spied on. "Well, I don't think I've pissed off anyone yet."

"Everyone appreciates a hard worker and a balanced opinion. That's why Tommy followed you."

"He followed for the women!"

"And your friendship, too."

Hunter looked across at him, where he now flirted openly with Morgana. "He's incorrigible."

"He's fun! We all need friends like that. And I'm pleased for Maverick, actually. He's a good alpha." She lowered her voice and leaned in. "I'm glad we're all friends again. Us witches and Storm Moon, I mean. We haven't had the easiest of years since Arlo and Odette had their differences. I think it's all behind us now, though."

Looking around him, at the happy security team that mingled with the witches and their human friends, Hunter couldn't disagree. He just hoped that it would last, and that Maverick could find some common ground with his brother.

Morgana was trying to relax and enjoy the party, but she kept thinking about the tower room that they needed to cleanse, and the huge demon trap on the drive that had to be removed somehow, and couldn't settle, despite Tommy's terrible flirting.

"Morgana, please, forget tonight and have fun!" Monroe told her, topping up her wine glass as Tommy was pulled aside by Jet.

"Sorry. I'm just thinking about the house." Plus, she was distracted by the memories of naked shifters and their impressive physiques, Monroe included. He might be fully clothed now, but she had an excellent memory. She felt the heat rising in her cheeks just thinking about it. "We have so much to do tomorrow."

"We'll help. I'll round up some of the team. Me and Tommy, plus Hunter. I bet Arlo will come, too. And Maverick, of course."

"You don't have to. We'll manage!"

"Morgana, we want to help. I do, at least. It's been a rough few days, and you put up with that madman in your house. It was very generous of you."

"I don't think of it like that. You needed help, and we could offer it. Besides, it was as much in our interests as yours."

Monroe smiled, his white teeth gleaming. "All the more reason to pitch in. Besides, I want another look at your garden. It's an interesting place."

"I'll give you a tour if you're that interested. Best you don't go alone. It resists newcomers." She wasn't lying, but there was something nice about the idea of showing the grounds to Monroe. She brushed the silly thought aside.

"Some of your cakes wouldn't go amiss, either." Monroe wiggled his eyebrows, looking hopeful.

"I can manage that. We won't start early. I think we all need a lie in, especially after this party!"

Shifters clearly knew how to enjoy themselves. Someone had turned the music up, and Fran, Jax, Cecile, Jet, and John were now dancing energetically in the middle of the room after moving a few tables to the side. A few others joined them, and she started tapping her toes and wiggling her hips. Morgana loved music.

Monroe took her glass and placed it on the bar, his own next to it. "Time to let your hair down."

"Oh no, I can just watch."

He grabbed her hand and pulled her across the floor, and her heart raced. "I don't think so. I can see those moves, Morgana. You were born to dance."

And before she could resist, she was dancing with Monroe and the others, and enjoying every moment of it.

"Why don't you stay for a few days?" Maverick asked Canagan, raising his voice to compete with the music. "You could meet my pack properly, and we could talk, hang out. You know, brotherly stuff."

Canagan smirked. "Did we ever do brotherly stuff?"

"We did when we were younger. We could hunt together again."

"You could say that we did that tonight."

Maverick laughed, but he was trying to disguise his worry. Despite his earlier intentions to never see or speak to his brother again, it seemed fate had already thrown them back together. And Canagan had travelled here to help. However, he sensed him withdrawing, and he needed to stop that. "We did, but it was hardly for fun. I mean that we should go hunting in Richmond Park and over the common. Throw off all this crap from the past few days."

Canagan met his eyes briefly before looking at his drink. A neat rum, just like Maverick drank. "I'd like to, I guess. I'll have to run it by my mate." He looked around the bar. "It's weird being in England again. Colder."

"Well, what do you expect after Italy?"

He laughed. "True. You have a great bar, though, and a good pack. Loyal."

"For the most part." Maverick didn't mention his recent issues.

"There are always a few problems, but there's nothing serious here. I can tell. A female security lead is an interesting choice." He glanced over at Domino.

"You have a female alpha! Your partner, no less!"

"We must like strong women. Something good we got from our parents." He held his glass up. "To them. I hope they forgive me, wherever they are."

Maverick raised his glass, unsure of what he thought about the afterlife, although after seeing Ivy's ghost, perhaps he shouldn't question it. "Of course they will. I'm sure they're happy we're talking now. And Aunt Abigail. You'll stay, then? I have a spare room. I'd like to know about your life. Fill in the endless blanks."

"Are you sure? You might not like what you hear."

Maverick's throat felt tight again. "There is only us now. Of course I want to know. I thought you might be interested in what I do, too."

"I've kept tabs on you for years, I told you that. But yes, details would be good. If you're sure. But," he held his finger up, "you have to promise to visit me. By the way, who was that witch you were at the casino with?"

"Ah. That would be Birdie's niece."

Canagan smirked. "She seemed helpful."

"She was, and that's all I'm saying about her."

"So, you're single, then?"

"Very, and I like it that way."

He laughed. "Fair enough. I must admit that I expected you would have settled down with someone by now."

"I've been busy building all of this."

"And still young enough to do anything you want."

"You sound regretful, but so are you."

"My choices have shaped me. Besides, I'm happy where I am. I have found a measure of peace after all these years. Even more so now." He smiled. "It's been too long, and it's my fault, I know."

Maverick shook his head. "No more apologies. No more regrets. It's done. Owen is dead, and horrible though it sounds, I'm pleased he died horribly. I still find it hard to believe the level of deception and lies he'd built up."

"I think he planned everything, meticulously. He's planned everything his whole life. Especially when he succeeded with his demon. He killed his sister, came here, goaded you... I think he really needed me, though. Well, my blood at least. But I don't think he expected the witches."

"No? Maybe not. It's a recent thing, our renewed friendship with them. I wasn't sure, though."

"Planting seeds of doubt. That's Owen all over. But he certainly didn't expect your friends to track down his house and survive the traps he set there." Canagan smirked.

"Finding his place was thanks to Maggie. She's proving to be more helpful than I expected." He watched her laughing at the bar with Grey and Harlan, and realised she was a party animal when given half a chance. "And her team found out about Ivy's death. She made a difference."

"Just like I said earlier. You have a great team here, Mav. Despite Owen's plans, he couldn't predict everything, and he failed. Arrogant prick."

"See? We have lots to talk about." Maverick couldn't explain his desire for his brother to stay. It was just something he wanted. Needed, even. But he wouldn't beg.

Canagan tapped his glass and then nodded. "All right. You're on, then. I'll stay. Just a few days, though."

"That's perfect. Thank you."

Maverick settled in his seat more comfortably, the tension finally easing from his tight shoulders. His security team was settled, their new friends already an extension of it, and he'd address the rest of the pack the next day. It was odd, but he somehow felt whole again, more than he had in years. His brother looked relaxed too, his arm stretched across the back of the booth as he watched the dancing and the chatter.

"So, tell me about your partner," Maverick said. "I think I should know about my new sister-in-law."

Canagan rubbed his stubbled jaw as if preparing himself. "That's a long, complicated story."

Maverick shrugged. "We've got time."

Thank you for reading *Dark Heart*. The next book in this series will be out next year. Please make an author happy and leave a review here:

https://happenstancebookshop.com/products/dark-heart-storm -moon-shifters-book-2-ebook

Newsletter

If you enjoyed this book and would like to read more of my stories, please subscribe to my newsletter at tjgreenauthor.com. You will get two free short stories, *Excalibur Rises* and *Jack's Encounter*, and will also receive free character sheets for the main characters in the White Haven Witches and White Haven Hunters series.

By staying on my mailing list you'll receive free excerpts of my new books, as well as short stories, news of giveaways, and a chance to join my launch team. I'll also be sharing information about other books in this genre you might enjoy.

Ream

I have started my own subscription service called Happenstance Book Club. I know what you're thinking! What is Ream? It's a bit like Patreon, which you may be more familiar with, and it allows you to support me and read my books before anyone else.

There is a monthly fee for this, and a few different tiers, so you can choose what option suits you. All tiers come with plenty of other bonuses, including merch, but the one thing common to all is that you can read my latest books while I'm writing them. I post a few chapters each week, and you can read them at your leisure, as well as comment in them. You can also choose to be a follower for free.

You can comment on my books, chat about spoilers, and be part of a community there. I will also post polls, character art, and some of my earlier books are available to read for free.

Interested? Head to Happenstance Book Club.

https://reamstories.com/happenstancebookclub

Happenstance Book Shop

I also now have a fabulous online shop called Happenstance Books where you can buy eBooks, audiobooks, and paperbacks, many bundled up at great prices, as well as fabulous merchandise. I know that you'll love it! Check it out here: https://happenstancebookshop.com/

YouTube

If you love audiobooks, you can listen for free on YouTube, as I have uploaded all of my audiobooks there. Please like and subscribe if you do. Thank you. https://www.youtube.com/@tjgreenauthor

Read on for a list of my other books.

Author's Note

T hank you for reading *Dark Heart*, the second book in the Storm Moon Shifter series. I wanted to explore Maverick's past, and it took me in directions I didn't expect. I hope you enjoyed it. I love the pack and their human friends.

There are real places in this story, such as the villages I mention in Kent, as well as Salerno, Amalfi, and Sorrento in Italy, but the casino and Giovanni's house are fictional. I was lucky enough to visit Italy years ago, and stayed in Sorrento. It really is a stunning town! Richmond Park and Wimbledon Common are also real, and I've tried to be reasonably accurate about their layout. Ham Polo Club, the stables, and other places along that stretch of the Thames also exist, but the characters are, of course, fictional.

A big thanks to my Ream subscribers Alan Green and Izzy Evans who supplied names for some of my characters: Mr. Skelton and his brief backstory, Mystic Banshees, Canagan, and Mr. Huntingdon Smythe. Canagan is Celtic for 'wolf cub'. Thank you so much for your input! They and my other Ream subscribers also pointed out inconsistencies during the early edits. It's a really fun process for me to share chapters as I write them with my subscribers. If you like seeing how a book develops and changes, joining Happenstance Book Club might be a good option for you.

I'm planning another book in this series, and I think it will be about shifter Gods. Don't hold me to that, though. Anything could happen between now and starting the next book! After a short break, I'll start writing the seventh book in the White Haven Hunters series. I'm thinking on a title right now, and can't wait to delve more into the storyline about Belial! After that will be the first full-length Moonfell Witches book. For the full list of my plans for books and other things in 2024, check out my blog post:

If you'd like to read a bit more background on the stories, please head to my website at www.tjgreenauthor.com, where I also blog about the books I've read and the research I've done for the series. In fact, there's lots of stuff on there about my other series, Rise of the King, White Haven Witches, and White Haven Hunters, as well. I also now have an online shop called Happenstance Books, where you can buy all of my eBooks, paperbacks, audiobooks, hardbacks, and merchandise: https://happenstancebookshop.com/. In addition, I offer a subscription community called Happenstance Book Club. This site features early access to works in progress, new chapters, and so much more! Check it out here: https://reamstories.com/happenstancebookclub

Thanks again to Fiona Jayde Media for my awesome cover, and thanks to Kyla Stein at Missed Period Editing for applying your fabulous editing skills.

Thanks also to my beta readers—Terri and my mother. I'm glad you enjoyed it; your feedback, as always, is very helpful! Thanks also to Jase, my fabulously helpful other half. You do so much to support me, and I am immensely grateful for you.

Finally, thank you to my launch team, who give valuable feedback on typos and are happy to review upon release. It's lovely to hear from them—you know who you are! You're amazing! I also love hearing from all of my readers, so I welcome you to get in touch.

I encourage you to follow my Facebook page, T J Green. I post there reasonably frequently. In addition, I have a Facebook group called TJ's Inner Circle. It's a fab little group where I run giveaways and post teasers, so come and join us.

About the Author

I was born in England, in the Black Country, but moved to New Zealand in 2006. I lived near Wellington with my partner, Jase, and my cats, Sacha and Leia. However, in April 2022 we moved again! Yes, I like making my life complicated… I'm now living in the Algarve in Portugal, and loving the fabulous weather and people. When I'm not busy writing I read lots, indulge in gardening and shopping, and I love yoga.

Confession time! I'm a Star Trek geek—old and new—and love urban fantasy and detective shows. Secret passion—Columbo! Favourite Star Trek film is the *Wrath of Khan*, the original! Other top films—*Predator*, the original, and *Aliens*.

In a previous life I was a singer in a band, and used to do some acting with a theatre company. For more on me, check out a couple of my blog posts. I'm an old grunge queen, so you can read about my love of that on my blog: https://tjgreenauthor.com/about-a-girl-and-what-chris-cornell-means-to-me/. For more random news, read: https://tjgreenauthor.com/read-self-published-blog-tour-things-you-probably-dont-know-about-me/

Why magic and mystery?

I've always loved the weird, the wonderful, and the inexplicable. Favourite stories are those of magic and mystery, set on the edges of the known, particularly tales of folklore, faerie, and legend—all the narratives that try to explain our reality.

The King Arthur stories are fascinating because they sit between reality and myth. They encompass real life concerns, but also cross boundaries with the world of faerie—or the Other, as I call it. There are green knights, witches, wizards, and dragons, and that's what I find particularly fascinating. They're stories that have intrigued people for generations, and like many others, I'm adding my own interpretation.

I love witches and magic, hence my second series set in beautiful Cornwall. There are witches, missing grimoires, supernatural threats, and ghosts, and as the series progresses, weirder stuff happens. The spinoff, White Haven Hunters, allows me to indulge my love of alchemy, as well as other myths and legends. Think Indiana Jones meets Supernatural!

Have a poke around in my blog posts and you'll find all sorts of posts about my series and my characters, and quite a few book reviews.

Please follow me on social media.

f facebook.com/tjgreenauthor/

P pinterest.pt/tjgreenauthor/

tiktok.com/@tjgreenauthor

youtube.com/@tjgreenauthor

g goodreads.com/author/show/15099365.T_J_Green

instagram.com/tjgreenauthor/

BB bookbub.com/authors/tj-green

https://reamstories.com/happenstancebookclub

Other Books by T J Green

Rise of the King

A Young Adult series about a teen called Tom who is summoned to wake King Arthur. It's a fun adventure about King Arthur in the Otherworld!

Call of the King #1

The Silver Tower #2

The Cursed Sword #3

White Haven Witches

This is an Urban Fantasy series all about witches! It's set in the fictional town of White Haven on the south Cornish coast in England. It's my most popular series, and features female and male witches. Low on romance, high on action and magic! I also blend lots of English myth and legend into the stories. And they'll make you laugh, too!

Buried Magic #1

Magic Unbound #2

Magic Unleashed #3

All Hallows' Magic #4

Undying Magic #5

Crossroads Magic #6

Crown of Magic #7

Vengeful Magic #8

Chaos Magic #9

Stormcrossed Magic #10

Wyrd Magic #11

Midwinter Magic #12

White Haven and the Lord of Misrule: Yuletide Novella

White Haven Hunters

The fun-filled spinoff to the White Haven Witches series! Featuring Fey, Nephilim, and the hunt for the occult.

Spirit of the Fallen #1

Shadow's Edge #2

Dark Star #3

Hunter's Dawn #4

Midnight Fire #5

Immortal Dusk #6

Storm Moon Shifters

This is an Urban Fantasy shifters spin-off in the White Haven world, and can be read as a standalone. There's a crossover of characters from my other series, and plenty of new ones, too. There is also a new group

of witches who I love! It's set in London around Storm Moon, the
club owned by Maverick Hale, Alpha of the Storm Moon Pack. Audio
will be available when I've organised myself!

Storm Moon Rising #1

Dark Heart #2

Moonfell Witches

Witch fiction set in Moonfell, the Gothic mansion in London. If
you love magic, fantastic characters, urban fantasy, and paranormal
mysteries, you'll love this series. Join the Moonfell Coven now!

The First Yule, a Moonfell Witches Novella.

Printed in Great Britain
by Amazon